**Also available from Angelina M. Lopez
and Carina Press**

Filthy Rich

Lush Money
Hate Crush

Serving Sin talks about topics some readers may find difficult, including sexual assault, PTSD and dissociation.

SERVING SIN

———

Angelina M. Lopez

carina
press

carina press®

Recycling programs
for this product may
not exist in your area.

ISBN-13: 978-1-335-45953-4

Serving Sin

This edition published by arrangement with Harlequin Books S.A.

For questions and comments about the quality of this book, please contact us at CustomerService@Harlequin.com.

Carina Press
22 Adelaide St. West, 40th Floor
Toronto, Ontario M5H 4E3, Canada
www.CarinaPress.com

Printed in U.S.A.

To every woman, everywhere.
May you feel mighty.

According to the World Health Organization, one in three women globally have experienced physical and/or sexual violence. Men are more likely to perpetrate violence if they have a sense of entitlement over women. Women are more likely to experience violence if they are surrounded by attitudes that encourage male privilege and a perception of women as subordinates.

These attitudes exist everywhere and aren't restrained by borders or wealth.

In the Filthy Rich series, I've written fierce, powerful women who are respected, honored and—most important—listened to by mighty men. My hope is that I can contribute in moving the needle away from entrenched anti-women attitudes.

If you need help, you can contact the National Sexual Assault Hotline at 800-656-HOPE (4673) or online: www.rainn.org.

Ni una más.

SERVING SIN

Chapter One

Monte del Vino Real, Spain

The people of the Monte del Vino Real cheered as a white jet slowly pulled up to the ramp decorated in billowing swags of green, red, and white. Mexican industrialist Daniel Trujillo had helped to change the fortunes of this small kingdom in the mountains of Northern Spain and the hundreds of growers, winemakers, and villagers waving banners and singing behind the security barricade wanted to show their appreciation. This day would be talked about in the village's *tabernas*, *cafés*, and *bodegas* for years to come. It was Trujillo's first visit to the kingdom he'd helped save. The people were used to almost daily interactions with the glamorous people that stood in a row at the bottom of the ramp: their winegrowing *rey* and beautiful billionaire *reina*, the adored eight-year-old twins who would one day rule them, their winemaking *princesa* and her rock star husband.

They still didn't want to miss out on a glimpse of one of the world's wealthiest tycoons.

All eyes were on the jet as it halted in front of the ramp and sparkled in the October sun. The two-man security team, dressed in dark suits and sunglasses, took their places on either side of the airplane door.

All eyes, that is, except for the startlingly bright green ones of thirty-nine-year-old Roman Sheppard. Standing at the end of the row of the beautiful royals, he scanned slowly over the cheering, shouting, singing crowd and made visual contact with his team. "Code white," they murmured through his earpiece, giving verbal verification of the quick, four-finger swipes they made across their foreheads.

All clear. No sign of anger, agitation, or suspicious behavior.

Next to report were the people he couldn't see: the sharpshooter watching from the air traffic control tower, the team monitoring the road leading to the airport, the four-person team maintaining ears and eyes in the village.

"Code white," they all verified.

Roman scratched his cleanly shaved chin against the bright navy shoulder of his Tom Ford jacket. "Copy that. Get a sitrep from Trujillo's advance team. Make sure they've coordinated with his people inside the plane so—"

A small-yet-painful elbow jabbed into his side. "Stop," his half sister muttered under her breath. "You said you were going to let Glori monitor security."

"Yeah, sir," his second-in-command deadpanned in his ear. "You said you were going to let me take lead."

Roman looked down at his little sister, Sofia. "I am. She is."

Sofia rolled her wide, pretty eyes and stuck out her hand. "Give me the earpiece."

His little sister was all balls. Roman gave her "the

look," his not-smile-smile that let terrified friendlies
know he wasn't about to blow their heads off. "Not a
chance," he drawled, laying his Texas accent on thick.

They were drawing an audience.

Aish, Sofia's husband, and their twin niece and
nephew smirked on the opposite side of her. His half
brother's billionaire wife, Roxanne, shook her head
while his half brother, Mateo, rolled his eyes. This
morning he'd commanded Roman to take the day off
and celebrate what he'd helped the people achieve.

Roman had read somewhere that he could still be
beheaded for defying a royal command.

Mateo Ferdinand Juan Carlos de Esperanza y Santos was the king of the Monte del Vino Real, a thousand-year-old kingdom that grew some of the finest
wine grapes in the world. Sofia Maria Isabel de Esperanza y Santos, a millionaire winemaking inventor, was
its *princesa*. And Roman Sheppard, raised in a Texas
trailer park and now head of an international security
firm, was technically a *príncipe*.

A reluctant warrior prince, proclaimed the tabloid
headlines that popped up again when his brother named
him the king's advisor.

Reluctant or not, he'd agreed it made sense for him
to be up here, in front of the crowd, with his siblings
and their spouses and kids. Thirteen years ago, as an
honorably discharged former army ranger still finding Iraqi sand in his gear, Roman had rescued Daniel
Trujillo's eighteen-year-old kidnapped daughter. When
he'd handled the bundle of brave, weeping girl to her
father—she'd been resolutely chatty and stiff-upper-
lipped for the four hours it had taken him to rescue her
and drive her to safety across the desert, and hadn't

fallen apart until she'd seen her dad—it had formed a bond that Roman had drawn upon when he'd asked the tycoon for a loan to preserve the kingdom.

Trujillo's loans to the Monte were now paid off. His loans to new wineries that had helped to create a booming wine and tourism industry in the kingdom had become investments.

And Daniel had recently stepped aside as CEO of Trujillo Industries, the family company that under his tenure rose to dominate the Mexican auto industry. Roman guessed that was why he'd gotten the surprising email that he was coming for a visit.

The tycoon finally had time to see all that his money had accomplished.

Roman was looking forward to seeing the older man. Their correspondence over the last ten years had always been short and sweet—Roman had included quick updates about the use of Trujillo's investment and the state of the kingdom along with the loan repayments. He'd also sent the occasional thank you note or birthday card. And Daniel had replied with useful advice, easy guidance, or sometimes just a good razzing answer. Roman asked questions or gave shit back.

The back-and-forth had sometimes included an invite to Mexico, which Roman had never accepted.

But now the retired CEO had come to the Monte, and the main reason Roman gave in and stood up here with his insistent family was to keep everyone safe. His hard-headed sister could poke him in the ribs all she wanted.

He was here to keep Daniel safe. To keep the royal family safe. To protect every single yelling, screaming, clapping person who called the Monte del Vino

Real home. That was Roman's job and it was what he was good at.

Glori's voice interrupted the stand-off with his sister. "The advanced team has signaled all clear. He's coming out."

At the top of the platform, Trujillo's men took a ready position on either side of the airplane door. The crowd noise went up. Half of the villagers sang a popular Mexican reggaeton song.

When the door popped open, the crowd's voice became a roar.

Then fell abruptly when a woman stepped out on the platform.

She seemed not to notice the sudden stillness. She slowly looked over the crowd as she walked toward the podium, a soft smile on her face, taking in the people and the view Roman knew by heart: the endless vineyards turned gold and rust after harvest, the red terra-cotta roofs of the village in the distance, the six-hundred-year-old Castillo del Monte, and the snow-peaked mountains protecting and dominating it all. She took her time, her hands pressed against her chest in her wide-collared coat, a look of wonder on her face. Then this woman, the newly named CEO of Trujillo Industries and one of the wealthiest people in the world, threw her arms out wide and waved exuberantly at the people of the Monte del Vino Real.

The joy beaming from Cenobia Trujillo's face popped the lid off the villagers' excitement. Roman had protected Nobel Peace Prize recipients and organized security when U2 played a surprise concert in Trafalgar Square. But he'd never heard a roar like this one.

He latched on to his two tours in Iraq to suppress his own emotion.

He hadn't seen Cenobia Trujillo in thirteen years. He certainly hadn't expected to see her today; according to the furtive googling he did every six months or so, this thirty-one-year-old newly minted CEO planned to launch a car in a month that would change the Mexican auto landscape.

But here she was, that eighteen-year-old girl who'd been terrified but resolute, dirty and scared but determined to chat through trembling lips, what she'd needed to do to keep herself from falling apart so he could focus on racing them away from the men who'd taken her. Now she was a powerful, dazzling woman stepping up to the podium, wearing a cream shawl coat that highlighted the dark golden brown of her skin, a handswidth wide leather belt that emphasized the curve of her waist, and a sienna brown leather skirt that smoothed over her hips and thighs to cover her to below her knees. Her black hair was coiled like a crown at the top of her head and her face—the slight hook of her nose, the rise of her strong cheekbones, the definitive line of her wide jaw, and the feline beauty of her dark eyes—was magisterially beautiful. She looked mighty and demure and no-nonsense.

And gorgeous. She was like a bolt of sunshine he had to squint against.

"Look alive, people," he said. "Leader one. Going dark." He was really going dim, slipping his phone out of his pocket to turn the earpiece down. His team would let him know if anything came up. But whatever she had to say, he didn't want to miss a word.

"*Muchísimas gracias,*" Cenobia thanked the crowd

enthusiastically as she waited for them to settle down. "The Monte del Vino Real is more beautiful than I could have dreamed."

Her warm voice ringing in Spanish across the valley just revved the crowd back up again.

Roman locked down the impulse to signal a code red, leap on the stage, surround her in a human shield, and hustle her someplace safe. Someplace with four walls and a ceiling, away from this wipe open spot with too many lines of sight.

Ranger up, he commanded himself. *Remain tactical.* Evaluate. Assess. Had anything about their security plan fundamentally changed?

No.

And he imagined this heiress who'd worked her ass off to earn her CEO spot wouldn't approve of a caveman maneuver any more than his powerful sister and sister-in-law would.

"I know you were expecting my father today," she said, quieting the crowd as she spoke into the microphone. "Ten years ago, we were shocked when we discovered that the American hero who rescued me was actually a lost Spanish prince. We learned that the Spanish prince needed funds to keep this kingdom afloat. My father had doubts about a loan. But I didn't."

Roman frowned.

"I knew this soldier-turned-royalty would never ask for a loan unless he was confident of its success. Unless he was confident in the ability of each and every one of you."

She paused, raised her chin, and looked over the crowd. Roman suddenly had an inkling how this thirty-one-year-old woman could control a forty-five thousand-person company steeped in machismo.

"I oversaw the loan to the Monte del Vino Real," she said, her words rustling through the crowd like a windstorm. "I managed the loan's disbursement and helped guide the Monte in its use. I also was responsible should the kingdom not be able to pay it back."

The crowd's quiet felt like Roman's shock.

I managed the loan's disbursement and helped guide the Monte in its use.

All those emails. All those notes. All those years.

Roman had come to think of Daniel Trujillo as a mentor and friend. Today, he'd planned to tell the industrialist that his guidance had helped improve a community and save a kingdom.

But the loan, the notes, the guidance—they had all come from her.

"Now I am here to thank you," she said with a warm, wide smile he felt in his gut. "The prosperity of the Monte del Vino Real was the final achievement that convinced my father I was ready to take his place as CEO of Trujillo Industries. Thank you for your tenacity. Thank you for your dedication. Thank you for your resolve to create a better future."

Cenobia Trujillo crossed her hands over her heart, then, with all the impact of a shock and awe campaign, looked at Roman for the first time in thirteen years. "I wouldn't be standing here today as CEO without you," she said, eyes like a bombardment that blinded him. "You've made my dearest fantasy come true."

Chapter Two

Monte del Vino Real, Spain

After, after soldiering up and doing his job, greeting
her at the bottom of the stairs in the roar of welcome
and introducing her to his family and escorting her to
the public luncheon in the courtyard of El Castillo then
stepping back as Mateo and Sofia took her on a tour of
the Monte, after watching his family and their people
adjust quickly to the fact that they had her and not her
father to thank for their financial salvation while he was
still seeing contrails from the bomb she dropped, after
she asked if she could have a private word with him
and he escorted her to his castle office in the waning
twilight of a surreal day, Roman sat on the edge of his
ancient carved desk and tried to wrangle his thoughts
and feelings into an orderly line as Cenobia "Cen" Trujillo wandered his office.

"Cen," she'd asked everyone to call her.

Cen.

Sin.

Goddammit.

She paced his office, slow and a little dreamy, looking out at the vineyards and mountains from his leaded

glass window, walking on fine leather ankle boots that got her up to 5'5" or so. He'd forgotten she was short; she'd been a titan on the podium. Sunset turned her cream cashmere sweater and russet full-grain leather skirt various shades of buttery gold over her curvy body.

Her clothes had been torn and dirty last time he'd seen her. Somehow she'd still managed to fill the cab of his truck with the smell of honeysuckle.

When she turned to face him, Roman realized he was staring.

"Who could've imagined this is where we'd end up thirteen years later," she said with a soft grin and real wonder, motioning to his office. The Spanish accent was light in her voice; she'd gotten all of her education in the U.S. "Both of us CEOs and you a *príncipe* and king's advisor."

He gave a nod, acknowledging the surreal.

Last time she'd seen him, he'd been a twenty-six-year-old kid, the ink still wet on his Sheppard Security business cards, just six months out of third batt and most comfortable in his ACU pants and sand-colored T-shirts.

Then, when he was twenty-nine, his biological father had called wanting to give him a kingdom.

It had been bullshit—the greedy, self-consumed man Roman had never known had really just wanted to take the kingdom away from Mateo, assuming a dumb American soldier would be easier to keep under his thumb. Roman had given the old man the finger and offered his sword to his half brother and half sister, who wanted to make their little kingdom a nice place to live. It'd been simple: good people had needed Roman's help. He could help them.

Then, six months ago, Mateo had gone and complicated it.

Now, Cenobia Trujillo was seeing a thirty-nine-year-old clotheshorse who claimed an office with ancient tapestries and a six-hundred-year-old mosaic ceiling in a medieval castle. Roman's dark high-and-tight haircut now had expensive product in it, his Tom Ford suit was bespoke, the burnished calfskin of his dark brown Berluti oxfords was as smooth as silk, his dinged up memorial bracelet now cozied up to a stainless-steel Jaeger-LeCoultre, and his Gucci pocket square was a birthday present from his rock star brother-in-law.

Cenobia's brown eyes, coffee bean dark and velvety, traveled over him as she walked closer. "You certainly look the part of CEO," she said, voice soft.

Roman straightened.

"Yeah, I'm CEO of a firm that employs two hundred and fifty-five of the smartest private-security minds in the world," he said. "I'm also advisor to the guy who runs this place. Right now, they should yank me off both jobs."

She paused, confused, just a few feet away between the two high-backed chairs in front of his desk.

"A stranger had her pretty fingers playing around in this kingdom and I had no clue."

The surprised hurt was instant on her wide, expressive face. "You're upset," she said, raising her chin.

"Damn right," he growled out. "Why didn't you tell me you were the one okaying our money, Cenobia?"

"Please," she said. "Call me Cen."

Like hell he would. He looked at her steadily.

Everyone talked about how bright and green his eyes were, brighter and greener surrounded by dark lashes.

Interrogation hadn't been his primary skill as a Ranger. But his eyes, his silence, and the sense of threat that ran closer to the surface than anyone understood had always been his best tools at getting people to talk.

His best tools weren't often greeted with a direct, cat-eyed gaze.

"Roman, imagine how that would have looked," she said, the fingers he hadn't meant to call pretty running absently along the back of one of the wooden chairs she stood next to. "A great and noble kingdom receives aid from a twenty-one-year-old girl?" She gripped a finial. "It would have looked like I was adopting the Monte as my puppy."

He shook his head. Focused. "Screw everyone else. Why didn't you tell *me*?"

He'd spent the day trying to rewrite ten years of understanding. All those emails and notes hadn't been with her father. They'd been with her.

A thread had woven between them when he'd extracted her from the bunker, held her up while she was physically ill from seeing the death he'd delivered, then raced her across the desert to safety.

But those short, quick notes had created a bond.

Those notes had transformed her into the only former Sheppard Security client Roman expected the truth from.

"If the loan came from my father, you would assume it was a business decision," she said. "From me... I was afraid you would think it was pity." For the first time that day, she dropped her gaze. "Or teenage...fancifulness."

Fancifulness?

A CEO in cashmere and leather stood before him

saying she hadn't revealed herself in a decade of jointly overseeing a fortune because he'd think she had a crush?

He wasn't touching that with a ten-foot pole. "You didn't tell me in the beginning? Fine. But ten years, Cenobia."

"Cen."

He crossed his arms and glowered back.

She clasped her dark hands together and ran four fingers over the back of one. "I did repeatedly invite you to Mexico with the intention of telling you in person."

Well…shit.

He'd repeatedly found an excuse not to accept.

"I never wanted to hurt you," she said quietly. Her dark eyes were velvet soft as she looked at him. "I admire you so much for what you've accomplished here."

Okay.

What was he doing?

This woman had given him a fortune and helped him figure out to use it. How long was he going to browbeat her for it?

"I didn't do anything," he said, gruffly. "It was you, you convincing your dad to loan us the money. Don't think I don't appreciate it."

"I know you do," she said gently. "You still have a right to be angry."

He shook off his glower, which wasn't the easiest thing to lose on the best of days. "Look, if Mateo and Sofia aren't pissed, then I shouldn't be. They're the ones who did all the work."

Her head with that heavy crown of shiny black hair tipped as she looked at him. "That's not true."

He wasn't gonna go round-and-round with her the way he did with his siblings. The Monte had been able to pay off the loan in half the time because of his brother's plans, his billionaire sister-in-law's financial oversight, and his sister's idea to begin a winemaking industry that matched the Monte's winegrowing reputation. Roman had just watched the money.

She nodded at Roman's bicep. "The reluctant warrior prince has become the king's right hand," she teased gently.

He looked down and saw the mammoth gold ring his crossed arms showed off there. Saw the finger next to it with its missing top third. His other hand was rippled and tight with a burn scar covering the back.

His brother had shoved the king's advisor ring with its family crest and ode of loyalty on Roman's middle finger six months ago, after their father's stroke had made Mateo the official king he'd already been acting as for the last ten years. The thing was tight and surprisingly heavy.

"It's a role worthy of you," she mused. "Your careful management of our money helped make me interim CEO."

"Interim?" That word kept him from hiding his hands in his pants' pockets. His tailor made sure his hands wouldn't fit anyway. "What do you mean interim?"

Cenobia crossed her own arms and absently stroked her earlobe. "My father wants an opportunity to observe me in the role before he names me his successor in truth. The heart condition that was reported as the reason he stepped back is a ruse. Only me, my father, and his doctor know."

On that long-ago four-hour drive, she'd filled the air with words, and many of them had been about her family's company, Trujillo Industries, Mexico's largest producer of foreign cars and parts, and her future hopes and dreams for it. In his occasional googling, he'd read how hard she'd worked to earn the CEO seat.

"Sorry," he said. He watched a peach pearl earring wink between her fingers as she continued to stroke her ear.

"Actually, it's why I've come." She dropped her hands and raised troubled eyes to look at him. "I need your help."

Roman felt the cool warning tingle at the base of his spine.

"A month ago, my security began seeing emails that concerned them. They didn't read different to me than any other ugly, misogynistic emails, but apparently there's been the right combo of words and an escalation of aggression…"

Roman pushed off his desk, moved a step closer to her. "Okay, send them to me." He would fix this. "I'll have my team analyze them and—"

"Then last week, someone left a note on my car."

Everything stopped. "In a secure lot? With your driver in it?"

Her strong, wide jaw went up. "No, I'd driven myself. It was…personal business. But I know my security protocols; I drive to avoid a tail. Still, someone followed me. Or knew where to expect me. They knew I'd be there."

Roman let her choice of words sink in: *escalation of aggression, security protocols, tail.*

She was a brilliant, beautiful, wealthy woman who shouldn't waste her superior brain power on her security. She was supposed to be building cars and changing the world and leaving her safety to ground pounders like him.

He began putting a team together. Glori would serve as point. "My second-in-command will fly home with you and the team will meet y'all there." His best risk mitigation analyst was in Venezuela but he'd swap him out. "They'll interview your security team, review the last six months of chatter, and then we'll figure out—"

"I need *you*," she said. Her eyes were pleading and silky.

He licked his always-dry lips. "My people are good."

"You're the only one I trust."

She let go of the chair and stepped closer in a shush of leather and cashmere, her heels clicking against the tile. She still smelled like honeysuckle. "I know it's too much to ask, for you to drop everything and come to Mexico. But I'm concerned there's a breach in my security. How else would someone know where I'd be?" He could see the weight of her frustration and concern on her fine, wide forehead. "It's such a critical time. I don't have the energy or mental capacity to deal with a threat. Not when I have the launch of La Primera in thirty days and so much I have to prove to my father."

La Primera, her affordable hybrid car, was going to be the first automobile entirely conceived, designed, and manufactured in Mexico. A fascinated auto industry—split between those who believed the car was a revolution long-in-coming and those who thought she was a spoiled girl killing her dad's company—would get their first look at the Frankfurt Auto Show in a month.

Roman already had his ticket and a civvies bag packed with the disguises that helped him blend into crowds.

He'd thought the launch of La Primera was a victory lap for Cenobia; instead, it was a test run. She'd helped him save a kingdom and had never once asked for anything in return. And she said he was the only one she trusted.

Damn.

"Okay," he said. "Okay." He mentally ran through his duties in the Monte. "I can be there in a couple of days."

Relief relaxed her like he'd cut her string. He hadn't realized, through the warmth and joy she showered everyone with today, how tense she was. He'd never imagined that Cenobia's gorgeous smile beaming from the society pages covered the fact that she'd learned to avoid a tail. He'd assumed—hoped—she'd left those ghosts behind in the bunker.

But when her relief made her sway closer, stirring up her smell of summer and sunshine, and reach for him, Roman stiffened. She tentatively slipped her hand inside his coat and pressed it against his shirt and chest and heart.

"Thank you," she said, her eyes brimming with gratefulness. "Thank you."

He dropped his crossed arms, and used one hand to pat hers, channeling her dad. His burned hand gripped the edge of his desk.

"We'll figure this out, Cenobia," he said. "Everything's gonna be okay."

She smiled ruefully. "You're the only man I believe when he says that. And please, if we're going to spend the next couple of weeks together, call me Cen."

He'd find the bastards threatening her and free up her big brain to focus on her launch. He'd make sure she was safe.

But he wouldn't call her by her nickname. Not with the way it added kindling to an ember lit when she stepped off the plane. And he'd minimize the amount of time he spent in the company of one honeysuckle-sweet CEO.

He patted her hand again with all the protective condescension he could muster, stepped away from his desk and her touch, and pulled out his phone to start sending messages.

The only man she trusted? He'd fix this.

That's what he was good at.

Chapter Three

Guanajuato, Mexico

Behind her large desk in her corner office, Cenobia Trujillo crossed her legs in her form-fitting black-and-white houndstooth dress and leaned back in her chair. Her hands… She threaded them over the small red belt at her waist. Then she tried resting them on the leather-covered arms of her desk chair.

No.

She uncrossed her legs and put both of her red Stuart Weitzman pumps on the floor. Hands on the keyboard. There. Yes. Position of authority. But Roman Sheppard was here to help her because she'd begged. He wasn't interviewing for a job.

She tried resting her chin in her palm, keeping her fingers away from her newly applied red lipstick. She could be—she grabbed a piece of paper—reading a document.

She tossed the paper back down on her desk. She looked ridiculous.

She felt ridiculous.

Her assistant's text that Roman was on his way up shouldn't have stirred this flurry of butterflies in her stomach. She collaborated with top engineering minds and faced down the most demeaning of misogynists in her industry. She was CEO—for now—and she'd earned this corner office that still smelled of her father's sandalwood cologne.

She surveyed her space with its updated bronze and marble fixtures, its private bathroom and kitchenette, its large white-acrylic conference table for serious meetings, and sleek couch and seating area for casual ones. Would he be impressed? Would he be able to see it at all? The Trujillo Industries headquarters, situated on a bluff on the outskirts of Guanajuato, Mexico, was a modern building of steel and glass with incredible views of the Bajío, the lowlands and hills of this region of Central Mexico. The land was covered in lush green during the rainy months and showed off golden rock dotted with nopal during the dry.

But Cenobia kept her navy drapes closed against the floor-to-ceiling view.

Perhaps she needed to turn on more lamps?

She rushed across the room and flipped on the designer bronze lamp next to the couch. It showed a smudge on the glass top of the side table, and she hurriedly raised the edge of her kick-pleated skirt to wipe it off. It was then that Paloma tapped on her door and opened it, just as Cenobia had instructed her to do.

Because of course.

Instead of seeing her majestically displayed in her white leather CEO's chair, powerful and calm and confident, the man who'd occupied too many of her thoughts for the last thirteen years walked in to see her revealing a decent amount of thigh as she cleaned a table with her skirt.

And, of course, he looked incredible. Like a mirage shimmering to life in her doorway. Wide shoulders. Steely jaw. Dark-brown hair militaristically perfect. Dressed like he'd stepped off a fashion shoot. Every inch of him the resolute warrior prince.

And then he pursed his mouth.

Drew attention to that horrible, horrible, *boca tan horrible*.

She smoothed down her skirt and straightened. "Cleaning," she said.

"You can hire people who'll take care of that," he drawled.

"I'm very hands on."

He didn't smile but at least he looked amused, those slight lines raying out from his captivating, heavy-lidded, sea-glass eyes.

"Welcome to Mexico," she said, bolstering herself with her thirty-one years of being an heiress, an engineer, the Trujillo Industry torchbearer, and one of the most-watched women in Mexico as she strolled to meet her savior, the warrior *príncipe*, in the center of her corner office.

He was here.

Roman Sheppard was actually here.

He wore an unbuttoned dark sports coat and a crisp white shirt that perfectly fit his muscular chest. A pendant on a leather cord dangled in the open collar of his shirt, in that shadowy space against his skin. Khaki jeans showed off long, strong legs that ended in black, sleek boots.

A foot away from her, he clasped her outstretched hand in his hard and callused one, then leaned close to kiss both of her cheeks in the Spanish-form of greeting.

The smell of leather. His smoothly shaved jaw. His plush, warm lips.

She fought the urge to go still and quiet so she could brand this moment into her memory.

"You've become very Spanish," she remarked quietly as he stepped back, glad her voice didn't reflect her emotions. "You even speak the language now."

Roman leaned back on a heel. "I get by," he said. "My sister and sister-in-law speak about a dozen languages between 'em. So they keep me humble."

"An ideal position for a man," she said with a teasing grin.

"My sisters think so."

She didn't know him, not really. Knowledge of a person couldn't be based on ten years of intermittent correspondence and overzealous pinning on Pinterest. But still, she could marvel at how this once-orphan—his mother, the only family he had growing up, had died when he was in Iraq—now had sisters and brothers, a niece and a nephew, family who wanted to give their reluctant *príncipe* a place of honor by making him king's advisor.

Family she'd pulled him away from.

"Thank you for coming," she said. How did she express how much his presence meant to her? "Your people have been wonderful but you being here is a relief."

His eyes narrowed. "Trust my folks. They'll keep you safe."

"I know they will," she said, clasping her hands in front of her. "I do trust them."

In the days since she'd asked for his help, his eight-person team had been busy. His second-in-command, Glori Knight, had flown with her to Mexico and taken a place on her private security detail, escorting Cenobia and staying in her guest bedroom. Others were analyzing the threatening emails that had triggered her team's worry. The anonymous emails expressed concern that Cenobia's brand of womanhood would pollute the waters, then went into gory detail—a gore that increased with each message—about the exact abuse they would impart if she didn't step back from her role. The specificity of the violence and the lines like "just when you think you've escaped and are safe, we'll find you in the tunnel" was what had red-flagged the emails.

Very few knew about the safe room in her Guanajuato home and its exit out a secret, natural tunnel. Roman's team was reviewing her past and present security personnel, looking for a possible leak.

She rubbed her thumb over the back of her hand. "I've always trusted my security teams; there is too much wasted mental energy if I don't. One of our longtime guards is like a family member. To suspect one of them now, during such a critical time…"

She saw him glance down and realized she was stroking the thin, silky skin on the back of her hand. She crossed her arms. "I feel vulnerable in a way I haven't felt in a long time."

She centered her hips, planted her feet in her elegant heels, met his green gaze. She wouldn't shy away from what she needed. The presence of the man who saved her, this soldier-turned-royalty, made her feel safer.

He nodded. There was a divot between his dark brows. "You want to show me the note left on your car?"

"It's with the head of security. I'll take you to his office. Let me grab my phone." She walked to her desk.

Roman wanted to get right to work. That was good. She had plenty of her own work with the launch of her

car in just under a month. And with him here, she could
focus without her mind wandering off to tunnels and
bunkers and the dark lifting to reveal something she
didn't want to see.

She slipped her phone into her houndstooth dress's
sleek pocket, turned around, and was struck—in just
those few seconds of looking away—by his perfect profile. She stared at his dark hair, strong forehead, thick
eyelashes, ski-slope nose, and plush lips as he looked
around her office.

Roman was here.

"Perhaps we can have dinner together this evening?"
she tossed out casually, crossing the room to her closed
door. "I can show you my fair city since you did me the
honor of showing me yours."

"That village wouldn't be so fair without your help,"
he replied. "It's more yours than mine. And I'm gonna
be pretty busy getting up to speed."

"Oh," she said, glad to be facing the door. "Well,
after you are caught up then we can…"

She startled back when she opened her office door
and found her vice president of marketing and publicity
standing in the doorway, her assistant just behind him.

"*Por favor*, Señor Vasquez…" Paloma was pleading.

"This is important and—*ah*. Perfect." Laurencio
"Lance" Vasquez looked at Cenobia like her job was
to open doors for him. "We need a moment."

We? Also standing in Cenobia's light-filled waiting
room was Barbara Benitez, a representative from the
state-owned oil and gas company Pemex. Wonderful.
Here were the two largest flies in her ointment.

"*Lo siento, señorita,*" her assistant said.

"*No te preocupas.* Lance, Barbara, I have an opening later this afternoon but now—"

Fit and slim shouldered in a tightly tailored Armani suit, Vasquez pushed past her and into her office. "Now," he said. "The future of the company depends on…"

"Señor," Roman drawled ominously. The way Vasquez lit up when he turned and saw Roman Sheppard proved he was too stuffed with ego to comprehend the warning.

"*Príncipe,*" Vasquez exclaimed, smoothing back his wavy, blond-highlighted hair before offering a hand. "It is an honor."

When Benitez excitedly rushed into her office as well, Cenobia begrudgingly made introductions. The two lauded and name-dropped. Laurencio Vasquez was a member of one of the most powerful families in Mexico and the sleek-suited and black-haired Barbara Benitez, as Pemex's public face, dined with prime ministers and kings.

They were still starstruck meeting the warrior prince famously reluctant to step into the limelight. The fact that Roman ducked the paparazzi didn't protect him from appearing on lists of the world's sexiest bachelors. His incredible story—war hero, Medal of Honor winner, finder of lost heiresses, protector of superstars and human rights activists, and an American-born prince of a now-flourishing Spanish kingdom—lit the public's interest in him; his reluctance to reveal himself added gas.

"You will have to allow my family to host an event in your honor," Vasquez oozed. Roman hadn't uttered a word, but the VP hadn't noticed. "I will introduce you to the crème of Mexican society. We were thrilled to learn about Cenobia's involvement in your kingdom.

That is where a woman's energies are best spent. *¿Ver-dad, Príncipe?* Helping a man. Building a home."

Cenobia cut him off. "Why did you need to meet with me?"

She caught the flare of his annoyance before he covered it with a thin-lipped smile. "Later. We'll return after *su alteza* departs and we can…"

"Now," Cenobia said, echoing his words from earlier. "Apparently the future of the company depends on it."

Born pale skinned with the ability to trace his family back to Mexico's earliest conquerors, nothing in Lance Vasquez's worldview had prepared him to report to a woman whose roots *indígenas* were evident in the skin, hair, and bone structure passed down from her nomadic Guachichil ancestors. He was visibly stewing. But after six months of Vasquez's disdain, obstinacy, and increasing hostility, she was unwilling to let him hide them from the *príncipe* now.

"If I must…" Vasquez said, the offended courtier. "The executives believe you should slow down. We want more testing before you make fools of us all with the car."

"You've been empowered to represent the entire executive team?" Cenobia asked deliberately as her heart rate picked up. The sunny fall day outside of her curtains never suggested the chance of a coup.

Vasquez ran a hand through his blond highlights. "Not officially."

Cenobia's stillness hid her sigh of relief.

"But several of them have come to me. In private. They're concerned that your youthful enthusiasm has us rushing La Primera to the Frankfurt Auto Show without you considering the consequences."

Youthful enthusiasm? She knew what he really wanted

to say. Her inexperience. Her naivete. Her winding her *papá* around her little finger and taking advantage of nepotism that gave her what was supposed to be Lance's due. It was the thought of many who didn't know her, hadn't worked with her, or simply needed a woman to fail.

When she'd stepped into the role of CEO six months ago, she'd felt sorry for Vasquez. The man had a past president and two senators in his family tree and her father had plucked him fresh from of his Harvard MBA program and groomed him to occupy this office. Ten years older than her, Vasquez had actually been supportive of several of Cenobia's projects during her twelve years working with the company; he'd considered her as much a threat to his future as the bats who sometimes nested in the rafters of their factories.

"Trust me, I've considered all the consequences," she said. "Our made-in-Mexico hybrid car will show off the talents of Mexican engineering, allow us to increase the wages of our workers, and help improve the environment for all Mexicans."

"The stockholders don't care about the greater good." Vasquez scoffed. "They care about making money." It was a sentiment often said by her father. "Your car puts us in direct competition with the companies we rely on for the bulk of our business, it creates a need for highly skilled employees we won't be able to find, and it makes enemies of our government allies. They don't want to hear us babbling about cutting fuel dependency when our gas industry is one of the country's main sources of income."

Barbara Benitez, one of the smartest and shrewdest people Cenobia had ever met, had watched the conversation like a hawk. Now the woman jumped in with a

coo. "Enemies? Never, señor," she said, raising a pacifying hand. Pemex had apparently assigned her to deal
with the problem of Cenobia. "But perhaps, *niña*, you're
not fully aware of the ways the relationship with Pemex
has benefitted Trujillo Industries over the decades?"

Cenobia returned the sleek-bobbed woman's dismis-
sive diminutive with a smile full of teeth.

"I'm aware," she said. "I'm also aware of the exploratory trips Trujillo Industries is funding to allow you
to find new oil reserves as your production continues
to fall. Pemex debt passed the forty-billion-dollar mark
this year, didn't it?"

Barbara had the kind of non-reactive face Cenobia
could learn a lot from. "Even more reason to dedicate
yourself to the good of the state," she said coolly.

Cenobia swallowed her frustration. Affordable, envi-
ronmentally friendly, and emblematic of what Mexicans
could achieve, La Primera *was* for the good of the state.

"I continue to invite Pemex to join our alternative
energies task force," she said. "Wind, solar, and hydro
energy show long term…"

Vasquez's loud and belligerent sigh stopped her
words. Indeed. What was the point?

She glanced at Roman. His strong shoulders were relaxed. But his brilliant green eyes would have terrified
Vasquez if her VP had dared to look his way.

The quiet support of *el príncipe* bolstered her.

"I've heard you both," she said, then aimed her gaze
at Vasquez. "But with a month until the show, we need
to present a unified front. We've invested half a billion
dollars in this effort. The testing is complete and satis-
factory. Our factory is the first of its kind in Mexico, and
the assembly line is ramping up as we speak. The launch

will happen now, before foreign manufacturers monop-
olize the same market with an inferior product made
by Mexicans making half of what our workers make."

Alphawind Autos, whose chassis, shocks, wind-
shields and leather seats had been produced by Trujillo
Industries since the American company's inception, had
felt emboldened enough to ask Cenobia to postpone La
Primera's reveal for a year while they rolled out their
own hybrid car in Mexico.

That's how accustomed foreign car companies were
to steamrolling their way through her country.

"Our partners will have to get used to some competition," she said.

"Or they will go somewhere else and you will disem-
bowel this company because you've ignored the advice
of those with more reason and experience," Vasquez
said, drawing himself up. "Don't be surprised when
people start choosing the future of this company over
your shortsighted car."

Cenobia simply answered with a nod that dismissed
him from her office. The pale skin he prized flushed
red. A brown-skinned younger woman had embarrassed
him in front of the prince.

He swung to leave without farewells.

Benitez gave a respectful "Señorita Trujillo" before
she followed him out. Apparently, Mexican oil and
gas—and by extension, the Mexican government—
wasn't ready to declare a side.

Vasquez slammed her door closed.

"Thank you," she said, staring at it as reverberations
echoed through her office.

"For what?" Roman's low, deep voice had reverberations, too.

"For looking daunting while staying out of my way."

"Guy's lucky I didn't turn him into a pretzel."

"I believe he practices yoga. It might have been possible."

"Sorry you're dealing with more than threatening emails. I assumed you'd just slid into the CEO's seat. You're last name bein' on the building and all."

"*¡Ay!*" she exclaimed, turning to look at him. "The only chair my father would allow me to slide into is one with bonbons next to it and a pedicurist at its feet."

To Daniel Trujillo's eternal dismay, the engineering, entrepreneurship, and revolution that ran through various Trujillo branches all concentrated in the body of his one and only *hija*. The writing was on the wall when, at six, she offered her brand new porcelain-and-silk doll to an engineer if he would sketch out a braking system she'd dreamed up and present it as his own. The man worked his way up to division head before he admitted to Daniel what he'd done.

La Primera was an effort twelve years in the making, first drafted and researched in her rare spare time between school and Trujillo internships during breaks and holidays, then discussed with various trusted Trujillo engineers, designers, and marketers while she climbed her way up the corporate ladder in Mexico City, then finally greenlighted for investment and development when she'd taken a role at the Guanajuato headquarters four years ago. She was still irritated that her father and executives like Vasquez reacted with shock when she made the launch of her car the tent pole of her new chairmanship.

Mexico was a world leader in building cars for foreign car companies, and Trujillo Industries dominated the Mexican auto industry with its multitude of factories producing parts and automobiles for American, European, and Japanese brands. Her father was satisfied with that. Cenobia wasn't. Unless they started their own car company based on Mexican ethos and ingenuity, she'd gone round and round with him, they would always be considered inferior.

Why must you always push uphill, mijita? her father had asked.

Her future as the leader of Trujillo Industries rode on the success of this launch. But, as the pointed questions and growing skepticism at their Sunday *comidas* pointed out, so did her final chance to make her father recognize that she could be more than the pampered heiress he always wanted her to be.

Roman stepped close and tugged away the hand she hadn't realized was stroking her ear lobe. "I'm gonna take care of what's troubling you," he said, a little furrow between his brows as he squeezed her pinkie between his strong fingers and warm palm. She could feel the gravel of his low voice in her chest. "Don't you worry about it. I'm here now, and you can focus on making that asshole eat his words."

She smiled, squeezed his hand, and then pulled hers away before motioning to the door to escort him to the office of her head of security.

She'd had to pull away.

His touch, his stare, his declaration…curling into his chest and attaching herself like a limpet was probably a common response when women were confronted with the reality of the reluctant warrior prince.

But it was a little early in the day for CEO Cenobia Trujillo.

Chapter Four

Late that night, Roman rapped a knuckle on Cenobia's office door.

He'd spent the day meeting with the building's head of security, touring the headquarters' security infrastructure, interviewing Cenobia's personal guards, and getting up to date on what the team had learned.

He'd been waiting for Glori's message that she was escorting the CEO home.

Instead, he'd gotten a text from Cenobia asking him to her office.

"Come in," she called.

With his dark Brioni blazer tucked under his arm and his Italian cotton sleeves rolled up, Roman nodded to the guard stationed outside her door who was sipping a cinnamon-and-coffee-scented drink. Then he opened the door.

He snapped it closed before the guard could see what was inside.

Candles. Linen. White porcelain and wineglasses of delicate crystal.

The end of Cenobia's conference table was set for a romantic dinner for two.

"Good evening," she called from across the room, standing next to the whirring microwave. "Have a seat."

She turned to look into the microwave, and Roman saw that she'd taken down the bun her hair had been in earlier. It was now in a low ponytail. Her thick, black, wavy hair trailed in a long curlicue to the small of her back. Bent over slightly, her round hips and her…hips were displayed in the figure-hugging houndstooth dress, the thin red belt at her waist showcasing everything below it. The kick pleat revealed the dark, tender skin at the bottom of her thighs. She was barefoot. Her narrow Achilles tendon looked edible.

"What's up?" he called, still near the door.

She tossed a smile at him over her shoulder and he didn't need to see that: her arched back, the dimple in her cheek, the slippery slide of her hair. "You're too busy to eat out. So, we eat in. Glori said you were wrapping up."

He was gonna have words with his second-in-command. Glori was supposed to keep Roman apprised of Cenobia's movements. Not the other way around.

Because he was a thirty-nine-year-old man and not a kid, Roman walked into the room and laid his blazer over a chair. He also bumped the dimmer switch as he passed it, brightening her office and making the candlelight less potent.

Cenobia looked up but didn't comment as the microwave dinged.

"Hay vino," she called as she pulled the cartons out of the microwave with a towel and plated the food.

He glanced at the wine bottle as he approached the table. It was his sister's label, Bodega Sofia.

"I don't drink when I'm working," he said. "You want some?"

"Oh." He watched her expressive face fall as she held the two plates. "No, then. None for me. I could make you a *café de olla*. It's ground coffee and boiled cinnamon sticks. I make it for the guards working the third shift—"

That's what the guard outside had been drinking. It'd smelled heavenly.

"Water's fine," he said, taking the spot at the side of the table, catty corner to the head seat. She placed his plate on the porcelain charger in front of him.

"You don't have to serve me—" he began, but she cut him off as she pointed at two bottles chilling in a sterling silver bucket.

"¿Con gas o sin?"

"Con," he answered.

As she opened the bottle of sparkling water, sat, and poured for them both, Roman placed his linen napkin in his lap. "You should keep on like I'm not here, Cenobia."

"Cen," she said. She kept her eyes on the gurgling water. "So the man who saved my life is in my world for the first time, has dropped everything at a moment's notice because I coerced him to, and I'm supposed to let him fend for himself while I eat dinner at my kitchen counter and catch up on emails?"

He stayed quiet because it seemed safest.

She put the bottle carefully down then looked at him with her wide jaw set. "Please don't minimize what you did for me before and what you're doing for me now. I feel awkward when you do."

"Okay," he said. She was a plain talker. He appreciated that. He'd do some plain talking back. "You didn't coerce me."

She raised her chin and picked up her fork. "I revealed that I'd been the source of the loan to the Monte and then begged you to come."

He pushed his sleeves up his forearms before picking up his knife and fork. "Staying objective working security is tricky," he said, starting to saw at his unappetizing-looking chicken breast. "Guards see clients at their best and their worst. And when you're protecting doctors in war zones or celebrities who treat people like their personal robots, that bar can get pretty high and low. But you gotta stay detached; it's the only way you can keep a client alive."

He speared a piece of chicken and looked at her. "Today, I discovered that your personal security team and the crew that guards the headquarters would throw themselves on a bomb for you." He motioned with his fork to the closed door. "Those men and women are dedicated, nearly indoctrinated, and they've balled up their objectivity and kicked it right out of the stadium. If you're doing things like making that incredible smelling coffee for them every night, I understand why they've lost their detachment."

She smiled cautiously. "That is the most words I've ever heard from you in one sitting. Would you like a *café de olla*? I still have some warm."

"God, yes, please," he said, conceding to this one little desire if it would wipe the remaining discomfort off her face.

When her smile widened and softened, he looked down at his limp zucchini medley. She obviously had more important things on her mind than the quality of her meals.

"Finding out who's threatening you is not gonna be easy," he said as she returned to the kitchenette. "If it was, your qualified crew would've found 'em already. Not that I'm ruling them out as the leak; it's too early for that. But I'm glad you called on me. I would have been pissed if you hadn't."

And that was the God's honest truth, for her to hear and for him to absorb. There was a job here that needed the excellence of Sheppard Security. Cenobia needed him. Them.

He would fix this. He would help her. He would keep her safe.

The way she looked at him as she padded back on bare feet with the two handle-less terra-cotta cups had him gripping tight to his detachment. The candlelight shimmered in her glossy eyes, like sunlight rippling over river stones. "I'm still sorry I didn't tell you about the loan sooner," she said softly, placing the cup in front of him.

She'd been planning on telling him. He didn't want to go into why he'd always turned down the invitations.

"It's fine," he said as he picked up the warm, painted cup. He took a sip and, damn, it tasted even better than it smelled. "Don't know how you squeezed in saving a kingdom between getting your undergrad and masters in five years and then working every spare second at the company, but I can't complain about it now."

She pushed aside the porcelain and crystal and picked up her own clay cup. "Your file on me is very thorough," she smirked before closing her eyes and inhaling the aroma.

Roman licked his lips, which were always as dry as the Ramadi desert. He didn't know that stuff because of a file.

When she opened her eyes again, he was focused on his coffee.

"Is that from your niece?" she asked, nodding at his wrist. Settled against the dinged-up, black metal KIA bracelet he never took off was the pink-and-yellow friendship bracelet his niece Liliana had woven for him.

"Yeah," he said, rubbing his thumb over it fondly. "She broke a vase. I took the fall. She's been paying me in friendship bracelets ever since."

"Blackmailing an eight-year-old for your accessories. Ruthless."

Roman huffed a laugh and met Cenobia's sparkling eyes. Her smile curved her cheeks up into rose-tinted balls. Her skin was marble smooth.

He was staring.

"Tell me about discovering that note," he said. It came out gruffer than he meant it to. Her smile settled before she put her cup down and folded her delicate hands into her lap.

"As I'm sure my security team has already told you—"

Ouch.

"—I was coming back from a personal meeting. I'd parked my car out of the way, on a side street. I thought it was just an advertisement left on the windshield; I was about to throw it away when I saw the words on back."

The note had been written in jagged block print on the back of a black-and-white flyer for a gordita stand.

We've warned you.

Stop.

Now.

We kept you blindfolded last time. This time, we'll cut off your eyelids so we'll be the last thing you see.

Both teams had already gone over the note with a fine-toothed comb and Roman had looked at it through a laminate sleeve. But nothing was more valuable than talking to the witness.

"Did you see anyone watching you? Anything that raised your hackles?"

She shook her head. "I didn't look around until I was safely in the locked car with my panic button pushed. But no. When my security arrived and investigated the scene, they couldn't find anything either."

"You reported you were blindfolded during your kidnapping," he said. "That intel could have been googled."

She was looking down at her lap, her gorgeous tail of hair over one shoulder. Roman knew she was stroking the back of her hand.

"You think what's happening now could have any connection to then?" He watched her closely, but didn't get much out of her shrug-head wobble.

Kidnapped from a park near Rice University in Houston, Texas where she'd been a freshman, she'd been blindfolded for six days before he rescued her. Daniel Trujillo had called Roman, who'd gotten some press as an American war hero starting his own security company, because the tycoon had been concerned that the American and Mexican governments were giving up hopes of finding her. Paying the paltry ransom the kidnappers had asked for hadn't resulted in Cenobia's return.

Roman had been sitting on his couch watching game shows with a three-day beard when his brand-new Sheppard Security mobile phone had rung for the first time.

"I know I don't have time to fret over it," she said. "If someone wanted to distract me, these emails and notes are a perfect way to do it."

He felt a rush of irritation. "If it's such a critical time, then why the hell would you go someplace alone?" There could have been so many worse things waiting for her than a note: an incendiary device, an assailant, a sharpshooter.

Her eyes snapped up to meet his. "Don't," she said firmly. "Don't question me like that."

Shit. He'd had clients sneak out of their hotel rooms, bribe bus boys, run traffic lights, dress themselves in glaringly bad outfits to escape the people they were paying good money to protect them. But Roman—who his sister teased was a *cara de piedra como* Easter Island— hadn't lost his cool with them.

"Sorry," he said. "Sorry." He took a breath then pointed at her. "But keeping you alive thirteen years ago is the first thing on my resume. If you screw that up now, I'm going to have to rewrite it."

He surprised her into a smile before she bit it away. "Well, we wouldn't want that."

"Not to mention what it'll do to my website."

He was glad to see her shoulders relaxing as she gave him a begrudging grin and took her cup back into her hands.

This woman needed someone to lift some of the load off her.

"Can you please talk to me about why you'd go some-place without your security detail?" he asked gently.

She blew into her still-steaming cup. "It's how I manage my anxiety," she said. She shot him a look over the rim and then blew again, her unpainted lips shaped into a perfect kiss. "Exposure therapy. I do what I'm afraid of."

"Your therapist has recommended that you go places unprotected?" he replied, processing the fact that she hadn't left what had happened to her back in the bunker.

Processing her mouth.

"No," Cenobia huffed. "Of course, my therapist hasn't recommended that. It's just…" She flung her hand out at the closed door. "I get so tired of being watched over. Of the need for it. I go months meditating and watching my caffeine and exercising and following every dictate of my security protocol and still out of nowhere, I'll see a man with a certain hairstyle and find myself dissociating."

He hated the thought of this powerful, sparkling woman going under and seeing herself through a thick fog.

"I stay in this padded lane, but the fear still seeps in. So I think *¿Para qué sirve?*" She linked her fingers and gave him a look of cautious defiance. "Then I get into my car and drive very fast."

"How fast?"

She smiled. "Very, very fast. I drive a Lexus LC 500."

He whistled and it made her dimples come out. The head of Mexico's largest automobile conglomerate had dimples. He didn't care what kind of precision team she had tuning up her luxury automobile; Roman was going to go over her car.

He leaned back in his chair with his cup. "I've managed some PTSD," he said. "After serving."

She leaned back in hers, too. "Anything now?"

"Insomnia," he said gruffly. "Nightmares. The occasional day when I feel like I'm trying to walk carrying a ten-ton weight. A therapist on speed dial I pay more than my mortgage."

He met her rich, brown eyes. Neither of them spoke for several moments.

The silence was far too comfortable.

"Thank you for telling me," she said softly.

"Thank you for telling *me*," he said. "But if you try to take off without your security detail while I'm here, I will proverbially kick your ass."

"How do you do that in proverb?" she asked, glancing up at him from under her long, black lashes.

He focused on pulling his phone out of his pocket. "Don't make me show you. You about ready to go?"

Suggesting it had his intended effect. She yawned. "Yes." She rose from her seat as Roman also stood and summoned her crew on his phone.

"Glori and the team will escort you home. In the morning, I'll meet you here to discuss—"

"You're not staying with me?" she asked.

He looked up from his phone to find her standing too close, right in his shadow. Her smoky-brown eyes stared up at him in confusion. They were end-of-day soft and exhausted.

A trace of her perfume clung to her like a last petal. "No."

"I assumed you'd be…taking…Glori's place," she said, each word slower than the one before it. Embarrassment grew in a warm flush across her pretty face.

It was the first time she reminded him of that eighteen-year-old girl.

"No," he said. "Glori will maintain her position in your home."

"Oh." If another man had made her look the way she was looking now, he would have eliminated him. "*Bien.*"

He turned and grabbed their half-eaten plates, carried them to the sink, rinsed them off, and put them in the dishwasher, even though she told him the cleaning crew would take care of it. After he'd stacked the rest of the precious tableware by the sink, he folded the tablecloth and bagged up the trash. When Glori still hadn't arrived, he opened the door and chatted with the guard until she did.

They all escorted Cenobia to her car and driver. Her black Rolls Royce Phantom would be the center of a three-car caravan for the foreseeable future.

"You good?" Roman asked as she settled into the white leather backseat.

"Yes. Thank you again, Roman," she said softly, her eyes luminous in the dim. "*Buenas noches.*"

He straightened and closed her door. Knocked on the hood and watched the caravan roll away. As he walked to his own rented car, he monitored her journey on his phone to make sure she made it safely.

The irony that he wouldn't have had to monitor it if he'd just gone with her didn't escape him.

Chapter Five

The next day, Cenobia was in wall-to-wall meetings and saw little of Roman after he gave her a morning update on his team's efforts. She invited him to join her for lunch in her office, but at the set hour, her assistant knocked on her door with a takeout container and a note. Roman apologized for not being able to make it, but he sent a *torta* stuffed with *chicharrón*, lettuce, tomato, avocado and salsa, and a cold Topo Chico.

The sandwich was a mess—she'd had to finish it over the sink—but only after getting up from her desk did she realized how delicious it was. She offered the boxed meal the catering company filled her home and work refrigerators with to her assistant, but Paloma always turned down Cenobia's food.

At the end of the long day, Roman, Glori, and the guard stationed outside her office door escorted Cenobia to the garage, her heels in her hand. Roman looked broad-shouldered and commanding in the garage's harsh light; the look of him both soothed her and riled a frustration she'd been trying to tamp down. He was here to protect her. He hadn't offered to befriend her.

But was he avoiding her?

He had no escape the next day. Her father had invited Roman to their family's Sunday *comida*.

"Román!" her father called as they entered the dining room, the early afternoon sun shining through the long wall of glass and burnishing the room's heavy wood furniture. Her family home was in the middle of a high-security compound on top of a flat mesa with stunning views of the dry grass-and-limestone Bajío. The tall walls and security force made it one of the few places she felt safe enough to enjoy views.

The staff delivered an excess number of dishes on the stone-and-marble-inlaid table then quickly kissed her cheek before they went back for more. She'd take the *príncipe* back to the kitchen later to meet them.

Her father pumped Roman's hand and pounded his shoulder. "The years have been kind, *compadre*," Daniel said, looking him over.

Y qué ricos, had they ever. Roman was wearing an unstructured blue-grey jacket, a light grey sweater that highlighted his body, and flat-fronted trousers. The tan leather cord around his strong neck matched the leather band of his TAG Heuer watch and his cap-toed camel leather oxfords. His dark hair, short on the sides and styled on top, looked softer than it at work. The whole effect of the brunch-chic look on his warrior-ready body was…delicious.

Cenobia caught her father's too-observant gaze before she looked away.

"And the tacos have been kind to me." Daniel laughed, white teeth flashing in his wide, dark face as he patted his belly. Daniel Trujillo might be one of the wealthiest and most powerful men in Mexico. But on

Sundays, he dressed down. His thick black waves with silver at the temple were brushed back with no product, there was black scruff over his wide cheeks, and he wore jeans and a white *guayabera*, an embroidered, short-sleeve, button-up shirt over his thick shoulders and round belly. His white teeth always sparkled like he'd polished them, part of his astonishing smile that calmed crying babies, pacified government officials, seduced American investors, and made friends of strangers everywhere he went.

Their family was descended from the Guachichiles, nomads who'd opposed the silver mining of their lands and fiercely fought the Spanish in the longest war of Spain's invasion of Mesoamerica. Ultimately, they'd been assimilated and worked the silver mines that made the city of Guanajuato rich and beautiful. During the Mexican revolution, Cenobia's great-great grandfather went from a worker to a revolutionary leader to a mine owner. Along with the family fortune, he also passed down his Guachichil ways, following the cycles of nature as he established business deals and calling on his eagle spirit to guide him.

Cenobia's father had wound his Catholic and indigenous beliefs into his own religion, a mix of lunar cycles and Virgin of Guadalupe prayers and feelings delivered from the earth and the heavens that had helped him transform his father's successful vehicle-seat factory into a monolithic corporation that reigned over the Mexican automotive industry.

Daniel looked to the doorway. *"Ah, mi hijo. Ven, ven aquí."*

Cenobia looked as well and swallowed the joy she

knew wouldn't be welcome as a boy and his bodyguard-companion crossed the room toward them.

She stepped away and put her arms around the massive shoulders of the bodyguard, Bartolo.

He kissed her cheek. "You look lovely."

She looked down at her ivory blouse with its pan collar, her voluminous olive-green skirt with its wrap tie and large floppy bow defining her waist, her burnt orange cardigan, and high heels. Her hair was in a high, sleek ponytail.

"Is it too much?" she whispered. He'd been with them since she was a girl and had once been head of her security detail.

Bartolo had a huge shaved head, a wide, busted nose, a scar on his lip, and black, understanding eyes. "You're perfect."

She grimaced and kissed his cheek before they turned to focus on the main event.

"Román," her father announced, his hands on the narrow shoulders of a twelve-year-old boy who was almost as tall as him and whose shiny, medium brown curls caught the noon sunlight. "I would like to introduce you to my son, Adán Trujillo, who also happens to be your number one fan."

"Papá," Adán whined softly. But nothing in his wide, slate-grey eyes disagreed as he looked up at the man who'd been a primary topic of conversation during these Sunday *comidas*.

"Nice to meet you," Roman drawled, a soothing smile on his face and a directness to his gaze as he shook Adán's certainly sweaty hand. He might be a reluctant prince but he'd mastered this role. "Don't think I've ever met a person with a comet named after them."

Adán had her father's smile—wide and glorious and heart tugging—and he gave it to Roman now, surprised and delighted that his hero knew such a thing about him. Cenobia was surprised, too. They kept Adán's media exposure to a minimum, but when he'd discovered what turned out to be an important comet with the telescope he'd begged for, they'd allowed him to be interviewed for a few academic journals and astronomy magazines.

"Welcome to our home, *Príncipe*," Adán said formally with a bow, his voice unnaturally somber, and Cenobia had to bite back a grin as she felt quick tears pop into her eyes. She wondered how often he'd practiced that in the mirror.

She could see in the austere edge of Roman's jaw that he was fighting back amusement. "You can call me Roman," he said, patting Adán's shoulder. Adán looked like he might shoot off and join those stars he admired.

"Say hello to your sister," her father said.

And Adán came crashing back to earth.

His thin shoulders slumped, his hair tumbling in front of his eyes, and Cenobia got to see the view of him she'd grown accustomed to over the last couple of months. Her father and Bartolo blamed it on the first trickle of puberty. But puberty seemed to be angry just at her.

He slouched to her, eyes on the ground, and gave her a half-hearted, one-armed hug. His clothes—pressed khakis, a tucked-in chambray shirt, and a polka-dotted bow tie—highlighted how tall and skinny he was getting. He smelled strongly of the Armani Privé she'd given him for Christmas, as if he'd layered body wash, body spray, and cologne. He'd kill her if she sneezed. Still, she squeezed him closer for a few seconds more.

He was changing rapidly from the boy who had squeezable baby fat just a few months before.

Her father introduced Bartolo and then they all took their seats at the mammoth table covered in food—Daniel and Cenobia at the ends, Roman on one side, Adán and Bartolo on the other—and began serving themselves.

As the mountain on Daniel's plate grew higher, Roman started with menudo, like Cenobia.

He savored a spoonful then looked at her. "You grew up with delicious food like this?" he asked.

"*Sí.*" She wiped her lip. "When I was home." Her school days had been spent in United States boarding schools. "Our chef Josefita has been with us since I was a girl."

He had a way of looking at her that made her feel like a puzzle.

He turned his gaze on Bartolo. "How long have you been with the family?" he asked politely.

Her father's eyes went spotlight wide. The arrival of Bartolo in their lives was a favorite of his many stories.

Within a minute, they were all laughing into their linen napkins.

"So this huge *luchador* in his black *demonio* mask comes flying out of the ring toward me and my guards instantly pounce," Daniel said, scattering *ensalada de nopales* like confetti as he waved his fork in the air. "But he won't let go of the neck of this little skinny *bolillo* that he landed on. So he breaks free from *my* men, big men, to show me what's in the guy's hand. There's a little pig sticker. That skinny *pendejo* would've stabbed me if this *hombre* hadn't stopped him."

Cenobia laughed along and watched Roman—his

white teeth flashing, a full laugh rumbling out of his chest, the rays at the corner of his eyes shining—as he tipped his water glass at Bartolo. The Afro-Mexican ex-wrestler gave a quick shrug, but Cenobia could tell he enjoyed this story being shared with the decorated warrior prince they'd discussed so often at this very table.

Adán had been young when he learned about the kidnapping from his friends, and when he first asked questions, Cenobia had left the room while her father and Bartolo made it clear that the topic was to be treated carefully. The empathetic boy quickly realized that the mood would tank if he brought it up, but that the atmosphere picked up considerably if he mentioned her rescuer. The four of them had spent many a Sunday *comida* marveling over Roman's latest appearance in the international press, his company's most recent miraculous rescue, his growing reputation as a reluctant royal, or his ranking on another world's most eligible bachelor list. He'd become the unofficial mascot of the *comida,* the playing card they collected throughout the week then traded on Sundays, and the bandage they used to cover the difficult spots in their relationships.

Now—in a surreal turn of events—he was sitting here, serving himself a helping of *tamales de alcega* while Cenobia watched, foolishly pleased. Food was simply fuel, and she didn't care to waste time focusing on it. But the creamy, Swiss chard tamales were her favorite.

Her father jabbed a tortilla toward Bartolo. "I hired him on the spot and he's been with us ever since."

Bartolo shook his head at Roman. "It wasn't quite that dramatic," he said in his deep-chested voice, his *lucha libre* days still apparent in his massive torso, mashed nose, and lip scar. "It was nothing like recovering five Armenian ministers from terrorists."

As Daniel, Adán, and Bartolo excitedly recounted Roman's meteoric rise from American soldier to international hero to Spanish royalty, Cenobia watched a muscle tick repeatedly in Roman's jaw.

"I leave the royal stuff to my siblings," he said, shifting in his seat.

Daniel pointed his sterling fork at Roman's hand. "That's not what the gold on your finger says."

Roman clenched his powerful fist around the king's advisor ring.

"This ring's partly your fault," he said. "Or…hers. I still get mixed up after ten years of thinking you were our patron."

Daniel chuckled. "Why would I come clean and give up all that admiration?" He used a scrap of tortilla to scoop up a bite of *frijoles*, chewed, swallowed, then shrugged. "Cenobia thought she knew better than my analysts. It's the bane of being the papá of a girl too smart for her own good. I decided to let her experiment and learn from being wrong."

Roman put down the fork that had been halfway up to his mouth and turned to look at her. "I thought you were just monitoring the money," he said, green eyes pinning her to the heavy, wooden chair. "Did your analysts deny the loan?"

"Sí," her father said gleefully.

"No," Cenobia cut in. "They used the wrong model. I put the Monte's debt and growth potential through a better statistical model and came up with a different number. They would have come around eventually. But since I was able to use my trust fund as collateral I just—"

Roman's face hardened to stone. "Your trust fund?"

This table, always surrounded by storytellers with illustrative hands and proud opinions, very seldom encountered silence. Now, you could hear a pin drop. If her father, Bartolo, and Adán wanted a glimpse of the warrior prince, they were getting it.

Cenobia raised her chin and met his eyes.

He pursed his lips and gave her one meaningful glance—*later*—before turning his attention to Adán. "You know who's gonna make a great prince? My nephew, Gabriel." He told a story about a camping trip he took with eight-year-old Gabriel, his twin sister, Liliana, and their "dumb-as-a-stump" cocker spaniel Benito that had the table laughing uproariously. And that effectively changed the subject.

Cenobia laughed along, but she was distracted by the promise of a future argument with him, like a bruise she couldn't stop stroking. She was accustomed to men disagreeing with her; they were usually just roadblocks to overcome. But with the warrior prince, she felt an alien desire to go toe-to-toe and eye-to-eye.

What was the taciturn soldier like when he wasn't so taciturn? Would a good brawl make him more comfortable with her?

Her father lifted the bottle of wine toward Roman's glass, but Roman shook his head.

Daniel filled his own glass. "*Pues*, let's talk about your plans to keep my daughter safe," he said.

Adán side-eyed Cenobia as worry crinkled his eyebrows. She'd stroked those feathery brows when he'd been a baby sleeping in her arms. "Papá, why don't we excuse Adán before we discuss that?"

Bartolo spoke up. "Adán needs to eat and stop trying to hide his *tamal* under the *sopa*." She remembered that voice as she'd once stared miserably at a plate of liver and onions.

Adán glanced from under his lashes at Roman, then stared down at his plate. "*Alcega* is gross," he said mulishly.

No, it wasn't; the tamales made with Swiss chard were way more moist than the meat tamales. But as much as twelve-year-old Adán was starting to stretch into a longer body, he was still a little boy.

"*Está bien, mi sueño*," she said, smiling at him. "You don't have to eat it. I think we're having *pastel de tres leches* for dessert. Go ask Josefita if you can have a slice."

Adán popped up. But then he hesitated, looking at Roman.

"Let us talk," she said. "And then you can show Roman your fossil collection before we leave."

Adán gave her a begrudging smile before he flew out of the room.

Bartolo, however, was slower, looking at Cenobia as he pushed back his chair and placed his napkin on his plate.

Just fifteen years older than Cenobia, Bartolo had been head of the security team meant to keep her safe in Houston. Now, he took his job as Adán's protector and companion—no one had ever dared call the man a *niñera*—very seriously.

Cenobia looked away from his pointed gaze and lifted her glass. She took a sip of the crisp chardonnay she'd been nursing throughout the meal as Bartolo walked out of the room.

Roman outlined what his team had learned so far

and the new safety measures they'd put in place. "I'm here to make sure she doesn't have to worry about this so she can focus on the launch of her car and her new role in the company. Lord knows, I don't want to upset your delicate ticker."

Cenobia choked on her wine as Roman's heavy-lidded gaze fastened on her father.

Daniel leaned back in his seat, threaded his fingers over his belly. He was enjoying this time off a little too much. If he kept eating and drinking the way he was, he might develop a true heart condition rather than the one he'd faked as a convenient ruse.

"So she told you her role as CEO is on a trial basis?" her father asked. "You think I'm being unfair?"

"Seems like an unfair thing to tease someone with," he drawled.

"A tease?" her father repeated, bushy black eyebrows raised.

"She's either qualified or she isn't."

"Oh, she's qualified. There's no doubt of that. She's done nothing but breathe, eat, and plan to run this company since she was a little girl."

She was sitting right here. But it was surprising to hear Roman leap into the fray.

"But what about boys?" her father said, his meal forgotten as he waved both hands around. "What about clothes? What about hobbies that involve something other than finding her in her bed at three in the morning reading Chilton repair manuals?"

Her humiliation and frustration flared. This endless argument. "If I was born a boy—" she began.

"But you weren't," her father cut her off, as tired of this ceaseless back-and-forth as she was. "And no amount of bemoaning the inequality of the sexes in the world, in Mexico, and in this industry is going to change that. Your only goal is to spend your life pushing uphill when my only goal has been to make your life perfect."

Pues, *it was too late for that*, she could have muttered with all of Adán's sullenness. But that was too far.

Her father was her best friend and biggest detractor.

After the kidnapping, he'd stood resolutely by her. He'd allowed her to bury herself at Rice University while coming home for summers and breaks to work for the company. He hadn't fought her resolve to dedicate herself to work when she'd taken a full-time position at the Mexico City headquarters, where she learned to wine and dine the right people to benefit Trujillo Industries. But as she made deeper strides into the company and finally earned a position in Guanajuato, she watched her father's empathy turn to impatience as Cenobia continued to choose work over the jetsetting and leisure he would have preferred for her.

"I want you safe. I want you healthy. I want you to have a husband."

Cenobia's face burned hot. "Says the man who lost his wife thirty-one years ago and hasn't been in a sustained relationship since." Her mother died of diabetic complications soon after Cenobia was born.

"I thought…" Roman stopped but then continued. "I thought you'd gotten married again. To Adán's mother."

Daniel smiled. "It's a marriage Cenobia likes to forget," he said smoothly.

He leaned back in his chair, rethreaded his fingers over his belly. "My daughter has worked hard and I won't deny her a chance," he said. "But I won't allow her to subsume herself to the company. I will take it away from her, and I will yank that car off the line if necessary."

More than Vasquez's misogyny, or Pemex's road blocking, or the partners and competitors who wanted Cenobia to fail, this was her biggest challenge. The lines of this lifelong battle were now drawn out for Roman Sheppard, an almost stranger and a man she admired more than any other.

Roman was wonderfully princely when he met the staff and appropriately impressed when Adán showed him his fossil collection. Adán gave her a half-hearted hug goodbye and she hoped for a mood that swung in her favor by next Sunday.

The sun was winking away on the horizon when they settled into the white leather backseat of the Rolls Royce Phantom, "Sorry about your Dad," he said before they'd even left the compound. "I know from my brother's situation, it's not easy when your parents stand in your way."

She sighed as she kicked her heels off into the lambswool-carpeted foot well and looked out the heavily tinted glass. "Yes, but my father loves me."

"Almost makes it worse."

Her heart squeezed. He really did understand. "Yes."

"You should've told me your trust fund was on the line, Cenobia."

At the abrupt change of subject, she turned to look at him. He kept his voice low, in respect of the presence of Arnol, her driver, but his green eyes looked fierce in the soft glow of the interior lights.

"Why?" she asked, his empathy forgotten in the flare of her temper. "So another man could doubt my intentions, advice, and expertise?"

His mouth pursed before he relaxed it. "Because, for all intents and purposes, I was your partner."

Oh. He wanted equality. "And as my *paaaartner*..." She drew the word out, making him inhale, irritated, through his nose. "What would you have done when I told you?"

He was proud and protective; she knew exactly what he would have done. His answer did not disappoint. "I would have figured out a way to return the money."

"Right," she snapped, her frustration sizzling like a lit firework. "You would have beggared a kingdom instead of trusting me to know my capabilities and limits."

The grip of his jaw, the narrowed intensity of his eyes, the tense set of his wide shoulders, she'd finally made him angry. He had the right to be. So did she.

But instead of defending himself or blaming her, he turned his chin away and looked out on the empty road. "I won't be the reason you get hurt, Cenobia."

No. They were near the heart of this. She didn't want him retreating behind his soldierly facade now.

"Cen," she said, entirely to irritate. Why was he so opposed to her nickname?

But he didn't even give her a jaw tic of reaction. She leaned across the plush leather armrest between their seats and grasped his big, hard hand, forcing his eyes back to her. "You listened to me and followed my advice when it was a battle with everyone else." She curled her hand around his. "Yes, you believed I was my father, but the trust you placed in me still meant so much." She pushed her fingertips across the calluses of his palm, explored his warm hand, until she could mesh her fingers with his. "I needed that faith." His fingers gripped hers back and she could feel it in her spine. "I still do."

His engulfing hand clasping hers against his hard thigh was one of the most pleasurable sensations of her life.

"I'd hoped we'd get to…know one another while you were here." She'd come this far, but his stillness was becoming more that she could stand. His eyes flicked to Arnol. She dropped her eyes to their joined hands. "But I never see you and…"

His phone buzzed a distinctive pattern.

She rubbed her thumb over a hard callus at the base of his palm. "I would like to get to know you."

The buzzing phone cracked the held-breath stillness in the car.

"It's Glori," he finally said, voice floorboard deep. "I have to take this."

She unwound her fingers from his and clenched her hand in her lap. "Of course."

As he spoke in a low murmur, Cenobia turned toward the window and considered asking Arnol to aim the car off the steep canyon road.

Roman was on the phone for several minutes.

When he hung up, he said, "Cenobia?"

She could scream.

But then he said, "Look at me."

Her eyes blinked wide in the reflection of the tinted glass. She could see him, too, the precisely drawn warrior prince staring at her. The interior of her opulent sedan suddenly seemed much smaller than it had a moment before.

She did as she'd been told.

There was a deep furrow between his dark eyebrows. "We've got new intel. We thought the threatening emails were coming from the University of Guanajuato library, that someone was using their public computers. Turns out the sender has masked the origination point."

Cenobia frowned. "Then where are the emails from?"

"We don't know." His face, his voice, wrapped those three words in cotton. "They're using a high-level encryption that isn't easy to break."

The person or people sending emails to her were using the kind of technology that even Sheppard Security found challenging?

"We're raising the threat-level concern," he said solemnly. "But you stay focused and do what you need to do. You let me worry about the rest. You'll hardly notice the changes."

"Changes?"

"The one you will notice… I'll be your point man during the day." He raised his chin, just a touch. "I'll be with you from the time you leave your house until you return to it."

"Bueno," she said, nodding. *"Gracias."*

She turned back to face the window.

She would get her wish. She would get to spend more time with Roman Sheppard.

Maybe she should be grateful for the escalating threat against her. It was far more successful in gaining his company than her wants and the words out of her mouth.

Chapter Six

Guanajuato, Mexico

Roman showed up at Cenobia's home the next morning five minutes before her scheduled departure time. Yes, he'd be near her more as her principal daytime close protection. But he'd minimize the amount of time he spent with her padding around her luxury mini-fortress of a home, built around a courtyard that used the original fronts of three pastel-colored townhomes to camouflage it within a busy residential neighborhood. CEO Cenobia Trujillo had a habit of relaxing her retro-glam billionaire look—taking down her hair, kicking off her shoes—and he would manage how relaxed he saw her.

She needed him. The threats against her were growing, and her obstacles were real. She needed him protecting her back so she could push forward, past bad-mannered employees and stuck-in-the-past oil companies and her own damn dad. He would help her.

But, to do it, he wanted her shoed and work-clothed and surrounded by observant eyes. Last night, she'd slipped off her towering heels and rubbed her toes into the arches. He'd barely resisted pulling her feet into his lap, using his artful thumbs to thank and punish her for risking her trust fund on him. Then she'd gripped his hand with a ferocity that made it feel like their bones were melding, careless of his stumpy finger. She'd stared into him with her mink-pelt eyes and told him she wanted to get to know him better.

She knew plenty. He'd keep her safe, do his job, and maintain his distance.

His plan was instantly blown to hell when Glori Knight, who was supposed to be waiting in the follow-up vehicle, walked into Cenobia's granite-and-stainless-steel kitchen to tell him that the driver had already left.

"He was told to meet us in the plaza. It's a mile walk down the hill, sir," she said as she delivered the news, a black scarf holding her chin-length curls off her face. Glori was former Army with military running through her veins. Both her African-American dad and her Mexican-American mom had served. She'd been one of his first hires. They'd gotten drunk together; they'd even saved each other's bacon a time or two. She still insisted on calling him sir.

Roman wasn't going to okay a jaunt through Guanajuato. He jerked out his phone, ready to rip the driver a new one, when he heard high heels tapping down the circular staircase. Between the gleaming wood steps, he could see shell-pink heels then smooth, mocha-colored calves and then a silver-grey, body-curving dress covered in white polka dots then a tiny pink belt around a squeezable waist, and then…

"*Buenos días.* Isn't it a beautiful morning?" Cenobia asked as she reached the first level, eyes sparkling and the balls of her cheeks rosy. She'd sleeked all that thick black hair into a bun high on her head. "I want to show you my city."

She slipped on a pastel pink blazer as she hummed.

"Put her two most experienced people in front," Roman told Glori. "You back us up."

Glori, who had one of the best poker faces he'd ever seen, worked it hard now as she gave a nod.

When they stepped out on the street in front of Cenobia's home, the sky was a rich true blue, the morning October air cool. Old-town Guanajuato was built into a canyon, and Cenobia's home was part of a neighborhood at the very top. Below them, brightly painted row houses, red terra-cotta roofs, and the rounded cupolas and spires built during the city's wealthy silver-mining days glittered like candies in a bowl. With her guards walking ten paces in front, Cenobia led Roman across the street to a narrow set of stairs.

As they began to descend the brick-and-mortar steps, Cenobia explained that much of Guanajuato was accessible only on foot using the *callejones*, the tiny alleys and stairways that they were walking along now.

"It has limited development but it's preserved a way of life," she said, motioning to a doorway with a cobalt-blue door and bright fuchsia bougainvillea hanging over the top of it. "You can only access the center of Guanajuato by driving through a tunnel, so American tourists driving past on the way to San Miguel de Allende think there's nothing here. The Mexican tourists know what a jewel it is."

"That's like the Monte," he said, keeping an eye on their surroundings. Revolutionary murals, carved wooden shutters, antique fountains that used to be the primary source of water, and vistas between the homes of the bright city and green hills provided something new to see with every step they descended. "The mountains kept out invaders and preserved the kingdom, but without proper care in modern times, the isolation almost did 'em in."

Cenobia smiled at him. "You and Mateo have certainly opened doors to the Monte, with all the transportation upgrades," she said. "I was disappointed I didn't get to see the train depot renovation."

Roman was about to grunt a response when he remembered. He narrowed his eyes on her. "Sad you didn't get to gloat with Mateo that y'all were right?"

Her smile grew. "The initial plan you approved was very...secure," she teased.

"Mateo called it a concrete igloo; he never worries himself too much about tact." Roman hadn't wanted to be in charge of the capital improvement project, but his siblings' hands had been full. "What'd he think he was going to get from an army grunt?"

"He just believed maintaining the view of the Picos was a touch more preferable than turning the depot into a very safe but mildly depressing holding cell." She wasn't doing a great job holding back her grin. But then her eyes traveled down him. "Your design eye doesn't always fail you."

He was wearing grey on grey on grey—a light grey fresco wool suit over a sleek Egyptian cotton grey shirt and a slim grey silk Hermes tie—and he'd just been thinking how glad he was that he'd sacrificed the monochrome of grey by going for his tan, hand-stained St. Crispin derby boots, which had some give to them.

He didn't know how her feet were handling the descent in those high pink heels.

He checked their two and ten. "At the time, I sure as hell didn't appreciate Mateo getting Daniel—you—to weigh in like he—you—was our dad."

"You two seem to have found a system that works."

The steps had flattened out to a narrow, stone-paved pathway winding between homes.

"Yeah," he said. "We go a few rounds, he gets hot under the collar, I let him get it out of his system, then we meet somewhere in the middle." He wouldn't mention the occasional headlock.

He and Mateo were almost as close in age as two brothers could be—Roman was actually a couple of hours older than the king—although they couldn't be more different. Mateo was born into Spanish royalty; Roman grew up in a Texas trailer park. Mateo was a scientist; Roman was a well-aimed gun. Mateo led emotions first, thinking about consequences later. Roman gauged the ripple effect of every move before he made it.

He glanced at her and saw her watching him with a look on her face. A glow.

"It must be quite a thing to find a brother," she said softly.

In the continued slow reveal of the way he and Cenobia were intertwined, he realized how enmeshed this woman was in his relationship with the most important person in his life.

"Report," he said. The *callejón* was about to open up into a plaza. The employees ten paces ahead and behind them could hear everything they said through his earpiece.

He put his hand out, bringing her to a stop, as he got status updates.

Then he looked at Cenobia and gave a nod. "Okay. All clear."

Her eyes were watchful, observant, and she lightly licked her lips, painted a pink like the inside of a seashell.

"Let's go," he said, motioning with two fingers like

he was her squad leader. They moved out into the stone-paved plaza. In front of her, he took a big, honeysuckle-free inhale of air.

Vendors selling churros and colorful *liquados* in front of a pink sandstone church called *"buenos dias"* to Señorita Trujillo as he hustled her across toward her waiting car. Cenobia replied by name.

"Please tell me you change your route on these morning strolls," Roman said.

"Constantly," she said without dropping her smile. "Religiously. And with intense paranoia."

Though, really, it didn't matter.

She was so gloriously beautiful in the morning light he was sure she blinded anyone who saw her.

When he'd finally—finally—gotten her to the safety of her corner office in the Trujillo Industries headquarters, Roman met with his people in a spare conference room they'd taken over.

Glori led the meeting from the other end of the table. "Trujillo's threat level has been elevated from moderate to substantial and the University of Guanajuato team is now going to augment her personal security."

The two people who'd been monitoring the university library nodded as they rooted through a couple bags of candy.

"The tech folks say the encryption used to camouflage the emails is going to be tough to crack."

The crunching and wrapper rustling paused. Glori had started the tradition of bringing local candy of wherever they were stationed to meetings, and bags with names like *Chupa Chups*, *Bolitochas*, and *Bandera de Coco* were scattered over the conference table.

The rule was that you had to finish whatever you put in your mouth, and it had made for some hilarious moments to lighten the load of their topics.

But there was no hilarity now as the implication of what Glori said sunk in. Sheppard Security was the best and no one was shy about that fact. The firm employed the kind of hackers that world security leaders checked in on regularly to make sure they were content, well paid, and busily occupied. Around this conference table alone were two former Marines, a team guy, two former Army, and three of the brightest minds from the Farm.

Right now, this elite group was getting played. The encryption was going to be tough, they hadn't identified a leak, and the source of the now-verified threat against Cenobia was still unidentified.

The analyst who'd been researching the note left on Cenobia's car gave an update. "The fact that she was blindfolded is in twenty-three percent of the online information about the kidnapping." He took a bite of a bar he was holding—*Pulparindo*, it said on the wrapper— then grimaced. "So it's not widely known, but it's not hard to discover."

He sighed and bravely took another bite of the candy.

We kept you blindfolded last time, the note said. *This time, we'll cut off your eyelids so we'll be the last thing you see.*

He swallowed then looked hesitant to keep talking. He was a newer hire to Sheppard Security.

Glori motioned for him to continue.

He focused on Roman. "Sir, is there any off-the-books info we should know that might draw a clearer line to Las Luces Oscuras?"

It was generally agreed that the drug cartel Las

Luces Oscuras was responsible for kidnapping Cenobia, although there was no one sitting in jail to pay for
it. Thirteen years ago, her father had been planning to
build a factory that would have loosened the cartel's
hold of an area in Zacatecas, and they'd sent numerous
threats before the kidnapping.

"FBI and Mexican intelligence thought it was Las
Luces Oscuras," Roman said. "The tiny ransom they
asked for was just the kind of taunt they liked."

Daniel Trujillo had received a ransom note demanding one hundred fifty thousand dollars, pocket change
for his most precious treasure. He'd paid it immediately, of course, but his daughter hadn't been returned
to him. The fact that she'd been kidnapped Mexican-
cartel style in the U.S. made the event huge news. Six
months home from Iraq and barely sleeping, Roman had
been keeping up with the news reports from the couch
in his mom's trailer while half-heartedly spreading the
word about his fledgling security company.

Leads for the FBI to investigate were drying up, the
tycoon had told him when he called. And Daniel was
worried that even if they did locate her, the corruption
that plagued the Mexican government and law enforce-
ment would mean the drug cartel would be notified before his daughter could be rescued.

He'd begged Roman to find and extract her.

Between Odessa and Houston, Roman had made
four stops: his storage locker to kit up with equipment
the Medal of Honor selection committee would have
frowned upon, an army surplus store, the home of a
former Ranger buddy working on tech, and the printer's
shop to finally pick up the business cards he'd wondered
if he was ever going to use. *Sheppard Security—Roman*

Sheppard, founder and CEO, they said on a thick card-stock that was soft to the touch.

He'd felt more at ease than he had in six months.

It was easy for a good ol' boy to ask a few questions of the people invisible to everyone else: the cleaning staff at Cenobia's college dorm; park maintenance in Hermann Park, where Cenobia liked to hang out with friends; transit drivers working the same routes, who noticed the unusual in their routines like a firework show in March.

He'd followed the kidnappers' trail north. When the service station clerk outside of the blink-and-you'll-miss-it town of Channing, Texas told him about a caravan of shiny Escalades heading west into nothing but scrubland, Roman had felt the full-body thrill of riding a C-130's combat landing into Bagram, followed by a snap back into absolute calm and focus.

He'd craved that feeling since the instant he'd returned to American soil. Using his innate gifts and military training, he'd crafted himself into one of a handful of people on the planet who could save her. This is what he was good at. He'd made a brutal choice to commit himself to the warrior life, and this was him putting that commitment into action.

The surprise when he'd descended on the decommissioned military bunker was absolute, the violence he'd applied to take out guys without alerting others who could use her as a human shield was surgical. She'd been a wild thing when he'd found her, kicking and biting until he had to restrain her to get her blindfold off so she could see his face.

To prevent an ambush or a mole on the inside giving away their position, Roman had waited until he was minutes away from delivering her to her father to contact the FBI. They'd swooped down on the decommissioned base, but in the four hours between her rescue and return, the site had already been scrubbed clean.

"The FBI couldn't put together enough evidence to go after Las Luces Oscuras," he said. "And the Mexican government, they made a few condemning speeches but…" He shrugged. "I told Daniel what I've told y'all—Las Luces Oscuras might have carried out the kidnapping but no way they organized it. Those guys in the bunker were blunt instruments; getting her away from her security team and out of Houston was precise and organized. I was a one-man team without enough to prove my theory, and the FBI didn't care about my gut."

He'd helped Daniel and Daniel's investigative team as much as he could. But when all the leads were exhausted, the tycoon felt he had to focus on the future of his daughter and business rather than getting hung up on the past. That failure made Roman understand he couldn't go it alone in the States any more than he had in Mosul—in the Rangers, one became two, two became a team, a team became a squad, and so on.

He'd ultimately built a squad that had saved hundreds of people, saved the kind of people who saved thousands of others.

Rescuing Cenobia Trujillo had given Roman a clarity of purpose outside of the military. Establishing Sheppard Security had given him the motivation to seek counseling for his pretty obvious PTSD.

He knocked his knuckles on the conference table. "If Las Luces Oscuras is back, why? What's their motive? They're fucking scary but they got away clean from the country's scariest billionaire. What makes it worth getting back in his cross hairs now? Mexico's most danger-

ous drug cartel is one of any number of enemies looking
to hurt our client; last time, investigators got hung up
on them too early and missed the real bad guys. I don't
want to make that same mistake. Let's do what we do
best and keep her safe."

Each team member gave a decisive nod as they
grabbed favorite bags of candies and finally got to spit
out what they couldn't stand to swallow.

When he went to pick her up that evening, he found her
on the phone. She beckoned him into her office but continued on the call with a grimace as he sat on a couch
arm at the back of the room.

Her lips were naked, licked clean, and she'd redone
her hair into a long, wavy ponytail at her nape. When
she swiveled in her chair, he caught sight of bare, dark
feet and shell-pink toenails before he was studying her
chandelier.

Someone needed to tell her not to get so comfy in
her office. Someone needed to hang up the receiver and
carry her to her car.

She looked exhausted. His crew guarding her home
commented that they didn't know when she slept. She
served them *café de ollas* at random middle-of-the-night
hours and lights went on and off throughout the night.

Roman dealt with insomnia, too.

"Yes, I understand that Alphawind Autos is releasing a similarly energy-efficient car, but I never agreed
to share our time slot with them," she said with forced
patience. She rubbed her ear where a dangly earring
hung. "Our car is unique in every way. Your coordinator has already assured us that the Frankfurt Auto Show
would be thrilled to showcase such a…"

Her face suddenly scrunched in consternation.

"Who said we'd be amenable to a joint showcase?"

Cenobia's face hardened as her jaw tightened, her wide mouth drew into a line, and her eyes widened and blazed. "I see," she said into the receiver.

He wondered if those two chill words shriveled up balls on the other end of the line like they were doing here in her office.

"I will have a talk with him. In the meantime, please ask your coordinator to speak to me or my assistant directly until I get this confusion straightened out."

After she said her farewells and disconnected from the call, she stared sightlessly at her phone for several minutes. Roman stayed silent and allowed himself the pleasure of watching that big brain of hers work.

He'd gotten accustomed to the feeling of Cenobia being aware of him, just like he was aware of her. His thoughts had never traveled far today from the fact that she was in the same building.

But she was more than the teenaged girl he rescued, the young woman who loaned him a fortune, and the gorgeous CEO who asked him to keep her safe. She was a powerful, world-changing industrialist who had a lot more to think about than her bodyguard.

Watching her ignore him as she cogitated stirred him as fiercely as the grip of her silky hand.

"My vice president of marketing and publicity has told the Frankfurt Auto Show that we would be interested in sharing our showcase with a competitor," she said without preamble, looking at Roman as she leaned back in her chair and crossed her legs. "Señor Vasquez explained to the organizers that sharing the spotlight would benefit Trujillo Industries when our car garners a tepid response."

"Do you want to go talk to him?" Roman asked. He had a way of dealing with Lance Vasquez that would blow the highlights right out of the guy's hair.

"He's gone for the night." She closed her eyes, then kept them closed a tired second too long. "Tomorrow is soon enough."

Roman stayed seated on the couch arm and worked to look docile as a house cat while he wrestled with an unholy need to feed her, bathe her, pleasure her until she slipped into a good night's sleep, then eradicate one of her problems by knocking on Vasquez's door.

"Let's go home," she said.

But they didn't go home. She told her driver to drop them off at a different plaza. Roman started to argue with her but couldn't sustain it under the barrage of her tired eyes.

Her guards in the car in front and Glori in the car behind were alerted.

He let Cenobia set the slow pace in her curvy, polka-dotted dress, her pink heels tapping on cobblestone streets that once again reminded him of the Monte. The night was quiet and although they walked Guanajuato's most touristed thoroughfares, past baroque churches, Diego Rivera's boyhood home, and sites of the Mexican revolution, only the occasional couple or group of twentysomethings passed them. Roman kept an eye on rooftops and dark doorways and trusted the qualified guards. In the Jardín de la Unión, where they waited for the gorditas Cenobia ordered from a street vendor, a mariachi band played a slow, heartsick song from a gazebo.

They stood beneath a tree lit with fairy lights that twinkled in Cenobia's eyes when she looked up at him.

"Alphawind Autos is the competitor trying to horn in on your show?" he asked.

They were an American car manufacturer founded in the '80s. He'd almost bought a used Alphawind truck when he'd returned from Iraq.

Her eyes blinked slowly before she nodded. "We've been manufacturing parts for them for years and have always had a good relationship. They're adjusting to the idea of us as competition."

"Not well," he said, and Cenobia bobbled her head as the vendor signaled that their gorditas were ready.

They walked and ate. As Cenobia sighed *"Que rico"* in a way that raised the hair on Roman's nape, he finally understood that she wasn't immune to good food. She was just indifferent.

He needed to learn how to make these.

After taking the same steep walk up that they'd walked down that morning—Roman tightened the perimeter, bringing the guards closer as they walked through narrow, moonlit, honeysuckle-soaked passageways— they entered through the fake facade of her home and into her courtyard.

His team handed off patrol positions as Cenobia stood in her open doorway, looking up at him with the smudge of her sleepless nights showing beneath her pretty eyes.

"Would you like to come in?" she invited, motioning inside. "I could make you a *café* before you…"

"No," Roman said abruptly. "Maybe you should lay off, too."

Her eyebrows quirked. *"¿Por qué?"*

"That much caffeine this late isn't good for you."

Her sparkling flash of irritation was getting to be familiar.

"Muchas gracias, padre," she said, putting her hand on a hip he'd been working to keep his eyes off of as they'd walked up the canyon. "I've lived on my own for the last thirteen years; somehow I've managed my bedtime routine just fine."

As he took a half step closer, his hand was in his pocket muting his earpiece on his phone.

"But when you do you actually go to bed?" he asked, urgent but hushed. "I know you see the finish line, but you got to get some rest to reach it."

Her cat eyes were suspicious as she looked up at him. The only way she'd become the woman she had was through mutiny. But she had to realize he was on her side.

"I know what it's like," he whispered. "Your brain ping-ponging from one worry to the next, the anxiety getting bigger and heavier in the dark."

Her long lashes blinked. She scraped her teeth against her bottom lip. "What do you do?" she asked, also in a whisper.

"Planks. Sit-ups. Push-ups." He leaned his shoulder against the stone wall of her entryway as he looked down at her. "I get back in bed, set my timer for thirty minutes, and if I'm not asleep, do 'em all over again." He lowered his head. "I avoid drinkin' heavenly tasting coffees after midnight."

She rolled her eyes and looked away, but gave him a view of her shy dimple. That little press of amusement in her skin was better than any medal. It lured him a step closer. "Trust that I'm gonna take care of you, Cenobia." We. He meant we. "Lay your troubles down for the night."

When she looked up at him, he realized he'd overshot. Like, by a mile. He was way too close to her and she had to tilt up to meet his eyes, offering up her gorgeous face—luminous forehead, velvety skin, bitable end of her nose—and her wide mouth.

Her lips were soft and shiny, not bone dry like his had gone.

Her sweet scent filled the entryway, becoming deadly when he inhaled it this close, this late, in the dark. Her eyes traveled over his face and landed on his mouth. Then she tilted up her wide chin, and stroked her bottom lip with her wet, pink tongue.

Will you go to war with me, brother?

Before every mission during his second tour, when his squad was hot and jacked and already loaded down with sixty-five pounds of equipment, the preacher would make a cross in the dirt and say a prayer. Then he'd look at Roman, the squad leader, and ask, "Will you go to war with me, brother?"

Roman said yes with excitement in his heart every single time.

He'd made himself into a man who couldn't accept Cenobia's invitation.

He stepped back. "If it'll keep you from tossin' and turning, I'll bring the crew coffee." That crew could come patrolling through the courtyard any second.

"They won't like yours as much as they like mine," she said readily, as if nothing had happened.

"I know. I won't either." Nothing had happened. "But we'll survive. Night, Cenobia."

He turned on a heel and turned his earpiece back on.

He ignored her soft, mocking reply—"Cen"—instead of hanging on to it as the excuse to follow her inside.

Chapter Seven

Guanajuato, Mexico

Cenobia didn't sleep well.

But she enthusiastically stayed in bed. The time she spent twisting and arching and fantasizing in her high-thread-count sheets was…very refreshing.

If the gorgeous *príncipe* had wanted Cenobia to sleep, he shouldn't have come so close in the shadows of her doorway, his broad shoulders blocking out all the light, leaving her blind to everything but his fiery green eyes staring into hers and his sulky lips gleaming like they were carved out of pink marble. He shouldn't have worn that fitted supermodel suit that showed her the faint lines of the chest harness he wore to hide his gun holster; he shouldn't have smelled like expensive cologne and gun oil.

He shouldn't have challenged her like she was a child, then shared with her his own challenges as if he trusted her. As if she was one of the few people he could trust with his own struggles.

He shouldn't have looked at her at her like he was considering which inch of her he wanted to devour first.

The next morning, she was almost grateful for the

dawn call about a crisis at the plant outside of Guanajuato where her hybrid car would be manufactured. That emergency kept her occupied and unable to exchange more than the briefest words with Roman as he escorted her to work and then back home to change for the Pemex-hosted cocktail event. She would have skipped the party entirely if her father wasn't the guest of honor. The oil and gas company wanted to present an award in acknowledgement of her father's supposed retirement.

If her father decided Cenobia was not fit to lead and took the company back, would he return the plaque?

When Roman stepped out of her car, Cenobia swallowed her gasp. He'd dressed the part of a fairy-tale prince—a slim-fit black tuxedo, black bow tie, white-silk pocket square—and every dark hair on his head was perfectly styled. But no one would mistake him for a fairy tale; the breadth of his shoulders, the scars on his useful hands, those life-filled lines around his intense eyes all spoke of a man too real, too warrior, to be a child's fantasy.

As they drove through the tunnels into old-town Guanajuato, shutter-like bars of light showcased him glamorously then turned him into a creature fiercely guarding her in the dark.

He gave her his arm and led her into the grand neo-classical hotel built for silver barons and Porfirio Díaz's acolytes. They'd already discussed the fact that he'd be immediately recognized in this room full of the Mexican and international elite.

For tonight, the reluctant warrior prince Roman Sheppard was her date.

When she heard the sharp intake of Roman's breath

behind her as he helped remove her shimmering white-silk *rebozo* to hand to the coat clerk, it was the first time in twenty-four hours that the ground felt firmer beneath her feet.

Her evening gown was a black lace over sleek black satin that covered her from its high neck to the tip of her heels in front. Tight cuffs gathered the full sleeves at her wrists and fastened with black pearl buttons, and she'd echoed those pearls in the black seed pearl chandelier earrings that dangled almost to her shoulders. She'd darkly lined her eyes, slicked her lips a fiery red, and parted her hair down the middle and into a tight bun at her nape.

While the dress covered her completely in front, her entire back was naked down to where the dress scooped to cover her just above her *culo*.

She'd stared down boardrooms full of men, taken on disbelieving foremen in their cigarillo-choked factory offices, and convinced skeptical international trade groups to give her a chance. But she had no bravery when it came to this dance between one man and one woman. Not usually.

Tonight, however, she hoped Roman Sheppard lost a bit of sleep as well.

He was the sensation she knew he would be in the vast room with its spectacularly decorated high ceiling of stained glass, its giant chandeliers gleaming off marble floors, and large, gold framed mirrors that made the room boundary-less. National and international representatives of the auto, oil, and gas industries, many who were wealthy enough to buy small nations, weren't immune to the presence of royalty, no matter how reluctant the royalty was.

Roman shook the hands and said the words, but quickly demurred to Señorita Trujillo. His silence, his sharpshooter stare, and his pleasant but resolute nonsmile was effective at shutting down even the most gregarious, clueless, or entitled. They were able to make their way quickly to her father to give their greetings and congratulations.

Daniel welcomed her with a huge, pearly white smile and a big, bear hug. He ruined his greeting when he said, "I heard you had a problem at the plant."

Cenobia swallowed her surprise and Roman bought her time by grabbing champagne flutes and shoving one into her hand. She took the tiniest sip. Of course her father had people reporting to him.

"It was a mix up," she said. "I'm handling it."

Her father, with his thick wavy hair brushed back and tamed with a bit of pomade, looked at her steadily. In her heels, he was only a couple of inches taller than her. But he was every bit as imposing as one would expect from a wealthy industrialist.

"You've made many promises about the quality of La Primera, the skill of the Mexican worker, and the excellence of Trujillo Industries. If that plant isn't running smoothly by the time of the launch, you will immediately break them."

The only reason her father was taking this pretend health sabbatical was so she could hang herself with her own rope. He didn't want to drive her away. Instead, he believed he was allowing her to make a half-a-billion-dollar mistake so she that would finally realize she was better suited to be the pretty, pampered heiress—with perhaps a quiet VP role in the company as a consolation prize—that he always wanted her to be.

Now, with so many powerful people in tuxedos and gowns watching, and with Roman Sheppard standing by her side, she gave her father her most confident smile. "I'll be visiting the plant tomorrow," she said. "We'll be ready for the onslaught of orders after the car is revealed at the auto show. Don't you worry, *mi padre*."

She leaned forward to kiss his cheek, but her father tightly gripped her hand as she did so. "Be sure you want this, *mi hija*." The worry in his voice was sincere. That was the hardest part. He sincerely loved her and sincerely wanted to protect her. "Be sure it's worth it. There's still time to slow it all down."

She squeezed his hand back with a reassurance that she wished her father could offer her. Roman escorted her away.

"You know what the problem with you two is?" he murmured as he moved them toward the hors d'oeuvres table. His bicep felt tantalizingly firm under her hand. "You're too much alike. Watching y'all argue is like watching someone yell at a mirror."

Cenobia sniffed as he handed her his glass, filled a small plate for both of them, then led her toward the edge of the room, away from the bright chandeliers and loud conversations. He wasn't wrong. She and Daniel could match point for point on stubbornness.

"My father wouldn't be disgruntled if the reflection he saw didn't have *chichis*," Cenobia grumbled as Roman raised a shrimp to her mouth. She took it and chewed.

"It's more than you simply being a woman." He took a shrimp for himself then wiped a dollop of yogurt from the corner of his mouth. "It's bigger than that."

Her father's protectiveness, devotion, and worry.

The obsessive eyes he'd kept on her in the weeks after Roman had returned her to him. She knew her father's issues were more than just about sexism or a Mexican traditionalist's point of view.

"I know," she said. Roman held out a tiny empanada, which she bit into, then he popped the rest into his mouth. It tasted of sweet corn and crabmeat. "But you do understand that half of the issue is simply my gender, *verdad*? I'm allowed to be angry about the disadvantage assigned to me because I have breasts."

He cleared his throat. "You are," he said. "It's not fair and it's something that I as a white male born in the U.S. won't ever fully get." The little toast of *mollete* he fed her was topped with pâté and bright salsa. "I also know it would be helpful while I'm in this tight tux if you'd stop talking about your *chichis*."

The shock of his words, his acknowledgement of his awareness of her, a simple joke between friends but they didn't joke this way, they weren't…had never been…this way, had her startling to realize that he'd been feeding her. With his thick, capable fingers, this warrior prince had been feeding her. Right now, he was holding up a small taco and she'd been about to take a bite.

"What are you doing?" she asked, rearing back.

His green eyes looked darker in the shadows here at the edge of the gilded room. "Have you eaten today?"

She realized she'd skipped lunch. "No."

"Then you need to eat, Cenobia." His voice was like black silk over sand. "I said I'd take care of you."

To any curious eyes, they simply looked like two longtime friends juggling a plate and two champagne glasses.

Heart pounding, she slowly tilted her head and

opened her mouth. He kept his eyes on hers as she fit her lips around the corn tortilla and bit into it. She'd never been more aware of the simple mechanics of eating. He lifted the rest of the taco to his mouth and finished it in one bite. He'd been sharing food with her as if their mouths had already shared other intimacies.

He wiped at a sheen on his plush bottom lip with a knuckle. "How'd that taste?" he asked, low, and how had he learned to make benign words sound like that?

The taco had been filled with crispy *carnitas*, fresh onion, a heavy squeeze of lime. "Good," she answered. Not at all breathlessly.

He gave her that smile that was more in his eyes than on his mouth. "I thought you were allergic to tasty food."

"Food is fuel. It's a waste of time. If I could just take a pill…"

He closed his eyes in what looked like agony and those tempting lines around them shot out like sunrays. "Oh, sweetheart, I have so much to teach you."

In a crowded room full of her peers, in front of the man she'd had an increasingly embarrassing crush on since she was eighteen years old, Cenobia suffered through the single most erotic moment of her life. If he breathed on her, she would go up in flames.

In an instant, his demeanor changed. He seemed to grow taller and broader as he received information from the almost-invisible device in his ear and looked over her shoulder, into a mirror that showed him a reflection of the whole room. "We've got incoming," he said as he put down the plate, took his champagne glass from her, then turned to step just behind her.

It was like having a warm brick wall at her back.

Her vice president of marketing and publicity was charging toward them as the head of Alphawind Autos followed halfheartedly behind.

The diamond studs in Lance Vasquez's tux shirt twinkled brighter than the candlelight. "Cen, what good does it do Trujillo Industries when our brightest jewel hides itself in a corner?" he said, curls slicked back and his smile as wide as a shark's. "We've been looking everywhere for you."

Vasquez had abandoned all efforts at obsequiousness with her. Only family and friends called her Cen; her employees called her Señorita Trujillo.

"And now you've found me." She took the American's hand in both of hers and shook it warmly. "It's good to see you, Blake."

Blake Anderson was the same age as her father and had that long face, square jaw, and blond hair mellowing to silver that was the trademark of television dads from American '80s sitcoms. As the longtime head of Alphawind Autos, one of Trujillo Industries' top clients, Blake had watched her grow up, and smiled down at her now with that affection as he patted her hand. "It's good to see you, too. Belated congratulations on your new role as CEO. It was well deserved."

"I appreciate the engraved Montblanc," she said of the luxury pen he'd sent when her position was announced. "It's helped to sign many of the important documents that have gotten La Primera off the ground."

She could see Vasquez's scowl as Blake chuckled. "Then maybe I should have given you a leaky Bic."

The email had been labeled exploratory when Alphawind Autos had written to inquire about Trujillo Industries putting off their eco-friendly car launch for a year to make way for the Americans' hybrid car in the Mexican market. Trujillo Industries had replied with a polite and emphatic no.

"I've instituted changes that will affect our partnership, but I'm sure we can agree that the Mexican car-buying market is big enough for the both of us," she said sincerely with a final squeeze before she let go of his hand. "I'm looking forward to our continued working relationship."

"As am I," he said. But a troubled frown etched his brow as he continued looking down at her. "I want to apologize for the mix up at the Frankfurt Auto Show."

Vasquez cut in, "And I was explaining to him that it wasn't a mix up. We'll benefit from the strong hand of an American ally supporting us when there are questions about the viability of our car."

The plant emergency had kept Cenobia too busy to deal with Vasquez. But if he wanted to play this out in front of a client and competitor, so be it.

"The principal voice questioning the viability of our car is yours, Señor Vasquez," she said. "Which is a concern. As the VP of marketing and publicity, you should be its most vocal champion. Perhaps we should discuss whether you are the best person to be in that role."

Lance Vasquez's connections to the top tiers of Mexican government, industry, and society were why her father had recruited him. Those same connections would make him a formidable enemy, which was why Cenobia had put up with his growing insolence. But she was done. When he undermined her, he kicked at the legs of her company, her employees, and all the Mexicans who needed her to chart a new way.

Vasquez stiffened and looked at her with outraged

fury. She imagined no one, and especially not a dark-skinned woman, had ever talked to him that way.

He glanced up and just behind her. Then blanched.

She didn't need Roman Sheppard standing behind her for this conversation. But his reassuring presence was like a hand pressed against her naked back.

"Perdóneme, señorita," Vasquez said through gritted teeth.

Blake looked like he wished to be anywhere but here.

She put her hand on his tuxedoed arm. *"Lo siento*, Blake," she murmured. "I'm sorry that you were given bad information. Please have your people contact my assistant while you're in Mexico and we'll have dinner."

She slipped her hand through Roman's arm as her cue that she was done. As he led her across the ballroom, she caught glimpses of them in the gold-framed mirrors—her with her black, sleek hair and black fitted gown, him with his dark hair and classic tuxedo—and marveled at how otherworldly beautiful that mirror-couple looked.

"I'm sorry," she said. "I didn't introduce you."

"I like being the fly on your wall, Cenobia," he said. He led her to where the guests were taking their seats for the ceremony. "You got more weapons than my people do. You melt 'em with your smile and dagger 'em with your eyes."

It was the best compliment she'd ever received.

She enjoyed watching her father receive his award—the speeches, the bawdy jokes, the truly astonishing stories about all he'd accomplished—even with all their current difficulties. Her father swiped at the occasional tear in his eye, and when she did the same, Roman handed her a soft white handkerchief. Daniel had grown up wealthy, had money his whole life although not the world-dominating sums that Cenobia had grown up with. And still, her bright-smiled father loved these events, loved the French champagne and gold-edged plates of *antojitos* and beautiful people and glittery rooms. Her father had never taken his wealth for granted, but instead enjoyed it, valued it, and appreciated that he had a responsibility with it, teaching her through example with his charitable endeavors and efforts to provide fair wages and benefits to his workers.

With his enormous crystal award in one arm, her father instructed everyone to raise their glass to Cenobia, "the future of Trujillo Industries."

She wished the future could be as easy as that straightforward toast. With her glass in the air and Roman's warmth by her side, she fantasized what this moment would feel like if the foundation beneath her was set and she truly was the pillar of Trujillo Industries.

People began to mingle again. Roman leaned close to say something, but stopped. He straightened abruptly then scanned the area around them. His entire bearing transformed, the prince instantly subsumed by the warrior.

She saw the two other guards making their way quickly toward them from the room's edges.

"We've got to get you out of here," he murmured, taking a firm grip of her arm. "You just got another email. It's a credible threat. They know the layout of the room and what you're wearing."

Cenobia's heart leapt into her throat. This was happening under the glitter of chandelier light, at an event where her ascendency had just been toasted. "Roman,

I need every single person in this room to believe I can maintain control of Mexico's auto industry."

If she—a young *indígena* woman in a backless dress—went scurrying from this room in front of the power brokers she desperately needed on her side, she would be mocked, derided, and undermined, regardless of the reasoning.

His eyes narrowed and the edges of his jaw clenched. He looked a second from slinging her over his shoulder. But he gave a quick nod.

"Maintain a close perimeter," he ordered the guards as they reached them. "Head straight to the door; the driver is already in the portico. We're not stopping—" He'd shot that command at Cenobia. "But keep it cool."

The four of them moved as quickly as they could through the throng of people toward the door fifty feet away. Cenobia kept her eyes constantly shifting, focusing on people just beyond the group they were about to pass, as if there was always someone more valuable than the individual she was about to encounter. She'd been an heiress her entire life; this game was as effortless as walking and talking. The game kept her occupied so that terror didn't take out her knees.

Fifty feet shrank to forty then thirty then twenty faster than she could have hoped. Roman's steely presence kept her from whirling to protect her exposed back.

Ten feet from the door, she began to feel the heady relief of escape.

Then she met the eyes of Barbara Benitez, the Pemex representative who'd joined Vasquez in her office. She stood at the door speaking to a man Cenobia had read about but hadn't met. They both stared at Cenobia.

Her heart rate picked up, but it felt like the rapid

heartbeat of a twin standing next to her. She was aware of her constricting breath and clammy palms, but she was safely observing the effects of panic from outside herself. She slowed, then stopped. Low, against her skirts, she held one hand in the other and rubbed her thumb across the silky back.

"Cenobia?" Roman's warm, vital voice sounded hollow and distant, like he was speaking through a tube. "We need to keep going. What's wrong?"

Barbara and the man—Hernán Rodriguez—were still talking. Still focused on her. Barbara gave her a simpering smile. Cenobia felt like she was seeing it from a mile away as they all but blocked the doorway.

She rubbed faster, the skin heating up.

Roman took her arm as appropriately as any gentleman but pulled her close against his side. "Cenobia, I got you. Let's go."

A guard fell back and another one stood directly in front of her.

"Bueno," she said. Her voice came from somewhere up in the stars.

He got them out of the ballroom and into her car with no fuss. She realized, as she came back into herself, the car and its caravan moving quickly out of central Guanajuato and Roman communicating with his people, that he'd escorted her out without forcing her to release her grounding press into her hand. She stretched out her fingers now and they ached.

He told the crew to assemble at her home and that he was going mute.

"Who was that man?" he asked quietly as he slipped his phone back into his jacket pocket.

"Hernán Rodriguez," she said, her voice giving an unexpected shudder.

Roman undid his seat belt, moved close to the leather divider that separated them, and slid his hard palm against hers, enfolding their fingers. His strength could crush her hand and she gripped it tight. "He's an attorney appointed a year ago to negotiate for the government with the most powerful drug cartels. He was lauded for bringing a new era of calm." She breathed harder and Roman rubbed his thumb across her hand.

"Now there are rumors that he is the principal bagman for Las Luces Oscuras."

The inside man for the drug cartel who'd kidnapped her and a representative of the oil and gas monolith desperate to see Cenobia fail were discussing her at a cocktail party.

"I think…" Cenobia felt herself starting to telescope out of her car. "I think I know what they want."

"Stay with me," he urged, close to her ear, squeezing her hand. He was the rock holding her down. "We'll get you home. I'll keep you safe."

Chapter Eight

Guanajuato, Mexico

Late that night, all but two of Roman's team, the head of headquarters security, and all of Cenobia's personal crew—including those who were off duty—were assembled in the kitchen, dining room, and living room of Cenobia's open-plan downstairs as Glori stood on the first step of the circular stairs and updated everyone on the night's events.

"At twenty-one hundred hours, the primary Trujillo Industries email address received a communication that threatened an immediate attack on Señorita Trujillo. They knew her location, what she was wearing, and who she was with. You all have a copy of the email."

There was a rustling of paper as everyone took a moment to read it. Roman, standing behind the couch in the living room with his back up against the stucco wall, already knew it by heart.

Your dressed-up mutt won't see us coming. We'll slip close then penetrate. That slutty birthmark makes a perfect target.

Tux coat off, his bow tie draped around his shirt, and
his sleeves rolled up, Roman watched Cenobia from
under his lashes. She stood on the other side of the living room, near the gargantuan fireplace with its giant,
white-stone mantel of carved flowers and leaves, the
fire roaring. She was still in her dress and heels, but
she'd wrapped her white shawl around her a couple of
times, like she was trying to get warmth out of its silk
and dangling tassels. With her arms crossed beneath it
and her eyes down, she wasn't reading the email either.

Roman had seen the birthmark the email referred
to. When he'd helped her remove her shawl earlier,
he'd also seen her delicate shoulder blades, the shadowy curve of her spine, and a landscape of soft, touch-
able golden-brown skin. He'd been slapped stupid by
the surprise of her dress. He'd stared at the thumb-size
dusky birthmark, low and just to the right of her spine,
where the small of her back began to curve into her
fine, round ass.

He'd wanted to slip to his knees and lick it.

That anyone would use that vulnerable, beautiful bit
of her to shame, taunt, and threaten her...he breathed
through the anger that kept trying to crawl to the surface.

"We've got two of our people at the scene now questioning the staff and going through security cameras,"
Glori continued, wearing a black Sheppard Securities
polo, black cargoes, and boots, her hair in a poof at the
top of her head. "They'll bring back the guest list and
we'll take that apart. But until then, Señorita Trujillo
has a theory about what might be going on here. I'll let
her explain."

Roman watched Cenobia grip the silk tighter around
herself. He uncrossed his arms and slid them into his

tux pockets, ready to amble over if she showed any unease.

He'd launch over the couch if there was even a hint of that nightmarishly blank look on her face.

But Cenobia relaxed her shoulders and raised her chin. "My people already know about the *huachicoleros*," she began, her voice strong to reach the crew who craned around the kitchen wall to see her. "But for Roman's team, *huachicoleros* are a new strain of drug lord in Mexico. Instead of dealing in narcotics, they tap exposed pipelines and sell the gas at steeply reduced prices. It sounds like petty theft, but it is highly profitable, corrupt, and destructive; their crude drilling practices cause spills, explosions, and biohazards that have been responsible for many deaths.

"For a time, *huachicoleros* were *de moda*. When the government was cracking down on the narco traffickers, it became much easier to puncture a pipeline and sell the gas to communities, bus companies, long-haul truckers, or to smuggle crude into the U.S. and sell it to American factories. But the Mexican president has cracked down on gas theft, so the *huachicoleros* are getting desperate. There's more fighting between gangs for territory, more innocents caught in the violence. They threaten the people with *pan o palo*: turn a blind eye and accept the bread of discount gas or get the *palo* of a beating."

He watched her take a steadying breath. The firelight sparkled over the black lace and white silk covering her. "One of the best organized and most dangerous *huachicolero* networks is run by Las Luces Oscuras, the drug cartel who kidnapped me." Cenobia had connected the dots for Roman and Glori when they'd arrived at her home. "Some estimates say Las Luces Oscuras is stealing thirteen thousand barrels a day. They earn more in gas and oil than they ever could in drugs."

Roman wanted his team to know that he supported this line of inquiry. "A popular and affordable hybrid car in the Mexican market that made people less dependent on gas would further cut into the cartel's profits," he said from his side of the room. "And tonight at the event, the principal bagman for Las Luces was talking to a Pemex representative. Cenobia called a contact in the government, and they told her that Pemex would rather pay off the cartels than fight them because it was cheaper than repairing the pipelines and cleaning up toxic spills."

Glori jumped back in. "The quality of the email encryption also seems to point to Las Luces," she said. Powerful drug cartels had learned to hire the right people to make the Internet their friend. "So let's sharpen our focus. Let's find proof. Then we'll make a decision."

A payoff or a black ops mission. Roman knew which one he'd choose.

One of his guards who'd accompanied them to the event raised his hand. "Has there been any discussion about relocating Ms. Trujillo to a safe house and maintaining her position there? Or getting her out of the country?"

Locking her down or forcing her to run away. Roman bit back an unreasonable flare of anger. Any other operation, and Roman would have suggested it.

Out of the corner of his eyes, he could see Cenobia shaking her head.

"That's not an option," he said. "The mission is to keep her safe so she can launch this new car. She can't do that from an isolated location."

He barreled on.

"I'll be taking Glori's place so that she can focus on overseeing the investigation. I'll be eyes-on Señorita Trujillo 24/7, so mark me as the last line of defense."

He injected his years as a CEO into his voice and met everyone's eyes. He didn't find what he was looking for: someone looking back like they wondered about his "real" reason for wanting to stick close to Cenobia Trujillo. Glori had recommended it—she was better at keeping a million plates spinning, and he was better at reacting quick and effectively on the ground—and Roman hadn't disagreed. Becoming Cenobia's principal close protection full-time made sense and was the best decision for the operation.

This was the first time Cenobia was hearing about it.

Earlier tonight, he'd hoped a little good-natured flirting would help clear the air between them. Their intwined past was creating too much gravitas in the present, he'd told himself. She was a good-lookin' woman and he knew what was in the mirror; no wonder there was an attraction. But he needed to stop making such a big damn deal out of it.

Earlier tonight, he'd been a self-deluding jackass.

How he was drawn to her when she took on antagonists, what he felt when she was in danger, and the way she trusted him when she was fierce and leaned on him when she was afraid was a huge fucking deal. The way she looked in that dress made her the only person he could see.

Now he'd be staying in her home.

He'd needed thirty people in the room, sixty eyes, eyes of his employees, eyes of her people who loved her, eyes of top-tier security professionals who knew that rule one was that you did not get romantically involved with a client, before he could tell her where he'd be sleeping tonight.

Glori gave final orders then dismissed everyone. Roman looked anywhere but at Cenobia while the team shuffled out. He said a few words to Glori before she left, then listened through his earpiece as the crew checked in and took their positions. Only then did he switch his phone to mute and look across the room to Cenobia.

Her back was to him. She clutched the shawl, protecting all that gorgeous skin. But still she shivered, a heartbreaking silhouette limned in fire.

He walked around the couch and approached her side slowly. It was a furnace here in front of the giant fireplace, and the flames jumped high.

He slid his hands into his pockets, using all his willpower to resist pulling her into his arms as she shuddered.

"You'll be staying with me," she said, abrupt and to the point without taking her eyes off the fire.

"Yep."

"Beginning when?"

"Immediately. Glori's already packed up her stuff and your driver got my bag from the hotel."

She stiffened for a moment, regal and tall, before she began shivering again.

She was still in that hair and those earrings and those shoes and he knew how much she liked to unwind. "Look," he said. "I got things covered. Why don't you go relax and—"

"Why?" she shot out.

"What?"

He saw her press her jaw together to keep her teeth from chattering. *Oh, baby girl*, he thought mournfully.

"Why are you staying with me now?" It was a demand even as she shivered.

"I..." He was surprised by the question. "It's the best use of our resources. It's the right call for the mission."

"Right," she snapped. "The mission."

Roman was missing something. He looked her over for clues. She was a tactile person, easy with a touch and a hug. Right now, she held herself stiff as a board although she shivered. She was tilted away from him.

Fuck. Did she not want him here? Did she not want him...close.

"Cenobia, in your office," he said haltingly. "You said you assumed I'd be taking Glori's place. I thought you wanted—"

"That's right," she said, whirling to face him. She was in half dark and half light, and the fire blazed in one darkly lined eye. "In my corner office, the office that says—no matter how temporarily—that I'm in control, I essentially begged you to stay with me. You shot me down." She planted her hands on her hips, and the shawl slid open, the shimmery tassels dangling around her thighs. "In my $230,000 automobile, I told you I wanted to get to know you better, as a person and a man, not just a scribbled note over the Internet. But it took the high-end technology of a bully to make that interesting, didn't it, *Príncipe*?" The shawl slipped off one shoulder, trailing to the floor. "And in my doorway, in a home I designed to keep me safe because until recently I'd been doing a damn good job of it all on my own, I...asked you to come inside."

The slight hitch in her breath, the way she looked at him, defined what Roman could no longer avoid:

more had happened in that doorway than an invitation for coffee.

Cenobia Trujillo wasn't shivering because she was afraid. Cenobia Trujillo was quivering with rage. At him. As the white silk slipped down her black-lace-and-satin-covered curves to fall to the floor, Roman took in the glory of Cenobia Trujillo vibrant with anger.

"When I have felt strong and brave and confident—" Her voice was a fierce punch. "I have repeatedly asked for your company and attention. But tonight, when you see me at my lowest, my weakest, my most pitiable—"

"No, Cenobia." Jesus. He'd never thought of her like that.

"Cen," she hissed. Her eyes were wide and terrifying. If she could have thrown him in the fire, she would have. "Call me Cen. When you respect a woman, you listen and acknowledge her. But when you think of her as a child, as a victim, when you see her unhinged and—"

He grabbed her biceps. "Stop," he demanded. He knew this reaction; he'd also punched the dark. It was easier to be angry than afraid. "Stop talking about yourself that way."

Her eyes flashed up at him. "But it's how you see me. I told you I need you, I told you I feel safer with you around. You think I need a monk to protect my virtue or a prison guard to watch over the nuthouse…"

He pulled her against him, felt the impact like a horse kick. "Stop it," he demanded into her upturned face. "You know I don't think that. You did nothing wrong."

Finally, he said something to snap her out it. He saw it in her eyes, felt it in the sudden sag of her body. Her eyes slid down to his chest.

Her hands crept up to rest on his tuxedo shirt. So quiet that he could barely hear her, she said, "I never wanted you to see me that way."

He looked down at the part in her hair and resisted putting his nose to it. "I never wanted to have a panic attack in front of prospective clients. Sometimes shit happens. It's not your fault."

She nodded slowly. She fingered the ends of his dangling bow tie.

"I know." She took a deep breath, and said it again, this time stronger. "I know it wasn't my fault and I did nothing wrong." Another breath. "I still never wanted you to see me that way."

Both could be true.

He felt her breathing under his hands. This woman who'd come up with her own design was gathering and reassembling her pieces. Her biceps were warm with a surprising amount of muscle beneath her dress. He should let her go.

But for the life of him, he just couldn't.

"I'm glad I was there," he said softly.

She'd gathered the ends of the silk tie into her fists and was rubbing the fabric with her thumbs.

"Do you dissociate often?"

She shook her head. "Not in a while."

"It kind of makes sense that it happened tonight, right?" he prodded gently. "If you look at the pieces?" The increasing threat. The stress of her upcoming launch. A code red warning. And then the reminder of her past trauma.

The gun had been loaded, and the sighting of the Las Luces bagman pulled the trigger.

"I owe you my career for getting me out of there

without incident," she said. The heel of her fists pressed warmly against his chest. "How did you know?"

"I used to mentor vets getting started with their PTSD therapy. I know the signs."

Her shoulders slumped in his hands. It was like his words cut the string of her building strength. When she raised her dark eyes to him, they shimmered with tears.

"I don't want to be someone you mentor," she said in a voice too rich with despair to be called sad. "Yes, you were the first person I thought of when alarm bells started to ring and, yes, I feel safer when you're near. But I'd hoped, with this time together, we'd get to meet as equals. That we would get to just…get to know one another." A tear reflected the flames as it trailed down her cheek. "I'd give anything for you to be here because you chose to be."

She was tearing out his heart. "Cenobia, I'm not forced to—"

"Why won't you call me Cen?" she cried, bending her head away from him. For the first time, he was seeing her give up and throw in the towel. And he was the cause.

Her father, her vice president, her competitor, and her anonymous antagonist had all tried to steal her power tonight. She hugged and applauded her father, kicked the legs out from under her vice president, patted the head of her competitor, and found a way to root out her antagonist. Only Roman, who admired her as fiercely as he admired his family, had succeeded in taking her power.

Only Roman had made her cry.

He had one way to give her power back.

His hands did the unthinkable and traced up her biceps, over her shoulders, and up her neck until they surrounded her jaw. She straightened and stiffened in surprised. He cradled her face in his palms and ran his fingers across her delicate neck and into her hair, her earrings teasing and tickling his wrists.

"Listen to it," he whispered, and Cenobia's brows furrowed in confusion. "Listen to it in English. Cen…" He said it softly, drawing it out, but when he said it in his voice, with his accent, her widening eyes showed that she finally heard what he'd avoided.

Sin.

"Sin, Cenobia. Sin." It was as erotic and addicting as he'd known it would be. "I can't call you that."

Her velvety-dark eyes searched his and, for this moment, he let her see the truth in them. Her fingers that had been resting against his shirt began to dig into it. Her face felt irresistible and precious in his hands, the Ark of the Covenant at the end of his quest. He licked his dry lower lip and instantly knew his mistake—it sharpened the sensation of her breath against his mouth.

She pulled with her fingers and he gathered with his hands.

Then, with a grunt, he looked down blindly at the floor.

Fuck. What was he doing? He was here to protect her.

Anyone patrolling the courtyard could see them through the sliding glass door at the other end of the room.

"Roman?" she whispered. Goddamn him. He wouldn't be the cause of that doubt in her mighty voice.

"Turn around," he growled, still looking down. Down at her dress and her thighs and the tips of her heels. Down at the silk that had shielded her beautiful back from him.

"What?"

"Please, just…" He tried to breathe some of the gravel out of his voice. "Just turn around."

She did, in a cautious slither of lace and satin, showing that he hadn't entirely destroyed her trust in him. Her breath had picked up, little huffs of nerves. He let his eyes wander up, up her legs, her ass, up to what the dress revealed.

He was going to hell.

He stepped close and knew he could warm her better than any fire. His eyes flicked to the glass door—the courtyard was empty—then he bent, took a second to inhale her, and pressed a soft kiss to the base of her neck, just under the collar that created the dress's high neck. At the very top of her gorgeous, exposed back.

She sucked in a sharp, surprised breath. He waited for her to say something. To say no.

She didn't. So he nuzzled, took in the scent of her at the source to discover that her perfume only enhanced the sweetness that already existed. She shivered under the warmth of his breath and he knew he had to keep moving.

He was on a clock.

He switched sides and kissed her left shoulder blade. He touched the tip of his tongue to her and got the flavor of her skin for the very first time. "Is this okay?" he breathed, tickling against this taut golden brown.

She nodded once, slowly. Then faster.

He dragged his lips across her spine and bit into the dip at her waist.

She gasped and moved her legs apart.

Fuck. Time was running out.

He got down on his knees. He stared at that thumb-sized birthmark. Memorized it. He curled his hands into fists at his sides and refused to let them stray. Then he leaned close and kissed every millimeter of that mark. Tasted it. He put his mouth over it and gave it a suck.

She broadened her stance again and when Roman looked up that gorgeous naked sweep of skin, her dark head was thrown back. Away from the door, both of them dressed in black, Roman wondered if he was even visible. It would be a matter of a couple of minutes to slip his hand under her skirt, smooth it up her leg and thigh, find her where she was wet, work her until she was soaking, loving on that mark until he made her—

Time was up.

He rose slowly, his breath and mouth and nose tracing over her spine.

When he stood, she was trembling. He stepped close enough for her to feel him. Close enough so that she would have no doubt that she affected him, too.

The courtyard was still empty.

He bent to her ear. "I can't, Cen." He kissed her lobe, once, because he already wasn't sleeping tonight. "That doesn't mean I don't want to. Now please, baby girl, please. Go to bed. I'll see you in the morning."

As *morning* left his mouth, the two-person patrol walked into view. Roman stepped back from her.

"*Lo entiendo,*" she breathed. "*Buenas noches,* Roman." Her words, said in a soft sigh, raised every hair on his body.

She took two wobbly steps, paused, then firmed those glorious legs and strode out of the room and up the stairs without looking back.

Roman put his hands behind his back and turned to face the fire, forced himself to remember the sacrifice he made to become the man who couldn't follow her upstairs.

Chapter Nine

Guanajuato, Mexico

Early the next morning, Cenobia could hear Glori and a night guard murmuring downstairs as she stood dressed for work in her bedroom doorway with a cold bottle of water and a guava in her hands. She stared down the hall at the closed door of her home gym and listened to the creak and crash of the Nautilus machine like it was delivering Morse code. When a few seconds of silence from the gym turned into ten and then thirty, she rolled out the tension in her shoulders and was glad for the coolness of the bottle in her sweaty palms.

With a final calming breath, she crossed the hallway in her heels. And timed it perfectly. It looked like she'd just arrived and hadn't been stalking Roman when he opened the door.

"We'll be leaving for the factory in half an hour," she announced as he took a step back, startled.

Cenobia forget what she'd planned to say next.

Roman Sheppard was wearing the shortest shorts she'd ever seen. They were olive green and they over-lapped at the sides, giving room for his thigh muscles— his thick, bulging, delineated thigh muscles—to flex and move. His sculpted legs had little hair this high up and his skin, sleek over muscle and paler than hers, showed a maroon flush that disappeared beneath the nylon fabric. She wondered how far up that flush traveled.

"Cenobia?"

"Hmm?" Just the lightest swath of shiny cloth separated her from…

"Cenobia!"

"¿Mande?" she jumped, her eyes skirting up him. His black t-shirt was sweat soaked and showed off the mounds of his chest. He had a night's worth of shadowy scruff. His hair was spikey and dark with sweat. It made his green eyes brilliant.

Warrior prince Roman Sheppard had slept in her home and this is what he looked like after rolling out of bed and working out.

He gave one fierce breath out of his nose, as hot as a fire-breathing dragon. "I asked if you needed anything else." He looked annoyed and amused and maybe, just maybe, a little aroused.

She was ogling him in her hallway.

"Sorry," she said quietly, holding out the bottle and fruit. "I wanted to catch you before things got weird."

She surprised a huff out of him. "Nice job," he murmured.

They could hear their employees talking downstairs. But he took the guava and water, leaned against the doorjamb, and opened the bottle, taking a long drink while watching her. In the morning sunlight, his eyes looked as cool as the flesh of a lime.

She simmered. She let him stare at her in her starched white blouse buttoned to the neck, a charcoal-flannel skirt with a peplum-kick, a bedazzled zebra pin and killer silver heels. It was only fair. She'd been measuring all men against Roman Sheppard since he'd rescued her.

She was a mathematician and engineer, so the equation made sense. Take a handsome twenty-six-year-old war hero and have him rescue an eighteen-year-old girl, have him treat her with respect, admiration, and care during the worst of circumstances, and, yes, a painful crush will result.

But then…turn him into a lost Spanish prince. A prince who asks for help for a family he's known for a few weeks. Add that he's the kind of man who saves a trailer full of women smuggled into Dubai and a human rights activist kidnapped in Colombia. Then multiply all of that with ten years of notes that prove him to be funny and conscientious and empathetic and willing to learn and desperate to take care of his family and his community.

What does that painful crush become then?

"Did you sleep okay?" she asked. He was in her home. She wanted him to like it.

"Yeah," he rumbled. But his eyes, warming, said something different. "You?"

"I slept fine." Once she'd slung off the pillow she'd buried her face in so he wouldn't hear her, she'd slept the limp, sexually gratified sleep of the dead.

Those plush, perfect lips that fit itself to the guava had turned her nickname into pornography. Those strong, white teeth that bit into the green rind had branded sex into her body in spots she'd never imagined were erogenous.

I can't, Cen. That doesn't mean I don't want to.

What did the math equal when your painful crush perhaps had a bit of a crush, too?

"I'm glad you're here," she said softly, with all the honesty in her.

"Me, too," he said, voice deep and low like it was a secret they shared as he wiped his soft, shining lips with his wrist.

"Pues, bueno."

She'd served him breakfast and, hopefully, circumvented his retreat. She wanted him. *Madre de dios*, she wanted him with a hunger and clarity that ached. But she empathized with how complicated the wanting could be in these circumstances, surrounded by employees and orbited by danger.

More urgently than desiring him, she wanted to get to know him.

"Be ready to leave in half an hour."

She turned, but she didn't have to see his face to hear the smile-not-smile in his voice.

"Sí, señorita," he said, slow and gruff.

Last night, he'd called her *baby girl*.

She imagined a relationship that could include both was a great place to start.

Later that morning when Cenobia handed out the safety goggles just outside the swinging doors of the assembly floor where La Primera was being manufactured, she planned on going straight to the plant's general manager to discover what was going on with the cobots, the machines necessary to ensure manufacturing could meet demand. But when Roman slipped on his goggles and said, "Lookin' forward to finally seeing this car I heard about thirteen years ago," she figured they could take the long route to the manager's office.

Last night's interviews of the catering staff and surveillance tapes of the ballroom hadn't revealed more about the threatened attack. Glori and the team were talking circumspectly to those on those guest list today. They were also building a plan to monitor Rodriguez's movements and communications.

Roman was by her side and she fervently believed everyone in her home last night was doing everything they could to protect her. She was even beginning to doubt her fears that someone close to her was working against her—Sheppard Security had yet to find proof of a leak.

So she could lose herself in the moment as she explained how the interaction of an electric motor, gasoline engine, and a braking system captured energy and used less gas to a gorgeous, dark-haired man who watched her with absolute focus in a fitted navy-blue suit with a chest-defining waistcoat and a chocolate paisley tie.

As she went into regenerative braking systems, he looked around. Even her perfect warrior prince had a breaking point.

He pointed up into the air with his burned hand. "I thought it was going to be loud."

It was a better compliment than the one about her eyes.

"We built a plant that is people focused; it's quiet, light filled, and easily altered," she said at a normal volume. There was noise—the buzz of drills, the whish and whizz of air compression, chatter—but it wasn't the ear-splitting roar of automation one usually encountered in car manufacturing. The ceiling of the assembly floor was high and ringed with windows that filled the factory with natural light, giving an expansive feel different than cramped and halogen-flooded factories. "Rather than relying on fixed lines and technology bolted in place, we have cobots that work alongside our people and can be moved, added, or stored, depending on car demand."

Cars in various stages of production moved on individual, motorized dollies in an S-line along the floor. Absent were rolling belts and huge robotic arms. "Because there are no hoses or electric cables, cobots can be wheeled wherever they're needed. Our lines can be effortlessly lengthened or shortened, depending on demand, and when we add a new car to our hybrid collection, we can change the line in a weekend. In other plants, that effort takes months and millions."

The furrow on his brow, the lines of his concentration around his eyes, were nearly as pleasurable as his kisses. "I always thought total automation was faster and cheaper."

Cenobia smiled. "Not when you're trying to appeal to customers whose car-buying tastes change as quick as the flavor of the month." She paused behind a plexiglass wall to watch cobots hold parts to the chassis while workers welded. Sparks flew and she saw Roman's hand stutter out before he pulled it back.

She tilted her head and glanced at him from under her lashes. *I saw that.*

He hooked his thumbs into his pockets and shrugged.

She nodded to a quiet corner of the factory just beyond where they were standing. "Want a closer look?"

"Try and stop me," he said.

Behind a series of guardrails sat several rows of unassuming cars. Soon, the cars would be transported to a holding garage where they would wait to be disseminated throughout Mexico and the world after their big reveal at the Frankfurt Auto Show.

The three guards stayed beside the guardrails as Cenobia and Roman walked toward a shiny red model.

"Mexicans like small cars that don't feel small," she said as her fingers petted over the subcompact sedan. *Hola, niña.* "So, we made sure La Primera had a roomy backseat and a large trunk."

She patted the trunk lid, proud of the car's proportions. The four-door looked like a good-sized sedan that had been shrunk by a third.

She came around to open the front passenger door and nodded at Roman. He opened the driver-side door and leaned down to look inside. "We packed the car full of budget-plush amenities like faux leather, driver-assist warnings…" she went on, pointing out all the details. Then she straightened and relaxed her hands on the roof. Roman did the same. "But what's truly revolutionary is what we packed under the hood: our 2.0-liter engine will provide class-leading fuel economy of fifty-two miles per gallon while delivering one hundred fifty horsepower. No one else has been able to offer than kind of conservation and power at the price we offer it."

His concentration had her going into pound-feet of torque and kilowatts of lithium battery power before she realized it. She stopped herself because he wasn't going to.

In the quiet, he kept staring. She was swept back to last night, when he held her face in his hands and mesmerized her with a look of naked desire.

"Most people don't actually do the country-saving at thirty-one that they dreamed of doing when they were eighteen," he finally said, his words low enough to vibrate over the hood of her car.

It was a lovely thing to say. But Roman had lost track of the company he kept. "You and your brother saved the Monte del Vino Real before you were thirty," she said, folding her hands together. "Your sister reinvigorated it before thirty as well. And you received the Medal of Honor when you were just twenty-six."

His brother had planted a new vine to improve the fortunes of their winegrowing kingdom, and he and Roman had wrested control of the kingdom from their greedy, do-nothing father. Their sister Sofia had launched a winery that revolutionized the kingdom's tired winemaking techniques and opened the door for a host of new wineries that brought tourists, jobs, and a much-needed vitality to the once-sleepy village.

While a squad leader in Iraq, Roman had single-handedly saved his squad when they were ambushed. Not one of his men had been injured and they'd been able to extract the valuable target who'd been the goal of their mission and whose information had helped to thwart other attacks.

But instead of agreeing with her, Roman looked away and twisted that thick gold ring on his finger. Had he been in contact with his family since he'd been here? She again felt the pang of pulling him away.

"I'm sorry you're here when you have so much going on in the Monte. I hope they're managing okay without—"

"They're fine," he said, still focused on the other end of the assembly floor. "I'm just the muscle."

Was he kidding?

Her thoughts were interrupted when she saw Edgar Tena, the plant's general manager, come around the guardrail. Cenobia introduced them, then Edgar led them all to a group of huge crates stacked in an empty spot of the factory. Cenobia quickly explained to Roman that these were the cobots they'd been planning to add to the line to manage the deluge in orders they expected in a month. Initial projections had them selling three hundred thousand cars in the first year.

Beside one opened crate was a machine that looked like a bent arm with a tray for a hand.

"We were uncrating and going through the initial tests for shipping integrity when we saw a wire sticking out," Edgar said. Tall and skinny in round glasses, Edgar believed in hybrid technology more fervently than she did. "It took us a while to trace what it was, but we found it."

He picked up a nearby laptop and hit some buttons. The cobot that would lift heavy manifolds and give them to the workers began to move. Then he leaned over and hit a large red button on the side of the machine.

Nothing happened.

Feeling a slow burble of dread in her stomach, Cenobia crossed her arms and chewed on her bottom lip.

"What's wrong?" Roman asked.

"This a kill switch," Edgar explained. "It allows the worker to shut the machine down quickly if it misbehaves. Without it, a glitchy machine could hurt someone."

"Those buttons don't come standard," Cenobia said, doing a quick calculation of the number of machines they'd gotten in the most recent shipment. "We pay extra for them in case our network gets hacked. Invading our system would be the easiest way to sabotage the line."

Sabotage. There. She'd said it out loud.

She saw Roman check their surroundings, then shoot a look at the guards, who'd heard Cenobia. They stepped away and started relaying information over their earpieces as Roman stepped closer to her.

"How many machines have been compromised?" she asked, dreading the answer.

"We don't have a full count, yet," Edgar said. "But at least a third of what we've tested so far."

Cenobia sucked in a breath.

"How bad is that?" Roman asked.

Even in this, now, he was beautifully soothing to look at. "We need to add these machines to the line in order to meet the demand we're anticipating," she said. "Without them…"

Her words dropped off as she met Edgar's eyes. This was really bad.

With the launch of La Primera, they were trying to do more than add an affordable hybrid car to the marketplace. They were also trying to prove that Mexico and its people were as capable of designing, engineering, and producing a quality car as any foreign company. As brown, Spanish-speaking mestizos who were always underestimated, this launch had to be more perfect than perfect. Delays in production and shipping would only feed the stereotypes that already existed. If Cenobia failed, the legend of La Primera—the first car for Mexicans, by Mexicans—would become another bad *gringo* joke and would give one more excuse for Wall Street to undervalue Mexican companies and megabanks to continue withholding access to afford-able credit.

The personal threats to her safety were widening to include attacks against her company and country.

Close to her side, Roman asked, "Have you contacted the distributor? And gone over the shipping manifest? When could these have been tampered with?"

"It would have been in Mexico," Edgar said.

"Then, for the time being, we'll arrange to have our own couriers meeting shipments at the border and trav-eling with them."

Roman looked to Cenobia for affirmation, and she gave it with a quick nod.

Don't waste your brain power on this, he'd told her repeatedly. Now, she truly understood the value of that advice. And the value of the man standing beside her. It was going to be an Olympian task getting these ma-chines fixed in time. Roman—his team, his efforts, his presence—allowed her to focus fully.

"Edgar, continuing testing and make a list of the damaged machines in terms of priority," she said. "The manufacturer can send us blueprints or we'll fly in a couple of their engineers, I don't care which, just con-tact them to…"

She ticked off marching orders as she led Edgar, Roman, and the trio of guards back to the plant man-agement offices.

Cenobia worked late into the night securing the top ro-boticists from Trujillo Industries, the Instituto Politéc-nico Nacional, and the cobots' German manufacturer to find and fix the damaged machines. Checking for further sabotage and repairing the damage was going to be slow and intricate work, and she needed the very best starting the task immediately if the cobots were going to be up and running in time to take the flood of orders expected after the Frankfurt Auto Show.

She refused to panic. The German manufacturer, a young robotics firm that had planned to piggyback its initial public offering on La Primera's success, was so horrified by the sabotage that two of their engineers were already on their way to Mexico.

Through the day and into the night, she was soothed by the quiet murmur of Roman's gravelly voice. He was working from the couch in her assistant's office to tighten factory security, develop a new strategy for investigation, and discover who messed with her machines.

It was past midnight by the time they entered her kitchen from the garage, Roman with his snow-white shirtsleeves rolled up as he held his jacket and Cenobia carrying her black heels. Roman had grumbled about how she should keep flats or slippers in her office as she'd walked barefoot down to her car, and Cenobia had smirked at his use of "flats." She slumped on a bar stool at her grey-granite kitchen island as Roman briefly spoke to the third-shift guards, then went to her fridge, pulled out the catering containers neatly stacked in there, and frowned as he opened each one. He found the two that were apparently the least objectionable and stuck them in her microwave.

When he turned toward her, Cenobia had pulled the band out of her high ponytail and was running her fingers through her hair. Her hair was too long and heavy to wear down, and she was too busy to bother with a cut that needed daily styling. She began to plait it over one shoulder.

He turned back to the cabinets.

She enjoyed watching him, unobserved, as he got a glass, filled it with water, and drank deeply. The muscles in his forearms, exposed by his rolled-up sleeves, flexed, and the large luxury watch and leather cord around his wrist showed off his arm's thickness.

Every time this perfectly put-together man rolled up his sleeves, it stirred something primal in her. That she was seeing him this way in her home, in the middle of the night, while he made himself comfortable in her kitchen and warmed them food, was better than her fantasies.

The microwave trilled that the food was ready. Roman clicked his glass down on the granite. "We need to have a conversation about getting you someplace safe," he said abruptly.

Cenobia's hands slowed as she tied the band around the end of her braid. "I am someplace safe."

He opened the microwave and pulled out the cartons. "Safer."

As he opened cabinets until he found plates, emptied the cartons, fussed in the silverware drawer, she realized he was purposely keeping his back to her.

"What are you saying, Roman?"

He rested his fists, curled around the silverware, on the countertop. The position pulled the white shirt tight at his shoulders and highlighted the inverted pyramid of his torso. With the shirt tucked in and the camel leather belt grasping his slim hips, his navy pants perfectly defined his hard, round...

"I'm saying we should get you hidden and keep you there until we figure out who's responsible."

Cenobia breathed through the concrete "no" that instantly filled her. "You said yesterday that wasn't the mission."

"The mission has changed, Cenobia."

"Why?"

He turned around with the plates and she wondered how he could look so glorious—white shirt and tired eyes and short hair mussed on top—when he was saying what he was saying. "Why?" he said low, practically growling it, like he was holding on to patience as he put her plate in front of her. He put his plate down and sat on the bar stool next to hers, one shoe on the floor and one on the rung. "Because we're playing whack-a-mole right now."

Roman and Glori had had a brief meeting with Cenobia that evening. They were still gathering intel, but the team had assessed quickly that the sophistication and subtlety of the sabotage was totally outside of Las Luces Oscuras' regular MO. Which left them with the uncomfortable possibility that there might be more than one bad guy in play.

"Maybe there's a leak and maybe there's not," he said, looking at her intently. "Maybe they had inside information to know exactly which shipment to hit or maybe they didn't. Maybe a motherfucking drug cartel wants to stop you from launching your car, or maybe it's the Mexican government."

The knob of his volume went up slowly as he spoke.

"There are too many maybes and I'm…" He licked his bottom lip. "I'm worried about you."

When Roman looked at a person like that, he didn't need a gun to be lethal.

Suddenly, she was aware of how late it was. She was aware that if she slipped off her stool, she could lean on him and soothe his worry. She was aware that she didn't care who saw them.

"If I was another client," she asked softly, "...would you make me hide?"

"Yes," he said immediately. He pursed his mouth. "Maybe." That mouth. "Fuck," he said. "I don't know."

His eyes were heavy lidded with honesty. "It's hard to think clearly with you, Cenobia."

She heard what he wasn't saying.

Cen.

The thing growing between them was beginning to have shape and density. It was more incredible, more unbelievable, than anything she could have fantasized.

It was more terrifying than anything she could have imagined.

Her rescuer, CEO and warrior prince Roman Sheppard, was black text under an email subject head or a strong, hasty scrawl on a card or an image she pinned on a secret Pinterest board titled *The Prince's Dirty Mouth*.

That was a secret she would take to her grave.

But Roman, the man, was flesh-and-blood sitting in her home, seeming to want her and not want her with the same equal pull because of the ferocity of his honor.

She had something she had to show him.

He needed to know. More importantly, centering herself because she had to, she needed to know how he would react.

"I can't leave," she said definitively, using the shadows under the island to slip her hand into his. He instantly gripped her fingers. Why had no one told her about the glory of handholding? "There's too much to do. We need to get the cobots back online, Vasquez is still agitating to push back the launch, the team is still putting together the details... If I left now, you might as well shoot me."

His hand squeezed hers tighter. "Don't say that."

"Then keep me safe," she murmured. "I trust you."

She slipped her hand from his then turned to pick up her fork, jabbing it into the pasta he'd warmed. He watched her for a moment more before he turned and picked up his fork as well.

She did trust him. When she had an opportunity to show him what he needed to see, she would know whether she could trust him absolutely.

Chapter Ten

Roman had never been tortured. But he'd gone through days at Ranger School that had felt like descending the circles of hell, a mind-and-body smashing rotation of fire drills, battle drills, and PTing at a pace that made him hurl, only to sleep a few hours, wake up, and start it all over again.

The next two days watching over Cenobia kind of felt like Ranger School. He saw her in every state of dress except naked: in her pinup-girl corporate wear, barefoot, even in loungewear when he'd gone down for coffee too early. He'd gotten one look at the cream sweater slipping off her shoulder and walked into a doorjamb. He was an arm's length away from her most of the time and a room's length away always, which meant he was constantly fighting the urge to pull her into his lap. He watched her power with his jaw dropped and worried about her vulnerability with fingers that ached to grab and shove her behind him.

His clothes and his hands smelled like honeysuckle. He was going to fire the tailor he'd been with for five years, who'd insisted on the slim cut of Roman's pants.

The only relief was that they were both preoccupied with work and surrounded by observant eyes from sunup to past midnight. Cenobia was relentlessly cementing the final details of La Primera's launch, monitoring the cobot repairs, shoring up support for her car inside and outside the company, and quietly lobbying for Vasquez's removal with influential members of the board, who would need to vote to fire him. Roman had brought in additional Sheppard Security team members to assist with the sabotage investigation and monitor Hernán Rodriguez, the Las Luces Oscuras liaison. He'd not mentioned again the need to sequester her, but he'd worked on a couple of plans with Glori in case it was abruptly necessary.

Their late-night rides home, when Cenobia curled her bare toes together and relaxed her hairstyle and filled the car with her soft, sweet, tortuous scent, were full of work and security updates.

It was of course right when Roman was getting comfortable with the torture that, early in the evening on the third day, Cenobia came out of her office dressed in body-skimming black Lycra capris and a red crop tank that showed just a slice of skin around her torso. Roman pulled his computer onto his lap.

"How upset would you be if I left without you?" she asked, tugging her ponytail out from the fitted workout jacket she'd slipped on.

"Very."

"I figured as much." She tossed a bag at him that her driver had sat on Paloma's desk minutes earlier. She'd sent her assistant home early after a lot of late nights. "Be ready to go in ten."

When he unzipped and looked in the bag, he saw it

was his workout T-shirt, a pair of track pants, and his sneakers.

She was walking back to her office with a little sauce to her hips. "Cenobia," he said, standing and taking out his earpiece. "Come here."

Cenobia paused, looked over her shoulder at him. They were alone. She turned around and came back. Slowly.

He beckoned with one finger for her to step closer.

"Are we going to where you sneak off to?" he asked.

She nodded, her eyes deep brown and watchful.

"Are you sure it's safe?"

"With you, it is."

Looking down at her thickly lashed cat eyes, her smooth forehead, her wide chin, and soft mauve lips was like looking at a plate of his favorite *tapas* and trying to decide which one he was going to enjoy first.

"So, if I don't feel it's safe, you're gonna listen to me?"

"Yes," she said, nodding solemnly, and for a moment, Roman felt the difference of the eight years between them. "I will listen to you."

He was glad she wasn't trying to go off on her own. He was honored she'd invited him. He felt a puffed-up pride that she was bringing him where she'd avoided taking everyone else.

He also knew Cenobia Trujillo was an excellent actress when faced with men standing in her way. She was going to do exactly what she wanted.

Roman followed Cenobia through a warren of narrow *callejones,* eating the roll that a *panadería* owner had given them as they'd walked through her shop to reach the alleyway behind it. Two of his team members were monitoring the bakery from down the street. Her people had stayed with the three-car caravan that had parked blocks away—they still hadn't ruled out a leak of information coming from the inside, and whatever this secret was, it was too precious for Cenobia to risk.

Roman took his cues from her silence and kept his questions for later.

After enough twist and turns that if she'd bolted, Roman would have been hopelessly lost, they entered the back door of a nondescript, concrete building. An automated bell signaled their entrance and Roman noted the small security camera in the corner. She led him down a narrow flight of dusty stairs into a tiny alcove with a large, steel door. Cenobia raised her face to another security camera and pointed at Roman to do the same.

When they did, the door clicked and they pushed through. A round woman in a grey sweatsuit greeted them.

"Tía Elena," Cenobia said, giving the woman a hug. "Is this okay?"

The woman waved away Cenobia's concern. *"¿Hablas en serio?"* she asked in Spanish. "Half of them are in there checking their lipstick."

When they walked into the next room, Roman saw that a few women going through warm-up exercises near the wall of mirrors did have bright lips. The concrete walls were spray painted with pink-and-red Venus signs and raised fists, and a couple of large metal cabinets were lined up against the back along with a stack of mats and several punch dummies.

As Cenobia took off her jacket and crossed to the

other women, Tía Elena kindly but firmly told Roman to stay at the back of the room and only speak if spoken to.

He noted the two small cameras focused on the room, another steel door, the quality of the wood flooring—probably foam backed to absorb shock—and the well-fitted mirror in the row of them that could be pressed and opened. An emergency exit?

"Ay qué sabroso está," floated toward him and he glanced to see Cenobia and two women checking him out as they warmed up. One full-figured woman was young and looking at him dreamily. The other woman—with a wiry strong body and coal-black hair pulled back—was stretching her hamstrings.

"He has cold eyes," she said, with no effort to lower her voice.

He kept his eyes tracking around the room, making sure not to stall on any one thing or person. Worked hard not to stare as Cenobia began stretching her shoulders. He'd felt it when he'd held her biceps or she'd pressed against him, but he could see it now. Cenobia was strong with useful, purposeful muscles.

After touching her palms flat to the floor then high-kneeing in place, Cenobia walked to the front of the room, her back to the mirrors, as the ten women formed a line facing her. Tía Elena handed her a large pink conch shell that filled Cenobia's hands, then joined the line at one end.

Cenobia briefly met Roman's eyes over all of their heads. For the first time, he saw an edge of worry.

She raised the conch shell to her lips and blew, sounding a loud primal horn that would have loosened the bladders of ancient enemies. The women crossed their arms over their chest, their hands in fists. When the bellow of the shell died away, Cenobia chanted with the other women. *"Permanecemos. Peleamos. Pero más importante, vivimos. ¡Ni una más!"*

We stand.

We fight.

But most importantly,

We live.

Not one more!

They hit their chests with their fists, then bowed.

Roman felt like they'd pounded his chest. All the air was knocked out of him. A shelter for women, he'd assumed. Services and safety for battered women, he'd figured. But he was beginning to suspect this was something more.

Something for Cenobia to hide and show only to him.

Cenobia set the shell aside and took a ready stance as the women spread themselves out.

Then the woman he'd come to Mexico to protect began leading her sisters through a series of open-hand strikes, knee and toe groin kicks, 360 defensive swipes, and downward side-fist punches. Only death could have made Roman immune to her glowing skin, her clenching muscles, her red cropped tank, the swish of her long black ponytail, but he worked to watch and not stare, worked to admire form and not covet shape. Cenobia was training the women in Krav Maga, a fighting system that would allow them defend themselves regardless of their size or fitness. Roman was a fan of it because it encouraged the defender to go for the nuts.

Their sharp exhales of breath—a harsh "shh" of purpose with each punch—filled the room.

Once they were sweating, Cenobia called for everyone to pair up and grab a pad. The women kicked and punched the pad, grunting together, smiling when a blow forced their opponent back in surprise, and Cenobia circled the room checking technique. She stopped the young woman, who had a bad habit of connecting her with toes. "Josefina, you're going to break something if you kick like that," she said, patting the top of the woman's laces. "Remember to kick with this part of the foot. It's stronger and will hurt more."

She circled the room one more time before she said, "Today, I'm introducing a different model for a defensive strike. Tía Elena is going to—" She stopped. Then she focused on Roman.

"Un momentito," she told the group.

She approached him where he stood at the back of the room. "Sometimes I bring in martial arts experts to act as attackers," she said. "It gives the women a chance to experience the emotions they'll feel when they have to defend themselves in real life."

Roman was already nodding. He did the same for clients he trained in self-defense; they needed to practice reacting during the rush of fear and fury. He'd also noted that she'd said "when" they have to defend themselves. Not "if."

"Would you like to be our expert today?"

"Of course."

"There are pads that should fit you," she said, motioning toward a supply locker. Sweat gleamed on her smooth forehead. "Suit up and—"

"If it's okay, I'll go without for the demonstration," he said quietly.

Sans pads was the best way to see where strikes would have the most impact.

She frowned. "I want to show them the hits—"

"That's fine," he said, slipping his hands into his track pants. He was honored to be invited into a space not meant for him. He wanted to give her something in return. "Just pull your punches. I trust you."

She met his eyes, then gave a quick nod.

They walked toward the front of the room. As he moved in front of the women, he was conscious of his height, his width, his power to hurt. He relaxed his shoulders, kept his big hands at his sides, made sure his face was howdy-y'all friendly.

"We know one of the most common attacks against women is the two-handed front choke hold," she said, turning to the group. "Today we're going to practice an extended defense if you're dealing with an opponent who won't go down."

She faced Roman expectantly.

Two-handed front choke hold. He looked at her dark delicate neck, exposed by her high ponytail and the V of her tank.

This, instantly, became a different beast than the close-combat training he'd performed with soldiers, staff, and clients. Cenobia waited and the women watched. They trusted that she knew what she was doing and believed that she could teach them to protect themselves.

You would have beggared a kingdom instead of trusting me to know my capabilities and limits, she'd said when they'd argued about the loan.

He had no doubt in her towering capabilities.

The room was quiet as Roman put his huge hands around her throat. He could feel the thin hot skin against his calluses. He had a flash of cradling her face while he begged her to understand the temptation of her name.

"What we want to prevent is being backed up against a surface," she told the women.

She looked at Roman again, then smiled as she sensed his discomfort. "I trust you, too," she murmured.

He gently maneuvered her back against the mirrors.

"We eliminate many options for movement when we're backed up," she said, showing her inability to get the 180-swing of her arm or rearing back strength of her leg. "You have six to ten seconds before the constriction of blood flow will make you pass out."

She put her hands over his, and pushed with her body, moving them back to where they started.

It suddenly felt like dancing.

"So, we use his forward momentum to break his hold."

Cenobia stared at him with an intensity that he recognized. This was how he worked with his squad and his team, communicating with eyes and expressions, putting absolute faith in each other's skills.

With a quick nod from her, he squeezed infinitesimally harder and pushed her backward.

Cenobia caught herself on her left leg, slapped her left hand over both of his wrists, raised her right arm high in the air, and then turned a sharp rotation to the left so his own momentum shoved his hands off her throat. She then caught his arms, bringing his face closer, and mimed two elbow strikes before actually connecting with his chin and snapping it with a light hammer strike that didn't hurt but jammed his jaw up. Turning her body forward, she faked two knee-raises to the groin before applying light punches, her fists tapping him backwards, until she had enough distance to turn and run.

He was so glad she was training them to run. Yes, they would stand and, yes, they would fight. But they would live by getting away from the people that threatened them.

At the door, Cenobia spun around, huffing. Roman put his hands on his thighs, breathing hard, staring at her. Adrenaline had his heart racing.

She met his eyes. Then her wide chin went up, and she gave him a slow, warm smile.

"*Dale*," the wiry woman said, as the other women began to hoot and clap. "You gave it to him good."

He felt a rush of heat like the high-end air conditioning had died in her deceptively low-rent building.

Her dark eyes dilated and became darker.

He couldn't hold it back any longer. The desire that began as a single drop during a curious Internet search when he'd asked for the loan, then became a worsening rain shower over the years of guilty googling and a deluge in the last ten days, finally drowned him. In front of these cheering warrior women, a roomful of survivors who expected him to keep her safe, Roman could no longer hide how fiercely he wanted Cenobia Trujillo.

Chapter Eleven

Guanajuato, Mexico

After getting padded up and allowing the women to pound on a *príncipe* while Cenobia offered hints and tips, Roman gave autographs and posed for selfies, even taking pictures with women who slipped in after news of his presence had filtered through the building. He and Cenobia got a boisterous farewell as they escaped into the now-dark night, but they were both quiet as they made their way back to the caravan.

They walked fast.

Roman was glad to see Cenobia matching his steps. There was a lot he wanted to say, to know, and he needed to get her alone to say it and know it.

When they entered her home, he didn't hesitate to draw the heavy drapes that covered her sliding glass door.

Cenobia walked to the living room and clicked the button to start the fire roaring in the fireplace. "I'm going to take a quick shower," she said.

They were her first words since leaving the shelter.

Roman showered, checked in with his team, left his earpiece in his room, and was on the couch drinking a glass of wine in his jeans and black T-shirt when she came down the circular staircase in linen lounge pants and a cream, wide-neck sweater. Her hair was down her back and still damp. Beyond a brief sighting that had almost crippled him in her kitchen, it was the first time he'd seen her with her hair down.

"You're drinking wine," she said as she walked toward the couch.

He'd needed to calm the urgency pressing against his skin. "Do you want a glass?"

She shook her head. Her face was washed clean of makeup, her skin in the firelight all coffee-cream and gold. She sat down on the couch, just a cushion away.

He should have drunk his wine faster. "I noticed you nurse a glass to look like you're drinking," he said.

"I don't like feeling tipsy. It's too much like dissociating."

He finished his wine in two large gulps and set the glass aside.

"Is Krav Maga the only martial art you've mastered?" he asked. He fought the drumbeat demand of *now* in his head.

This was the most important moment in his life to take his time.

"I've also learned judo, jujitsu, and aikido," she said, curling her legs up on the couch as she faced him. "Some boxing."

That goddamn sweater fell off her shoulder, showing him the tiny strap of a cream camisole against her gleaming skin.

"And you learned all this…"

"I started in Houston. But I didn't like the group classes." She raised her round chin to meet his eyes and he wanted pull her into his lap, slowly kiss her chin and cheeks and nose while she spoke. "So, I hired a master and trained with him in Mexico City. I never imagined training others, but the group gave me so much that I wanted to give back."

Those magazine articles and Trujillo Industries newsletters and society page pictures and communications in the guise of her father had never hinted at this.

"You own the building."

Cenobia scraped her teeth against her bottom lip.

She'd taken him there because she'd wanted him to see, but this was still hard for her. She was so incredibly brave.

Finally, she nodded. "We provide the women no-to-low-rent apartments, a food kitchen, classrooms and meeting space, a medical clinic and other services."

"I could go over the building's security," he said, carefully, not wanting to defile the temple she'd built with his white, male, American overstepping. "Just me, not the team. I can recommend updates and get you the latest equipment."

She nodded again. He'd paint her temple in biometric keypads and AES-256 encryption.

"I could also do it for other buildings the group uses," he hazarded.

"I'll get you the addresses." Because of course there were more than just the one.

She was looking down at her hands. One thumb was rubbing over the other's back. He now knew how silky and soothing that skin was.

"Cenobia," he said quietly, drawing her eyes back up to him. When he saw what was in them, he wanted to pull her against him and swear that she'd always be safe. He kept his voice cotton soft. "You provide safe houses for assault survivors?"

She crossed her arms around herself, then lifted one hand to stroke her earlobe.

"One of the women you met today was molested for years by her stepfather and no one would…stop him," she said. "Help her. With us she has a job and an apartment and…joy.

"Another had a sister who was abducted, raped, and killed in Ciudad Juárez," she continued. The hundreds of femicides unsolved and ignored by authorities in that border city were infamous and horrifying. "We've gotten her additional martial arts training and she teaches when I'm not there."

"Nine women are killed every day in Mexico," she said, her eyes dropping back to his chest as she rubbed her ear. "When men become angry and say *no más, como* Che Guevara *y* Emiliano Zapata, they're celebrated for it. When it's women demanding justice, we're treated like Sirens who will force society to dash itself against the rocks. But I refuse—refuse—to be okay with the fact that forty-one percent of Mexican women have experienced sexual violence."

Her thumb desperately working her tender lobe, she again met his eyes. "The group is for sexual assault survivors," she said, now fierce and defiant. "I was raped when I was kidnapped."

He couldn't help the sting in his nose and throat as she confirmed what he'd feared.

"Did I kill him?" He thought of the bodies he'd left behind in the bunker.

She shook her head. "The person who raped me wasn't there when you came."

He closed his eyes. "Fuck, Cenobia." He'd sold his soul to excel at this one thing. And still, he'd failed her. "I'm so sorry."

"Don't." Suddenly she was standing, standing and glaring down at him. "Don't pity me. I'm still the same person. You knowing I was raped doesn't change me."

"Hey," he said, putting his hands up. "I don't think it does."

"You said you felt sorry for me—"

"No," he said, scooting to the edge of her couch, but keeping his shoulders relaxed and hands up.

He recognized this now. He'd seen Cenobia stay as cool as a cucumber with everyone else. But she gave him power she gave no one else when she chose to make herself vulnerable with him.

She'd rather be mad than afraid.

"I'm sorry I didn't kill the person who hurt you. I'm sorry I didn't lay his body at your feet." He lowered his hands to his lap, felt hulking and ineffective in front of her taut, worthy anger. "And I'm sorry that you trusted me enough to share this with me and I'm fucking it up. But I don't pity you. There's nothing to pity."

Never had he felt his lack of grace with words more. "You and those women you're training, y'all survived a battle that you didn't want and wasn't your fault," he said. "What is there to pity? Look at you." He motioned to her, her house, her world she'd built. If he could just plug her into his brain… "Look at what you've done. And you choose to share it all: your car and your hurt and those warrior women…with me?"

She was still and firelit as she stared down at him, a golden goddess, and Roman, who'd worked so hard to keep his guard up with her, let her see everything.

"I can't pity you when I'm down on my knees, Cen. You put me on my fucking knees."

He'd slide to them if that's what it took.

Her stillness was towering. Her gorgeous face was so wary.

She took a step closer and put her hand, slim and cool, against his neck. She slowly slid it up, caught his jaw, and tilted his face to her.

He offered up his throat.

Cenobia Trujillo bent forward, her hair sliding around his face, and kissed him. In the honeysuckle-scented hideout of her hair, the girl he rescued and the woman he wanted pressed soft mauve lips to his as she kept her eyes open and Roman was swallowed in brown velvet.

Cenobia was kissing him. Soft. Slow. Warm presses. Then… Cen tasted him. The tiniest lick of her tongue. She did it again across his bottom lip. Slower. A longer drag. He wanted to scrape his teeth across it to ease the tingles. She sipped at his top lip. Like it was *café de olla* soaked. Gave this…sound in the back of her throat. She tilted her head, the wavy cloud of her hair stroking against his cheek, and sucked the generous pout of his bottom lip into her mouth. Nursed at it.

He felt like candy. He felt sugar sweet and dipped in chocolate. He could feel the soft suction in a straight line down to his cock.

"Cen," he mumbled, concussed with the feel of her, the taste, her smell.

"Are you going to kiss me back?" she sighed against his mouth. "You feel so good."

Good. God. He could make her feel good.

"Yeah, sweet girl," he breathed out then inhaled her

air. He put his bloodless hands up to her beautiful face. "Yeah," he said, tilting his head.

And then she was climbing into his lap and he was stroking into her mouth and then her tongue. His tongue.

She tasted... God, she tasted. It was hot and soft and wet in her mouth, in Cenobia Trujillo's goddamn mouth, and even though he was eight years older than her, Cenobia was the engineer of their pleasure. She pressed flush against him from pelvis to chest, squeezed his hips with her knees, anchored her hands in his hair. She was warm lips, tactile tongue, eager, grabbing hands. And he was still trying to figure out which end was up on the blueprints.

She was a fantasy made oh-so-fucking real by lush breasts and warm thighs and silken hair and the greedy grind of her against his cock.

He gripped her waist, the firm, warm, flesh of Cenobia Trujillo in big hands, and tilted her to slide against him.

She moaned into his open mouth.

Yeah. This was never supposed to happen. But no power on Earth could make him push her away now that it was. Her people could break in and tase him, his people could shoot him. Nothing was going to make him let go of her now.

He gathered her hair into his hand and wrapped it around his fist, the tug causing her to shiver as he tongued at the sensitive corner of her lips. She followed the pull of his hand like a good girl, let him gently fuck her mouth while he rolled up between her legs.

He tugged harder, breaking their kiss, the only way he was going to be able to give up her addicting mouth, and slid his lips and nose down her neck, licking at her heartbeat.

"So good," she panted up into the fire-warmed air. He bit at her clavicle and mouthed over her deep brown shoulder, exposed by the sweater trying to kill him. "I always hoped it would feel this good."

God, the whirling, grinding friction of her. He tilted up to let her ride faster. Harder. He hadn't gotten off like this since he was a kid. But he could do it. She could do it to him. He could do it to her.

All the things he could do to her.

Her hips began to move in faster, tighter circles. "I never thought it could feel this good with someone," she gasped, nails digging into his shoulders.

I always hoped it would feel this good. Her words were jabbing his lust-crazed brain. *I never thought it could feel this good with someone.*

She was trying to tell him this, too.

He let go of his clench on her hair, smoothed it down against her back.

His body whined. He relaxed his hips.

If she kept moving, he was going to blow.

Holding her against him, he slid backwards until his back was against the couch. "Cen," he said, rubbing her waist as he tried to catch his breath. Her hips slowed. "Cen, sweetheart…what're you saying?"

She pressed her face into his hair and breathed. Just breathed. Then they breathed together.

"I haven't had intercourse since then," she said.

God.

"Why?" he asked. Why no one else? And, most astoundingly, why him?

"I get…very uncomfortable," she said against his

scalp. "I tried to push through it in college and had a couple of panic attacks. We've been working on it in therapy and I've dated, used toys…"

At the thought of Cenobia using toys, of being used like a toy by her, his stupid, infantile cock jolted. She was tight enough against him to feel it.

She leaned back and searched his eyes with both hesitancy and shy amusement on her face.

"I don't feel any discomfort with you," she said. "The thought of sex, with you, has always been very… inspiring."

His cock jolted again and he closed his eyes. He could feel sweat in the small of his back.

She leaned close and kissed him. "I want to be with you, Roman. Not because you can fix me or protect me or pleasure me. I want to be with you because I desire you." More kisses. "I admire you." Kissed again. "I have for years."

Years.

Her desire was like swallowing a helium balloon and a cannonball at the same time.

Cenobia Trujillo wanted him. She had for years. He wanted her, too. For years.

He wanted to be her lover, one in a collection of boyfriends and loves and hot one-night stands, a collection owed to a woman of her age and sophistication. But he couldn't be *the* lover. He couldn't be her one.

He curled his hand around her nape and selfishly took her mouth while he still could.

"Cen, beautiful," he breathed against her lips. "I want…" She gave a slow roll against him as she kissed her way to his ear, sucked his lobe into her mouth.

"Fuck…" He grabbed her hip. "You can feel how bad I want you. But this is really fucking complicated."

She pulled off his ear and leaned back. He hated the sudden wariness he'd put into her eyes.

"Because I was raped?"

"No," he dismissed instantly, squeezing her hips in his hands and jostling her once to emphasize it. He slid his hands up under her camisole, held her waist to stroke his thumbs soothingly and greedily over her soft stomach.

He made sure not to look away from her dark, measuring eyes. "Because I don't take the fact that I'd be your first lightly. Because you're the eighteen-year-old girl I saved. Because we're both so fucking busy and overwhelmed I don't know when I'd find the time to make love to like you deserve. Because you're a client…" He said the word heavily and his shoulders slumped. "And being with a woman I'm supposed to be protecting breaks every code I've established and every rule I've hammered into those employees outside."

She looked down toward their laps.

He had to convince her. She had to know how much he admired and desired her.

He ran his hands up so his palms covered her skin, bracketed her torso, held her completely. She had to take her hard-earned confidence with her when she gave this firm, warm, beautiful body to another man.

"Cenobia?"

When she raised her eyes back to him, he was stunned by the naked craving in them. "Everything you said just makes me trust you more. Want you more." She pressed her hand low against her belly, looked at him with awe. "I'm trembling with it."

She was. Trembling in his hands. "Baby girl," he breathed.

"You make me wet when you say that."

He gripped her tight and closed his eyes.

He felt her lean close. "I crave you," she whispered, dream words against his lips. "I believe and trust you desire me back. The ball's in your court, *Príncipe*."

Her lips touched his in the sweetest, hottest press and he gathered her face to hold her there. But she broke the kiss, nuzzled into his palm, and climbed off. She gave him a tremulous smile—she was so fucking brave— then turned to head toward the stairs.

He never took his eyes off of her. When their eyes met on her final rotation of the stairs, he let her see every drop of his desire.

After she disappeared, he put his elbows on his knees and buried his face in his hands.

Yeah, he desired her. He might want her more than anything he'd ever wanted. More than kingdom or family or retribution or the addicting adrenaline rush of being the perfect battle weapon.

But years ago, he'd made a choice. That choice led him to saving the lives of his squad and turning his back on the President so the man could hook the blue Medal of Honor ribbon around his neck.

That choice meant he could never be the one and only in Cenobia Trujillo's bed.

How was he going explain that to her for the remainder of his days in Mexico?

Chapter Twelve

Guanajuato, Mexico

Cenobia stared out the tinted window of the Phantom, letting the morning sun shining across the low, flat constancy of the Bajío—its low trees of mesquite, its ubiquitous *nopal*, its grasses turning to yellow with the end of the rainy season—soothe her while she slowly traced her fingers over the back of her hand.

What did Adán want to talk to her about?

"Did I upset you last night?" Roman murmured, providing both balm and scrape to her thoughts as he leaned over the leather divider to slide his hand into hers. "I want to take things off your plate, not add to it."

She glanced at Arnol, who was resolutely keeping his eyes on the road. The former Mexico City *pesero* driver had faced down would-be rapists and drug runners on his graffitied bus and could be a pleasant source of jabber at the end of a long day. She'd earned his eternal loyalty by always suggesting the perfect gifts for his many nieces.

"No," she said softly, giving Roman what she hoped was a sincere smile. "It's just the usual worries: career on the line, future of the company in the balance, intrigue and terrorism at my doorstep. And I was a little restless in bed last night."

She felt like she pulled off the under-the-eyelashes look just right. But her hand was curled around his and she was rubbing her fingers over the large, satiny burn scar on the back of his hand.

"If it helps," he said, so low she felt it more than heard it. "I didn't get much sleep either." The etch of those lines at the corner of his eyes were deep. She wished she could lean over and kiss them.

Roman wanted her.

Yesterday, she'd stripped herself bare for him. She'd let him see everything down to her bones and viscera: her sisters, her efforts to protect herself and them, her rage at the injustice, her hurt caused by another, her fear of being defined by it. Her inexperience.

She'd revealed herself to the only man she wanted to see her and the only man who could have destroyed her by perceiving her as weak because of a horrible ten minutes not of her choosing and out of her control.

And he'd shown her with his words, his eyes, the sacrificial offering of his pornographic mouth, and the unflagging readiness of his body that he wanted her. He'd seemed undone by her kiss and touch. She'd made this huge, hard-muscled, experienced man stagger. Her memories of being young and carnal had been tainted, but last night, he'd made her feel what other girls at seventeen, eighteen, nineteen must feel: that greed. That desperation. That power.

She'd been nothing but the skin that reveled beneath the touch of those dreamt-about lips, the scalp that tingled as he pulled her hair, the fingertips that clung to the heat and muscle of him, and the *michi* that danced and rubbed wildly against his hard, eager, throbbing, long, thick penis.

Roman's long, thick, hard penis for her.

He'd been militaristically precise in laying out how difficult being together would be. She didn't disagree. But if he believed outlining his discipline, honor, and respect would dampen her desire, he wasn't as good as a tactician as he thought he was. Only looking away from him and performing measured belly breathing had prevented her from unleashing thirteen years of stored-up sexual fantasies and frustrations on him on the couch.

She would give him time. She would be patient— as patient as her innate impatience allowed. She would hold on tight to the belief that wanted her and saw her as powerful, and that his knowledge of her rape hadn't weakened that. She'd gone to bed exultant and a little in shock. After all this time, her warrior prince was here, and he was gentle and dominant and empathetic and bloodthirsty and…perfect. Better than a fantasy.

It should have been a morning for celebration.

But Daniel's call last night reminded her that, no, Roman didn't know everything.

Her father had said Adán wanted to speak to her immediately, first thing in the morning. About what, he didn't know.

"But I love that boy, too," he'd said, "and if he has something to ask you, I will support him."

Carajo. She almost forgot. She gently tugged her hand from Roman. "When we arrive at my father's house, I need to meet with my father and brother alone." She'd texted Roman last night about the change in the day's itinerary, but she hadn't mentioned the need for privacy.

Her words bounced hollowly around the tinted glass.

Never one to react quickly, Roman's silence still spoke volumes. It was the first time she'd spoken to him like he was staff.

"Okay. Glori was planning to interview Daniel's security while we're here." She was in the front car. "I'll join them."

Could someone from inside her father's household be providing information about her movements, her home, her work, her past?

We kept you blindfolded last time. This time, we'll cut off your eyelids so we'll be the last thing you see.

The men working for Las Luces Oscuras believed they'd kept her blindfolded when she was their captive. But her eyes hadn't been covered the whole time. And only one person in the world knew that. He'd been a young man, then. Or at least, she'd thought he was a young man.

He'd been her first lesson that someone could take all of her resources—her might, her wealth, her high IQ and inductive reasoning and problem-solving skills— ball them up and throw them away like used tissue.

They pulled off the highway and onto the miles-long private road that led to the flat-topped mesa where the compound loomed. The dry grasses and jacaranda trees that they passed hid the kind of deterrents usually found surrounding American military bases. Locals took the fence and *"Peligroso. No entrar."* signs that had gone up twelve years ago seriously after one elderly nopal picker was swarmed by her father's SWAT team.

Her childhood home, the place she'd dreamt about when she was excelling in her American boarding schools, hadn't always been called a compound. Her father had transformed it for her.

And yet she was only here for one meal a week. Sometimes less.

Arnol made a *harrumph* of sound from the front seat. "Some *pendejo* is driving down the road like he's racing the Carrera Panamerica," he said.

Cenobia glanced out the Phantom's front windshield to see dust billowing behind a car speeding in their direction.

Roman spoke to his team through his earpiece. "Alpha Team, we've got an unknown vehicle moving fast toward us. Contact the main house and make sure—"

Suddenly he winced, dug his finger into his ear, and pulled out his earpiece, throwing it to the lambswool carpeting. She could hear a tinny feedback squeal.

He grabbed for his phone. "Communications are out," he said. Cenobia glanced at hers, heart pounding, and saw that it also showed no reception.

"Señorita," Arnol said, his voice hard in a way she'd never heard it. "That's your father's car."

They were close enough now to see that it was her father's black S-560e Mercedes barreling toward them.

What was happening?

The black, bullet-proof Escalade at the front of their caravan swerved sideways and screeched to a stop, blocking the road. Arnol braked behind it.

"You stay down," Roman ordered as he pulled the gun that she always forgot he wore from the holster inside his coat. His face looked marble-carved.

This was the soldier who'd dragged her out of the bunker, held her up when she was sick, then raced her across the desert to safety. This was the man who did the things no one else wanted to do, but did them because they were necessary and he was called and he could do them best.

He cracked his door open.

Through it, she could suddenly hear automatic gunfire, sounding like the crackle of fireworks, coming from the top of the mesa.

Someone was shooting in the compound.

Terrified, horrified, Cenobia looked at Roman.

Her father. Bartolo.

Adán.

"I've got you," he told her, reassurance in every warrior-hard line.

With the Mercedes almost on top of them, Glori and the Escalade's driver leapt out of his door and positioned themselves behind the hood, aiming their guns over it. The two guards in the rear Escalade came running up to join them. Roman opened the passenger front door then stood behind its bulletproof wing.

"As soon as we find out if the oncoming car's a tango or friendly, we need to exfil," he called to the guards, aiming his gun over the door frame. "Keep your eyes on your quadrants, we don't want to get flanked."

Cenobia watched over Arnol's shoulder as the dust plume filled the road in front of them. He crossed himself. She'd stopped praying years ago, but she hoped his murmuring lips had power.

She could save a kingdom and build a car from the ground up and kick a man so that he couldn't support his weight for an hour. But she'd never felt more helpless.

At the last second, the car screeched to a sideways stop across the road. It was still shuddering when Bartolo stuck his head above the driver side door, waving his hands.

"I've got Daniel and Adán," he shouted. His shaved head was bleeding and there was blood on his shirt. "Daniel's hurt. We've got to get out of here."

She scrambled to get out the passenger door and to him, but only made it a step before Roman grabbed her arm.

"Please," she begged, inches from his face. "I need to see if they're okay."

He breathed out a harsh breath. "Stay behind me," he commanded. He signaled to his people. "Cover us."

She crouched behind Roman as they ran.

"We've got to go," Bartolo yelled as they scrambled to his side of the car. "It was an ambush. They were waiting for you." She wrenched open the back door and gasped at what she saw: her father, stretched out on the seat, his head in Adán's lap. They were both covered in blood.

"¡Papá, Adán!" she cried. Daniel was pale and glassy eyed. Adán held a thick compress against her father's side.

"It's okay, *mija*," her father croaked. "I'm okay."

The amount of blood meant he was not okay. "Adán, *mi amor, ¿estás bien?*" He nodded. He wasn't shot, but his eyes were glassy and sweat dampened his lank curls. He was probably in shock.

All she'd ever wanted was to protect him from this.

"I don't know how they got in and I don't know how long they were there undetected," Bartolo told Roman, pressing his palm to the bleeding cut on his head. His knuckles were torn and bloody. "They were waiting for Cenobia. But someone jumped the gun and the alarm was sounded. I got the staff safely into the panic room, and I was able to trap the *chingados* behind the compound gate, but I don't know how long the lock code will hold them."

A moment of total stillness blinked over Roman.

Cenobia watched him as the moment grew uncomfortable.

Then, as if it hadn't happened, he looked over and yelled for Glori. He ordered Arnol, the SUV's driver, and her two guards to turn the rear van around and head for the exit. "Send up a flare if we've got a second front forming," he called as Glori jogged toward them. "We can drive out over the desert but I don't want to."

The stunted trees and cacti would make that escape an obstacle course. And while Cenobia had been adamant that her father reject using land mines, she didn't entirely trust the decisions he made about protecting her when she'd first come home from the kidnapping.

Roman focused again on Bartolo as Glori joined them. "Did the house security know we were coming?"

Bartolo shook his head.

A dreadful sadness passed over Roman's beautiful face as he looked at his second in command. "Our people knew," he said.

Glori's dark eyes flashed wide and Cenobia could see the instant objection in her face before she swallowed it. "Yes," she said. "I informed our people and Cenobia's people last night."

Adán gave a scared sob. Still crouching in the car, Cenobia reached for his blood-sticky hand.

He turned his face to the window.

"We've got to get them out of the country," Roman said.

"I can't leave!" Cenobia cried, standing.

He stepped close and she could feel the force of a man who commanded elite soldiers. "We've run out of options," he said through gritted teeth. "They know your locations. They sabotaged your shipment. Now, they got inside your dad's compound."

Conscious of the terrified boy in the car, he held her elbow and whispered into her ear, "If they've corrupted someone on my team, there are few places they can't get to you."

He could've shaken her and it wouldn't have had the power of the tortured look on his face.

He stepped back, his jaw turned to granite.

"We need to get you and Adán out, someplace remote, someplace safe. Bartolo should come with us."

"Not without Daniel," Bartolo barked, eyes blazing. But there was so much blood.

"Glori will get him to the hospital and protect him." Roman's voice was surprisingly soothing as he answered the ferocious bodyguard. "I trust her with my life."

Glori gave an affirmative nod. Cenobia was so glad he had this unyielding woman watching his back.

"Yes, *compadre*," her father insisted, his voice weak. "Go with them. Help Roman. *Protege a nuestros hijos.*"

Protect our children. "Papá," Cenobia croaked, not wanting to leave him alone either.

Even weakened, her father looked back at her with fortifying love. "Nothing is more important than the life of…of Adán. Of you and Adán. *Por favor, mijita.* Go. Be safe."

He was right. Nothing was more important than Adán's safety. Not a car. Not her legacy. Not her employees or the people of her country.

Adán. She had to keep Adán safe.

She nodded, and Bartolo cursed then agreed deso-
lately.

The next half hour was a crazy, desperate dance.
She only got to give her father a tiny kiss before Glori
was tearing off in the Mercedes with him. He would be
safe in the Trujillo wing of Hospital Angeles in León.
The idea that it was her people who'd betrayed them
was torturous—for Roman, the thought that it was his
people would be deadening.

She, Adán, Roman and Bartolo escaped in the Escalade. Two miles up the road, driving away from Guanajuato, they threw their destroyed phones out the
window. Five miles up, they traded their Escalade for
a farmer's truck and a flip phone.

On a tiny airstrip outside San Miguel de Allende,
they boarded billionaire Roxanne Medina's private
plane. The pilot knew where they were going. But Adán,
Bartolo, and Cenobia didn't.

Cenobia was flying through the clouds with her warrior prince. The trust she'd first placed in him based on
memory and fantasy was now as real as life and death.

Chapter Thirteen

"Es un chiste," Adán yelled at Bartolo as Roman drank his coffee in the kitchen doorway of his sister-in-law's vacation home and watched the kid from under his eyelids. "There are people I need to stay in touch with."

The twelve-year-old was long and skinny, growing into his adult shape, but still swimming in Mateo's track pants and T-shirt. Right now, with twin spots of color in his too-pale cheeks, he looked on the verge of a full-on tantrum.

After a day and night of resting and recovering in this lake-house-on-steroids just outside of Roxanne's hometown of Freedom, Kansas, Bartolo was planning a trip to Wal-Mart to pick up clothes for him and Adán. Right now, the big man was barely holding on to his patience.

"I've told you, repeatedly, that no one's getting a phone," he said, rubbing his hand over his dark, shaved head. "We've all got to stay offline."

"I thought you were kidding," the kid accused.

Roman wondered if Adán was getting a wink of sleep.

Roxanne's lake home of rock and cedar planks, rag rugs and rocking chairs, wide windows and a big stone fireplace was tucked into the woods right up against the steely grey Big Lake, which was good for boating and bass fishing. Roman had designed the security, and the home was off the grid. When he'd called Roxanne from the side of a desolate airstrip in Mexico asking for the use of her plane and home, his brother had asked him to come to the Monte instead.

But Roman was determined not to bring his fuck up down on his family's heads.

Only Roman, Cenobia, Daniel, Cenobia's security, and Roman's team had known they were visiting the compound that morning. One of them had shared that info with the bad guys. If it was one of her people, he'd fucked up by not finding them after a week of looking. If it was one of his people that was compromised…

The only way he could protect Cenobia and her little brother was by taking them entirely off the board. Not even Sheppard Security knew about this place. He was communicating with Glori using their black box system, which also allowed Cenobia to send and receive notes from her staff.

His second-in-command was doing a yeoman's level of work keeping Daniel safe, overseeing the team, and conducting a secret investigation into the leak while Cenobia was sitting here with her hands essentially tied.

All because Roman had wandered off the path he'd stayed on all these years—do what you're good at, keep people safe, Ranger up, remain tactical—and allowed himself to be distracted by daydreams of her. He'd gone into the weeds and failed at his job. Failed at keeping her and her family safe.

The brazen daylight attack on one of Mexico's most important families was being covered 24/7 by the international press. On the now-muted TV over the crackling fireplace, Roman kept track of the updates. Daniel was stable and steadily improving. The attackers, who'd been trapped behind the compound walls while the family escaped, had unfortunately gotten away before the Federales descended. No one among the staff had been hurt, to Cenobia's relief. And yesterday, an ashen-faced Barbara Benitez had decried the assault and offered a reward for information about the attackers.

Clearly, Pemex wanted the Trujillos to know that the government entity was not involved.

It's good to know my little car did not inspire state-sponsored terrorism, Cenobia had said archly from the couch.

She sat there now in Roxanne's borrowed rolled up jeans, a red-and-white flannel shirt she'd tied at the hips, and a red bandana holding back her long hair, looking like his own Rosie the Riveter. Her bare toenails were painted a candy cane red.

"Maybe we can get you one of those games," Cenobia offered Adán. "*Como* PlayStation?"

Adán shot her a furious look. "Stop talking to me like I'm a baby!" he shouted.

Bartolo immediately snapped his fingers. *"Cálmate,"* he demanded, the scar on his lip making his mouth more daunting. "You've been through a lot but so have we all. You're not getting a phone and that's it. Now apologize to your sister."

Adán stared stubbornly at the floor, his lank medium-brown curls falling in front of his face.

"No hay bronco," Cenobia said, brushing off the in-

sult. "You're just hungry, *es cierto, mi amor.* Why don't you get a bowl of cereal?"

As Adán stomped out of the room, Bartolo rolled his eyes with an *Are you kidding me?* expression.

The boy had refused to accept a drop of comfort from his sister since they'd raced from his home, holding himself away from her even when he'd been drooping into an exhausted sleep on the plane. Cenobia obviously adored him, but this woman who was sincere and tactile with gordita vendors and society's elite and assault victims and American auto executives was surprisingly awkward with her little brother. She would jump into cooing or pacifying rather than really talking to him.

Maybe she just didn't know him well; she'd been in school or living in a different city for most of his life.

"What were you going to discuss with your father and Adán?" Roman asked Cenobia once he could hear her brother slamming down a cereal bowl.

Every line of her went rigid. She looked at the muted television. "I don't know. My father had called to say Adán wanted to speak to me."

Bartolo shot her a surprised look.

"Do you know what he wanted to talk about?" Roman asked him.

Bartolo shook his head, still eyeing Cenobia. "This is the first I've heard of it."

"How often did you visit during the week?" Roman asked her.

"Seldom," Cenobia replied at the same time Bartolo said, "Never."

Bartolo had already shared with them the little that he'd gotten out of an attacker with the help of his now-bandaged knuckles; they'd infiltrated and hid in the compound with plans to target Cenobia, and the plan would have worked if someone hadn't tried to grab Adán, who'd pushed a panic button. Roman needed more details, but right now was obviously not the time.

After Bartolo left to run errands, Roman hauled Cenobia into the kitchen where Adán sat at the butcher block island finishing his cereal. The boy looked at him suspiciously as Roman began to pull out ingredients from the fridge and pantry. Roman's mama, who was always good at getting people to set down their worries, used to say there was no problem that couldn't be solved over a slice of peach pie.

He hoped to be as successful with Texas chili.

"As much I'd love to do all the cooking while we're here, I don't want to do all the cooking," he said as he dumped an armful of ingredients from the fridge on the island. "I'm teaching y'all how to make chili, which is impossible to screw up as long as you don't do one thing: don't add beans. What do you stay away from?"

When no one said anything, he looked at Adán, who was glaring down into his empty cereal bowl. "Man, I'm talking to you."

"Beans," Adán muttered.

Cenobia sat on a stool on the other end of the island. Without a drop of makeup and her wavy hair held back by the bandana and trailing down her back, she looked so young. Her eyes wandered over him, and Roman suddenly had a sense of how different he must look; instead of bespoke suits and hair gel, he was barefoot in old, faded jeans, a soft grey Henley, and a two-day old beard. Being here meant family and relaxing—he maintained a bedroom here with clothes and weapons—

and he'd slipped into the creature comforts of this place without considering the hazards.

Like the hazard of Cenobia's velvety eyes traveling over him while rain hit the windows and a fire crackled in the fireplace and twelve-year-old boy who'd be relieved to be sent to his room serving as their only observer.

"Beans," Cenobia said.

Roman swallowed before he looked away. "Right." What had he been doing?

"Right…okay, now everyone knows all good meals start with bacon…" He diced bacon slices and then dumped them into a large Dutch oven he'd set on one of the six burners.

He showed them how to cut top round against the grain into chunks. The across-the-island stand-off didn't make his instruction easy. He added the meat to the sizzling pot, then picked up a bell pepper. Because it was easier to focus on Adán, he showed him how to cut off the stem, clean out the pith and seeds, then break the pepper down in strips then bits. Roman was being showy with his knife work—you could hold a knife one way and kill a man, hold it another way and impress a twelve-year-old boy—but he wanted to help this kid forget, at least for the moment, the terror he'd been through.

Terror that was Roman's fault.

He handed a cored green pepper and a much smaller knife to Adán. "Now you," he said.

Adán halved the pepper, but the cut was ragged.

"Okay, it's going to go a lot easier if you turn the knife over," Roman said, twisting the handle in Adán's hand.

The thin sleek knife didn't have the easily identifiable serrated edge. But Adán flushed an instant red and let his hair hang in front of his face. "This is stupid," he muttered. "I don't—"

"No, dude, don't be embarrassed," Roman said, nudging him with an elbow. "The first time I cleaned an M-16 in basic, I was so nervous about the other guys watching I tried to jam in the bolt carrier the wrong way. My sergeant asked me why I thought it was going to work ass end up." He looked at Adán from under his heavy lashes. "Guess what became my nickname 'til I went to Ranger School.'"

Adán replied like he couldn't help himself. "Ass end up?"

Roman leaned back. "It's got a nice flow to it if you say it all together. New guys just thought it was my last name." He fanned his hand in the air. "Assendup."

A surprised laugh huffed out of Adán, and Roman felt it like a Cenobia smile.

Roman picked up the butcher knife and began chopping an onion. "Trying and getting it wrong takes guts." He nodded at Adán's pepper. "It's not even tryin' that's embarassin'."

Pushing his curls out of his face, Adán began to cut the pepper just as Roman had shown him, much slower, but ending up with nicely sized pieces.

Cenobia had stayed quiet on her stool. Roman could lead a horse to water but he couldn't make the beauty drink. So, he was pretty darned thrilled when she came around the island to stand next to Adán.

"The closest I've come to cooking is building an engine that runs on used fry oil," she said, picking up a knife. "I don't know how to cut a pepper either. What would you like me to do?"

Cenobia Trujillo had never and would never have to cook her own meals. She hadn't shopped once a week with her mom on payday, then stretched out the cheap meat and canned veggies and unending bowls of off-brand mac 'n' cheese until the next paycheck.

But she stood ready to learn with her small, dimpled smile. Good Lord, she was pretty.

Adán's thin shoulders stiffened up.

She reached for her ear lobe. "Or I could just watch and—"

"Do you know how to cut a jalapeño?" Roman asked.

She shook her head.

Adán kept his head down, chopping another pepper as he stood between them, and Roman showed her how to slice open a jalapeño, scrape away the seeds and membrane, and then mince it into tiny pieces.

Cenobia worked on a couple of chilis while Roman turned to flip the browning meat.

"If I threw your peppers up in the air, it would look like confetti *para el Día de la Independencia*," she said to Adán.

The kid stayed silent.

"Cenobia, don't touch your face until you've scrubbed your hands good," Roman said, prying up a stuck meat cube with his tongs. "My lips once swelled up to peach-slice size after cutting chilis."

"Has Cenobia told you about her Pinterest page?" Adán asked.

When Roman looked at them, Adán was still and Cenobia stood liked she'd been freeze rayed.

He put down the tongs. "Nope," he answered. "Maybe you should let her…"

"It's called *The Prince's Dirty Mouth*. Do you have a picture of your swollen lips she could add to it?"

Cenobia looked over her shoulder at Roman and her face—eyes wide, mouth slightly open, brow miserable—was a dictionary's example of mortification.

Roman kept his face blank. It would be his death if he smiled. It would be even worse if he leaned close and showed her what he could do with this prince's dirty mouth.

Daniel had praised their Guachichil blood for giving the Trujillos a perceptive sixth sense about what made people tick. Adán knew exactly where to cut.

"My mouth used to get me punched a lot," Roman said as he turned back to the pot and started scooping meat cubes into a bowl. "'Bout the time girls started noticing my mouth, the boys did too. I was on the small side, quiet, with big green eyes and a purdy mouth that made a good target. And, *whoo*, it sucked until I punched back."

He put down the spoon and came around the island, motioned for Adán to put the bell peppers in the pot. The fat at the bottom popped and hissed. Cenobía scraped in the jalapeños from her cutting board, and Roman dumped in chopped onions and garlic.

He topped the vegetables with a good pinch of salt and black pepper, stirred it, then handed the spoon to Adán.

Adán moved closer to the stove while Roman leaned back on the island, crossing his legs at the ankle.

"When I punched back, I realized I was good at

punching," Roman continued. "And I liked it. I liked it a lot. I started hittin' more guys and kissing more girls."

He pointed at Adán, who stood at the stove, rain-sky eyes wide and mesmerized. "Don't let that burn," Roman said. "You gotta stir it."

He thought about that time, when his talents were running wild, untethered, and powerful for the very first time. That feeling had been a narcotic for a poor, runty kid who lived in a trailer park in Odessa, who'd been at the bottom of every ladder he'd ever encountered except the one that measured how much his mama loved him.

"I was on the verge of getting kicked outta school, and girls kept callin' and cryin', and finally, my mama sat me down. Here's the thing: my mama was a great lady."

He didn't talk about her much. He gave single-word answers when the press asked; he didn't want them speculating about a domestic flight attendant with big dreams. Her training run working an international flight between Houston and Madrid had ended with her spending the weekend with a king, missing her flight, and losing her job. Ended with her pregnant, unemployed, and unable to get a response from the man who'd sworn love at first sight.

With his family...he didn't talk about her much.

"She was beautiful," he went on, resting the heels of his palms back on the island. "I mean, drop-you-dead-in-the-street beautiful. And kind. She worked so damn hard; all that kindness and hard work sapped her after a while but she was always beautiful to me."

He wanted to bring her to life for these two.

"My mama sits me down and tells me that with great

gifts come great responsibility. That my looks, my ability to fight, those were gifts—they came natural, I really didn't have anything to do with them but I was responsible for how I used 'em. I could use 'em to hurt people or help people. She coulda used her looks to get us out of Odessa, but knew it wasn't good for me, so she didn't. I found out later my biological dad used his gifts to make his people poor and seduce women with promises he never intended to keep."

Although his mother never shared with him who his biological father was, already understanding the man's greedy nature, she had written the man a number of times looking for a small amount of child support. The son of a bitch had ignored all her letters. Had ignored Roman until he wanted to use him.

"So, I had to decide. What was I gonna do with my gifts?"

He pushed off the island and looked into the pot, putting his hand on Adan's thin shoulder. "Looks good. Real good," he said. The steam from the vegetables was wafting over the boy's face. He looked straight at Roman for the first time with his unusual slate-grey eyes. The kid was going to be a lady killer.

"Roman," Adán said hesitantly. It was the first time he'd heard his voice without anger since they'd arrived. "I think your mom might have borrowed that line from Spider-Man."

Roman chuckled, and it had been too long since he'd done so. His laughter sounded like pop rocks in his chest. He squeezed Adán's shoulder with his burned hand, the rain making the skin tight. "Caught that, did you?"

He let go of Adán and turned the burner down to low.

"Point is, kiddo, you're smart, rich and loved." He spoke while he pulled cans of tomatoes and broth from a cabinet. "You got gifts and a lot of power, although I know it doesn't seem like it sometimes. You're gonna have crappy days. You're gonna have awful days." Roman squinted to find spices in the rack. "It's up to you to figure out whether you're going to use your gifts to take those crappy days out on people or find something better to do with all that power."

He set the cans and spices on the counter, then glanced at Adán. "You get me?"

He didn't want to embarrass the kid. He wasn't Bartolo or Daniel. Or Cenobia. He had no right to impart life lessons. Adán could have stormed out or just acted like he didn't "get him."

But he didn't storm out or act clueless. The dude nodded, a thought-filled notch between his flyaway eyebrows.

And for once, Cenobia didn't jump in to baby him.

"What was your mom's name?" Adán asked gently. From the corner of his eye, he watched Cenobia turn her head away and blink quickly.

Roman really dug this kid. He smiled, missing his mom something fierce and wishing she was here to meet these two. "Madeline," he said. "Everyone called her Maddie."

When Adán repeated it, it was like he blessed the room with her name.

He turned and glanced guiltily at Cenobia. "Sorry, Cici," he croaked.

Roman could see Cenobia fighting her discomfort. But she put her hand on Adán's shoulder, just like Roman had. "Thank you," she said. "I'm sorry, too."

That thick, cloudy air between them felt like it was clearing.

"Will Papá be okay?" Adán asked.

"Yes," Cenobia said, instantly.

Adán breathed and smiled, full and relieved, and Roman recognized that smile. It was Cenobia's. Adán looked at her as if her assurance—more than the reporter's or the doctor's or Bartolo's—was what he needed to stop the rain and bring out the sun.

"Adán," Roman said. "Why'd you ask Cenobia to come to the compound? What were you gonna tell her?"

Cenobia shot him a furrowed glare.

If part of doing his job was pissing her off, then so be it.

"Just that I was tired of her treating me like a baby." Adán looked guiltily at Cenobia. "I'm good enough to be included in company stuff just like you were at my age."

"Of course, you are," she said, her eyes wide and surprised. "I hadn't realized... I'm sorry I made you think differently."

"Did you tell anyone she was coming?" Roman asked.

She scowled at him again.

"No!" Adán declared.

Roman watched him for a beat longer before he glanced at Cenobia, then put his hands up and laughed. "Whoa, okay, I gotta ask. Y'all put away the eye lasers."

She and Adán glanced at each other, and Roman watched them give each other the same smirk.

"Okay," he said, picking up a teaspoon. "We're gonna throw in a heap of spices, then let them cook in while we get these cans opened up."

As they finished off the chili then made cornbread, Adán's laughter grew easier. Bartolo looked at Roman like he was a miracle worker when he came in carting bags. When they all sat down to eat, Cenobia gave Roman the softest, sweetest smile.

Good. Today he'd done his job. They were fed, warm, comfy, and breaking the knot of fear and worry that bound them. Cenobia and Adán were clearing the air between them.

Today, he'd done what he was good at and seen to the health and welfare of his clients.

He'd also effectively reminded himself of what he'd sacrificed to fully embrace his gifts. He wouldn't again let Cenobia's sweet smile distract him from the path he'd chosen or the memory of what choosing this path cost the person he loved most.

Chapter Fourteen

Freedom, Kansas

Two nights later, Cenobia softly knocked on Roman's door. She had a completely reasonable excuse for wanting to speak to him in the middle of the night. Still, Bartolo and Adán were in guest bedrooms down the hall, past a study and the twins' playroom, and Bartolo was a light sleeper.

She felt like a teenager sneaking into her boyfriend's bedroom.

When there was no response, she pushed open the door. If he was asleep, she would go back to her room. If he was asleep, she would stand and stare. Then she would go back to her room.

He wasn't asleep. With the full moon streaming across the lake in a silvery carpet that ended at his glass wall, Roman was shirtless with white earbuds in his ears doing sit-ups in the tiny army-green nylon shorts she adored.

Cenobia stepped into the room and shut the door behind her.

He didn't stop the smooth motion of his sit-ups when he saw her, but she barely got to see the crunch of his magnificent abs under a soft patch of dark hair—he had a hairy chest and his nipples were hard and the muscles gleamed lightly with sweat—before he was pulling a black T-shirt on, not stopping his sit-ups to do it.

As he continued to exercise, huffing slightly at the top of his rise, she stared at his thick thigh muscles bunching and lengthening in the lamp light. The hair on his legs was sparser than on his chest.

Roman Sheppard had a hairy chest. She could rub her nose into the hair. Search for his nipple though it with her tongue. Run her fingers into it and use it to hang on.

He fell back to the braided rug with a grunt and flung his arms out wide. The hard pale underneaths of his biceps looked tender. Bitable. After several recovery breaths, he pulled his ear buds out and asked, eyes closed, "You need something?"

Oh, yes.

She crept in and sat on an ottoman near his feet, stared at the lips that had gotten her into trouble. He'd stopped shaving in the days since they'd been there, and the dark, unholy scruff only highlighted the pink perfection of his mouth.

"I wanted to apologize for that ridiculous Pinterest board," she said. He continued to breathe deep and heavy, and he'd turned his muscular arms so his fingers dug in between the rug coils. "It was immature and—"

"Don't worry about it. That was just your brother being twelve."

When Adán had outed her, she'd prayed for a trap door in this deceptively luxurious house to open beneath her feet and send her into the deepest depths of the lake.

Their Pinterest boards—*Roman Sheppard's Res-*

cues, Fashion of a Prince, Roman in the Monte—had been a way for Cenobia and Adán to connect beyond the Sunday *comidas*. They hid their real identities behind benign names, and they shared pins like trading stats about a favorite *fútbol* player. She'd been horrified when nine-year-old Adán mentioned a board he'd found and wondered why it said Roman's mouth was dirty. It always looked clean to Adán.

Bartolo had almost laughed himself out of his chair while Cenobia squirmed and her father had graciously changed the subject. She'd locked down the board she'd made under a different alias and ramped up Adán's online filters.

Now it was clear to Roman that while she'd been offering him advice on loan restructuring and tax-free municipal debt, she'd also been childishly objectifying him.

Strangely, in the quiet of these woods, she hadn't yet had the chance to apologize for it. When Roman wasn't out on a run, monitoring the news, orchestrating a meal, or leading a hike, he was off using his secret black box system to communicate with Glori.

Cenobia wasn't complaining; the black box system had allowed her to send lengthy messages to her staff and receive memos in return. Everything she could do to ensure the success of her car launch, she'd done, and now she had to trust her people to deliver the car in time to the Frankfurt Auto Show and to have the factory ready for the high volume of orders they expected. The outrage over the attack and the fact that Cenobia and Adán had to go into hiding was actually giving them a PR boost. But she knew Vasquez, without her intercession, could still throw wrenches into the works.

For the first time in her life, she wasn't sure how much she cared.

She'd been adamant about staying close to midwife the birth of La Primera. Then her father, who'd always agonized over her safety, had been shot. He was steadily improving but he was still in the hospital. Roman was sidelined from his team and his family who needed him. And Adán…

All she'd ever wanted was to protect him from terrors like this. She thought he would be safe, guarded up in her father's citadel, kept close to home for his schooling, and attached to Bartolo. Had it been her decisions that had brought nightmares to his door?

How important was a stupid *carro*?

She looked down at Roman, who still had his eyes closed. She would love to discuss all this with him. But he'd been distant since their arrival in Kansas.

"Talking about your mouth that way was inappropriate and I'm sorry that—"

"Leave it, Cenobia," he said, startling her as he pushed off the ground. He turned to walk toward his bathroom and she watched his hard *culo* and thick thighs flex and his bare feet slap against the wood. Cenobia had new body parts to fixate on.

"I've offended you," she called desperately, standing. He was actually walking away from her. "I'd like to fix it."

He stopped, put his hands on his hips, and dropped his head. Cursed.

She had to fix it. She was growing concerned that all of his manic activity was a deliberate effort to structure space between them, and she didn't understand why.

"I'm not offended." He bit the words out like he

didn't want to say them. "But you being in here is a bad idea."

She flinched back. "I…" A pounding was beginning in her temples. Cruel thoughts she fought believing were whispering through her brain.

She straightened her spine against them. "If you don't want me anymore, please be a friend and tell me." She could take this. She'd survived worse. "If you've processed what happened to me and decided that you no longer want…"

"No," he whispered it, his back still to her. But the guttural, bone-deep denial blew away her building nausea. "Never think that, baby girl."

He calmed her nervous heart.

"Then why?" She didn't care that it came out plaintive. She didn't understand.

Five nights ago, she'd told him clearly that she wanted him, and he'd said and shown her, in a glorious way that was starting to feel more like a fantastic dream, that he wanted her back. *You can feel how bad I want you.* She'd been patient and said the ball was in his court but she could *still* feel it, in his heavy-lidded stares before he looked away, in the slow lick of his lips before he realized he was doing it. In his concern and care for her while they'd been here.

"As awful as the circumstances are that led us here, several of the complicated issues have been…put on pause," she said, directing her words at his tense, broad back. "We've gone from being very busy and surrounded by employees to having a lot of free time and very few people around." Those people were currently asleep and several rooms of thick walls away. She gathered her courage. "There are now many late-night hours for you to make love to this first timer as we deserve."

She didn't think it was possible for him to go stiffer, but she watched the myriad muscles of his legs and biceps stack up like bricks in a wall.

"Dammit, Cenobia," he finally groaned. "Someone's lookin' to hurt you." He spat the last two words. "Someone's looking to hurt you and because I screwed up, I can't do a damn thing to stop it."

He walked to the windowed wall and crossed his arms over his chest. His back looked massive against the lake outside.

"There are two highly skilled teams out there investigating who did this to your family," he said to the glass. "And because I got distracted and didn't do my job, one or both of those teams may be compromised. My crew is without their captain."

"I'm sorry that—"

"Your company is without their boss," he steamrolled over her. "On the verge of creatin' something that might make things better for your whole country, they're doing it without their leader."

"I don't blame you for—"

He swung around and glared at her, his green eyes blazing. Cenobia felt heat shimmer down beneath her cowl-necked oversized sweater and yoga pants. His eyes raked the same path and she realized that while she'd been looking her fill, he hadn't looked at all.

"Your little brother was terrorized. That's on me. Your father was *shot* and almost killed. That's on me."

He so effortlessly overlooked the enhanced technology and additional security teams he'd installed in her home and office and factory, and her father's reassurances that the compound was a step above America's Fort Knox and needed no enhancements. He shoved aside the long hours he'd worked to investigate the threats. He disregarded the reality that he'd upended his life to be at her side.

She cocked her head. "What distracted you?"

He straightened as his shoulders went back.

"All I saw was how hard you were working," she said. "What do you believe distracted you from protecting me and my family?"

Roman Sheppard's steely focus was legendary, had been mentioned in his profile in Forbes and when he received an award from the U.N. What did he believe was powerful enough to interrupt it?

She felt the strength of that monumental focus now.

He lifted his chin, his scruff making him look less prince and more warrior. He firmed his pouty mouth in it, like he'd come to a decision, before he spoke.

"Cen, you weren't the only one lookin' online and thinkin' dirty thoughts."

Her heart beat its way up into her throat.

"Why do you think you haven't seen me in thirteen years?" he asked, low and rumbly. "Why do you think I never accepted any of your invitations?"

Steely. Taciturn. Resolved. Those were the words others used about Roman Sheppard. But Cenobia had seen a man with a terrifyingly intense range of emotions—terrifying because of the way they affected her—and now, when this man dropped all of his barriers and let naked desire shine from his eyes, she felt it like the sun pushing against her body.

"I was looking online, too, baby girl," he said, heat roughing up his voice. "Every six months, if I could wait that long. Quicker if I couldn't." He scraped his bottom lip with his teeth and Cenobia felt it between her legs. "Most times, I couldn't."

Why did he say those words like penance?

"Why did you never contact me?" she breathed. "Why have you never said anything?"

"Because I'm a man and a soldier who knows better than to fixate on a client I once rescued," he said grimly. "So you can stop worrying about that board because I've done a lot worse—"

Cenobia dismissed his self-flagellation with a *pfft* of her lips. "Did you want me when you rescued me?"

"'Course not," he said instantly, scowling. The twist of his face would have been funny if he wasn't taking this all so seriously.

"Believe me," she deadpanned. "Most adult men aren't shy about desiring an eighteen-year-old girl. When did your illicit online attraction start?"

"Cenobia," he grumbled, that daunting furrow appearing between his brows.

Bueno, maybe she shouldn't tease him. But she'd just discovered that the man she'd been Pinning and pining for had been, across the Atlantic, indulging in an internet crush as well.

"I first looked you up when I asked for the loan," he said grumpily.

She'd been twenty-one.

"Was it the photos of me in a hardhat that got you hot?" she said, grinning. She slowly walked toward him, felt the sweep of her clothes against her skin, the warmth of the dimly lit room against her face, the leather and clean-sweat scent of him pumping through her veins. "Or my graduation picture from Rice, when

I thought short bangs were a good look?" She stopped. "You didn't see those society page pictures when I was dating Vasquez, did you?"

The warning look he'd been giving her as she approached him went laser hot.

"You what?"

"It was just a few casual dates." Roman's clenched fists at his sides, his tense jaw, was this all for her? "But I'm sure my father wanted it to be more. Vasquez *is* from one of the premier families in Mexico." She stepped up close to Roman, let herself simmer in all this male aggression aimed in her favor. "I imagine he and my father dreamed we'd reclaim Moctezuma's throne. It's another reason Vasquez is so angry; the wife he expected to keep under his thumb is now his boss."

"If that dickhead ever laid a finger on you…" he growled, green eyes searching hers.

She stroked her palm across the burned back of his hand and rubbed his white knuckles. "In that, he was very polite."

The back of his hand was tight and satiny in some spots, bumpy and ropey in others, and hot to the touch. It felt like some wish granted by her own fairy godmother to be here, in this quiet, moon-drenched room, stroking the hand of her warrior prince.

"It wasn't just the pictures, Cenobia," he grumbled like he didn't want to say anything. "It was who you are. What you were accomplishing. What you were strivin' to do." He gripped her fingers. "None of that matters. The one thing you asked me to do was to keep you safe so you could focus and stay in Mexico, but because I was mooning over you instead of doin' my goddamned job you— Why are you smiling?"

"Oh, I don't know," she said, with an exaggerated shrug of her shoulders. "Maybe I just discovered that the man I've had a crush on for eons has one on me, too."

All this time. All this time, she'd been feeding on fantasies as satiating as air, mesmerized by this warrior prince's beauty, ferocity, and nobility. All this time, she'd felt too mesmerized and out of her depth to do more than make feeble attempts to come out behind the cover of her father's email address.

But all this time, he'd been fantasizing, too.

She felt like a spark had ignited her combustion, tiny explosions of heat pushing her pistons and sending confidence and strength through her limbs. She swept her hand under her hair and pulled it over her shoulder, glad she left it down with all of its waves and curls, thrilled to watch his eyes trail over it.

All this time, she had power, too.

She raised his gripped hand and pressed it hard against her chest. "I don't blame you for the attack. I'm grateful for your intercession—who knows what would have happened if you and your team hadn't been there? Please stop blaming yourself."

"But Cen…"

"No," she said, squeezing his hand, feeling him squeeze back. "No. I might have been an eighteen-year-old girl when we met, but now I'm a thirty-one-year-old woman giving explicit consent. You, the only man I've ever desired, have ten years of fantasies about me?" She brought his hand up to her mouth and kissed the back of it. Then she kissed his big, middle knuckle. Lightly, wonderingly, she licked it as she looked at him from under her lashes. "I'd love to hear one of them."

She'd idolized him for so long. Now her golden idol

had transformed into an overwarm, hairy-chested, thick-thighed, barefooted man who looked at her like she'd performed a spell on him.

The thrill of her power was intoxicating.

Whisper-soft, she rubbed her lips back-and-forth across that knuckle, making them tingle. "Did you fantasize about my mouth?"

"Fuck me," he breathed.

This. This is what her therapist had talked about and she'd read about and seen in carefully curated pornography. This moment of a man, of her man, of Roman, spellbound by the promise of pleasure she could bring him.

The one time she'd tried to push past her experience and date like the rest of the girls in college, she'd come back to herself hyperventilating, pressed against the passenger door, the shocked boy pressed against his own driver door. When she started dating under the guidance of her therapist, the men followed Cenobia's cues and were slow and gentle in their physical courtship. And while she never told them about the assault, each of them seemed to know at some point that something was wrong. On the couple of dates she'd been on with Vasquez, humoring her father, he never tried to touch her beyond holding her arm. Her father had vehemently denied warning him.

After fearing that that was the sludge she was doomed to, this felt like the cryogenic propulsion of liquid oxygen and hydrogen. Pure rocket fuel.

"I've thought about using my mouth. With you," she said between slow kisses to his knuckles. His focused green gaze sent her higher. "But I have no practical experience. Could you tell me how to please you this way?"

"I…" She could see the desperation in him. Feel it in the death grip on her hand. But his hesitation was also palpable.

She pressed his hand against her heart.

"I trust you. I want you. I'm more than your client and you're more than my rescuer. Do you want to be with me?"

If that was a line he couldn't cross, this was his out.

For an instant, his hand clenched. But then slowly, like the uncoiling of all of him, his big warm hand spread out over her sweater and pressed firmly against the heartbeat pounding to greet it.

"Yeah, baby girl," he said. His heavy-lidded eyes, full of lust, could be mistaken for sad. "Yeah, I want you, sweet Cen."

Her *michi* clenched between her legs. "I love the sound of your voice," she moaned, her eyes, her body, her everything suddenly feeling heavy and warm. "Tell me what to do."

He rubbed his hand up to her neck, pushed his fingers into her hair and leaned close. "C'mere," he said, against her ear, his voice like the barbs of catnip felines liked to rub against. "C'mere, sweetheart."

The heat of him was a brand. Somehow he got them over to his large, low platform bed.

"I'm gonna…" He pulled off his T-shirt and leaned over to turn off his bedside lamp. It didn't matter. The bright blue moonlight lit even the shadows between them and she glanced down his muscular torso to see that his penis was a thick, gorgeous shaft in his tiny shorts. She'd done that to him. Her words. Her voice. Her. "Do you want to be up on the bed or on the…"

He abruptly stopped and she met his eyes. Floor. Did she want to be on the floor kneeling for this glorious man?

She sank down on the soft navy rug, rested back on her heels, and looked up at him from her knees. "What I want is for you to tell me about your fantasy. Tell me how I pleased you in it."

Then he was sitting, sliding his bare feet past her across the rug, surrounding her with the heat of his strong thighs, his dark hair and trim beard and his gleaming, nearly naked body making him look like a satyr lording over her, commanding pleasure from his nymph. But his cautious, careful, noble eyes…

"Tell me what I did," she breathed again.

"You…" he stopped, licked his decadent mouth. "You put your hands on my thighs."

At last. At last she could touch him. She put her hands on his thighs, his muscles feeling like the hottest of river rocks, and stared at him bathed in blue moonlight, his thick chest, his dark hair, the scars of his journey, the waves of his abs, the deep cuts at his hips. She felt him staring back. Her hair was pulled over her shoulder, all waves and curls. She wasn't wearing a bra.

"You…stroked up."

She did, stretched her fingers wide to caress those thighs, let her thumbs rub into the muscles as her pinkies stroked at the hair. She finally had her hands on Roman Sheppard's powerful body. Her fingertips encountered nylon.

"You pulled down my shorts."

Dios. She felt heat crawl up into her hairline at the

erotic command of his deep, gravel voice. The backs of her hands were darker than the pale skin of his belly. They looked so small compared to the width of him as she dug her fingers into the waistband, tucked up right against his skin and heat, pulled the shorts down, *espera*, she had to pull out, too, he was caught…

Roman Sheppard's penis slapped hard against his belly, making an audible *thwack*.

Horrified, she looked up at him. "I'm so sorry," she whispered.

With his lips pinched together, he shook his head. "That doesn't…" He closed his eyes, then opened them again, breathed deep. He was leaning back on both hands, his arms straight and anchoring him upright, muscles bulging. "That didn't hurt."

"Oh," she said, breathless over the banquet displayed in front of her. "Good."

He lifted up so she could slowly pull the shorts all the way down, down his thighs and over his knees and off his feet. She tossed them aside.

Then she stared.

She'd seen penises, in therapy and pornography. Many of them looked silly. Some looked terrifying. Some were quite lovely. But Roman Sheppard's penis, moving minutely every so often, had to be one of the more beautiful penises on the planet. Rising from a tuft of dark hair, it was thick and encircled with veins like vines climbing a perfectly straight tree. The mushroom-capped head was deep red and covered his slitted belly button. She could see the line where he was circumcised and she wanted to kiss that fragile scar.

"You trace your hands up my stomach, over my chest

as you look at my dick." He'd never sounded more imperial.

"Yes," she sighed relief. She felt the heavy warmth of *finally* through her thighs and in between.

So much skin. Every muscle. Roman Sheppard was completely naked for her, displayed and vulnerable, while she was fully covered. The satin smoothness of his body was interrupted by the bumps and twists of scars. Soft hair threaded through her fingers. She felt heat and hardness and muscle and then suddenly the delicate crinkle of a nipple. She scratched her nail over it and the "dick" that she'd never taken her eyes off of jolted then gave her a clear drop of fluid that came up from his slit then slowly, teasingly, trailed over the head and down the side.

The legs she was kneeling between warmed her like she was in a sauna.

"You take the tip of your finger and feel that precome."

Oh. Her fingertip, the painted nail, made his penis look even more beautifully barbaric in comparison. The head was spongy but hard; the little slit felt like it kissed her skin. She realized he was delicate, too. The fluid, as she rubbed it between fingertip and thumb, was silky. She ran her tongue over her bottom lip.

"You…you lick your finger. Cenobia, you sure?"

She looked up at him and realized how closely he'd been watching her, following her cues. His fists were gripped into the comforter and a fine sheen covered his naked body.

Oh, she'd done that.

"Yes, Roman," she said, eager. She wanted it all.

She licked her finger and it was salt and it was him and that made him groan.

"You put both hands around the top of my dick and run them slowly down to the base. You hold my dick up, yeah, that's it, nice and straight. And then you lean forward, yeah, just like that, Cen, push your hair back behind your shoulder so I can see…"

Following the command of his erotic storytelling and dream-fulfilling voice, she leaned forward and kissed him—"just the tip"—soaking in the luxury of his taste and guidance and praise.

"God. Look at those lips. Those pretty, pretty lips."

She followed his instruction to kiss the little dip, just under the head, then licked it. Her tongue buzzed deliciously, more of that clear fluid dripping on it, and her body almost floated off the rug in pleasure when she looked up to see the glorious sight of Roman, her beautiful warrior prince who'd reluctantly wanted her for years, leaning on his hands with his head hanging back, one long line of moonlight-washed muscle and man from his Adam's apple to where she held him against her tongue.

"When do I put it in my mouth?"

His head shot up and he looked down at her, brow furrowed. "Cen, you don't—are you sure you want…"

He was holding back.

That *pendejo* was holding back.

She pressed his penis against his stomach and dragged her tongue over one of his tight balls. She'd seen that in a clip and always wondered…

He captured her chin and jerked her head up, eyes blazing. "I didn't tell you to do that."

She ripped her chin out of his hand. "Then trust me enough to make you come."

His penis was so big in her hand. So obviously throbbing. So effortlessly handled by every other woman who'd touched it. She imagined he demanded orgasms from those women.

"Trust me to know my capabilities and limits. Listen to me. Don't deny what we both want. Don't make me feel like I'm not worthy to—"

He kissed her. With a grunt of denial, he swept up her face in both hands and kissed her, deep and rich and all tongue, his beard scratching her face. He took and tasted her mouth, twisted her head like he was desperate to touch and savor and know. His hands stroked back to clench into her hair and anchor her against his lips, and her hands slid up to grip him to her by his neck.

"I'm sorry," he huffed into her mouth. Kissed her. Soothed her with his tongue. "I'm sorry."

She could survive like this underground, underwater, for decades in the *cenotes* of the Yucatan, his breath panting into her mouth, live on his words and devotion. "I've only thought about protecting you," he growled into her. "It's dangerous to dream about having you."

"You can have everything."

She broke from his lips as she realized her words. Their hands still holding tight, they stared at each other, Cenobia trapped by forest green. This, right now, was the most intimate she'd ever been with him. She'd said too much.

His eyes narrowed like she should be afraid.

"What I want right now…" he said as he gently let go of her face to lean back on both hands. "Is for you to hold my cock by the base again. Yeah. Like that. Feel it? Feel what you do to me? Feel how much I want you?"

She could. She could feel his desire pulsing in her hand.

"Now, you play, Cen," he urged, his eyes heavy as he watched her. "You do whatever you want to that big cock in your hand. I'll tell you how it feels."

Oh. There was safety in his fantasy. Now she had to come out from behind it. Now he was asking her to take the reins and truly embrace her power.

She leaned close. Kissed the tip. Smoothed it over her lips. Slowly opened her mouth over the hard, silky head. Her tongue fluttered against him. She closed her eyes and her breath shuddered around the fullness in her mouth. He tasted…he tasted of brine and skin and woodsmoke. He smelled warm and musky, filling her head. He surrounded her body with heat.

"Yeah…yeah…when you…" She heard the gulp of his swallow. "When you rub your tongue under the head like that, *fuck*…fuck." He shivered and shifted under her hands and her *michi* felt slick and eager. She sucked. "*Ungh*…not too…not too deep, baby girl, takes practice, just…oh God, that. Do that." Her lips had accidentally caught on the ridge of his head as she'd pulled back up, but the hungry gravel in his voice said he liked that, so she focused there. "Yeah, yeah, most of the nerves are in the head anyway… Good fucking Christ, your mouth."

Still sucking and licking, she looked up at him from under her lashes, and moaned at the back of her throat at what she saw. He had all of his weight on one arm, his body twisted and rippling muscle, with his face hidden in the crook of his other thick, muscular arm.

Oh, she loved this.

Oh, she loved him.

Here, where a man could dominate and humiliate her completely, Roman had put himself under her thrall, made himself vulnerable. She was beginning to understand why he'd been so cautious with her. Lovemaking wasn't about naked bodies. It was about exposing yourself completely and trusting your lover as they looked.

She pulled off of him with a lick. "You're so satiny," she cooed against the sensitive head, rubbing her lips over him. "I had a satin blanket, a *mantita* when I was young. I used to rub it on my cheek." She tilted her head, rubbing him against her cheek. "When I rubbed it, I made this sound…"

And then she did it, a soft, wet, repetitive click at the front of her palate with her tongue, something she'd once done to him in a sweat-soaked dream and now she could give to him in reality as she stroked her lips over the head, down the shaft, her tongue giving the tiniest kitten licks while her lips gave the softest sucks.

He fell back to the bed and covered his face with both hands.

"*Fuuuuuuck*," he groaned mightily behind his hands. "Baby, fucking… *Cennnnn*." His hips bucked up then shoved down, like it was involuntary, and Cenobia pushed closer in between his legs, gripped into his rock-hard thighs, and took as much of him into her mouth as she could manage.

He was going to take practice.

Up and down and up and down and up and down, mostly around his head because he said that was enough, and she hoped all the wetness was okay because he made her mouth water and she could feel him, she didn't know how it was possible, getting even harder in her mouth, and she put her hand around his shaft, she'd seen this and read about this, began to use all that wetness to stroke him and his hips jerked again, just barely, and his hand gripped into her hair, and that she could make the cautious Roman Sheppard grab her made her preen and she swirled her tongue around his head and caught more of that salt, so much brine, and it was going to happen, he was going to...

He tugged her hair until she had to let his penis slip out of her mouth.

He lifted her jaw as he struggled to sitting.

"It's so good, so good..." his voice shuddered as he looked at her with his heavy-lidded eyes and his thumb traced clumsily over her mouth. "Just not in your mouth, sweetheart. Not the first time. Please. For me."

She had to trust him to know his limits, too.

Her tongue touched her lips. They felt swollen. She stroked him in her hand. "I want to see," she said, stripped of everything but want.

"O-okay," he mumbled in a shiver. "Okay." He covered her hand with his then pulled her close to kiss her. His big hard hand began to move hers, squeezing then releasing, up and down. He was hot and lurching in her hand.

He let go of her hand and pressed his forehead against hers. "Do it," he whispered. "Make me come."

Breathing his breath, smelling his smell, hearing the stroke of their skin together, she watched it in the shadows they created with their bodies as she stroked this beautiful, vibrant piece of him, as his hips rolled almost helplessly into her touch, as she squeezed hard and soft, stroked faster then slower, listened to him groan and pant and mutter absolute filth.

"Look," he gasped, leaning back on an arm ridged with tension. "Look what you do to me." The full naked front of him was washed in moonlight. "Look what you've always...fuck...please... Cenobia!"

He shouted her name through clenched teeth as his warrior's body lurched and the first thread of liquid shot up high on his chest, surprising her, making her stomach jolt with the satisfaction of it. There were more, more strings of his come, over his chest, over the clenching muscles of his abs, and her nails dug into his thigh and his hips twisted beneath her touch, trying to get closer and away at the same time, and she was doing this to him, she'd done this to him. She glanced down to see his toes clenched into the rug.

She let go of his still-spasming penis and threw her arms around his neck, kissing him.

"Oh...oh baby, your sweater," he groaned, worrying about her sweater when he was still shivering through his orgasm, and she kissed him harder and licked him deeper.

Oh, she loved this.

Oh, she loved him.

Chapter Fifteen

Freedom, Kansas

Roman tried not to curse or take the Lord's name in vain for the same reason he'd never gotten a tattoo or taken up chew, although the latter two deeds had verged on a religion to his Ranger brothers.

His mama wouldn't have liked it.

But Maddie Sheppard was gone and as he'd tried to pretend the next day was as normal as any other day in hiding, as he surveyed the news for nonexistent new info then went for a jog by the lake, made a big country breakfast for everyone, then took his second cold shower in twelve hours, three words kept popping into his head.

Jesus fucking Christ.

Actually, it was four words. *Jesus fucking Christ, Cenobia.*

Cenobia. He breathed it out, his fingers splayed on the shower's chill tile, as he thought about the way she looked at breakfast—black hair piled on top of her head, her huge dark eyes watching him with sleepy, shy want. Last night, after she'd given him the most bone-shattering orgasm of his life, she'd vibrated as if she was the one who'd just been decimated, so he'd stripped off her sweater—thankfully she'd been wearing a camisole underneath it—wiped himself off with a mental reminder to burn the borrowed sweater and claim ignorance if Roxanne ever asked, and held her tight under his covers until she fell asleep.

He'd snuck out of bed for his first cold shower, pulled on pajama pants, then slept with her in his arms until he carried her to bed before dawn.

In one of those late night, good-bourbon-sipping online searches he'd fessed up to last night, he'd discovered that Cenobia, or Zenobia in its original Ancient Greek, meant force of Zeus. Cenobia didn't derive her power from any man. The men in her life generally tried to siphon it off her. But her full name was queenly and majestic; her nickname was… *Jesus fucking Christ*, he thought as an image of her seared his brain: between his legs, her black curls draped over his naked thigh, her mauve lips wrapped and moving around the head of his dick while she hummed pleasure in her throat.

Last night, she'd become his Cen.

Roman turned his face into the ice-cold spray.

The first time he'd googled her, he'd ignored that lifesaving tickle of warning at the base of his skull as he read the top article. In the three years since he'd rescued her, she'd accomplished so much; she'd already been more than halfway through her combined bachelor's and master's degree at Rice while she spent her summers and holidays spearheading various efforts at Trujillo Industries. He kept typing in her name until he had to disable his autofill; just typing CE would make her name pop up. Keeping tabs on her over the years had been easy. The media made sure to feed the world's fascination about the once-kidnapped girl who raced her way through engineering degrees and into the male-dominated auto industry.

He'd ignored that warning tickle that had saved him and his squad from IEDs and let his curiosity about Cenobia Trujillo go from interest to fanboying then yearning. At least he'd heeded it when "her father" had offered the occasional invites to Mexico.

He'd already been doing enough daydreaming about her when she was a continent away.

Maybe his mama felt the same premonition the first time she got a call from the principal.

Maddie Sheppard had been scared of Roman's suddenly powerful looks and fists when he'd roared into puberty, and she'd laid out for him the man he could become if he used his powers to hurt people, hurt men, hurt women. His biological father had provided a blueprint for the kind of man Maddie never wanted her son to be. Although she'd been devastated when Roman had enlisted, taking him so far away from her right after high school, she'd ultimately agreed that it was the best way to channel the pain giving that came so easy to him.

With women, he'd always been cautious and careful. They called him considerate. Maybe there was an edge of control he liked to take in bed—enough to recognize that Cenobia had been shaking from the emotional rush of what she'd done to him, not because she was afraid—but he *never* let his mouth run away from him the way he did last night.

"*The Prince's Dirty Mouth.*"

Roman gave a hopeless huff of a laugh through it, put both hands against the wall, and hung his head in the freezing stream.

Trust me to know my capabilities and limits. Don't make me feel like I'm not worthy.

The hugeness of what he felt for her, the enormity of her worth, and the imperative to wipe any doubt from her mind was why he'd closed his eyes and stepped off his path last night. And who was he kidding, he'd lost all nobility the instant she'd traced her full mauve lips with his knuckle. He'd wanted what he wanted and would have charged into a minefield to get it.

But that blind stumbling wasn't good for her. He'd kept his family in the Monte safe for ten years by firmly sticking to his chosen tightrope.

You can have whatever you want.

He really couldn't.

His dick, still bobbing in the frigid water, didn't give a damn.

Later that afternoon, he stood in the huge, well-lit garage in a denim shirt, old jeans, and work boots with Cenobia. Although she wore tight jeans, canvas sneakers, and a fuzzy pink sweater that offered up her breasts like cotton candy, his erection was finally under control thanks to the presence of a frowning Bartolo and an excited Adán, who was bouncing a skinny leg.

Gone was the sullen kid. Instead, Adán was wide-eyed and hope-filled when he pointed a finger at a fiery red Porsche Boxster, one of the ten cars parked in the long garage along with a boat trailer, a couple of four-wheelers, and an all-purpose Kubota tractor that made Roman useful whenever he'd overstayed his welcome.

"That one?" Adán asked, his grey-blue eyes lit up like school was out for the summer. Right then he reminded Roman so much of his nephew, a happy-go-lucky kid. They even shared the same floppy curls, although Gabriel's hair was dark, as dark as Roman's. People sometimes said Gabriel looked like Roman's son.

Cenobia tapped her soft lips consideringly while Bartolo adamantly shook his head.

"Nice choice," she said. "But maybe we pick something with less power for your first lesson."

Bartolo scowled. "Or maybe we wait for the lesson until he's legal driving age." The heavy frowning forehead over the ex-*luchador*'s mashed nose would have scared anyone else off.

But Cenobia, whose ponytail kept flicking Roman's arm, was on a mission. "He's past age," she exclaimed. "I can't believe you or my father haven't put him behind the wheel already."

"He's twelve," Bartolo said. The glossy whites of his big eyes bulged a little when he was outraged. "He can't drive in Mexico for another six years."

"In Kansas, you can get a license at fourteen," Roman said quietly.

When Cenobia swung her head to beam at him, he was glad he picked a side. Adán, who'd switched to bouncing the other leg, watched the back-and-forth like it was a death match.

Roman had no doubt who was going to win.

Cenobia hadn't been faking her shock when she discovered her twelve-year-old brother hadn't driven yet. She'd immediately marched them all out to the garage with an insistence to begin his lessons right away, to Roman's bemusement, Bartolo's irritation, and Adán's complete and total joy. Cenobia and Adán's mutual adoration society was growing more and more powerful every day, and if it meant that he and Bartolo were getting outvoted more often in matters of dinner planning, hiking trail selection, and board game choosing, he was okay with that. If a better connection between these siblings separated by eighteen years was something that came out of this shit show, he'd take it.

"Papá put me in the driver's seat the moment I could reach the pedals," Cenobia prodded Bartolo. She enjoyed teasing the big guy. "We run *una companía de coches*."

"*Sí, claro.* A car company that will still be in operation when he's of legal driving age."

Cenobia flapped her hands at him. "When did you become *una vieja*?" she asked, accusing him of becoming an old lady.

Bartolo's wide, dark face went still. *"Sabes cuando."* *You know when.*

Cenobia dropped her grin. She reached out and squeezed his thick arm. *"Pues, lo siento, compadre,"* she apologized. "I took my teasing too far."

The ex-*luchador* had been with Cenobia's family a long time; he'd been head of her protective detail when she'd been at Rice. It was known famously that Cenobia had snuck away from her security to meet friends when she'd been kidnapped. Did Bartolo blame himself for that?

The bodyguard's quick thinking had saved the lives of Daniel, Adán, and all their staff. Roman had been impressed when he'd fully questioned them about the attack; he would have tried to lure Bartolo away to Shepherd Security if he hadn't known it was a waste of hot air. Whether Bartolo and the Trujillos realized it or not, he was more than a bodyguard to them, and they were more than his clients. But the lives in the plus column still didn't let Bartolo take himself off the hook for whatever error he thought he'd made thirteen years ago.

Bartolo sighed heavily and patted her hand. "Maybe I have become an old woman."

They ended up picking a Ford F-150 for Adán's first lesson. It had an extended cab, so Cenobia jumped in the back as Bartolo waved goodbye and Roman drove them to a flat stretch of road on the private property with no ditch and no chance of oncoming traffic. He'd never been more conscience of keeping his hands at two and ten as Cenobia pointed out the speedometer, the turn signals, mirror position, and other details of the truck.

When they all switched positions, it did something to Roman to watch Cenobia jump into the front passenger seat in her rolled up jeans and fuzzy sweater, wearing the same sparkly eyed, rounded-cheek, dimpled-grin look of excitement as her little brother in the driver's seat. As she took Adán through the steps of checking the seat position, steering wheel height, and mirror, then turning on his signal and looking over his shoulder, the boy looked like she was explaining how to turn lead into gold.

Cenobia and Roman surreptitiously checked their seatbelts, and Adán stepped on the gas. The truck started forward slowly, began gaining some momentum, then lurched to a quick, hard stop.

"That's fine," Cenobia instantly soothed. "It's a big machine in your hands, isn't it?"

Adán nodded, wide-eyed. "It's doesn't feel like *Gran Turismo*."

Roman caught Adán's quick, nervous glance in the rearview mirror. "Remember, buddy, *assendup*," he said. "It's okay to make mistakes. You'd pretty much have to flip this truck to earn an embarrassing nickname today."

When Adán giggled and Cenobia shot him a grateful look, Roman felt about twenty feet tall.

Adán's shoulders relaxed and he tried again.

Twice more the truck built up a small amount of speed before Adán hit the brakes with too much force.

Cenobia spoke in a logical voice. "Instead of relying on the brake to slow down, it's easier to gently ease off the gas." Her hands showed the movement like a release of bellows. "Try it."

At her confident nod, Adán got them up to the breakneck speed of fifteen miles per hour then slowly eased off the pedal. He snuck a grin at Cenobia before returning his eyes to the road as the truck slowed down. When he hit the break this time, the lurch involved less whiplash.

"Muy bien, guapo," she praised, grin huge and clapping. "That move will help you make friends with your car. It's more fuel efficient and easier on the tires and breaks. Imagine the car crying *'¡Ay, mis patas!'* whenever you hit the brakes too hard."

Of course, she would talk about a vehicle like it was a pet. Adán giggled in the front seat, and Roman had a sense again of how young and innocent this junior billionaire was. Roman had protected enough children born into wealth to know how rare it was to find a twelve-year-old richling who acted twelve. Like his brother and sister-in-law, Adán's family had done a great job normalizing the life of a kid growing up in an extraordinary situation.

Outside the truck, the unseasonably warm November

day was grey and blustery. But inside, Adán and Cenobia's smiles made it feel like the sun was out.

Adán practiced driving and braking until they reached a "T" in the road. Adán and Cenobia switched positions, and she performed a tight-and-fast turn-reverse-turn to get the cumbersome truck turned around in the narrow country lane that was a thing of beauty.

Adán drove back the way they came as Cenobia gave him spare, gentle notes about staying in the center of the lane and glancing at the speedometer instead of focusing on it.

Then she laid her arm across the seat back. "What do you drive?" she turned to ask Roman.

Adán shot a quick glance at her, shaking his curls out of his eyes, before focusing back on the road.

Roman had been using his psychic powers to steer the car back into the center of the road and wasn't sure he wanted to give up that control. But she gave him a steady look with her pretty feline eyes, and he understood that easing up was going to be the best way for Adán to get comfortable with driving.

"A Range Rover Westminster in the Monte. With all the mountain driving I gotta do. And then in Tallahassee, I've got a few: a Lexus RC F, a Chevy Colorado ZR2, and a couple of bikes."

"You're not worried about your U.S. carbon footprint," she smirked, flicking her high ponytail in his direction.

He gave her his look. "If it's any consolation, I can't remember the last time I drove any of 'em."

"I forget that you have a home in Florida," she said.

So did he. Tallahassee was home to Sheppard Security's corporate headquarters and a forty-five-minute drive from the camp in the Florida swamps where they trained clients in defensive shooting, scenario defense, and tactical mobility. But with the international nature of their work, Sheppard Security's conference-room meetings were usually held over the Internet.

And with his home and family in the Monte… "Mateo's mentioned me selling my Florida place a couple of times. I think he's afraid I'm going to slip away and not come back."

Cenobia looked at him a little longer before glancing at how Adán was doing. It was supposed to have come out funnier than it had.

"Why would he think that?" Adán asked, hunched close to the steering wheel as they crawled along.

"He doesn't," Roman said. "I'm kidding."

"You're a prince of the Monte del Vino Real," Adán said, with that child's lack of irony Roman had learned from his niece and nephew. "That's where you're supposed to be. And now that you're the king's advisor, they're really depending on you."

The kid knew exactly where to jiggle the knife. The Monte was growing at a fast clip and, right now, there were emails waiting for Roman's response and contracts on his centuries-old desk needing signatures. His brother would finally understand the mistake he made. Roman already had a mission.

He used his thumb to scratch the itchy skin under the gold ring.

"I hope I can visit one day," Adán whispered to the windshield.

Cenobia met Roman's eyes.

"Why don't you stop for a second," she said gently. Adán brought the truck to an almost smooth brake, then put it in park. He leaned back against the seat, looked down at his lap, and let his curls flop into his eyes.

Roman put his hand on the boy's shoulder. It felt bird thin under the kid's hoodie.

"Hey," he said, although the kid didn't look up. "You can come to the Monte anytime."

"Are you sure? We've never been and then Cici went as a surprise and I didn't know if we could go again…"

Huh. This was about more than an invite.

"Adán, are you upset I didn't take you with me?" Cenobia asked, eyes wide.

Adán shrugged his shoulders and shook his head in a way that said *yes* without committing to it.

Cenobia wilted for a second before she gently reached out to take Adán's hand. "I'm so sorry," she said. "Of course, I should have brought you."

"It's okay," he mumbled.

"No, no it's not," she said fervently. "You know more about the kingdom than I do."

Adán moved out from Roman's hand, but it was to turn and peek over his shoulder at him. "I think it would be a good place to bring my telescope."

"Hell, yeah," Roman said. Sometimes the stars were so clear and close in the Monte he felt like he could touch them. "I've been over every inch of the kingdom, but I don't know anything about its skies. You can teach me."

Adán gave him a shy smile until Cenobia said, "And you could have Aish Salinger autograph your ticket stub."

She looked at Roman and whispered, "He's a fan."

Roman calmed Adán's horror-stricken face with a

manly nod before he said, "Aish would definitely come stargazing with us."

He needed to remind Cenobia how uncool it was to out a dude's fanboying.

"Yes," Cenobia said declaratively. "Once La Primera is launched, we will go for a visit." She smiled at Adán, who looked thrilled at the turn of events, but her gaze on Roman was quick and hesitant. She instructed Adán to start driving again, and she moved her arm off the top of the seat to face forward.

Every single heart-pounding moment since she'd asked for his help had been focused on the here-and-now. Roman hadn't had one clear thought about the future. But Cenobia was as woven into the Monte as he or his musician brother-in-law was. Even when she no longer needed his protection, she would always have a connection with the kingdom she helped save.

She would always be present in his life.

"Yeah," he said. "I'll give you a tour of the Monte. Liliana and Gabriel can show you around the castle."

Adán quickly shot Cenobia a dazzling bright smile that she answered with its twin.

Then she looked over her shoulder at Roman. Her smile warmed. And her eyes said thank you with a promise to properly thank him later.

Chapter Sixteen

Freedom, Kansas

Roman drove them back to the house and was holding the door of the garage open for Adán when he saw Cenobia pause beside a mint-condition '55 Ford Thunderbird Roadster convertible, its pale, powder-turquoise flanks gleaming under the halogen lights.

"Hola, bonita," she sighed to the car, running a finger along its right tailfin.

All the hairs stood up on the back of his neck.

"Do you want to take it out?" he asked without knowing the words were coming.

Cenobia looked at him, eyes wide. "Would Roxanne mind?"

"Her lawyer restored this car and gave it to her," Roman said. "He put in an upgraded Thunderbird Special V8 engine. You should hear the sound of it."

Cenobia moaned and Roman casually moved so that his hips were turned away from Adán.

"Yes!" Adán said.

"No," Bartolo replied, stepping into the garage. One look at his face made it clear that, this time, he was not budging. "You have school, señor."

The three adults had found enough books in Roxanne and Mateo's library to keep up a nominal level of education for the boy.

"We will practice again tomorrow, Adán," Cenobia said. *"Te lo prometo."*

With the promise of more driving lessons and more time with his sister keeping the smile on the kid's face as Bartolo dragged him out, Roman tossed the keys from the key locker to Cenobia. She settled into the driver's seat and lit up when the car roared on then settled into a grumbling purr that throbbed through the garage.

Roman got into the passenger seat and draped his forearms over his lap. She drove them out of the garage and down the long driveway, pausing where the driveway met the road and looking in both directions.

The grey November day was windy and threatening rain but unseasonably warm. She lowered her window. Roman rolled his down, too.

"No one else is going to be on these roads?"

He shook his head. "Not as long as we stay on Medina property."

"Ay, que bueno," she said. She eased the car out onto the road, gave the car some gas and then ambled along, aiming away from the lake and into the woods. Roman rested his forearm in the open window, his denim shirtsleeve rolled up, the air balmy against his skin.

And then he was shoved back against his seat as she opened it up.

She focused on the road, shifting the manual transmission smoothly without a hint of a hitch, faster and faster, until the trees looked like they were whipping not because of the wind, but because of the Thunderbird's trajectory. She followed the slight raises and dips of the well-maintained private road like she was on rails, never wavering from perfect center. She slowed down for the first turn, testing the car's responsiveness, and that's when Roman noticed she was braking with her left foot.

When she whipped around the next turn, fast and in total dominance of the pretty car, Roman got hard.

"Who rebuilt this?" she shouted over the roar of the wind and motor, the curls of her ponytail dancing. "Roxanne's lawyer? I'll have to contact him. He's got the front and rear drive balanced perfectly. It's always more effective in older cars without the electronic clutch pack, but he's an artist."

Her feet in a pair of black Converse looked like they were fingers on a keyboard, quickly typing over the clutch, brake, and gas to tell the car what she wanted it to do. Sometimes she skipped the clutch entirely and relied on the RPMs to give her an opportunity to shift.

Roman needed to get his jaw out of his lap. "Where'd you learn to drive like this?" he finally got out as they took another cock-stroking turn.

"I grew up on test tracks," she said, grinning. Her hands gripped the turquoise-and-white ball of the shifter like a scepter, loose but with authority. "I went on a couple dates with a master sergeant in the *Fuerzas Armadas* and he showed me some tricks."

Roman didn't want to think about the tricks the man had wanted to show her, not when she'd looked like this, hair whipping, cheeks flushed, lips wide with a daring, devilish smile.

"So you just love cars," he shouted, feeling that grin that didn't come out too often crack his face. "If you'd been born into a family of candlemakers, you still would have gone and made cars."

She downshifted and slowed down, looked at him for a second longer than she could have at breakneck speed. "I guess I do," she said. Now they were able to speak at a normal volume. "I like how all the intricate pieces fit together to make a smooth-running whole. It's like an equation, isn't it?"

"Or a company," he said.

She smiled. "Or a kingdom."

Roman could smell the rain in the warm air whooshing through the car.

"Do you love being a soldier?"

What a question. Roman focused on the straight road and the oak and hickory trees hanging over the lane, clinging to their last bits of fall color. He looked ahead, saw the gentle slope and its unpredictable next rise.

"I do," he said.

This fast drive with the windows open felt cleansing.

"I'm good at it. It comes naturally. I feel guilty 'cause I like it."

Not the killing. Never the killing. But he liked the calm before the target revealed itself, the instant assessment, the rapid response, the variety of combat, the coordination with a team. He liked the sensation of racing blood and pounding heart and crystal-clear mind.

He liked knowing he was the perfect tool for the craft.

"I still take part in the Sheppard Security training exercises because I'd look like a real jackass as the prince who had to jump out of planes to feed a need."

"You want to charge into what everyone else avoids,"

she said succinctly. "Every person you've saved is grateful you've embraced your innate talents."

Cenobia made it sound so easy.

He made a decision.

"Pull over and let me drive," he said. "I want to show
you something."

They changed places and Roman turned around and
aimed them back towards the lake. Roman pointed out
landmarks as he drove: the hiking trail where he and
Sofia had briefly lost the dog, and the twins almost
killed them; the fishing pier where he'd taught Aish
how to bait a worm, and the LA-born trust-fund rock
star had been very *ew-ugh* about the whole thing; the
horseshoe court where Roxanne had succinctly kicked
his and Mateo's ass, although she'd been cheating because she'd been hugely pregnant and had brought out
the good scotch.

"I'm not kiddin'," Roman said as he pulled up to the
spot he wanted to show her. He had her laughing too
much for her to notice the gentle rise they'd been driving up. He loved that grumpy-ol' him could make her
laugh. "I still dream about that scotch."

As he put the car in park, she finally looked out the
windshield. *"Mira,"* she breathed. *"Maravillosa."*

He leaned across her to unlatch the convertible's soft
top, unlatched his side, and then pushed a button. The
white top accordioned back, letting in warm air, and
disappeared behind the seat.

He turned off the car then patted the top of the white
bench. "Sit up here for the best view," he said.

She scrambled up, her feet in the seat, and sighed
again happily.

There weren't many hills in this part of southeast

Kansas, but there were natural flint cliffs around this manmade lake. A little gravel road wound through trees until it ended here, higher than one would have imagined, with a view of the cliffs and the water. Right now, the lake reflected the cloud-heavy sky, made it look like a bowl filled with the heavens.

The air was rain-thick and warm; it was getting ready to storm. But Roman wasn't ready to go back. Not when Cenobia was looking around with that smile on her face, the heavy copse of trees protecting them from the wind.

"Hey, I was wonderin'," he said. He looked down and saw the dark skin of her ankle exposed between sneaker and rolled-up jeans. He slid his thumb and forefinger around the delicate bones and tender skin, cuffing it. "What's a good girl like you know about a prince's dirty mouth?"

Her foot twitched in his hold.

He looked into her surprised wide eyes and waited patiently for a response.

"P-practically nothing," she finally got out.

"I figured," he drawled, solemn and straight faced. He held her jeans-covered calf in the cup of his palm and slowly rubbed it—her, her flesh and her warmth— up to the bend of her knee. "I mean, how many princes could you know?"

He smoothed his hand over her knee, and those pretty mauve lips fell open.

"Even if there'd been a dozen of 'em…" He shifted up onto his knees as he lightly stroked up her firm thigh and leaned close to her. "They won't have a mouth like mine."

She let out the tiniest little gasp and her breasts were

rising and falling fast in that fuzzy pink sweater. *I love your voice*, she'd moaned to him last night, and now she knew what he was doing with it. Seducing her. Initiating this. Touching first for the very first time.

He was a soldier, and she'd reminded him that he was damned good at his job. That he liked it. That he liked helping people.

And she'd asked him to help her.

Every person you've saved is grateful you've embraced your innate talents.

If one of his talents wasn't helping the worthiest, bravest, most daring woman he'd ever known learn pleasure and revel in the gift of her beautiful body, then what was the point. She'd stated clearly, plainly, what she wanted, and he could do this for her, during this weird time-out time with few responsibilities and fewer eyes. That dance of bodies he got to learn as a teen experimenting in back seats was ruined for her. He would take her through it slowly, carefully, with her pleasure being his only mission.

Then he would let her go.

The breeze had stopped rustling the leaves and no birds chittered or squawked.

"There's a lot I can do with my lips…" He gently pushed her thighs apart and got between them, staring her down. "…And tongue…" He held her hips in his hands and scooted her forward, the metal squeaking beneath her. "…And teeth." He nestled against her, let her feel the hardness of his chest and cock through denim, let her know he could take care of her in all ways.

Leaving the playground didn't mean he'd stopped hearing about his mouth. Women praised it. Assholes said it looked good for cock sucking. Some decent guys sighed with a tear in their eye when Roman let them down gently.

But never in a million years had he imagined that Cenobia was having her own filthy fantasies about the feature that had given him so much trouble. Holding her close and looking into her dark eyes swirling with lust and overwhelm and hope, he ran his teeth slowly over his bottom lip now, and got a gut jolt at the helpless, hungry way she watched him do it.

"You want me to show you what a prince can do with his dirty mouth?" he purred, looking down at her through his heavy lids.

"Dios mío, por favor," she moaned.

He smiled lazily, like he was going to take all day with her, when giving himself the go-ahead made him desperate. He lowered his mouth and kissed her, kissed her the way he wanted to at the breakfast table and in the shower and after she'd made her brother beam and when she'd put the pedal to the medal. He kissed her first, kissed her without a request from her, kissed with lips and tongue and teeth, holding her face in his hands so she couldn't get away, kissed with claim and ownership and the glory of finally giving himself permission to do it.

But a storm was in the air and their time was short. He ripped away from her succulent mouth to nip at her ear. "I trust you," he breathed into it. "I trust you'll tell me if I do anything that makes you uncomfortable."

"Te lo prometo," she sighed against him.

Her throat was long and dark and got him that much closer to the sweetness of her as he kissed and sucked at it, the smell of her pulsing through him. He dragged his hand up her torso, pulling up her sweater, and held her breast in his hand for the very first time. He undid her front-clasp bra—pink, too, goddammit—and licked across her marble-hard nipple, blew on it and then took a look as she panted in his hair.

Cenobia's perfect, full, soft breast. He kissed the heavy underside, making promises for later as he rushed along.

"Gonna spread you out," he swore as he kissed down her stomach. "Gonna eat you up."

She gave a high-pitched whine, her stomach trembling under his lips, and urgency beat like a storm in his veins.

He dug his fingers into the waistband of her jeans, around the closure, felt baby soft skin against his knuckles. He looked up into her eyes.

"Please," she gasped, giving a little shove of her pelvis that covered Roman in a fine layer of lust like Texas humidity. "Please."

He ripped open her fly, reared up and took her mouth while he hitched her up so he could pull her jeans and underwear down, her not helping at all as she devoured his mouth and got in the way. He plopped her soft, naked ass back down on the car as he blindly reached back for her shoe, yanked it off, then tugged one sleek, muscular leg out of all that fabric.

Fuck. She had him like a kid, eager for his first taste.

She wrapped that naked leg around his jeans-covered ass and ground herself against his cock. She was no fucking help at all.

He yanked her leg off him and held it out wide so he could nuzzle into the tender crease of her thigh, where the smell of her was rich and intoxicating.

She slapped her hands against the fine car. "Roman," she called, her hips rolling and begging for more.

He pulled her by her knee until she slid to her back. He bit the side of her kneecap. Kissed the edge of her obvious thigh muscle. Rubbed his beard, slowly, slowly, up the soft, tender skin.

He was going to savor this.

When he nosed at her trim, black curls, she let her thigh fall wide.

"Good girl," he praised, sounding like he was at the end of a three-day whiskey binge. He gently separated her with his big thumbs then looked his fill. She was burgundy rose, soft and puffy, wet and glistening. For him. "Pretty girl, you let me in there."

He kissed that wet, rosy skin. Licked out with his tongue and took a good, long taste. He swallowed and memorized—salt and tang and skin and sweetness. His Cen. He edged his tongue around her tiny oval pearl of a clit, felt her jerk, heard her startle, then he took that little innocent clit between the dirty lips she adored and laved it wetly.

Cenobia cried out, sending a few crows flying and cawing, and tried to jerk her hips away.

He chuckled, made sure to do it against the hot slick skin of her pussy as he picked up her knees and pulled her thighs over his shoulders. "Where you think you're goin'?" he growled against her, holding on to her hips, adding the gravel of his voice to her cunt.

"That can't be… It's too…"

Giving in to what he'd always wanted, what he'd dreamed of doing, he tongued her clit, wet-mouthed, licked and caressed it, over and all around, stroking her words into moans. He fed himself as much as he pleased her, kissing lower to taste, test, exploring with his mouth to find all her sweet spots, then getting into all that sugar. He pressed his tongue inside her, gave her a tiny little fucking.

Her hips shoved up against his mouth.

Yeah. His Cen liked that.

He pushed his tongue deep and pulled it back slow. Her thighs started trembling.

His raised his head and rested his chin on her pelvic bone, let the slight breeze cool his face. He faked calm and control, drew on a lifetime of focusing on the mission, while greed and need were growling in his head.

"Cen?" he asked, looking up at her then quickly pressing the heel of his palm against his throbbing cock as he took in her brown-satin flesh against gleaming turquoise, that pervy pink sweater lifting and falling with her heaving breaths. He shoved up the sweater to expose those beautiful tits to the rain-heavy air, then squeezed a tight, dark nipple, his cock jolting against his hand.

She gasped and clenched her eyes tight.

"Cen?" he sing-songed again to cover the strain in his voice.

"¿Mande?" she asked weakly.

"Don't you want to watch your warrior prince lick your pretty pussy?"

She gave a whimper in the back of her throat and he thought that if he pushed his fingers into her right now and just right…

She forced her eyes open and struggled up on her elbows.

Cenobia Trujillo, her pussy spread for him, mostly naked and stretched out over a classic car, looked devastated. His Cen looked one fragile second from coming all over his face.

Roman was the general of self-denial, had mastered the agony of waiting in the freezing cold, boiling heat, surrounded by enemies, alone in the dark when time became meaningless as he waited for his prey.

But he was like a green recruit during his first day of basic with the way he wanted to plunge inside her.

He fought it as he locked eyes with her and circled both arms around her thighs, separated her pussy lips, and nestled his mouth between. He kept his eyes on her as he pursed his lips in the way she liked so much and used them to suck on her clit.

Her beautiful face squeezed into a rictus of pleasure.

He trailed his tongue down the center of her, focusing his hunger on her pleasure, and pushed his tongue into her body.

He had to grip her thighs with his arms to keep her from rocking away. Her heels beat at his back and then...then she was snapping her hips up against his mouth. She'd found something to put her feet on—the dash? the windshield?—and she was helping him fuck her, forcing his mouth deeper as she trapped him in her midnight brown eyes.

His baby girl was filthy. His CEO was using her prince's dirty mouth.

He might come.

He tilted his head so he could fondle her clit with his thumb while he fucked and sucked at her without breaking eye contact.

"Roman," she demanded. His bossy baby girl. Her hips were speeding up and he shoved his tongue deeper. "Roman, make me come." Her face was so sweet, so desperate. "Make it happen. Make me come." She had no way of knowing that he never wavered once he set his course. "I want it, I want it, please, please."

He leaned up, moved his thumb between her legs to push it into her dripping body, and surrounded her clit with his lips, vibrated over it with his tongue.

Her scream was long and crystalline and perfect. So was the sluice of moisture over his hand, the silky, soaking channel that clenched his thumb, and he kept moving it, stroking her, wanting more, tasting that delicious pulsing clit, devouring all her sweetness until she wrenched her pelvis away.

He slid his hands up her sides and gripped her around the waist, trapping her against his mouth, kissing and lapping, gently, wanting to feed and watch and make her come again.

"Roman." She was buttery with wetness. He'd done that to her. He was gonna sink his cock into all that sweet cream.

"Roman." Her gorgeous torso was covered in a wet sheen. He'd given her that. He was going to breath cool air between her breasts as he made love to her slow on the hood, give her a long, languid ride until she was coming again.

He could have everything, she'd said.

"Roman, the car. It's sprinkling."

He pulled back, wiped his mouth on his shoulder, rested his forehead on her thigh.

The light rain was starting to soak into his denim shirt. He was surprised it didn't sizzle when it hit his skin.

"You're gonna..." He gulped against her thigh. The

smell here…it wasn't helping him. "You're gonna have to drive back."

"'Kay." He could hear the laziness of carnal satisfaction in her voice. He'd put that there. "Or we could raise the hood and…find some way to pass the time."

The instant roaring "yes" of his body reminded him of that first delirious time he'd punched back and didn't stop until teachers had dragged him off.

Plunging into Cenobia Trujillo's body, hungrily, desperately, right now, wasn't the mission.

He was going to make love to her. The thing he most/least wanted was going to happen. But her first real time wasn't going to be in a car, no matter how gorgeous the car was. He wanted hours and a closed door and a bed the size of a small country. And she deserved to be teased wild before they got there.

Hours later, with the thunderstorm finally rolling out of the area, Roman and Cenobia took a fully clothed dip in the lake. When they showed up at the house—drenched instead of sweat soaked and shuddering with an afternoon of pleasure—they hoped it would look like they'd merely gotten caught in the rain.

Chapter Seventeen

Freedom, Kansas

Three nights later, Cenobia was humming along to the music playing on the kitchen sound system and handing the rinsed-off dishes to Adán who was stacking them in the dishwasher when she realized she hadn't thought of her car or her company once since she'd woken up.

Pleasantly stuffed on steaks and elote that Bartolo had prepared, and waiting for the men to return with firewood before beginning a comedy movie marathon—*Nosotros Los Nobles* then *No Se Aceptan Devoluciones*—she also realized that she didn't *care* that she hadn't thought about car or company.

Her father was out of the hospital and recovering with full-time care at home, his already beefed-up security augmented by Sheppard Security and a ring of *Guardia Nacional* surrounding the compound. With eleven days until the launch of La Primera at the Frankfurt Auto Show, her staff was seeing to the last details, all of the cobots were repaired and being installed on the line, and five perfect examples of La Primera were approaching the port at Duisburg-Ruhrort.

Sheppard Security had traced the cobot sabotage to

a small cell of eco-tech terrorists out of Jalisco, but the five teens and twentysomethings had already fled the country by the time the team arrived. They were now hunting them internationally, anticipating proof that Las Luces Oscuras had paid their bill.

The one cloud in Glori's latest report: she still hadn't uncovered the leak. In fact, all of her efforts to un-cover the leak—planting bugs, whispering false rumors, even hiring a subcontractor to offer bribes and favors to members of both teams—had been so fruitless, Glori wrote, that she would have declared there *was* no leak. Except for the obvious evidence to the contrary.

But Cenobia's loved ones were safe, Trujillo Indus-tries was churning along, and she was staying as en-gaged as circumstances would allow. She'd given the full decade of her twenties to the company. Now, in this strange forced vacation, it was difficult for her to care what was going on beyond the grey lake and tall trees.

She let her eyes linger on Adán as he figured out how to get a baking sheet in the dishwasher. She'd hated the sense that her father wanted her to be nothing but pretty and useless. While she'd never prioritized learning to cook, she now knew how to properly chop vegetables and get a good sear on a steak. Here Adán, too, had learned things that would see him through whatever life threw his way: how to fill a dishwasher, how to make an apple pie, how to fold laundry. How to drive.

She'd continued Adán's driving lessons, despite Bar-tolo's grumbles. She was glad for this time with the bodyguard who'd always stood by her side like it was a choice he'd made, instead of a job. He'd entirely aban-doned his own personal life to protect her, then essen-tially raised Adán. She hoped, in time, that he could forgive himself for what happened to her. The fault was all hers, none of his.

There was so much she was learning about Adán in the cab of a royal billionaire's truck. He could whistle like a bird, he was in a better mood in the mornings than at night, and he had an aptitude for math, like her. She understood why her father had resisted getting Adán's IQ tested.

It wasn't healthy for a child to know he was smarter than his teachers.

Adán liked rancheras and Kpop and flipped to stations on the satellite radio in the truck that fascinated Cenobia so much that sometimes they pulled to the side of the country lane and listened, chatting about nothing and everything. Adán wanted to travel to Arizona to look through its mighty telescopes and he missed his three best friends and he'd been making a claymation video with Playdough he'd found in the toy room and he liked to watch rock climbing competitions.

Roman had taken them fishing off a small pier and said their bright smiles were going to dry up the lake and kill all the fish.

She straightened as a wash of heat made her almost dizzy. Or perhaps she was just exhausted. The last three nights, she'd gotten very little sleep.

In the dark of the woods, against a tree, in her bathroom, straddling him on a chair, Roman had been occupying all of her nighttime.

We're gonna play, baby girl, he'd panted into her ear, stretched strong and naked over her trembling body, her thighs squeezing his hips, her *michi* dancing and clinging to the tip of him. *Before we make love, you're gonna let me play, sweet Cen.*

He'd taken the tremendous gravity out of what they were doing and made it joy-filled and sweat-soaked and sensation-focused, like two horny teenagers with nothing more important than figuring out all the iterations of pleasure their bodies could design.

It was one of a thousand reasons she loved him.

Strange that such a familiar feeling could be so overwhelming. She'd always loved him, but she'd thought that it was a young woman's first love that never had the opportunity to grow banal with exposure. Surely, a man she'd spent four hours with, regardless of what happened in those four hours, couldn't be the "one" and only love of her life.

She'd now spent almost three weeks with Roman Sheppard. He protected her and kept her safe, yes. But he also taught her how to cook and cooked for her. He acted as intermediary when small and big tempers flared. He supported her. He admired her. Most importantly, he adapted for her, listening to her words and trusting her. This Texas-born warrior prince didn't focus his self-worth on being the dominant voice in a room.

He was what he'd always been: the only man for her.

Help me I think I'm falling... She realized she was singing along to the music coming from the kitchen speakers. "I love this song," she said absently.

"That's why I put it on," Adán said, sitting on a kitchen stool reading a book, his curls hanging in front of his eyes as he bounced skinny feet off the stool legs.

Cenobia looked around. The dishes were done. How long had she been daydreaming?

She dried her hands on a kitchen towel. "How'd you know?"

He grinned quick at her then dropped his eyes back

to his book, like he didn't want to lose his place. "You used to sing it all the time when I was little."

She was glad he wasn't focusing on her as her smile dimmed. "Did I?"

When he was little, she'd lived hours and miles and most often a country away. She'd compulsively filled every spare moment with school and work, and that didn't change during her rare weekend visits. That he clung to details like that from the few memories he had with her...

No wonder he'd been furious at her. She didn't want him to cling to Pinterest boards and Sunday *comidas* and a few precious hours every week. He deserved more—always had—and she now believed she was strong enough to give more to him.

Outside, Roman was girding himself as he followed Bartolo to the wood shelter.

Roman had watched the former *luchador* singlehandedly carry in enough wood to set the house on fire. He knew why he was really being dragged outside.

They were barely out of earshot of the house when Bartolo growled, "The only reason I haven't yanked your sorry *culo* out of her room is because she would kick mine for attempting it. What the hell do you think you're doing?"

Roman remained silent as the leaves and pine needles crunched under his feet. Stars shined in the reflection of the lake. The night was clear and cold.

"You're too much of a *putamadre* coward to answer?"

They reached the lean-to and Roman began to fill his arms with logs. "You're not the only one afraid of getting your ass kicked. She'd kick mine for discussing what she as a consenting adult is doing."

Bartolo shoved him, a dirty trick, sending Roman's logs clattering to the ground. He jumped back to save his toes. The ex-wrestler had been a *rudo*, a villain of the script, so Roman should have expected it.

"Consenting?" Bartolo snarled, enraged by the word. "She's in *love* with you. She has no clarity where you're concerned. But clarity is all you should have right now."

Roman slowly breathed through his nose. Want? Yes. But love? No way.

"You're supposed to be protecting her." Bartolo would be yelling if he could. "Can you protect her when you're focused on sneaking into her room to…to…"

"Stop," Roman bit out, keeping his eyes on the dense, darkening forest in front of him. "Stop making it sound…"

They both were struggling for words like two old maids.

He respected Bartolo. He struggled to remind himself that he was listening to and respecting Cenobia. He was not discussing her sex life with him.

"I loved her, too, when I was protecting her."

Roman's eyes jerked to Bartolo, narrowed on him.

Bartolo sighed extravagantly and waved his hands. "*No seas tonto,* not like that. Not like you." He pointed a thick finger at Roman. "I loved her like a *tío* who would happily take you down for the *tercera caída*."

Roman had no doubt that Bartolo would win in the ring.

"Daniel saw her weekends and holidays and summer breaks, but I was with her every day. He asked me to care for her like he would. I was proud of her and I encouraged her and I corrected her, when necessary. She's always been so smart. Quick. Kind."

Bartolo ran his hand over his dark shaved head and

what Roman saw on his face as the anger eased away
was a heavy sorrow, more etched in than his battered
nose and lip scar.

"The night of her kidnapping, she did sneak out of
her dorm room, as reported," Bartolo said, his words
grim. "But I caught her in the hallway before she left
the building."

Roman's eyes widened.

"You know about the bait-and-switch she'd pulled
with the other girl—they'd met in the bathroom, exchanged pajamas and robes, then the girl passed us and
returned to Cenobia's room while Cenobia snuck out."

Roman nodded. He'd read the report during the
follow-up investigation—the crew of all-male guards
hadn't thought they needed to pull down her robe hood
to check it was her.

"It was God's will that I found her in the hallway.
But…I let her go." Bartolo shook his head. "She begged
me. I couldn't go with her to protect her; if I left my
post, the other patrol would know something was
wrong. The only way she could go is if I supported her
lie. It was her freshman year, she was eighteen years
old, a young woman. And she'd worked so hard."

Bartolo shook his head again, his head like an anvil
on his thick shoulders. "I loved her. I gave her what she
wanted. I didn't do my job. And it almost destroyed her."

Bartolo wasn't just talking about the kidnapping.
He could feel Bartolo's eyes searching for how much
Roman knew.

"She told me what happened to her in the bunker,"
Roman said softly, not wanting the words to seep out
of this foot of space.

The man closed his eyes and his face was awful in
its pain.

"Daniel fired the rest of the team, but me...he wouldn't look at me, wouldn't talk to me. I finally drove him out to a canyon and took the first swing. The staff had to retrieve us, and we couldn't get out of our beds for a week. I'd begged him to kill me. I wanted to die. He trusted me with his most precious treasure and I turned my back on her. I let him down in the most fundamental way when all I've ever wanted is to make him—"

Bartolo shut up and his eyes shot open. Roman kept his face impassive, void of judgement or surprise. Bartolo had only confirmed what Roman, who made his fortune on his skills of observation and assessment, had already suspected.

In the face of Roman's silence, Bartolo asked, "Did she tell you all of it?"

Roman never saw that coming; all of his skills of observation and assessment and Bartolo just swept his legs.

More had happened to her down in the bunker? More that she still hadn't shared with him? More than she didn't trust him enough to share?

Bartolo huffed a harsh breath. "I've said too much."

"Bartolo—" Roman began to object.

But the man cut him off. "No. It's not mine to tell." He breathed deep again. Then he turned to the woodpile and began loading up his arms. "But, I beg of you...do your job." He wouldn't look at Roman. "Keep her safe. Protect her better than I did."

He turned his back on Roman and began moving to the house, arms loaded down, as if he didn't want to see Roman's reaction. As if he already knew that Roman was going to let him—let all of them—down.

Again.

The only reason they were here was because Roman had already failed at keeping her and her family safe.

Do his job? Was he doing his job when he convinced himself they were in a time outside of their timeline? When he told himself he could make her his mission—for now—then return to his path? When he was racing to complete this mission and make love to her before there were more observers around telling him he couldn't?

Was he doing his job when he was too focused on his greed for her to realize that she still hid something vital from him?

He filled his arms with wood and followed Bartolo inside.

"There's going to be an announcement," Cenobia told Bartolo and Roman the moment they came into the living room with armfuls of logs. From the couch, where she was rubbing her ear lobe as Adán sat next to her, she nodded at the muted TV, which they always left on an international business news channel.

The men dumped the wood in the bin then turned to see what had greeted her and Adán when they'd come out of the kitchen: a scrolling message that announced an emergency update from Trujillo Industries as people set up in the press conference room of the Mexico City headquarters.

Still wearing his sheepskin jacket, Roman turned to look at her, worry on his face, and she wished she could get up and snuggle against him. He'd transformed in their time here from her crisply dressed warrior prince to a man who liked to rub his big hand over his beard and had a breathtaking collection of faded-seat jeans.

Roman shed his jacket and sat next to her, and Bartolo sat on the other side of Adán.

Cenobia's eyes widened when she saw Lance Vasquez walk up to the podium. Adán pointed the remote at the TV and unmuted it. It was nine p.m. What did he have to announce that couldn't wait until morning?

"Thank you for your attention at this late hour," Vasquez began, his highlights shining. It appeared he'd touched them up and polished his gold cufflinks for this event. "The board has taken an emergency vote, and as of seven p.m., I am acting CEO of Trujillo Industries."

"No," Adán burst out, shoving forward on the couch. "He can't do that!" Outraged and passionate, he was a Trujillo to his core.

"He just did," Bartolo shushed him.

Roman pressed the back of his hand against her thigh. He smelled woodsy and comforting.

"Señor Trujillo is in no position to return to his duties and Señorita Trujillo is nowhere to be found." Vasquez sneered. "But their absence has left a vacuum of power. We cannot allow our company, employees, customers, and most importantly, our stockholders flounder while we are on the cusp of detrimental changes to our mission and focus. There are still many questions about the viability of Señorita Trujillos pet project. We hope to resolve those questions in time to make sound decisions."

Sound decisions about what? All the decisions were made, and every detail was in place. The unveiling would have proceeded smoothly without Vasquez's power grab. But now…the acting CEO of a car that was to go to market in a week had just questioned its viability.

She grit her teeth through the rest of the press conference so she could record his every word, threat, and casual insult. As the camera pulled back to show the wall of people standing behind him, Cenobia recognized some of the faces of board members and top-level employees. Some of the faces she didn't know, and some important people were conspicuously absent. What kind of chaos had Vasquez brought down on her company in the last few days?

Suddenly, Adán stiffened. She put her arm around him and squeezed him to her.

"It's okay," she murmured against his curls. "I'll fix this."

Bartolo jabbed the TV off with a curse when the press conference ended. "This is the last thing your father needs right now."

Cenobia closed her eyes, took in a deep, slow breath counting to seven, held it for a count of three, and slowly and carefully pushed all her breath out.

Then she turned to Roman.

"I have to get back."

An hour ago, she'd been toying with fantasies of abandoning it all to live in the woods. That fantasy was quickly rejected with the reality that an entitled invader was trying to steal her company from her. From the Trujillos. She'd fix this, she'd promised Adán. She would fix this for her company, employees, customers, and stockholders. She would fix this for her country. Most importantly, she would fix this for the boy sitting next to her, the boy who'd attempted to sound casual as he asked more and more questions about his inheritance and birthright. A boy who deserved to know everything.

She needed to think very clearly about the steps to take next.

She focused on Roman and realized he was watching her rub her ear. She dropped her hand to her lap.

The look on his face…her heart that had been beating at a rabbit's pace suddenly felt heavy.

Their vacation was over.

"Go back?" Bartolo blustered. "Daniel would never allow it; I won't allow it!" He gestured with his giant, protective hands. "What if that is exactly what they want? What if they're betting this announcement makes you come rushing back directly into their crosshairs?"

She reached out and grabbed one of his frantic hands, squeezed it. "You'll protect us. Roman will protect us. But you know that staying here and giving Vasquez free rein is not an option. If he was able to bully and scare the board into voting for him, my father can't wrest back control on his own, not in the condition he's in."

To her shock, Roman nodded. "Your absence makes things real convenient for Vasquez. One thing I've been thinking: What if giving themselves away too soon when they attacked the compound wasn't an accident? What if they never wanted you and me behind the wall?" Roman ran his head over his trim beard as he thought. "These are terror professionals skilled enough to hide from my team, and yet they allow themselves to be seen so Adán can sound the alarm? It doesn't make any sense. But starting the attack before we're inside the compound means my team can't respond, we're freaked out, and we get out of the country and out of their way."

"They shot my father," Cenobia said, disgusted at the idea that the whole, terrifying episode had been a distraction.

Roman nodded. "Mistake? Accident? Or targeted? Where they hit him, it's scary, it's bloody, and it's survivable."

"Are you saying that…" Cenobia shook her head in

astonishment. "Are you saying that I may never have been in physical jeopardy this whole time? That the notes, the attack, they've all been a ruse to get me out of the way?"

Roman put a hand up. "This is conjecture. We're gonna proceed with the assumption that you're in danger. But I'm saying maybe we can proceed from Mexico. Using this theory, they don't want you…" He glanced at Adán. "… Eliminated. That just makes a martyr of you, and La Primera becomes a symbol. You alive means assholes can imply that you're tannin' on a beach somewhere."

"So when can we go?" she asked.

It would be "we."

Roman would come back with her to Mexico. They would keep Adán close. For the first time in her life, perhaps she could merge all the things that were important to her. Her family. Her company. And her… Roman.

"We've planned for this contingency, but we need to give Glori a day to activate it," Roman said. "I'll notify her and then we'll head back the morning after tomorrow. Sound good?"

Cenobia appreciated that Roman visually checked in with all three of them, even Adán, who gave a head nod. She understood why he gained such loyalty from his troops and employees.

Yes, their vacation was over. But perhaps in the midst of a hostile takeover and a life-threatening game of hide-and-seek, something much better was about to begin.

Chapter Eighteen

Freedom, Kansas

They celebrated their last day of freedom in Freedom.

Early in the morning, Roman took them downtown because they had special permission from the librarian for some off-hours browsing. In the sunrise light, Cenobia window-shopped the four blocks of Freedom's Main Street while Roman used his black box system to set up final arrangements with Glori. When Adán struggled out of the library with a stack of astronomy books they would ship back by their due dates, he asked why the library's computers were named Roman 1, Roman 2, Roman 3…

Roman squirmed. "I told them they didn't have to do that. I replaced a few machines and helped them beef up their alarm system after they were vandalized."

It had taken everything in Cenobia not to kiss him.

Then they enjoyed their final Roman-led hike, Cenobia-cooked meal, Adán-guided stargazing, and Bartolo-led sing-along, this time to one of Daniel's favorite songs, the *muy macho* "El Rey."

Bartolo sent an impressive *grito Mexicano* through the trees that had sheltered them.

They would be flying to Mexico City the next day. Roman explained that they would be installed in a comfortable safe house, protected 24/7 by Sheppard Security team members who'd had no contact with the case, and kept together at all times, even when they traveled at erratic and unscheduled hours in an armored car to the Trujillo Industries offshoot in the capital so that Cenobia could undo what Vasquez had done.

Cenobia burned with an unfamiliar excitement that, in the coming days, part of Adán's daily education would be the inner workings of Trujillo Industries.

But tonight, the last night before more watchful eyes returned to their lives, Cenobia hoped to convince Roman that it was time. She wanted to make love to him. She'd dressed to prove it.

She slipped into Roman's room and locked the door behind her.

And pressed back against it when she saw him. Big, bare chested, and bearded, he was sitting up in bed and watching her, one knee drawn up in his linen sleep pants and his scarred hand hanging off of it. Candles flickered on both bedside tables.

He'd been waiting for her. He'd prepared for her, too.

Usually, he overwhelmed her the instant they were alone, wherever, whenever, using his hands and mouth and body to tease and threaten and promise. His greed, encouraging hers, had been lightning flashes, with no time for seductive clothing and candlelight.

But tonight, he stayed quiet and commandingly still as his eyes traveled over her. She'd worn a bronze silk La Perla nightgown with a plunging neckline and filigreed lace over the swells of her breasts. She'd rubbed a bit of musk-scented hair oil into her hair to help it fight the dryness that came with central heating and fireplaces, but it still crackled and curled and waved down her back.

His slow perusal while he displayed that masterful body make him look like a lord in that bed, a pasha, *un príncipe* surveying his treasure.

"Come here," he said, a command from a green-eyed *tlatoani* of pleasure. She pushed off the door and walked to him feeling her heart pounding with dual injections of apprehension and excitement.

When she reached his bedside, he held out his hand. "Sit between my legs." The flames picked out flecks of gold in his eyes. "Lay back against my chest."

She shuddered out a breath, but kneeled on the bed then settled back against his hard chest and luxuriously hot skin.

"I had a plan," he breathed against her ear as his huge hands smoothed down her goose-pebbled biceps. "You almost ruined it with this fucking nightgown."

Cenobia's huff of a laugh released half of her tension. If she was his battle prize, he'd just kneeled in front of it. She snuggled back against him, and tilted her head so he could have better access.

"Far be it for me to ruin a good plan," she breathed as he delicately fingered her hair away from her ear, kissed it gently, traced his fingers down her neck and slowly down the edge of the lace.

"Cenobia, why don't you like your name?" he murmured, his hot breath soft and caressing. He skirted his fingers over her hard nipple.

"I…" Her brain, generally dependable, blanked.

"Cenobia," he drew it out, gravel over leather, spreading his fingers slowly over the silk until he held her whole breast in his hand. It was his right hand, with his shortened finger and thick gold ring and seeing it on her, on top of bronze silk, make her unexpectedly shiver. "It's a good name," he said, the grin obvious in his voice. "Did you know it's the name of a queen?"

"It is?" she replied weakly.

He caught her nipple between his index finger and the ring, squeezed gently, and she arched into his touch.

Her name was pretentious, overdone. It was difficult to spell and always had to be repeated. It was a waste of time. Cenobia was a literalist, not a romantic. She would have been fine with the effortless Ana.

They were all words she would have said if she could find the power of speech.

"Queen Zenobia, with a Z, was the ruler of a wealthy Arabian city called Palmyra," he said against her ear, rubbing his nose into her hair. "She conquered Egypt, Palestine, Lebanon, all the way into Roman territory. One of the names they called her was the Queen of the East, wise and ferocious." He was switching between caressing her breast, strong hand claiming her through silk, and squeezing her nipple, each time a little harder. "Eventually, she was captured by the Romans. But they were so impressed by her, they let her go, and she became a well-known philosopher."

The flickering candles created tiny wisps of light and shadow in the room, and in their glow, she realized she'd worked herself into a sprawl, her thighs spread and one knee resting against his, her hands gripping his sleep pants, her head lolling while she tingled with luxurious pleasure. He turned her into a creature of pure, thoughtless, decadent sensation.

"Roman—"

"Seems to me someone picked out your name pretty deliberately, baby girl," he said, nuzzling her ear. "Where'd it come from?"

When his thick scruff rasped against her skin like that… "My mother picked it out," she sighed.

"You never talk about her." His big hand now just held her breast. It was warm. Comforting in a way she didn't know a hand there could be.

She shrugged lightly, not wanting to dislodge him. His warm breath, the smell of him surrounding her, his strength and tenderness and erotic teasing… "I didn't know her," she sighed.

Francisca Pedron Trujillo died of complications from her lifelong diabetes soon after Cenobia was born. There were the appropriate pictures in the home, a picture that had gotten shoved further and further back in favor of pictures of Cenobia and Adán on her father's desk. But her father seldom talked about the beautiful girl from a good family who seemed groomed to make him the perfect wife.

"I don't think she and my father were very happy," she said, closing her eyes as he tenderly licked at her lobe. This was so different than every other time. "She wouldn't have put up with my whims the way my father has."

Roman huffed into her hair. "She did name you after a queen. Maybe you turned out just the way she wanted."

Her fingers dug into his muscular thighs. When he gave her careless, glorious praise like that…

She twisted around so she could look into his eyes.

"Why do you know so much about my name?"

He scraped his teeth over his succulent bottom lip as considered her, his eyes lazy.

"My sweet Cen," he said in a low, toe-curling drawl. "I wasn't lyin' about looking you up. I did everything but doodle your name on a note pad." He traced a hand up her shoulder and buried it in her hair. "One translation of your name is father's ornament."

Cenobia gave an unexpected but very un-fantasy-like snort.

His eyes searched hers.

"But Queen Zenobia had another nickname," he murmured, stroking his thumb over her cheekbone. "They called her the warrior queen."

Warrior queen.

How many times had she teased him by calling him a warrior prince? How many thousands of times had she thought of him that way reverently in her head? Not just a warrior prince but *her* warrior prince.

And now her much-fantasized warrior prince was scarred skin and built muscle and a pounding heart under her hands.

He worked so hard to convince her, the world, and himself that he was nothing more than a stone-faced soldier. But in the Monte del Vino Real, he had a royal brother who trusted him as second-in-command, a royal sister who'd embraced him as a big brother, and a niece and nephew who feted him with homemade jewelry. With their little family here, he'd become head chef and entertainment director, grocery list maker and boardgame referee.

He wasn't a taciturn soldier. He was a den mother. He was a devoted son and a beloved brother and a leader of heroes and the savior of lost causes.

Cenobia swallowed the three little words that wanted to pour out of her throat and blinked back her tears.

"Roman?"

There was no hesitation or holding back in his powerful gaze. "My queen."

She dragged his mouth down to hers and claimed it. It was hers.

He was hers.

He kissed her deeply then pulled back, panting into her mouth. "I want you more than I've ever wanted anyone." She pressed those words into her heart. "But Cen…" He searched her eyes and gritted his teeth. "That's all I can give you. My body. I can't give you more than that. And I don't want to hurt you."

He hissed *hurt you* like the inevitability of it already wounded him. He wanted her to push him away.

But she could never.

The moments when he implied he'd be a danger to her or he wasn't valuable to his family were rare. But there were enough of them for her to see the pattern.

Her reluctant warrior prince was reluctant to grab something for himself.

"You've already given me so much—trust, faith, respect, admiration, desire," she breathed against his mouth, staring into his fiercely intent gaze, meaning every word. She would fight tooth and nail for him. But if this was truly all he could give, she would walk away blessed to have had him in her life. "Make love to me." He bared his teeth like he was going to bite. "Let me give you something, too."

She saw it his eyes. Whatever reins he'd been holding…he let go.

His grip on her arms was real and vital and better than the best fantasy as he pulled her toward him.

The house turned off. Every electronic whir and hum went dead. Then flood lights blasted on outside, small safety lights lit up inside, and an alarm shrieked through the house.

Roman squeezed her biceps and pulled her close.

"Someone's coming," he said against her ear, immediate and exacting, switched in an instant from what they were to this, calm and in control despite the wailing alarm that nearly shattered her skull. "I'll keep you safe."

Safe. He'd keep her safe.

Adán.

She jumped out of bed alongside him, awash in panicked urgency, as he blew out the candles then started pulling things out from underneath the bed: a gun, a duffle, a sweater that he yanked on, shoes. He pulled out a bulky sweatshirt, yoga pants, and sneakers in her size that he tried to shove at her. But she motioned with her hands to the door.

Now. Adán. *Now!*

Instead of arguing with her, he grabbed her face and kissed her. The comfort of his mouth was the antidote to her panic as he pushed the clothes against her body. His mouth went to her ear. "You gotta get dressed so you're ready for anything. We'll get him. We'll keep him safe, too."

Yes. Yes. Not just her. Him.

She nodded, message received, pulling on the clothes as he checked the gun's chamber and slung the duffle across his body.

The alarm abruptly went off. She could hear its echo in the silence.

He motioned for her to follow him without saying a word.

She crept behind him as he walked to the door, illuminated by the small yellow safety lights incorporated unobtrusively into the wall paneling. He held the gun up as walked backwards, surveying the large window that looked out on the lake. He'd told her that the windows could withstand a bomb blast, that they could see out, but no one could see in. She saw no movement out there. At his bedroom door, they stopped to listen. She could hear nothing.

Roman opened the door soundlessly—of course nothing in Roxanne Medina's house creaked—peeked out, stepped out to fully check the hallway, then motioned for her to follow.

He pointed toward his brother and wife's room, Cenobia's temporary bedroom. It was in the wrong direction, away from Adán's bedroom. Away from Adán.

She shook her head, confused.

He leaned close.

"Safe room," he barely whispered. "I'll get Adán and…"

She gave one solid headshake, leaned back to meet his eyes, then pointed at her chest and then his. Together. *We'll keep him safe*, he'd said. They would do this together.

No fear was as massive as the fear of being locked behind a door while Adán was still out here.

Roman huffed once through his nose then motioned for her to follow him.

From the living room, they suddenly heard an attack, the sound of fists, bodies, and grunts, then a cry from the living room.

"You promised!" It was Adán.

Cenobia sprinted on Roman's heels down the hallway.

The bedroom doors of Adán and Bartolo were open, the rooms empty, and when she turned the corner, she saw Adán by the sofa, his shoulder held by a tall man dressed in black, a fitted black hood and slim goggles covering his head and face.

A knife glinted in the man's free hand.

Bartolo was on the floor.

Just inside the living room doorway, a flash of movement caught her eye. A second hooded man, just to Cenobia's right, raised a handgun on them.

"Down!" Roman roared. But Adán was in danger and she'd trained this scenario a thousand times so she did what instinct demanded. She slammed the man's wrist and the gun to the side with her left hand, made sure it pointed away from everyone, snapped up his jaw with the right, then kneed into his groin with all her strength. The gunman keeled over with a grunt and the weapon clattered to the floor.

Roman grabbed the man's collar, hauled him upright while he kicked the gun away, punched him in the cheek with side of his own gun, a meaty grinding sound, once, twice, but still he struggled…

"Stop."

The tall man crouched behind Adán with the knife up to the boy's throat.

Roman shoved the accomplice down on his knees and pointed the gun at his head.

The tall man huffed a laugh. "I don't care about him," he mocked in a Spanish accent. "Shoot him. This *niño* will be dead."

"No," Cenobia gasped. Adán's eyes were enormous with terror, showing the same color of steel as the knife against his tender throat.

"It's all right, Cenobia," the man said. His tone was intimate. Almost tender. "Roman's not an idiot."

She heard Roman's breaths. Once. Twice. Then he

pulled the gun away. The accomplice slumped over, breathing harshly, his hands on his thighs.

"Mira," the man said. "You finally picked a good man."

He stepped back several steps, dragging Adán with him as a shield, as he said, "Shove that useless *basura* toward me."

"You're not leaving the house with the boy," Roman growled.

Adán suddenly whimpered and even in the spare light they could see the trickle of blood down his throat.

She knew how to disarm him; all of her sisters knew what to do with a knife at her throat. If she'd just spent time with him, maybe she could have shown him. Maybe he'd know right now what to do rather than being helpless.

"Don't hurt him," she cried. All the weapons at her disposal and she'd left him helpless.

"I'm not going to hurt him, *guapa,"* the man said, cooing the words as he wrapped a gloved hand around Adán's slim throat. He flicked a thumb over the wound. "As long as *su alteza* there does what I say. Give me my man."

Roman hauled the man up, pushed him away with a grunt, then aimed his firearm at them both.

"I'm leaving you with your people, I'll be leaving here with mine," the tall man said as he backed up in a squat behind a terrified Adán and his accomplice staggered behind him to the entrance. *"Y óyeme,* you take the time to chase me, your giant there will die."

"Let him go," Roman ordered succinctly.

The accomplice barreled out, leaving the door open. The man squeezed Adán's neck. The knife slowly slid away as he moved back, still crouching, into the dark doorway.

"See you soon, Cenobia," the man called as he moved out of sight.

Then a car door slammed and an engine roared as Cenobia raced Roman to get to Adán. She pulled the boy against her as he crumbled, sobbing, and Roman tilted up his head to check his neck. Fortunately, it was just a nick. Roman charged outside, but Cenobia could already hear an automobile speeding away.

Roman ran back in and grabbed his duffel then slid over the floorboards to get to Bartolo.

He pulled out a medical bag then bent over Bartolo in a flurry of efficient movements.

Suddenly, she heard the bodyguard croak in the semi-dark, "Cenobia…"

Adán's sobs choked off. They both hurried to him, joined Roman on their knees.

The man—always such a mighty bulwark in her life—looked sallow and strangely small on the ground as Roman used cloths to staunch the blood on Bartolo's side.

"*Mija, mijo, están bien,*" he said, relief sighing through him.

She grabbed his huge hand. "Yes, we're fine."

"I'm so sorry…"

The white cloth was turning dark terrifyingly fast.

She pressed his hand against her chest, tears welling in her eyes. "No, we're fine, you're fine, don't be…"

"Tell Daniel I'm so sorry. Tell him… I thought we'd have more time…tell him… I wanted to tell him that…"

His strong hand went limp in hers. Cenobia felt a wail climbing in her throat.

Roman checked his pulse. "He's passed out, not gone. But we've got to get him to the hospital right now."

"Okay, okay," she said, gasping, wiping her cheeks. "Okay. What do you want us to do?"

Roman was ripping open a pack of sterile bandages. "You two are going to help me get him into the car. Adán!"

Adán sucked in a shocked breath next to her. Her poor boy.

"You with me, buddy?" Roman asked, urgent. "We can't do this without you."

She felt Adán grip into her sweater. But he nodded, his breath still hitching from his earlier crying, a sound she hadn't heard since he was tiny.

Cenobia willed herself to keep it together. All she'd ever wanted was to protect him from this.

"Cenobia." Roman said her name in a way that reminded her of what he'd just called her. His warrior queen.

She squeezed Adán against her and said, "Let's help Bartolo."

Roman grabbed keys out of his duffle and told Cenobia which car to get out of the garage.

"You're gonna drive hell bent for leather to get us to the hospital while Adán's gonna help me keep pressure," Roman said as he taped down a compress. "Then once we pass Bartolo off to the very capable hands at Freedom Medical Center—I promise you, they will fix him—then we're getting on a plane and I'm taking you where I should have taken you in the first place." He pulled a large piece of medical tape with his teeth and snipped it with scissors. "I'm taking you where whole armies with cannons couldn't get through."

He taped the final side of the compress down.

"I'm taking you home."

Chapter Nineteen

Monte del Vino Real, Spain

Roman stood at the window of his mountain-side home and looked down at the few lights still on in the village of Monte del Vino Real, the one thousand-year-old principality he was connected to by blood and luck in Northern Spain. He'd bought this spot where he'd built his small, stone home for the view, and from here he could see the slight glow of the lamps that lit the winding granite streets; the brighter glow of the world-renowned luxury hotel his sister built in the middle of Bodega Sofia, her monastery-turned-winery; the tower of the castle; and the snow-capped peaks of the Picos de Europa, the looming mountains that protected this small, warm valley from harsh winds and a millennium of would-be invaders.

El Castillo, the medieval Moorish-built castle that was a gift from Queen Isabella to her favorite wine suppliers, had few lights on. His brother was militant about making sure the castle was self-supporting and not a drain on the kingdom's coffers after he'd spent the last ten years fixing the financial abuses their father had almost destroyed the kingdom with. Roman had been happy to report after this year's audit that the castle was operating in the black. They'd opened a large portion of the castle to tourists, who were excited to see one of the best-preserved medieval castles in Europe, reserved several sacred spaces for kingdom affairs and village celebrations, and maintained a few living and staff quarters for Mateo's mother, Queen Dowager Valentina, who continued to live there after her husband died.

Mateo and his family lived in a gorgeous mountainside home on the other side of the valley, a good thirty minutes away. Still, Roman wasn't surprised when he got the text from the castle security team stationed at the bottom of his drive.

Roman tapped in the code to disarm his house alarm and then lugged open his wooden front door.

Rey Mateo Ferdinand Juan Carlos de Esperanza y Santos, king of the Monte del Vino Real, stepped into Roman's house in a grey parka and a red nose and tugged his brother into his arms.

Roman was a patter and a shoulder squeezer. But Mateo, he was a hugger. They were about the same size, and Mateo braced his forearms across Roman's back, squeezing him, before pounding his back hard. His brother worked in the fields—he'd been one of the top vine scientists in the world before he'd stepped away to focus on the Monte—and those vineyard-built arms could knock the wind out of Roman.

Mateo stepped back to pat Roman's freshly shaved face with his gloved hand. "You okay?"

Roman's nod didn't look like it comforted the guy.

"You handle this kind of thing all the time, right? I shouldn't worry, should I?"

Like Cenobia, Mateo got his education from kindergarten to PhD entirely in the U.S., so he had an Americanism that meant, when Roman had met him ten years ago, the man barely had an accent. Still, he was Spanish through and through, wearing his emotions—worry, anger, joy, love and lust when he looked at his wife—like a big, flapping cape.

People said they looked alike, but Roman didn't see it. Even though Mateo was king, the paparazzi still liked to call him the "Golden Prince," and with his wavy hair that got blond under the sun of a September harvest, his thick brows, and last remnants of a tan, Mateo looked more like a California windsurfer than a Spanish king on the edge of forty. At least Mateo was starting to get the lines at the corners of his eyes that Roman had had his whole life.

Mateo's billionaire wife liked to tease that the brothers shared the same manly facade.

Roman motioned his manly, hugging, handsy brother into the living room.

Mateo shed his outerwear—it got cold fast in this mountain valley once November hit—and sat on the couch as Roman took a seat on a nearby armchair.

"No, you shouldn't worry," Roman said. "I'm borrowing a few of your security guys but I'll return them as soon as this is resolved. We're going to stay out of everyone's hair so it'll be like we're not even here—"

"*¡Joder!* That's not what I meant," Mateo said, his hazel-brown eyes all lit up. You never had to wonder if Mateo was annoyed. "I'm not worried about us. I'm worried about you? Are you okay? Are they okay?"

Cenobia and Adán were currently sleeping in a guest bedroom in the same king-sized bed after Adán had quickly noped out of sleeping alone and Cenobia had quickly agreed. They'd both been quiet as they'd rushed Bartolo to the hospital and then met Roxanne's plane at a private airstrip. It was only when they were in the air and Roman got Bartolo's good prognosis from one of his buddies on the Freedom police force that Adán fell apart.

When Cenobia wasn't soothing the boy, she'd been deep in thought. Roman hadn't had the chance to tell her how amazing she was. She'd put all her practice to real-world use; she reacted as well as a member of his team to that traumatic event.

A traumatic event that Roman had been unable to protect her from. He filled in the blanks for Mateo now.

His brother asked the question that kept Roman awake. "How in the hell did they find you?"

Roman shook his head. "I don't know. Maybe someone in Freedom gave us away?"

Mateo's face reflected the dubiousness that Roman felt.

When Roxanne's family went back to her hometown for a visit, Freedom's citizens guarded their privacy from the press as effectively as the Monte's mountains had guarded the village from attackers.

But if Roman couldn't blame their discovery on a thoughtless social media post about a surprise sighting of the reluctant prince and the Mexican CEO…

"Another possibility is that I have an iceberg-sized leak in my team."

"You don't believe that," Mateo dismissed instantly.

"I didn't," Roman said. "I don't want to. Glori's the only person I've been communicating with." He and Glori were the only ones who knew the secrets of their

black-box system—a communication strategy that relied on the archaic technology of burner phones, Morse
code, and ancient message boards chosen in a random
pattern—and it had never been hacked. Even saying her
name in the context of this conversation made his stomach roll over. "Maybe I haven't been thinkin' as clearly
as I should be. Bartolo warned me that—"

Crap. He looked up to find his brother's gaze narrowing on him. *Crap crap crap.* He needed to get some
sleep.

"Bartolo told you what?"

"Nothin'" Roman said to the wood floor.

He could hear Mateo grinding his teeth. "I will
punch you because I love you."

Damn.

His whole life changed ten years ago when he found
out he had a brother, a sister, and a kingdom in its death
throes because of his womanizing, greedy, narcissistic
biological dad. After the initial meeting, he never cared
to get to know his father. But he'd taken to his smart,
funny, hard-working siblings, even though they both
raked themselves over the coals a little bit more than
a person should. He'd hung around because they were
good people with the best of intentions, and he could
help fix their woes. He had contacts with the Trujillos, he could beef up their security, and keep an eye
on things. But he'd never meant to spend more than a
few months at a time here in the house he'd built so he
wasn't always staying in one of their homes or the castle. He'd never meant to lure them into relying on him.

Six months ago, Mateo refused to be talked out of
naming Roman his advisor. Roman had threatened to
reject the position, to leave the Monte and not come

back. Mateo, that asshole, hadn't even looked up from signing the declaration.

Someday I'm going to convince you that this is your home, his brother had muttered as he shoved the king's advisor ring on his finger in a ceremony on the castle grounds, in front of what looked like all of the Monte's exploding population.

What did he owe this guy who kept forcing love, brotherhood, and a kingdom of responsibility on him, no matter how hard he resisted? What did he owe a man whose two a.m. visit and worried pat on Roman's cheek loosened the bind of worry around his guts?

How did he explain to him that this—a family to love, a community to call home—wasn't his path?

His hands hanging between his knees, Roman covered the ring with his burned hand.

"Bartolo said I couldn't protect her when I was…" He paused and swallowed. "…When I was sleeping with her," he finished as quietly as he could.

"*Gracias a Dios*, finally," Mateo said.

Roman shot a surprised glance at his brother.

Mateo rolled his eyes. "*¿Qué?* You think you were keeping it a secret, the way you twitched whenever her name was mentioned? We had a man loaning us millions of dollars—scratch that, a woman—and you never went for a visit? You think you're all cool, calm and collected, *hermano*, but your ears perk up whenever someone says Trujillo, loan, or Mexico. Those are not sexy words."

He made him sound like a leg-humping poodle. "You can barely keep it your pants when someone says billionaire," he scowled.

Mateo shrugged. "I don't have to keep it in my pants.

Cenobia got off that plane and looked at you like you were her favorite *flan*. You don't have to keep it in your pants, either."

His brother made it sound so easy. He wanted Cenobia Trujillo, so he could have her. He'd been on the verge of having her.

But Mateo hadn't taken into account that Roman himself—either his team or his inattention—had failed Cenobia entirely. Not once. But twice.

Mateo hadn't taken into account that, for all the ways she trusted him, admired him, desired him, she was still holding something back. *Did she tell you all of it?* Bartolo had asked. She didn't owe him her secrets. Especially not now, after the way he'd let her down.

And Mateo hadn't taken into account that he didn't fully know his half brother, who was related by DNA and a chance weekend and little else. Roman had probably been more honest with Cenobia in the last twenty-four hours than he'd ever been with the brother he'd known for ten years.

All I can give you is my body. I can't give you more than that, he'd told her, wanting her to have all the facts before she made love to him. *And I don't want to hurt you.*

If he'd said the same in Mateo's office six months ago, he wouldn't now be wearing this too-tight, too-heavy ring. *I can't give you more than I already have*, he should have out-shouted his brother. *And I don't want to hurt you. Don't let me hurt all of you.*

Six months ago, he should have gotten on a plane and not looked back. Cenobia's money was spent. They didn't need him here anymore.

Every day he wore the ring, he felt the weight of his mother's you-know-better stare.

"I'm glad you're here," his brother who didn't fully know him said.

"Sorry I've been out of the loop. We'll come to El Castillo tomorrow and I'll get caught up on emails," Roman said. "All the bids should be in for the kingdom-wide network upgrade and I gotta go through the top proposals for that hostel property. The Monte's gonna have a youth hostel nicer than the Four Seasons."

When Roman zeroed in on Mateo, he wondered what he'd said *this time* to piss the man off.

"I'm not glad you're here so you can do a job," Mateo said, his eyes flashing. "I'm glad my brother's around; I'm glad you're safe. I'm grateful you've brought the woman I owe so much to so I can get to know her better."

Mateo shook his head as he looked at Roman. "I don't know how to get it through your thick head that even if you never lifted another finger, I'd still want you around."

Roman met his brother's angry and determined gaze until he couldn't anymore. He licked his lips and looked out the window.

"Roman?"

He stood and turned as Cenobia's voice came from the hallway. So did Mateo.

She looked like the girl he'd rescued as she came into the living room, sleepy eyed, her hair tumbling around her, tying the robe over her nightgown.

She quickened her tying when she saw Mateo.

"Alteza, perdóneme," she said, calling his brother highness as she cinched the robe bow.

"No, *perdóname*," Mateo said. "I shouldn't be here so late. I hope I didn't wake you."

"My body clock is confused," she said, pulling her hair over one shoulder. She looked so vulnerable and beautiful and so fucking sexy that Roman wanted to command his king to shut his damn eyes and turn around. "I woke up craving a *café con leche*, but I see that Roman hasn't even slept yet."

Was that a reprimand in her tone?

Mateo's not-so-hidden grin seemed to say he'd heard it, too. "Well, I'll go so he can remedy that. I'm sorry for the circumstances that have brought you and your brother here, but we are glad for your visit. Please come see us soon. The twins are excited to show Adán all the secrets of El Castillo."

Roman led his brother to the door—the king's shit-eating grin became more obvious the second he turned away from Cenobia—and promised to see him the next day.

When he shut the door and turned around, he was surprised to see that Cenobia had followed him on her bare, quiet feet and stood just behind him. She instantly wrapped her arms around his torso and went up on her toes to kiss him.

Instinct had him enfolding her in his arms and kissing her back.

The kiss was lush and wet and slow and as comforting as a long, hot shower after a six-day ground fight. Roman had never had a kiss like this, a kiss for kissing's sake, a kiss that wasn't asking to be anything else, a kiss merely for the wonder and solace and miracle of it.

It was the first chance they'd had to be alone since he'd begged to make love to her.

Cenobia broke the kiss to nuzzle his cheek.

"You shaved," she said.

"Couldn't sleep," he answered. "And our time off is over."

She gave a heavy sigh as she settled back down on her feet and didn't disagree with him. Tomorrow, their time off would be over. Tomorrow, Roman needed to get back on mission and actually do some good for the people relying on him.

But tonight...he let her hold him against her warm, sleep-scented body, let her support him even though he was taller and broader, as she asked, "How are you doing?"

He clasped his hands at the small of her back and soaked up strength from her spine. "Tired," he said, honestly. "Worried."

"Yes," she said, her smoky brown eyes showing her worry, too.

He held her hand as he walked into the living room and then pulled her into his lap as he sat in his large, overstuffed armchair. He was too tired to fight his need to have her close right now.

He supported her with a hand around her back as he stroked her hip and thigh and hid his face against her neck, lost himself in the black cloud of her hair. She rested her chin against his head and squeezed his shoulder.

"I realized something I should have a long time ago," she said in a soft, wondering tone. "I think Bartolo and my father are in love."

He nestled his face in closer and let her muse on what he'd suspected.

"All the signs have been there, since he first came to us, but I never... I can't believe I didn't realize it."

"Bartolo loves you and Adán very much," Roman said against her neck. He'd called them both *mija* and *mijo* when he thought he was saying goodbye. *My daughter. My son.*

"Yes," she breathed. "He's been a wonderful father to us."

She smelled heavenly.

"It must be torture for them to not be able to express their love," she said.

He couldn't imagine living in the same house as Cenobia, sitting at the same table with Cenobia, raising children with Cenobia, and not being able to claim her as his.

"It must be so hard for my father." Her voice was full of sorrow. "Heir to a legacy and determined to dominate the auto industry. He felt he had to choose between being out or being a success in the world he wanted to inhabit.

"It never made sense how hard he tried to stand in my way..." She rubbed her cheek against his hair. "He loved me and admired me so it didn't... I've cried so many frustrated tears because I didn't understand. And now, I think I can. He wanted me to...fit in. To flow with society rather than shove against it. Not because he was ashamed of me or needed me as a token but because he wanted my life to be easier than his has been.

"He had something he felt he had to hide and I have something I want to shine, but for both of us, it makes life much more challenging. He wanted to save me from that."

Roman could understand the man's impulse. Even

knowing and reveling in what Cenobia was capable of—even having proof that she could disarm a man and protect them both—he still wanted to keep her safe in a silk-and-velvet lined box.

"The problem is," Cenobia murmured against his skull, "I've never gained anything from hiding."

He felt her spine straighten in his hands. He looked up at her. "I tint my windows and close my curtains and deny myself views, believing that will keep me safe. All while I'm facing down a roomful of men to build my car or presenting a plan to the world no other Mexican auto manufacturer would touch."

She stroked her fingers through his hair like the feel of it was comforting against her fingertips.

"On the plane ride, I kept thinking about lost opportunities. About…regret." With a last loving brush, she withdrew her hand from his hair and enfolded it with the other in her lap.

Her beautiful, deep-brown eyes searched his. She took a deep breath.

"Adán is my son," she said, lifting her chin bravely.

Roman suddenly felt the ache of tears in his throat. Adán's age, the timing…that poor, brave, terrorized girl he'd driven across the desert. "Sweetheart."

Even as tears filled her eyes, she kept her back straight. "I'm sorry," she said, sniffing. "I'm sorry I didn't tell you. No one but my father, Bartolo, and my therapist know. Not even…" She gave a tiny hiccup that surprised her; she covered it with her hand.

He tugged her until he could be the wall that she leaned on.

"No…" she softly gasped against his shoulder. "I don't…deserve your sympathy. I've lied… I've lied to

Adán his whole life. I've ignored him, I've shoved his upbringing on my father and Bartolo, you don't want to…you can't…"

"I can," Roman said into her ear. "I do."

For minutes upon minutes as she cried, he held her and squeezed her and murmured into her ear and urged his body to soak up her years of pain and sorrow and fear and regret.

She shuddered against him. "I was so afraid you'd feel how I feel."

"How's that?"

"Disgusted. Disgusted with me."

Which set off a fresh round of tears and he hugged her close. Disgusted. By her. When she was the bravest person he'd ever met.

As her tears quieted, he gently wiped her face with his thumbs.

"I'm here for whatever you need," he murmured, wanting to lick away her tears like a cat. "You tell me as much or as little as you want. You don't owe me that story. You don't owe it to anyone except Adán."

When she nodded, he knew that she'd already made up her mind. She was going to tell her son that she was his mother.

"I didn't…accept that I was pregnant for several months," she said, so quietly it was almost a whisper. "I was trying so hard to pretend none of it had happened. Or that it hadn't…affected me. Changed me. By the time I acknowledged it, I was very far along. Finally, my father intervened and brought me home from Houston for the last trimester."

He realized she was absently running a finger up

and down the button placket inside his shirt, soothing herself with the silky cotton.

"I told myself... I told myself it was better for Adán to believe he was the son of a tycoon and an absent socialite than the son of...what I had to offer him. My father's second wife, I forgot, she knows too. She's a tremendous friend of ours. She married him and isolated herself for months merely to provide cover for me."

Roman needed to check in and make sure Daniel Trujillo's ex-wife always had everything she needed.

"I told myself I was lying for Adán's benefit," she said, still rubbing that placket. "But that was a lie. Adán will know it's a lie. I was absent and uncaring and distant, and all of that was for me."

Roman pulled her hand from the placket and entwined it with his, caught her eyes. "You could have made a lot of decisions that meant Adán didn't grow up in your dad's house. None of those decisions would have been wrong. But you kept him close to you. You gotta add that to your equation, too, baby girl."

He never wanted her eyes to look so endlessly sad.

"I practiced the conversation so many times in my therapist's office but... I kept putting it off," she whispered. "I'm...I'm afraid he's going to hate me. I'm afraid he's going to feel ashamed. I'm afraid he's going to... he's going to ask why I didn't stop it from happening."

"He might feel and say all of those things," Roman said, gruff. "But you'll stand by him and take it until he realizes you're not going away. And I'll be here, helping you and supporting you."

Her huge, liquid eyes looked into his as their hands clung together. But neither of them said a word.

She needed him and he could help her. Hell, he'd

been walking this line with his family for ten years. He could stay on his path while giving her just enough, just as long as she needed him, without turning his back on the choice he made.

Without turning his back on the sacrifice he made to choose it.

I'm here as long as you need me.

"I'm done hiding, Roman." She lifted his hand with its burn scar to her lips and kissed it before she put it in her lap. "All my secret routes and walls and guards… and look where I've ended up. My family in danger and my company on the verge of being stolen from me."

The list of Roman's failures. "I know. I'm sorry. I'll figure it out…"

She shook her head. "No. *We'll* figure it out. Together. You've done so much already."

Roman began to scoff, but she caught his face in her hands before he could get it out. "You have." She gently shook his head. "You leave things out of your equation as well. I am alive because of you. Adán is safe because of you. I have a company and an initiative to go save because of you. Why don't you give yourself credit for that?"

Cenobia sounded like his brother.

What they didn't understand, what had been hammered into him and turned into his vow, was that the highest standard was the minimum level of expectation as a Ranger. When that minimum level was met—staying on mission, remaining tactical—every member of your squad came back to base. Good enough just got people killed. Or, at least, got them hiding in a house in Spain while their company and family were threatened.

But his stubborn, brave girl didn't see it that way.

She slid her hands to his chest. "I need to come out from behind all the people trying to protect me. I need to tell Adán. I need to take Vasquez head on."

Roman frowned. "What's that mean?"

"I don't know, yet," she said. "But the Frankfurt Auto Show is in a little over a week. And the only way I can encourage my people to support the launch and overcome Vasquez is if I'm in contact with them. I can't be afraid any longer."

He opened his mouth to bring up safety protocols and the sieve of a leak among their people when Cenobia cheated and kissed him, hard and mind-spinning.

"You'll keep us safe," she said urgently against his lips. "I know you'll keep him safe." She kissed him again, deeper and more demanding, and the inexperienced woman whose kisses had made his hands shake when she'd just started learning the art now had practice blowing his mind.

The days ahead were going to be hard. Her son wasn't just going to give her a pass for twelve years of lying to him. Neither were others, once the world knew. He'd been at the center of PR storms with his siblings, subjected to pundits and bloggers and people on Twitter judging and moralizing and fighting and condemning, spending hours talking about what they did not know and had no bearing on.

But Roman saw her, and he knew her.

And he loved her.

He loved her, even though he shouldn't. He loved her because how could he not, after the whole of herself she'd shown him. He loved her and he would use all his gifts to help her.

He loved her and would protect her from knowing it.

He would protect her and her son as long as she would let him. He would help her come out from behind her shields and take back what men were trying to steal from her.

You'll keep us safe. I know you'll keep him safe.

Yes, he would keep his love and her boy safe. And in doing so, he was going to wildly piss her off. Because there was a certain clarity that came with finally admitting he was in love. And Roman gave in to the one valuable thing he learned from that attack on the lake house, the one piece of information he'd been rejecting in his worry and exhaustion.

Adán knew the attacker.

He couldn't now, not with his hands and mouth occupied with worshiping his love. But in the morning, Roman was going to start dissecting how a smart, angry, innocent but misinformed twelve-year-old boy might be the center of all their leaks.

Chapter Twenty

Monte del Vino Real, Spain

Mateo surprised them all the next day when he showed up to drive them to his castle.

Cenobia had woken Adán with the wonderful news that Bartolo was recovering well from his surgery. Then she showed him the thrilling surprise in the smaller guest bedroom closet: the queen had filled it with clothes for him. With a flick of her magic wand, *La reina* Roxanne had provided Adán and Cenobia with correct sizes and fashion choices.

When Adán saw a king at the door, he nearly choked on his *canela*.

Roman swallowed his disgruntlement while he slapped Adán on the back.

Mateo grinned like a card shark who'd just won a round.

Adán was given the place of honor in the front seat of Mateo's Mercedes G-Class, and as they drove through the valley, passing mile after mile of vineyards, the bare, twisted vines resting after a season of growing the world's best Tempranillo grapes, Mateo pointed out the improvements that had been possible with Cenobia's long-ago loan.

He drove them past the airport, now a sleek hub, with improved runways that allowed them to welcome more tourists in and ship more wine and grapes out; the village's primary, secondary and upper secondary schools, all updated buildings; and the recently christened *Camino del Vino*, a winding road with new wineries, many of which were funded by low-interest microloans Cenobia had offered Monte vineyard owners after *Princesa* Sofia had revived the kingdom's wine scene. He spoke about infrastructure improvements that made the kingdom's energy and water use more efficient, updates not easy when trying to preserve centuries-old granite buildings and streets, as well as changes to the tithe system that made it more like modern-day, reasonable tax collection.

With every improvement, he pointed out Roman's contribution. Roman had overseen the dispersal, use, and repayment of every *centavo* of her money and had been an important advisor to Mateo before he wore the ring. But he'd also gotten involved in his own way. He'd streamlined airport security and updated training, insured that the schools had the best of appropriate safety measures and technology, and regularly worked with the *Policía Local* and castle guards to train them on policing justly, without bias, and with physical deterrence as the last resort.

"He's the reason this road is as flat as the horizon," Mateo said with a grandiose motion out his windshield. "When he didn't like the grade, he pulled the blade operator out of the cab and ran the tractor himself."

Cenobia grinned at Roman sitting next to her in the back seat.

"Worked on a road crew during my summers in high school," Roman muttered.

She had a blinding vision of a deeply tanned and lush-lipped young Roman sweating in the shimmer of Texas asphalt.

"Cici, Cici, *mira, mira*," Adán suddenly yelled, sounding all of five as he pointed out his window.

She instantly saw the sign he was pointing at. It was beautifully painted on tile, mounted on a stone shelter built as a refuge for a traveler or a resting spot for a vineyard worker. An image of the Mexican flag was surrounded by painted grapes and leafy vines. Ruta Trujillo was written in curlicue script. Mateo braked at the intersection. Down the road, Cenobia could see a large manor home set back among the vines.

"This used to be called Ruta Carrero," Mateo said as he looked out Adan's window. "The Carreros were among the Monte's earliest settlers, but when our father was done with them, they were out of time, patience, and money. I could offer them change, but not soon enough. They were about to sell their land and lose hundreds of years of history. The Trujillo loan allowed them to hold on."

Adán looked back at her from the front seat, his blue-grey eyes sparkling happily.

"They were the biggest proponents of naming the new bridge after the Trujillos, but after your father—" Mateo shook his head. "I mean, after Cenobia resisted, they felt this was the least they could do."

There was no shortage of buildings with her name on it. But Ruta Trujillo christened something she and

Roman had accomplished together and showed her son how their wealth could be used to balance the scales of an increasingly fraught world where those in power used it to harm instead of help.

This was the first time she'd allowed herself to feel the burning bright beam of her son's admiring gaze.

Mi hijo.

She'd already decided to tell Adán sooner than later that she was his mother. But witnessing Bartolo's despair at the belief that he'd lost his chance to reveal his love fully and finally understanding her father's reluctance to support her had slid so many pieces into place. Her father couldn't bend Cenobia or her world into an alignment that never hurt her, and Cenobia couldn't engineer some kind of perfect reveal that mitigated all of Adán's pain. But she loved him, she'd always wanted him in her life—no matter how much evidence she'd established to the contrary—and he deserved the truth.

She didn't want her son growing up banging his head against an impossible-to-understand question the way she had.

Roman's open-hearted acceptance of what she'd been afraid to tell anyone, especially him, a man whose every step was honor bound, had freed her from one of her chains. But she was still terrified. The truth was that she'd lied to this innocent child his whole life. He could condemn her. Once she was revealed as his mother, others would put together his timeline with her infamous kidnapping and make assumptions about his conception.

There would be repercussions. For her. For Adán.

But it was time to come out from behind her walls.

Roman said he'd be there for them. How long, she didn't know.

But she shook off that million-dollar question—for now—and smiled back at Adán, allowing herself to enjoy the complex and glorious joy of the words *my son, mi hijo.* She would give him a couple of days in this kingdom he'd talked about dreamily, a couple of days as a child who could fantasize about being a knight and rescuing a princess from a dragon, before she made him too old, too quick.

When Mateo pulled through a tall, granite archway and into the Castillo del Monte courtyard, Adán's eyes were as big as saucers. Standing to greet them in the wide-open space decorated in the Moorish style with checkerboard gravel pathways, potted trees, and mosaic-tile covered fountains were *la Reina* Roxanne Medina, her longtime bodyguard and now head of castle security, Henry Walker, and Liliana and Gabriel Esperanza y Medina, the next *princesa y príncipe* of the Monte del Vino Real.

They were all bundled up in luxurious winter coats, and Cenobia couldn't thank them enough for the welcome they were creating for Adán on this blustery winter day.

Adán bowed when Mateo introduced him to the beautiful queen. Roxanne, who seldom stood on formality, nodded her head majestically then declared that the kingdom would be honored if Adán considered it his second home.

When the stunned expression on her son's face forced Cenobia to turn away to hide her tears, Roman gave her one of his rare, gruff smiles.

The tawny-haired girl and dark-haired boy, both with abundant curls and gorgeous lashes, wanted nothing to do with formality. When Adán tried to bow to them, they immediately latched on and dragged him off to explore the castle. After a hug, Roxanne told Cenobia that their much-loved nanny Helen was waiting inside to prevent them from getting into too much trouble.

Now, the adults were gathered in Roman's castle office, brainstorming how Cenobia could reclaim her company while keeping everyone safe.

"One theory is that the attack on the Trujillo compound was staged to push Cenobia into hiding and disrupt the car launch," Roman said in his deep, low drawl. He wore dark grey jeans, a nearly black shirt, and a matching tie tucked into a grey wool vest that fit his torso like a dream. Leaning back against his desk with his sleeves rolled up and ankles crossed, he still looked as imposing as a four-star general. "Kidnapping Adán would have kept Cenobia distracted right when we were heading back, but the attempt felt like it was performed by the B team. They didn't have enough manpower, their positioning was wrong, and they didn't have the alarm specs. Every other attack was perfectly planned and executed with inside info. This was a hot mess."

"You engaged with the attacker," Henry said in a lazier Texas drawl. "Catch any clues to his identity?" The large blond American wasn't as fit as the brothers, but those linebacker shoulders were still wider than his plush middle. Henry had recently married Bodega Sofia's barrel maker, and Cenobia hoped they were enjoying lavish meals and long days in bed.

"He had a Spanish accent," she offered.

The crevice between Roman's brows dug in deep. "Or was he faking a pretty decent Spanish accent? Did anything about it sound off to you?"

Cenobia had worn a navy-blue Chanel dress, a cream

cashmere cardigan, pearls, and a high ponytail. She rubbed the silk skirt against her knees as she thought back. She remembered the red-hot urgency to get to Adán, the instinctive response to the gun, her fear about Bartolo's condition, and her wonder over what he revealed. She remembered her surprise, later, that she hadn't dissociated. "I think the gleam of that knife wiped away everything else," she said apologetically.

He moved toward her chair, stroked two fingers under her chin so she had to look up at him. "You did good; you remember that," he ordered, furrowed green eyes looking into hers. "You relied on your training and kept that situation from getting away from us. I've had years to practice observing and recording during action. You haven't."

The touch of his fingers felt hot and commanding against her skin. She couldn't hide her reaction to his touch, saw him register it, too. His mouth softened and she knew he was about to lick that fabulous bottom lip.

"Yes," Roxanne said, coughing politely. "I've read that eyewitness error is one of the leading causes of wrongful convictions."

Roman let go of her chin and backed up to his desk.

Roxanne and Mateo were sitting on a brocade love seat, his arm loosely draped around her. They were a queen and king on the verge of forty: one, a CEO with headquarters on four continents, and the other, one of the leading agricultural scientists in the world. They'd been married for a decade. And yet they watched Cenobia and Roman with the bitten-back grins of children.

They looked like they were about to taunt "sitting in a tree."

La reina Roxanne nudged her husband before she

said, "Maybe the outrage over the Mexico attack has spooked someone," she said, shaking back her brown hair, cut chic and blunt just below her shoulders. In her black pencil skirt and cream heels, she looked like a Latina Aphrodite after she clambered out of her shell, got dressed, and headed into the office. "Maybe all the players aren't as aligned as they once were, so they're working with fewer resources."

Roman nodded. "I contacted Glori to check something for me."

"You contacted Glori?" Cenobia asked, relieved. She knew there'd been a moment when Roman worried that his second-in-command was the leak.

"This morning," he said. "I'm hopin' we're about to get to the bottom of this thing."

Why did the clench of his brow and the purse of his mouth say he wasn't happy about it?

"I have to connect with my company immediately, though," she said, hating to pull him in twelve directions but having no choice. "If Vasquez torpedoes this launch, we won't be able to make back the losses."

"You can use our studio to make an announcement today," Roxanne said, leaning back and crossing her long legs.

Three deep voices immediately objected.

"I don't think…"

"We gotta…"

"Let's weigh our options before…"

Roxanne put up a hand. "Gentlemen." Cenobia recognized the move from her own board meetings. "You've worked tirelessly over the last ten years to make the Monte del Vino Real secure. This is the low season. We have few tourists, one major road kept clear of snow coming into the valley, one train station, and one air-port with two incoming flights a day. Right now, it is as close to a fortress as you could want. Let's put that fortress to use making sure she doesn't lose her com-pany. We owe her that much."

Cenobia sucked in a breath. "No, you don't owe me anything. Certainly not the security of your family or your people."

"We'll be fine," Roxanne said, turning her chocolate-brown, thickly lashed eyes on Cenobia. "That's what I'm trying to point out to these chest-thumping lunk-heads." Her warm smile said how much she loved the lunkheads. "They lose all logic when they're worried. But letting what you've built crumble without your in-tervention is not an option for you, any more than it would be for me or them in the same situation. I trust the security measures they've put into place. Roman, you have to trust yourself the way we trust you."

If Cenobia hadn't spent so much time staring fasci-nated at his face, she might have missed the tiny tics as he worked to keep his expression neutral. But the delicate jump of muscle in his jaw, the small furrow that appeared then instantly smoothed between his eyes touched a tremor in her. Pointed out a truth she hadn't understood. All of Roman's quiet denials—his reluc-tance to accept his role in the kingdom, his inability to understand how much his family needed him, and his insistence on claiming failures as "his" but never owning successes—they were because her warrior, her prince, the savior of humans, didn't trust himself.

He had confidence in his abilities, his gifts, as his mother had called them. But not in who he innately was. And that made him want to reject the family that put faith in him.

As if verifying her world-quaking realization, Roman said, "I should've fixed this already." His gravelly voice fell to the floor. "I'm sorry."

His response made her want to put her arms around him. Then give him a smack. Why couldn't he see himself as the miracle that he was?

"*Joder*," Mateo muttered, sounding as upset as she felt and more weary as he looked out the ancient leaded window. "You're not an island. If something needs fixing, we can help fix it."

Apparently, any reluctance the king had to the queen's plan had been cleared up by his brother's resistance.

Roxanne quickly squeezed her husband's knee and then stood. "We CEOs are going to work out how Cenobia's going to take back her company. You boys figure out how to keep her safe doing it."

She flourished a hand at Cenobia. "Shall we?"

Cenobia hesitated. She didn't want to abandon him.

But Roxanne gave her a look that said, *Trust me.*

Out in the hallway, after she'd closed the heavy door on the still-silent room, Roxanne whispered. "It's going to be all right. It's better if we leave." They began to walk, their heels tapping against the ancient terracotta tile. "They can *machismo* it out. Sometimes they have to punch each other before they hug and cry."

Cenobia stopped. "They're going to punch each other? I don't want to cause any—"

Roxanne tugged her forearm to get her walking again. "It's not you. This has been building for years; I'm glad they're finally getting a chance to clear the air." She sighed. "If I didn't have an excuse to leave, I might have taken a shot at Roman."

They walked under a ceiling decorated with beautiful dime-sized tiles, passed suits of armor and through archways shaped into the Moorish U. *La reina* Roxanne certainly seemed bloodthirsty enough to stroll the halls of a medieval castle.

Cenobia caught the women grinning at her, her smile a lush, glistening red.

"The shot you took hit its mark," Roxanne purred, hooking her arm through Cenobia's as they walked.

Cenobia was at a loss how to reply. She'd been eighteen and another person the last time she'd talked about her love life with girlfriends.

"Thank God you had lots of practice overcoming insurmountable odds," Roxanne said. "Roman wanted you, but he would have ripped out his tongue before admitting it."

"You knew?" Cenobia asked, surprise making her artless.

"Suspected," she said. "Then when you walked off that plane and announced *you'd* been the person behind the loan all along…" Roxanne's eyes widened scandalously as she pressed a hand to her chest. "That bit of drama made me miss my younger years. You'd finally found a chink in the armor of my impenetrable brother-in-law."

An intimate, enthusiastic Roxanne Medina was a thing to behold.

"That wasn't my intention."

"Sweetie, I'm thrilled," Roxanne said, patting her arm. "You're the first thing he's wanted that he's allowed himself to touch."

Cenobia dropped her eyes to the tile. "I feel like I've been chasing after him like a fan hungry for an autograph."

Roxanne's pat became a rub. "If it's any consolation, his brother was the same way," she said, softer. "I handed him my heart on a silver platter, and even then, he almost screwed it up."

They'd stopped walking. Roxanne faced Cenobia, looking at her, considering. Finally, she said in an almost-whisper, "You know you're going to have to tell him you love him. He won't say it first."

There was no use denying it. Cenobia's love for Roman felt as obvious as the clothes she wore, followed her into a room just like her favorite perfume. Of course, this genius of a woman would figure it out.

"I've faced a lot," Cenobia said, as quietly as she could. "Telling him I love him is still one of the scariest things I can imagine."

Roxanne gave her a heart-filled smile. "I know." This self-made billionaire, this woman who'd built herself up from humble beginnings then risked her whole self by admitting her love for a prince, did indeed know. "Please believe me. It's worth it."

The *reina* was like a glowing beacon of joy, an advertisement for wedded bliss. But if Roman maintained his penchant for self-denial with her?

"Let's bullet point it out," Roxanne said. "One CEO to another. If you don't tell him, you deny yourself a lifetime of access to that body."

Cenobia startled at Roxanne's mildly lecherous grin.

"I'm married, not blind," she smirked. Then her smile dimmed. "You go back to Mexico and live lonely. Or you find a man half as good, knowing he's going to love you a tenth as well."

She sobered completely and squeezed both of Cenobia's biceps. "And you abandon one of the best men in the world to his worst tendencies."

Roman, alone and lonely. There was no justice in the world if her warrior prince was cursed to that life.

"I told myself I wouldn't hide anymore," Cenobia whispered.

"Then don't," Roxanne said, her hold on Cenobia's biceps feeling valuable and fortifying. "The risk *is* scary. But the rewards are…"

For the first time, this titan of a woman fell speechless, unable to find the words as she searched for them in the air and looked around this castle hall where she was queen. She focused back on Cenobia with a helpless smile and tears in her beautiful, brown eyes.

The jarring scrape of stone against stone and then giggles behind a suddenly moving tapestry surprised them both. They quickly wiped their eyes then Cenobia watched, astonished, as Adán came out from behind the precious fabric carrying Liliana on his back, followed by Gabriel and an older women who must have been their nanny, Helen. The solemn-faced woman was impressively intimidating even though she was covered, like the children, in cobwebs.

"Mamá!" Liliana exclaimed, startled, her hazel-green eyes wide.

"Liliana?" Roxanne replied, her eyes narrowing.

"She tripped and she fell and she hurt her ankle," Gabriel chattered while Helen picked a crawling spider out of his dark-brown curls. "And Helen said she was okay but Liliana said she couldn't walk so Adán said he'd carry her."

Helen and Roxanne exchanged a look.

"*Sí*, I'm fine now," Liliana added quickly, all skinny

legs and arms as she clambered off Adán's back and hopped down on her sneakers without even twinge. "*Muchas gracias*, Adán."

He smiled at her and gave a bow. He'd worn khaki trousers and a white shirt which Roman had helped him pair with navy suspenders embroidered with tiny, snow-capped mountains. Adán had taken to rolling up his shirtsleeves like Roman.

"*De nada, princesita*," he said, shoving his wavy curls out of his slate-grey eyes as he smiled down at her. "And thank you for showing me those *chulada* tunnels."

Adán spoke to the princess with all of the gentle condescension of an almost-teenager.

Liliana looked up at him with eyes that were wide and soft, full of rainbows and pink hearts.

"Wanna see the throne room?" Gabriel asked, blissfully unaware.

"Yeah!" Adán replied like the child that he was.

The two boys ran off. Liliana wandered to Helen, folded her fingers through the older woman's, and followed behind, slow and dreamily.

Roxanne gave a wild-eyed look to Cenobia. "Oh my God. What was that?"

Cenobia shrugged. "I don't know. I don't know if that's happened to him before."

"That's never happened to her before!" Roxanne said. She ran a hand into her hair. "*Joder*."

Cenobia laughed gently. It was reassuring that *la reina* didn't have an answer to everything. She echoed Roxanne's earlier move and wound a supportive arm through hers.

"First, let's figure out how to save my company," she said as they started down the hallway after the children. "Then we'll discuss how to muddle through puberty."

Chapter Twenty-One

Monte del Vino Real, Spain

By that evening, they had a plan.

As always, Roxanne had been right. If they ramped up security personnel and technology to the high-alert summer level, they could use the benefits of winter and the way it funneled entry into the Monte to monitor the few people who came in through the handful of routes still available. Personal security for each family member, as well as the castle and Roman's home, would be beefed up. And guards would relaunch the summer protocol of patrolling the natural tunnels that ran beneath the limestone foundation of the Monte. Once a security sieve, the tunnels were now gated and equipped with cameras and sensors.

Anyone looking to hurt Cenobia Trujillo after she enacted her own plans tomorrow would run into the millennia-old walls of the Monte's snow-covered mountains and the twenty-first-century threat of Roman's talents.

Tomorrow, with the launch of La Primera barely a week away, things would begin moving very fast. Especially if the information Roman was waiting for from Glori turned out the way he expected.

Tonight, his sister Sofia had prodded gently once she joined them, they should enjoy Cenobia and Adán's company. The kids had already come up with their own plan, descending on the adults with three sets of puppy-dog eyes asking for a castle sleepover with Adán. Henry, who as head of castle security technically reported to Roman, promised the adults he'd spend the night there as well. Cenobia, with a gentle smile on her son, had nodded in approval.

Which was why Roman now found himself in a small rock-walled dining room in the wine caves beneath Bodega Sofia, his sister's winery in an ancient monastery, watching from under his eyelids as Cenobia charmed the living pants off his family.

"Now I'm teetering at the top of a twenty-five-foot pole in front of my entire executive team, expected to jump and grab this trapeze bar, and I realize, for the first time in three decades, that I am terrified of heights," she exclaimed, her eyes wide and capturing the candlelight, her wide smile slicked in some glistening color that reflected the overhead chandelier, her capable hands flaring out with her storytelling. She had the other six people at the round, linen-covered table roaring. "I'd just been too busy to figure it out before. I was stuck there in an orange hard hat and with a harness up my *culo* for twenty minutes. Some *pendejo* had to climb up and help me down."

"Oh no," Sofia said, gasping, using her linen napkin to wipe the makeup from under her eyes.

"It takes real *huevos* to wear construction orange in front of your employees," said Carmen Louisa, Bodega

Sofia's winery manager and a dear family friend that Mateo and Sofia had grown up with. In her early fifties, she'd brought as her date the new young chef of one of the Monte's long-established restaurants. She'd purposefully ignored Roxanne and Sofia's significant glances.

Roman had always admired how the swaggery, gorgeous vineyard owner lived life by her own rules.

"My people don't even get to see me if my manicure is aging," Roxanne said as she leaned back to hold her laughing husband's hand.

Cenobia picked up her wine goblet. "And that is why I will never again volunteer to go first."

"Wait, wait, wait," Sofia's husband, Aish said. The rock star's shoulder-length black hair was falling into his eyes and he was leaning in his chair toward Cenobia, giving her his dimpled half smile that made Roman's trigger finger itch.

He loved his brother-in-law. Really.

"You stepped up and saved the Monte's ass. Now you're attempting in Mexico what's never been done. And you say you don't go first?"

Cenobia primly put down her wineglass while she gave Aish her own dimpled grin. "Well…in matters of team building."

"And harnesses," Roxanne said.

"And heights," said Carmen Louisa, raising her glass in agreement.

Sofia put her chin in her hand and looked at her husband, her tawny-brown hair trailing over one shoulder. "There are many situations in which women don't mind going first," she purred, smile growing wide and sensual.

Mateo and Roman gave twin sounds of horror then

Mateo looked sideways into the dark depths of the wine cave. "I'm blind," he announced, palms up, blinking exaggeratedly. "Where have you gone?"

As Roxanne, Sofia, and Carmen Louisa jeered, prodded, and threw their linen napkins at him, Roman turned to meet Cenobia's eyes. She gave him a shy, sweet smile. Yes. She was having a good time.

He worked to keep his face easy and relaxed, to keep his hands lazily folded on the table, rather than gripping the carved arms of the dining chair. Or grabbing her. Roman wasn't drinking. But he felt drunk on her. Starving for his Cen.

Cenobia's mass of hair was in an easy ponytail, and she was wearing a cashmere sweater in camel, a black wool skirt, and suede high boots, a good winter-weather outfit for a woman used to Mexican heat. But the sweater hung to the very edge of her shoulders and crossed across her breasts, hugging her in cloudlike softness while revealing her glistening clavicles and the sleek dark skin of her chest. The wool skirt that covered her knees had a slit up the back, to the middle of her thighs. And the boots were stiletto-heeled and fit her strong calves—calves he knew the taste of, calves that had squeezed across his back as she'd come—like a glove.

As he sat next to this funny, smart, engaging woman who was charming the people he loved most and wearing a comfy outfit that asked to be ripped off of her, he couldn't let go of the awareness that when they went home tonight, it would be just the two of them. No one would be down the hall or patrolling just outside the door.

Tonight, for the very first time, they would be completely alone.

Feeling sweat under the crew neck of his fitted black

sweater, Roman leaned forward to take off his olive-green tweed jacket when he realized everyone at the table was looking at him. He straightened. He'd missed something while he was lusting over Cenobia.

"Sorry," he said, looking around "What's that?"

Carmen Louisa's date, Cristóbal, nodded. He was blond, blue eyed, and in his midtwenties. His family had run the same restaurant in the Monte's plaza for several generations, and he'd just returned from a prestigious spot in a Barcelona Michelin-starred restaurant to take over his family's kitchen.

"I was asking about your plans for *Nochebuena*," Cristóbal said. "Cenobia mentioned it had been some time since she'd enjoyed a Christmas with snow. The procession in the Monte is beautiful after *La Misa de Gallo* when the townspeople leave the chapel and walk the streets singing and carrying torches."

Roman said, "I'm not sure what her plans—" at the same moment Cenobia sighed, "That sounds wonderful."

They both stopped.

Cenobia recovered first, stuttering, "Not that... Yes, I don't know what I'm going to be..." as Roman felt the not-so-subtle glares of his sister and sister-in-law.

Mateo jumped in, all Spanish-cool with his pushed back wavy hair and soft linen scarf around his neck. "Then this is a formal invitation for you and your family to come spend the holidays with us at El Castillo," he declared, raising his glass. The others followed suit. "This year and any year to come."

As they all toasted, Cristóbal offered Roman a chagrined look of apology. He thought, as everyone at this table assumed, that Roman and Cenobia were together.

Roman had promised to stand by her, to offer her his sword and his shoulder. But she had her family to spend the holidays with. And Roman had his duties.

He leaned toward her. "I'll probably be in Florida," he said, meeting her eyes. He couldn't help the note of apology in his voice.

But while she gave him a steady look and an answering nod, his sister asked, *"¿Qué?"* sharply from across the table. Roman looked to see both of his siblings stabbing him with their eyes.

Fuck. "We got a lot of people booked for the Sheppard Security winter camp. Clients like to do their survival training over the break. I'm helping out this year."

His coordinator didn't know that. But now was as good a time as any for him to draw a line for what his future relationship with Cenobia would be. Hell, it was past time for him to be drawing one with his family. He'd be back in the Monte, straight after the camp, to get to work. But he'd spent the last three Christmas seasons here. It was a bad habit to get into.

If God ever answered a single one of his prayers, He was doing it now as their servers knocked on the room's heavy wooden door. Roman stood and pulled out Cenobia's chair, offered her his arm as Mateo's bright, brown-gold eyes caught his. They were going to be talking about this later.

He led Cenobia to a small nook shielded by a screen in the back of the room where they were hidden from the servers, a privacy tactic Bodega Sofia had developed for some of their famous guests. Roman himself had designed and redesigned the security for Bodega Sofia, and they trusted the staff. But if they wanted complete confidence that they were keeping Cenobia and Adán's location a secret until she revealed her plans, then extra precautions were best. The servers were to stay together and no one else would be down in these tunnels while Roman's family was dining.

From his spot shielding her, Roman watched a parade of staff delivering the third course: a pan of paella the size of a spotlight and a variety of side dishes.

Cenobia tugged on his jacket and leaned toward him.

"I'm sorry about that," she murmured, her velvety eyes looking into his.

"Don't be," he whispered. "I'm a jackass." He was making the right call for his mission and for her. But how else would you describe a man who wasn't stumbling over himself to make her Christmas bright?

"No, you're not," she urged, her eyebrows crinkling. "We'll—" she smiled helplessly, fluttering her hands in the air "—figure it out."

She was the sweetest tidal wave, and it would be so easy to let himself drown in her open arms, her powerful desire, her surety about him.

It would be so easy, so dangerous, and such a betrayal.

The servers left the room and he led her back to the table.

Rather than taking her seat, Cenobia picked up her purse. "Don't let anyone serve me clams," she said, wrinkling her nose. "I'll be right back."

He watched her walk toward the door—watched the naked top of her back and her swaying hips and her crisscrossing, suede-covered calves—tug it open and step out. He checked his Tag Heuer, noting the time.

Exactly one hundred and twenty seconds later, with

everyone starting to dig in, Roman stood. "Be right back," he said, ignoring Sofia's knowing look.

He closed the door behind him as he stepped out into the dim stone hallway, soft lighting from black iron finials lighting the way but just barely. Cenobia was safe here, he reminded himself. No one was else was going to be down in these tunnels. Still, it was easy to lose your way.

When he turned the corner and saw her marveling at an ancient mechanical winepress, the worry he told himself he hadn't been feeling eased. His sister had set up wine-tasting tables throughout these atmospheric, historic tunnels and this one, nestled in a small alcove with dramatic uplighting, had screw pegs as wide as his hands holding up giant gears as a tabletop. Six seats made from old wine barrels surrounded it.

"It's amazing the mechanisms humans were able to create before modern technology," she said as he approached her.

He couldn't help himself. He put his hand on her hip, the wool soft and warm. "People'll go to a lot of trouble for their alcohol."

She straightened, smiling, and rubbed her hands up his cashmere-covered chest. "I was waiting for you."

"You were?" he asked, squeezing her waist with both hands.

"You look painfully handsome." She hooked her hands around his neck and leaned against him. "I love spending time with your family but I wish we could've stayed home."

Fuck. *Home.*

Sitting next to him, she'd been thinking what he'd been thinking. Wanting what he wanted. He tugged her back with him, a step into the alcove, a little deeper into the shadows.

"We could…uh…" He licked his mouth, and, hell, the way she watched. "We could leave."

Her eyes widened. "We can't do that."

He slowly turned her, his hands gripping her waist, and she moved with him smoothly on her stiletto heels like they were dancing. "I'll text them," he murmured, walking them into the dark. He could feel the softness of her breath against his lips. "They'll understand."

"But we shouldn't," she said as her fingers combed into his hair.

"Do you want to?" he asked, his thumbs dipping under her sweater.

She breathed against his mouth.

"Yes."

In this, he could give her what she wanted.

He stretched an arm across her from waist to neck to protect her from the cold stone wall and pressed her back, held her head in his hand to take her mouth, wholly, wetly and with all the need building in him. She pushed her hands under his sweater and ran palms and fingers over his abs and around his back, scratching her nails and sending electricity over his skin. He throbbed against her. His world began to narrow to the thought of that slit at the back of her skirt and how easy it would make raising the wool to her hips, hoisting her up, and showing her what a tasting table could be good for. No one else was down here, and no one from his family would dare come looking. They were all alone. They had all night. He could pleasure her here and in the car and in the living room and then, by the time he carried her to his bed, by the time he slid inside her, she would know how good a good man could make it for her.

She would know how precious her pleasure was.

His hand was reaching for the bottom of her skirt when he realized that they were being watched.

No one was supposed to be down here.

He slid his mouth to her ear. "Stay relaxed. Someone's in the hall. I'll take care of you."

He made his murmur sound like love words, kept his shoulders easy, did nothing to telegraph his intentions. He raised his head slowly.

Then he shoved her into a crouch and bolted out of the alcove and across the hall where he grabbed the neck of a man spying on them from behind a wine armoir and slammed him back against the stone wall. Something clattered to the ground.

"Who are you with?" Roman roared, pulling the man forward then slamming him back again, hard enough to stun him. Roman patted him down with one hand, looking for a weapon.

Nothing.

The man's throat was a fragile thing in Roman's grip.

No one was supposed to be down here. He thought he'd locked these tunnels down. He kept fucking up and someone kept threatening his woman.

He pulled him forward to snarl into his face. "I could do this all day. Now who the fuck are you with?"

The man was nondescript, midthirties, wearing a Bodega Sofia staff shirt. Gasping.

If Roman hadn't come looking for Cenobia, this man would have been alone with her.

Roman's hand squeezed tighter.

"Goddamn it, tell me…"

He suddenly felt the stiletto point of a boot pressing meaningfully into the soft flesh behind his knee. "Roman." Cenobia's voice sounded like it was coming from the other end of the tunnel.

His name was echoing in the hall. She'd said it a few times.

"Roman, I think he's an employee. Look down; he dropped his phone. He was about to post a video of us. He's going to be in a lot of trouble, but he's not working with them."

Once, three days into a mission, Roman had taken refuge in a building to get some sleep on a concrete floor. He'd woken from a horrible nightmare to the sounds of incoming 120 mm mortar, the building exploding all around him, and his hand on fire. This felt like that moment, waking from a nightmare into a nightmare.

Cenobia had come face-to-face with what had scared his mama. And she'd had to threaten him to stop him.

"What's happening?" Mateo said, shocked, from the end of the hall.

Roman shoved the gibbering, sobbing man into the corner and picked up his fallen phone. The lit-up screen showed the beginning of a social media post. In the thumbnail image, Roman and Cenobia were pressed together.

When Roman moved toward the man, Cenobia stepped between them.

"What's going on?" Mateo asked behind Roman's shoulder.

Roman met Cenobia's eyes. She looked back at him squarely. Undaunted. Whatever he wanted to do to the man was not going to go unobserved.

"Get Sofia," Roman told Mateo, not shying away from Cenobia's eyes. "Tell her to bring her security chief. This asshole just ruined dinner."

The man was going to lose his job and pay a hefty fine for violating his confidentiality agreement.

But Roman had been as unsuccessful hiding in the shadows as the man had been.

Cenobia had seen what his mama had been afraid of. What he'd channeled into war and protection. What he'd restrained within the boundaries of his path for the safety of everyone around him.

As brave as his mama, she'd refused to look away from the truth of what he was.

His time with her was over.

Chapter Twenty-Two

Monte del Vino Real, Spain

It seemed to take years to talk to the security chief, reassure Roman's family that she was fine, endure the silent drive with him up the mountain, check in with security at the bottom of his long driveway, then finally, finally, walk into Roman's home.

Venga, she wanted to urge like the impatient twelve-year-old she'd been when she watched a car accelerate on the test track, anxious to see if her prototype engine could perform the way she believed it could. *Let's go.*

Her impatience and her confidence in its urgency had grown exponentially since she was twelve. The instant Roman flipped on the lamps with amber shades in his living room, she stepped in front of him.

"What are you thinking?" she demanded.

She'd changed in the three weeks since she'd stood in his office with her heart in her throat and her palms sweaty, wandering around his office instead of looking dead on at the warrior prince who'd become more blindingly magnificent than even her active imagination could have dreamed.

He kept his hands in his pocket, his beautiful eyes

on the ground. With his dark, perfectly styled hair and
rough olive tweed suit over his chest-defining sweater,
he looked like a bruiser dressed for a press conference.

"Cenobia," he grumbled.

"Talk to me."

Roman would discover that Texas recalcitrance was
no match for fiery-eyed Guachichil bullheadedness.

"It's late." He started to turn away. "We should go
to bed."

"Together?"

He stiffened and finally did look at her, a quick look
over his shoulder. Cenobia felt a drip of panic enter her
bloodstream. His glance carried the shame and guilt that
she hadn't seen since he'd finally admitted how much,
how long, he'd wanted her.

She refused to allow her vibrant warrior prince fade
once again into a man she only knew through emails
and glamorous pictures. She refused to be his warrior
queen he guiltily googled every six months.

"You think you reacted rashly," she said, on his heels
as he tried to move away. "You think seeing you as
the aggressor should scare me." His massive shoulders
flinched as she followed him across the rugs and wood
of his living room. "You think your job is something
people you care about shouldn't be exposed to."

Panic strengthened her spine. She didn't believe he
would rather spend his Christmas in a Florida swamp.
And she didn't believe that he would rather live without her. She'd been a fool back in Kansas when she'd
told herself that she could make love to him and then
let him go, if that's what he demanded. She'd fought
for everything that was important to her. She would
fight for him, too.

"You think people you care about will get hurt by what you do."

He spun on her, his bright eyes blazing ferociously, making her aware of his size and width in the narrow alley of space between his stone wall and a low slim table that she'd corralled them into.

"Won't they?" he growled into her face, drawl thick with frustration. "You saw what I did to a defenseless hotel worker. You want that near your son?" He splayed the back of his hands. "You want me touching you with these knowing what they can do?"

She grabbed his hands and pressed them against the plentiful skin revealed above her sweater. "Yes, I do."

He tried to tug his hands away and, damn him, she laced her fingers through his and anchored them against her chest, against her heart and heat. She could feel his burned skin. She could feel the thickness of the advisor ring.

"I saw you spot and neutralize a threat before it could hurt me," she said, trying to reach him through his eyes. "Were you angrier and more protective than you would have been under normal circumstances? Yes. But I'm not going to castigate you for it. You've put rules in place to protect your family, the staff who serve them, and the Monte's people equally. That man flaunted all of them."

She let him search her face, let him see the truth in it.

He squeezed her fingers. Then he yanked her close until her body pressed against his with their hands squeezed between their chests. He towered over, looked under his heavy lids down at her.

Suddenly her hold was his leather-scented trap.

"You had to threaten me with a hole punch through my knee to get me to stop," he growled.

If this was his tactic for scaring her off, he was going about it all wrong.

Especially when he allowed her to slip her hands from his so she could lean against his chest. Especially when he tugged her closer and made her feel safer with his hands on her arms.

"It wasn't a threat," she said, snuggling in. He was a hard wall of heat. "A reminder. You would've stopped in time."

His eyes narrowed in frustration. "You don't know that."

"Yes, I do." His fingers twitched on her shoulders as she let her smile grow slowly. "You want me more than you wanted that man's blood. And you've always maintained control with me, no matter how it ached."

She moaned "ached" with a pout in her lips like he'd taught her to, mimicked the way he teased her when he'd drawn out her pleasure until she begged for release.

His face was sculpted hunger inches from hers. "I was losin' control tonight, baby girl."

"You were?" she asked, simmering. "What did you have planned?"

She'd been astonished how fast he'd darted across the hallway to apprehend the man. Now she gasped as he spun her around just as quickly. She smacked her hands down on the waist-high table.

His big body bent to cover hers, becoming a blanket of dense, gorgeous-smelling heat as his hands trapped hers against the wood. "The slit up your skirt was driving me crazy," he said into her ear, vibrations traveling down her neck and to her peaked nipples.

One muscular arm, still in his tweed jacket, caught her around her waist. He stooped. Thick fingers tickled the back of her knee through her sheer black stockings.

His hot, hard palm began to rub up her thigh through the skirt slit. "All I could think about was the easy access you gave me." His hand's slow ride up her leg was hypnotic.

In front of her, through Roman's living room window, she had a perfect view of the fairy-tale village and castle.

Her blood pounded in her ears.

Halfway up her thigh, Roman's hand stopped.

"Cenobia?" The way he said her name caused an answering drip between her legs. "What are you wearin'?"

His hand was on the lacey elastic holding up her thigh-high stockings.

She leaned on her hands and eased her legs apart. "Tonight's our first night alone," she sighed.

She heard a *thunk* as Roman landed on his knees then felt one hard tug. The rip of the fabric was loud and shocking as he tore the skirt all the way up to the zipper. She moaned and arched her back, the pull of her ponytail heavy on her neck.

He groaned. The cool air of the living room caressed the curves of her bottom revealed by the black, lace, high-cut bodysuit.

His hand trembled against her skin as he gently traced the line of the lace.

"I'm gonna kill Roxanne," he growled.

Cenobia had to lean more of her weight on her hands to support her wobbly legs as he undid the zipper of her ruined skirt and tugged it down her hips. She could imagine what she looked like: high-heeled suede boots sleeking up her calves, sheer black stockings covering her to her thighs, brown curves revealed in black lace, a billowing sweater cuffing her waist and highlighting her shoulders.

The billionaire who'd stocked their closets had provided Cenobia an array of beautiful and sometimes shocking lingerie in slim, chocolate-brown boxes with gold script stacked in one dresser. This bodysuit was constructed with boning and held together with delicate lace that cupped her breasts.

He smoothed a hot, huge hand over her bottom.

"There are snaps between my…"

He squeezed that cheek. Not hard. But it got her lust-soaked attention. "I know how it works, Cenobia."

His hand gentled again and then he was rubbing both hands, so slowly, up her suede-covered calves, up her thighs and exploring the naked flesh, over her lace-covered bottom until she wiggled with the sensation, under her sweater and up, up her hips and waist as he rose to his feet, stroking the lace and boning, over her breasts where he pinched and rubbed her nipples, until he could pull the sweater over her head.

She was visibly vibrating with sensation when he turned her chin up to him. "All this?" he breathed against her mouth, his eyes crinkling beautifully at the corners as he stared into hers. "For me, sweet Cen? Don't waste yourself on me."

Her heart ached for him. Her hand holding his strong neck was the foundation they both needed right now. "It's not a waste. You act like the soldier in you dooms you to isolation. He doesn't." She squeezed the tendons of his neck, tendons that led to his world-bearing shoulders. "Roman, you do the work no one wants to.

You're good at it. But you're more than a man with a sword. Your focus on doing good and your resistance to the brutality proves that. I love the soldier, he saved me, but he's only one of a thousand aspects that I love about you."

His eyes widened. She knew what she'd said.

"I see you, Roman." She leaned up and kissed him gently. "I've always seen you. Just like you've always seen me. That's why I love you. That's why we're in love."

She would be brave enough for the both of them.

His face went absolutely brutal. "Jesus fucking Christ, Cen," he groaned, his hands singeing skin and lace as he ran them over her, tugged on her ponytail and pulled up her chin to devour her mouth.

The kiss flooded her with desire.

"Hold on," he growled into her ear; then all the spots he'd touched with his hands, he worshipped with his mouth: kisses down her neck and bites down her shoulder blades, teasing sucks to the lace over her nipples although he refused to let her turn around. He kept her bending over and back to him as his mouth traveled over the lace, his mouth plush and erotic even through fabric, his tongue delicious over her birthmark then across the prickled skin of her bottom.

One hand gently but resolutely pushed her forward until she was leaning over the table and across the back of the couch while the other hand carefully undid the snaps.

Dios mío.

He sounded like he was breathing prayers against her skin as he tucked the fabric out of the way. Cenobia widened her legs. "Good girl," he sighed, his hot breath touching her. "Good glistening girl…"

She'd thought, after all the ways he'd touched and

rubbed and kissed her during their days together in Kansas, that there were few surprises left. She'd thought wrong.

It was deliciously obscene to receive his kiss this way, feeling his nose, the long flat lick of his tongue, the drip of herself and him down her thighs, his willingness to kiss and taste and savor her everywhere. He pulled on her ponytail, made her arch her head up, told her he wanted to hear her, everything, all that he was doing to her.

Her weight was entirely resting on the table and in his hands, tears streaming down her face and her voice hoarse as he held her and feasted, when the pleasure edged back enough to let her think again.

Roman put her legs back on the ground and stood, pulling her up and back against him "I can't, Cen," he begged, cradling her lolling body, supporting her. "Not tonight, baby girl. I want to be gentle your first time. I gotta be gentle. And tonight… I want you so much…"

Only then did she realize that she'd been crying out for him to make love to her.

He pressed two fingers into her while he held her against his fully clothed body.

She opened her eyes as he began to move them inside.

"Bueno, querido," she said, looking into his eyes with the freedom of the love she was finally able to express. He would never hurt her. But she wanted him to trust himself the way she trusted him. "We'll take as long as you want. Just like you are. That's all I want. I want you just as you are."

Chapter Twenty-Three

Monte del Vino Real, Spain

By the end of the next day, Cenobia had firmly stepped out of the shadows.

First, she'd called her assistant, Paloma, who cried when she heard Cenobia's voice. Vasquez had demoted her and moved into Cenobia's office, but Paloma had managed to change Cenobia's password and secret away all of her personal and confidential files before he'd taken over. Cenobia swore her undying devotion and a fifty percent raise, then asked her to gather everyone still loyal. With the castle's elegant throne room as backdrop, she looked back at the eighteen women and men from upper-level management on the screen and skipped talking about the attacks against her, Vasquez's underhanded maneuvers, or the fact that it was the Trujillo name at the top of their paychecks. Instead, she reminded them of the vision that had gotten each and every one of them to devote themselves to this revolutionary idea. A vision of Mexicans seen globally as creators as well as makers, their ingenuity and engineering honored so that their innovators stayed home instead of taking their talents abroad. A vision of creating better transportation cheaper and cleaner for Mexicans. A vision of more Mexicans receiving a living wage.

We are days, hours, from seeing that vision bear fruit, she'd told them. *If you'll stick with me.*

Vasquez, she'd been pleased to discover, had yet to acquire all the votes to stop the gears of the La Primera launch. But he was close, willing to let the five cars in Frankfurt, the factory in Guanajuato, the millions of dollars invested, the thousands of woman-and-man hours spent, and the hundreds of workers dependent on a successful launch rust to nothing in his greed for power.

With eighteen votes of confidence and detailed next-step emails sent to each of them, Cenobia hoped to keep the gears moving forward.

Next, she called her father.

Her understanding of what he'd denied himself, her empathy for his motives, and the simple relief of hearing him healthy, worried, and desk-pounding had her breaking out into sobs that surprised them both.

"Mija...¿Qué pasa?" It reminded her of Bartolo's *mija*. All her life, they'd both strived to fix whatever was wrong.

She would never demand that he reveal himself. But in small steps, she could let him know that she loved and accepted him fully, and there was nothing he needed to hide from her.

"Nada," she said, wiping her nose. "I've missed you. What would I do without you wanting the best for me?"

That surprised him into silence. She told him that they suspected the attacks were a ruse to get her out of the way, and explained her plan to regain control of their company.

"If I am successful, my trial period will end," she said firmly. "I will be the permanent CEO of Trujillo Industries."

Rather than her father challenging her, which she'd prepared for, he sighed heavily. "Yes," he said. "But I wanted your life to be easier than this."

What an incredible, terrifying emotion it was to love your child.

"Papá, we are the Children of the Wind," she reminded him with tears in her eyes and a smile in her voice. "We're so good at fighting for what we believe in that we were the Spaniards' longest and most expensive war."

"Don't repeat your bedtime stories back at me," he harrumphed.

"That's right, *your* bedtime stories. How do you stuff a Guachichilean *and* a Trujillo into a little girl's body and expect her to want a calm and peaceful life? If I'd sought that, I would have denied what you and nature and history made me. And Papá, you know that denial makes for an unhappy life."

He was quiet for a very long time. Then he said. "Not entirely unhappy."

"I love you," she replied.

She told him about her decision to finally tell Adán that evening. This time, her father joined her in her tears.

Finally, she used Roxanne's PR resources to announce an immediate livestream. She touched up her makeup, then started the broadcast meant for her employees, investors, and the citizens of Mexico. First, she detailed the terrorism against her and her family, the sabotage against her factory, and the attack in Kansas.

Then she decried the hostile takeover while her family was hospitalized or running for their lives.

Even Roman, who was standing by the camera crew, looked surprised by the boldness of her tactic.

"I will hide no longer," she told the camera's black eye. "La Primera will launch in Frankfurt, and at long last, the world will see that the car that's caused so much fuss isn't fussy at all. It's affordable, eco-friendly, and understated. With its launch, I look forward to returning home."

Vengan, she aimed into the camera toward the people who wanted to hurt her. *Let's finish this.*

Roman had escorted her through the day with a gentleness as focused as the pleasure he'd pummeled her with the night before. She hadn't asked him to make love to her again, and he hadn't said he loved her. But she would take her time with him. This wasn't a fight she would win with one swift kick.

Anyway, she already knew he loved her.

If she'd needed proof, it was in the easy way he'd carried the load of the dinner conversation with Adán as they sat at the kitchen table, Cenobia too much of a bundle of nerves to be able to contribute much. He'd asked Adán about the sleepover and watching her son chatter happily about his night had almost made her delay, once again, what she had to tell him.

She hated the idea that she might curse his memories of this time in a fairytale kingdom.

But as she dried the last of the dishes, she knew that this was something she could not take more time with. She had to tell him tonight.

Roman suddenly strode into the kitchen holding a file folder. One look at his face had her heart pounding.

"What's wrong?" Cenobia asked quietly as she put the final dish in the drainer. Adán was in the living room but was playing his video game loud enough for them to talk.

"Glori went to the compound to check a hunch I had," Roman said, the furrow between his brows deep and worried. "The hunch turned out to be true."

He held the file folder out to her. "Adán was the leak," he whispered.

She shrank back from the folder like it was a desert *crótalo*, shaking its rattle at her. "No," she said firmly. "He couldn't…"

"He didn't know, not in the beginning," Roman said, soft but urgent. "By the time he realized, he was in too deep. He was afraid. Read."

With a trembling hand, Cenobia took the file folder from him. She turned away and opened it on the butcher-block island. With her hands clenched against the well-oiled wood, she began to read.

The messages were to an account she didn't recognize. As she read, she realized Adán had set up an account in a chat room using a VPN—a virtual private network—that allowed him to get around their internet security checks on his phone and computer.

Her son was certainly his mother's child, she thought with growing dread.

It was a chat room in one of his favorite online games, Swords of Mercy.

The first few messages from the handle "PazY-Guerra" were innocuous questions during game play, compliments about Adán's moves and choices. Over the course of a couple of weeks, they became more personal, offering information and asking about Adán's favorite food, size of his Pokémon collection, and then about Adán's school and life and family. After two months and almost daily communication, Adán brought up not having a mom.

Cenobia blinked back tears as she read. Adán never discussed his absent "mother." Daniel's friend had moved back to her family's estate in Chile.

PazYGuerra then told Adán who he "truly" was. He claimed to be a military operative who needed Adán's help to discover information related to "urgent national security." Information that could only be found on Daniel Trujillo's computer. Help him, PazYGuerra wrote, and he would share the true identity of Adán's parents.

Adán was not the son of Daniel Trujillo and his second wife, he told him.

Cenobia felt a shock of freezing cold. Did they truly know that Adán wasn't Daniel's son? Or was it merely a tactic to take advantage of a motherless boy? The person was using her deepest, most damaging secret as well as Adán's admiration for men like Roman Sheppard to manipulate a child.

Adán's responses went from furious denial to curiosity to confiding. He'd always wondered, he wrote, why his mother didn't love him.

Cenobia covered her eyes. She needed a moment. Roman would alert her if Adán was coming. He put his hand on her lower back. She didn't shrug him away, but neither did she invite him closer.

Then she wiped her eyes and continued reading.

His country needed Adán, PazYGuerra urged, jiggling the crowbar in the crack he'd found. No, Daniel had done nothing wrong. But the information would help all Mexicans. Did Adán owe loyalty to a family who'd never fully embraced him? Yes, Daniel had always loved him and always wanted a son and wanted to make him a true Trujillo, but it was Cenobia standing in Adán's way. Cenobia, PazYGuerra repeated, wanted to deny Adán a place in their family and company.

Ultimately, the person instructed Adán to install a code on his computer that would connect with the other computers in the house. He'd also requested a live, on-camera chat.

"The timestamp on that message is one week before you got the threat sent from the university library. The worm got into Daniel's machine, so they saw everything: security details of your home, email arguments about you ducking security to go to the shelters, updates from La Primera's factory manager," Roman said from behind her. "We don't know what was said in the live chats, but he apparently talked to Adán twice. We believe the live chat is when he told Adán to ask you to come to the compound."

Even with so much proof right in front of her, Cenobia still couldn't believe it. "No," she said. "Adán wouldn't have helped them…"

Roman came to her side and took her hand. She realized then she'd been frantically rubbing her ear lobe.

"Adán tried to end the relationship. He realized something bad was going on; he told him he didn't care who his true parents were. But PazYGuerra threatened to tell you and Daniel what Adán had done."

Cenobia's stomach rolled. Her poor, poor boy.

"That still doesn't explain the attack in Kansas," she said. "Adán had no way to tell them where we were."

"Look at the last page."

She flipped to the final message. It was in all caps.

"LEAVE US ALONE. I DON'T BELIEVE YOU. I NEVER SHOULD HAVE LISTENED TO YOU. YOU ALMOST KILLED MY DAD. MY DAD AND SISTER LOVE ME AND YOU CAN…"

Adán used an expression that a nun had once washed out of Cenobia's mouth.

At the top of each message was a timestamp and IP address. The timestamp was a few days ago, in the morning.

"Do you remember when Adán said he thought it was funny that all the computers in the library were named after me?"

Cenobia closed her eyes. The IP address would lead the attackers to the Freedom Library.

"I didn't catch it, either," Roman said gently. "Information about the lake house is hard to find, but not impossible. If they knew we were in the Freedom area, they could track us to the house."

"He was confused and angry," Cenobia said through a tight throat. She thought of how miserable Adán had been after Daniel had been shot. She thought of the weeks and weeks he'd been tormented by this mad man, a torment Cenobia could have prevented if she'd just been honest with him. "He knew *something* was wrong in our family, but not what."

Roman stepped close and pulled her hip against him. "I don't blame him, Cenobia," he said, his words urgent in her hair. "But we've got to find out what he knows."

"Let me tell him…who he is first," she begged, clenching his arm.

Roman looked troubled but nodded. "Do you want me to go in there with you?"

She shook her head. "No. I have to do this by myself. He needs the freedom to react however he wants to."

Roman rubbed his rough thumb across her cheek. "I'll be right here if you need anything."

She nodded and then turned before she lost her nerve and headed for the living room.

Adán's smile was sweet, but he was preoccupied with his video game when he glanced at her.

"*Mi amor*, I need to talk to you. Can you turn off the *tele*?"

He did as she asked, but when he looked at her again, she saw a shadow of fear fall over his fine, childish features, features just beginning their stretch into manhood. He could expect any kind of bad news: there'd been another attack against Daniel, Bartolo had taken a turn, they were forced to flee again. And he would blame himself.

She would do anything to free him from that crushing weight.

She sat next to him on the couch.

"Adán, what I am about to tell you is very difficult," she said, meeting his beautiful slate-blue eyes. She took a deep breath. She had to get control of her heart rate. "I have been lying to you, and I am very sorry. But my sorrow is not an excuse. My lie allowed someone to manipulate you into installing that code, and that is my fault."

Adán's eyes widened in horrified surprise, but she pulled his sweaty hand into her grasp and squeezed it between hers. "I love you, and you are not responsible for what has happened," she said urgently. "The only person to blame is me."

"Am I a Trujillo?" he demanded, high and wounded.

She fervently nodded her head and held on to her own emotions. "Yes, you *are* a Trujillo. You are our family. *Pero*, Daniel is not your father. He is your grandfather. I...I am your mother."

The words, stuck inside Cenobia for so long, felt like they had barbs that clung to her insides as they came out of her. She'd never been more afraid.

Adán ripped his hand from her hold and stared at her in stunned disbelief. Then he crushed his fist against his mouth, clenched his eyes shut like he couldn't stand the misery, and crumbled into weeping.

But he fell forward into Cenobia's lap.

She put her arms around him, hunched forward and protected him.

"*Lo siento...mi amor...* I love you..." she murmured as he cried and she cried, whispered words into his curls as she rocked him. "We all love you...none of this is your fault...*lo siento...* I'm so proud of you... I'm so sorry..."

They cried and they cried and they cried and his tears soaked her jeans.

An unknown amount of time passed. Still crying, his head still resting against her thigh, Adán croaked, "Why didn't you tell me? Were you ashamed of me?"

"Never," Cenobia said fiercely in his ear. "Never. I've always been so proud of you. I can't believe you came from me."

"But you never wanted to be around me," he cried, weeping harder.

She sniffed hard. She had to stop her tears. She had to give him some answers.

She stroked his silky, curly hair and squeezed his shoulder. "You know when you have a secret, the longer you hold on to that secret, the worse it feels? Adán, I was ashamed of *me*. Never you." She could feel his thin chest shuddering. "The longer I took to tell you, the more ashamed I felt. I want to explain *why* I took so long to tell you. But…but I'd like a family counselor there to help us. To help me. I want to make sure I answer your questions and don't hurt you more."

She'd spent his whole life denying them both so she could avoid telling him this fact of his conception. That would come to an end, it had to come to an end, the instant they were back in Guanajuato. But she wouldn't unload it on him now, not when her poor boy was already handling so much.

She gently lifted him from her lap so he was sitting, then looked into his tear-filled eyes. "I swear to you, I will answer all your questions. But until then, know this. You are joy and you are brightness and you are a blessing to me and our family. I'm sorry my lies ever made you think differently."

She would say it firmly and clearly now. She would say it tonight and tomorrow. She would say it if he slammed doors on her and she would say it if he allowed her to be part of his life. When they returned to Mexico, she would say it with the help of a family counselor, over and over again.

"I love you and I am honored to have been blessed with you in my life."

Adán tugged his hand from her. He used his palms to wipe his red nose and cheeks, then settled back against the couch cushions, looking down at his lap. Cenobia carefully settled back as well. And felt her heart grow three sizes when he tilted to lean against her.

"He said you didn't want me to be part of the company," he muttered. His bony shoulder against her bicep was the world's best feeling.

"I'm sorry I made him easy to believe. It isn't true. We were so happy in Kansas that I thought maybe I could just walk away from the company. But when I realized someone could take it away from *you*, I knew I had to fight to get it back." She thought of a private board on her Pinterest page. "Adán, can I show you something?"

She felt his nod against her shoulder.

"I've been talking to my therapist for a while about how to tell you," she said as she picked up the digital tablet off the coffee table and logged into her Pinterest account. "When we were planning to return to Mexico, I knew it wouldn't be long before we went home. So I asked Glori if she would contact a friend of mine I'd been working with. My friend, she's an interior designer. I shared this with her for inspiration." Cenobia found the board she was looking for and handed it to Adán.

Hundreds of images had been pinned on the board. They showed bed frames—some in rocket shapes—and bed linens, paint swatches in a variety of grey-blue shades, curtain finials and table lamps, posters of constellations, bedroom rugs, and several do-it-yourself kits for rooftop planetariums.

The board was titled *Adán's Room*.

He tilted his head against her shoulder and scrolled and scrolled. Every now and then, his breath hitched, and Cenobia let herself cry, too.

"It's not done yet, but it will be done in a week or so," she finally said, sniffing and swallowing. "And you never have to stay there, if you don't want to. But

I would like you with me as much or as little as you want. It's up to you."

He snuggled closer until she lifted her arm and put it around him.

After several minutes, Adán turned his face against her shoulder. "Papá and Bartolo got hurt because of me," he whispered into her shirt.

"No," she said, stroking her hand through his curls. "They got hurt because of the attackers. You were a means to an end, and without you, they would have just found another way."

Roman appeared in the kitchen doorway with a questioning look and Cenobia nodded.

He walked into the living room and sat on the coffee table facing Adán, who still had his face buried against Cenobia. Her son, who now knew he was her son, was resting against her.

"Adán, we saw the chat room messages."

Her son clenched his hand into her shirt and she rubbed his back, murmuring, "It's okay."

Roman squeezed Adán's knee with a big hand. "Those guys are experienced liars. And you still realized something was off. You tried to make them go away; that takes guts."

Adán pulled his head up to look at Roman through watery eyes. "I'm sorry I let you down," he sniffed.

"You didn't," Roman said. "And now, you're *our* inside man. Is there anything else we should know?"

Adán nodded.

"Did you know the man who attacked you at the lake house?" Roman asked.

Adán nodded again, and Cenobia looked at Roman in surprise. "That's PazYGuerra," Adán said. "I think he's

American. When he snuck into my room, he promised—"
Adán sniffed and wiped his nose. "He promised no one
would get hurt if I went with him."

"Have you seen him anywhere but online and at the
lake house?"

"Yes," he croaked miserably.

"Where?"

He looked up at Cenobia from the circle of her arm.
"During Vasquez's press conference. I'm sorry I didn't
tell you. That's when I knew he was still looking for us.
I thought I could get him to leave us alone."

She squeezed him again, full of anger at herself and
these miserable men. "It's not your fault." She would
repeat it two million times if she had to.

As she held him and rocked him, Roman started typing on the tablet. Then he handed it to Adán.

It was a video of the press conference. Roman pushed
play with the video on mute. "Point out the guy when
you see him."

Adán fast forwarded through the intro then stopped
it and pointed out a man standing with security in the
background. "That's him," he said.

Cenobia looked down. And froze. The man was as
noticeably tall as he'd been at the lake house. His hair
was brown, cut into a militaristic cut, and he had a neat
but thick beard. He'd been clean-shaven and a shaggy
blond the last time she'd seen him. But his eyes were
the same slate grey-blue.

She was looking at her first boyfriend. The man who
tricked her. The man who raped her.

Cenobia was looking at Adán's father.

Chapter Twenty-Four

Houston, Texas—Thirteen years earlier

As far as rebellions went, this one was pretty pathetic.

When she'd been in high school at an exclusive San Antonio boarding school, her friends had gotten tattoos. Or left school to follow a band. One girl invited the cast of an MTV reality show back to her home in the Malibu Hills during Christmas break and drank everything in her father's wine cellar, including a century-old bottle of Château Lafite.

But here she was, eighteen years old and a college freshman, attempting to stick it to her father by staying out past curfew to stand in the line of a popular taco joint in Rice Village while trying to befriend some punk-rock locals. She took an occasional hit off a passed joint as Bartolo gave disapproving glares from the other end of the parking lot.

"Stop obsessing about the company," her father had yelled earlier when all she'd done was call to ask if she could speak to one of his lead engineers about a summer internship. "Go be *una niña.*"

A *niña normal* was what was implied even if it wasn't said, which in her father's parlance meant engaging in the behaviors of a wealthy, young socialite while still remaining virginal, being home by midnight, and enduring the constant scrutiny of her security team.

"Give him time," Bartolo had urged when her father refused to change her teenage security protocols even though she was an adult in college. "He'll loosen up."

She doubted that—getting his approval to live in the dorms had been an all-out war—and she was beginning to take all of her frustrations out on the bodyguard who she loved like a *tío* but now just reminded her of her dad.

"You look like an angel." The boy standing in front of her surprised her and pulled her from her thoughts; he was tall, tall enough that a bright parking lot light created a corona around his head and all she could really see of him was that he was lean with shaggy light blond hair.

"Oh." It was a sweet thing to say. "Thank you."

"You're a Rice student, right?"

Her smile faded as she squinted to see his features with the light shining in her eyes . "I…"

"I work in maintenance," he said. He dropped his head, sending his shaggy hair into his face. "Sorry. Of course, you've never noticed me."

"No, I…" Feeling classist, she reached out and touched his hand. "I just can't see you. With the light."

But he shook his head without lifting it. "Sorry. I'm bugging you. I hope you have a night that's…that's as beautiful as you are," he mumbled before he walked away.

Cenobia would have followed him if Bartolo hadn't been bearing down on her. Rather, bearing down on him. Very few boys got the opportunity to say sweet things to Mexican heiress Cenobia Trujillo. She felt awful she'd inadvertently hurt him.

The next day, she was thrilled when she saw him— she was sure it was him, the same long, lanky body, the same shaggy blond hair, and he was wearing a navy uniform shirt with a Rice patch—sitting at a table in her favorite Rice Village coffee shop. Her guards had taken their standard positions outside. Bartolo watched the entrance while another guard monitored back exits.

She walked up to him, introduced herself, and asked his name.

Tyler McKinney had a normal face that blended in, but nice, grey-blue eyes, broad shoulders, and strong arms. He was older than she thought, twenty-two. He didn't plan on being a janitor forever, he told her shyly from under his blond hair. He was just saving money so he could finish his BS in mathematics before going on to graduate school.

He was sorry for approaching her, he said again. "You're just so pretty, I couldn't help it," he'd said into his coffee cup.

With a foreign but fantastic flutter in her stomach and an awareness that the seconds until Bartolo came looking for her were counting down, Cenobia wrote a secret email address her father didn't know about on a napkin and shoved it at Tyler, telling him with a shy smile that he could write her whenever he wanted.

By the time she got home and logged in, there already was an email from him waiting.

Tyler wrote her poetry.

He wrote her long emails about how smart she was, how capable, how beautiful and perfect. He wrote her about how she inspired him, how he was going to work harder to be worthy of her.

He told her she wasn't like other girls.

When she saw him on campus, it was like fire racing through her veins. A smile, a long stare would send her heart pounding for the next hour. He was incredibly romantic, leaving her a chalk-drawn rose, a single line of adoration rolled up into a scroll, or a candy heart in places he knew she would see them. They never spoke at school, not wanting to alert her security or get him fired, not when—like Cenobia—he had so much he wanted to achieve and so much standing in his way. But she went more and more often to Rice Village, where she would duck into agreed upon places—coffee shops, bookstores, clothing stores—and get five, sometimes even ten and fifteen minutes with him while her security guarded the entrances and exits but otherwise left her alone. There were always nooks, crannies, bathrooms, and fitting rooms that would hide them from other's gazes.

Tyler gave her her first kiss in the bathroom of the coffee shop. He was so slow and sweet, she'd had to beg him for it, had to touch her tongue to his lips before he returned the favor.

She first felt him hard against her in the dusty corner of an antiques store. He licked her nipple only when she'd pulled down her bra and tank top in a fitting room. She pushed his hand between her legs as they sat at a table pretending to read Russian poetry in a used bookstore, and she thought she was going to die.

For two months, they shared sips of time and endlessly passionate emails. Finally, Cenobia demanded that they had to find a way to be together, together for hours and not minutes. She couldn't stand it any longer.

For the first time, Tyler didn't immediately object. He said he thought he knew a way.

At Tyler's instruction, Cenobia got up during the night for the next three weeks, put on a robe, and passed her security to go to the dorm bathroom with her hood up. She also told a friend in her dorm—a friend the same size as Cenobia—her deepest, darkest secret: she had a boyfriend.

The friend was happy to help for true love.

On the night she was finally going to be with Tyler, bad luck had her running into Bartolo during shift change. She cried honest tears of frustration.

"Please," she begged, lying to him about a show she wanted to go to with her friends. "Papá says he wants me to be normal but what's normal about being an eighteen-year-old woman who is constantly watched and judged and weighed. I deserve one night to be free."

Bartolo cursed and fumed. But he let her go with a promise to be back by dawn and to call immediately at the first sign of trouble.

It was midnight by the time she finally met Tyler at the large pond in Hermann Park, across the street from campus. He wore sunglasses and a baseball cap, which was odd, but his huge, embracing hug burned away her nerves. He led her to a car.

She only discovered later that he'd slipped her phone out of her pocket during that hug and threw it into the pond. He'd parked in one of the few spots hidden from security cameras.

Cenobia didn't know when it was dawn. She'd already been in the back of a van, her hands bound, her mouth gagged, and her eyes blindfolded.

* * *

The men pushed her, prodded her, and jeered at her in Spanish, all which Cenobia experienced through slow, shutter-click transitions between paralyzed shock, ear-cottoning terror, and out-of-body disbelief. She couldn't believe he had done this to her.

But no one touched her. Not until, after what could have been days or only hours into her kidnapping, someone took off her blindfold.

The dim light was like twin spikes into her eyeballs. She cried out and shrunk back. Only when the light coming through her lids hurt less did she again try to open her eyes.

Tyler crouched in front of her. Behind him was a table set for two with candles on it, a towel and a bar of soap next to the barracks shower stall, and a freshly made pallet on the floor with a pillow.

When Cenobia saw the rose on the pillow, she started to cry.

Chapter Twenty-Five

Monte del Vino Real, Spain

Roman held her close in bed, her back against his T-shirted chest, his arms surrounding her in her thick pajamas, his legs bent and trying to shield her from the world as she told him everything later that night.

He'd seen her reaction to that photo and watched her hide it from her son. While Cenobia and Adán had continued to talk and sometimes cry, he'd stepped away to send the image, bullet points, and a flag to find the connection between Vasquez and the man who'd been at his press conference to Henry and Glori, who would disseminate it to all necessary personnel. Then he spent the rest of the evening with his love and her son, feeling privileged to be part of this moment.

Adán told his mother that he was going to sleep in his own room that night, and she understood. While he'd been getting ready for bed, Cenobia had quickly told Roman some of what he'd already suspected, some new and awful information, and the alias the man used in Houston. Roman had quickly forwarded that alias and the fact that he'd been instrumental in her kidnapping.

Now, with their position secured, the leak identified,

and multiple elite security teams once again able to do their jobs, Roman tuned out the world and held Cenobia in his arms, determined to carry as much or as little of her pain as she would allow.

The tears that had slowly trickled down her cheeks as she'd talked now had dried up, and she spoke in a flat and exacting voice. "He said if I didn't let him do it gently, he'd let all the other men do it rough. He'd said…since I was so eager for it, we might as well let our relationship reach its natural conclusion. So I kissed him and I held him and…and I didn't try to stop him."

Roman squeezed her tighter and listened, using his talents to record every bit of info that would help him find the man playing Tyler McKinney.

Cenobia's story slipped all of the square pegs into spaces that had once been round. Someone had paid this man to organize Cenobia's kidnapping, and he'd used Las Luces Oscuras as an effective cover. Now that man was back as PazYGuerra.

But who was footing the bill? And why?

Right now, it didn't matter. What mattered was that when he found him, Roman was going to do what he was good at. He was going to fix this.

Roman was going to kill him.

What mattered was ensuring that the woman in his arms and her precious son were never hurt again.

He ran his hands up and down her biceps and nuzzled into her hair.

"Logically, and with the help of my therapist, I can break it down and understand that it wasn't my fault," she said, so quiet. "I know I didn't ask for it. I know the entire…courtship…was just a way to separate me from my security. And I know the rape wasn't about sex or culpability, it was about power. He'd been paid to kidnap me, but the way he raped me—that was for himself. He took a confident girl with the world in her hands—money, influence, intelligence—and made her feel she betrayed herself. I've told myself that if he'd been violent or aggressive, I wouldn't have hidden it all this time. That, if I'd been honest, maybe he would have been caught. I can look at the rape. But my complicity and all the lies it bred, the way I hid myself from Adán, it's heaped shame upon shame."

She turned and pressed her forehead against his bicep. "One of the reasons I never told you that I was responsible for the loan was that I didn't think I deserved you to be nice to me."

He kissed her delicate nape. "You deserve it all."

"I just wish I'd fought him."

Roman gathered her up and breathed in her honeysuckle-scented pulse of life. "I'm so glad you didn't."

"The worst thing is, I don't think he would have hurt me. After, he washed me in the shower, even cleaned under my nails, then he dressed me and left me alone. I heard raised voices through the door. I couldn't hear much of what was said. But they weren't happy he'd been in there with me that long. I don't think they were supposed to touch me. Maybe if I'd just screamed…"

Roman and his team met with rape counseling experts annually to refresh their training on extracting victims of sexual assault from dangerous environments. His team worked triage rather than long-term recovery. But even in those first hours, the victims often centered themselves in the blame: if they'd only turned left, not smiled, hid somewhere different…if they'd only screamed.

Smart, wise, therapy-embracing Cenobia already knew it wasn't her fault. Just as Roman knew, with the help of his counseling, that his heavy guilt was an emotion that had served its purpose and was now only dragging him down.

"It's easy to look back and imagine a better path," he said into her hair. "Problem is, all that's real is the hard path we've already walked down."

She nodded against his bicep, then lifted her head and kissed it.

"When I role-played telling this story in my therapist's office to a love interest, I never imagined…I would feel like this."

"How do you feel?"

"Safe."

The feeling that lanced through Roman at that word was so good and clear and purifying that it hurt, like taking a drink out of an icy stream after a long, hot hike. He fought pride, wouldn't pat himself on the back, but right now that word was better than his Medal of Honor. He'd shine that word up and hang it on his wall.

All he'd ever wanted was to keep Cenobia Trujillo safe. He was a *príncipe* and she was a warrior queen. She was a CEO and so was he. He'd saved lives and, in so many ways, so did she. But they were also two plain people who'd faced the worst of what life had to offer and come out swinging. They could hold each other without their titles and shields and talk of their hurt knowing the other person would soothe it.

They were, according to Cenobia, in love.

Last night, she'd faced what he hated and feared most

about himself head-on and still given him love, told him she loved him just the way he was and encouraged him to play. Said he made her feel safe. How could he not love her back? He wouldn't say it, not right now. He wouldn't tell her what he regretted, the sacrifice he'd made. He wouldn't tell her what he planned to do to the man who'd hurt her and terrorized her son. There'd been enough revelations tonight and his girl was warm and safe and exhausted in his arms.

That was enough for tonight.

But perhaps, tomorrow, there was a way she could join him on the path he'd chosen.

Perhaps tomorrow could be a brand-new day.

Chapter Twenty-Six

Monte del Vino Real, Spain

When Cenobia came out of her room the next morning, looking dressed to kill in pearls, a high-waisted skirt that outlined her curves, and a siren-red blouse, Roman bounded over like a stray offering her a carcass and told her what he'd learned: Glori and the head of Trujillo Industries' security had gone to question Vasquez at his home, but—according to his staff—he'd left in a hurry hours earlier. Finding the worm on Daniel's computer had probably triggered an alert.

Sheppard Security was currently dismantling Vasquez's computers and hunting for the man.

She'd leaned on him and kissed him, relief trembling through her beautiful body. "It's almost over," she'd sighed against him.

He smelled the end like blood in the water. They were close. Soon Cenobia and her son, her car and her company, would be safe. They would discover who set this turbulence in motion. Roman would let the Mexican government deal with Las Luces Oscuras in public and he would deal with them in private. And when they discovered the location of PazYGuerra… If it was in the next few days, Roman would assign Glori to accompany Cenobia to the Frankfort launch.

His love accepted his mission. She understood. She was strong enough to withstand it. He could have her and it.

His family expected him to be devoted to them and a cause he couldn't embrace. Cenobia saw him. She knew him. She loved the soldier. So the Christmases at the training camp or the weeks away to protect a client or the way putting his gun to PazYGuerra would change him, she would understand that.

She'd asked to borrow his office for the day. While Roman got updates at his kitchen island, Cenobia video conferenced with her staff to get the launch of La Primera back on track.

They'd both taken a break when Adán had come out of his room. Roman had made him toast and a cup of weak, sweet coffee, which Adán liked to dunk his toast in, while Cenobia sat next to him at the dining table and asked if he had any questions.

When Adán had given that head tilt and half shrug of kids, Cenobia said, "I know it seems like you can't ask them, but you can. If I feel like they'd be better answered with a family counselor in the room, then we'll write your questions down."

Adán looked down into his cup. "I was wondering... about my father."

Roman immediately wanted to go to Cenobia, wanted to offer her his strength. But his girl didn't need it. She looked resolutely back at Adán.

"Of course, you'd be curious about him. I'm going to tell you the little I know. *Te lo prometo*," she swore. "I want you to feel free to ask whatever you want to ask, and I need guidance to make sure I'm helping and not hurting. Is that okay?"

Adán looked at Cenobia, his mother, and Cenobia looked back, unflinching and open. When the boy nodded slowly, it felt like the first shaky steps toward a new relationship, and Roman hoped like hell he would be there to watch it firm up.

"But until then, know this," Cenobia said, carefully taking Adán's hand. He didn't pull away. "Daniel and Bartolo are your fathers, just like they're mine. They love you, they've shaped you, they protected you, and they admire you. You are their own, *tu sangre*."

Cenobia told Roman later, in private, that she hoped Adán staying with her more often (she didn't say *living with me* but Roman could hear it) would give Daniel and Bartolo a chance to explore and fully experience the love between them. It was up to them whether they were going to tell Adán, she'd said. But she seemed to be setting the stage.

"I don't pray for myself," she'd said. "But I'm willing to pray that all of the members of our family can stop hiding."

Roman eyed his family now at the last-minute gathering Roxanne and Mateo had thrown together in their glamorous mountain-side home. Officially, the dinner was a chance for Cenobia and Adán to mingle with everyone. Unofficially, Roxanne had begged them to come over and put Liliana out of her first-crush misery, a misery that had given Roxanne and Mateo a jarring window into the upcoming teen years. Now the little girl—Liliana was still Roman's baby niece no matter how many crushes she had—sat next to Adán on the long couch in the sunken living room, staring at him with the same adoring eyes he was currently giving Aish, who sat in front of Adán on an ottoman and showed him how to play a "C" on the guitar the rock star had placed in his lap.

Aish leaned back and laughed, long and lanky with his black straight hair falling behind him, at something the boy said. Sofia who stood at the top of the living room steps chatting with her mother, Queen Valentina, broke off to smile warmly at her husband.

Aish and Sofia had once hidden their love from each other, Aish because he'd selfishly broken her heart and Sofia because she'd detested that she still loved him when her heart had been broken. They'd both worked hard to face truths and shake off misconceptions, and love shined off them now.

Near the dining table with its extravagant modern chandelier, Mateo chatted with Henry, his wife's former bodyguard, while Roxanne spoke to a pregnant Gina Pérez, Henry's wife and Bodega Sofia's head barrel maker. Gina's little girls and Gabriel huffed on the floor-to-ceiling window and wrote messages in the fog, totally ignoring the spectacular view of the mountain range beyond it.

Roman remembered a time when a drunk Mateo, trying to hide from his shame that he'd turned his back on the beautiful billionaire, would have punched her "centerfold bodyguard" before talking to him. And he remembered when Roxanne's efforts to hide her past almost made victims of them both.

They'd both bared their shame and revealed their secrets to the world in order to put the other person first.

Not one person in this room had to hide a betrayal as shameful as Roman's.

In a quiet corner of the living room, Cenobia sat on a

stool in front of Titi, the woman who'd been nanny and mother-figure to Mateo and Sofia. The tiny lady in her widow's black leaned forward in her chair, looking down as fascinated at Cenobia as Cenobia looked up at her.

Roman walked over to join them.

"Hey," he said, squeezing her shoulder in the red silk and running his thumb over her nape—her thick hair was coiled on top of her head—before moving his hand away. He wasn't sure how much she wanted people to know about them. If she wanted Adán to know.

But she reached for his hand and pressed it back against her shoulder where she interlaced their fingers.

Titi's sharp dark eyes watched like a pleased hawk.

"What're y'all talking about?" Roman asked.

"Titi asked about my mother," Cenobia said, smiling up at the woman. "I was telling her I didn't know her but"—she lowered her voice—"I just recently realized I was raised by two wonderful dads."

Roman looked down at his girl's beautiful, shining face.

"*Sí, vale*, a child only needs love," Titi said, her smile lifting her cheeks into soft, crepey balls.

"My mama loved me enough to count for two people," he said.

"Yes, *mijo*," Titi said. "She is looking down from heaven very proud of the person you've become."

Roman never knew what to do with the clear-eyed affection Titi gave him. She'd taken him in as one of her adopted children along with Mateo and Sofia, whose parents had pretty much ignored them when they were little. But besides making sure her small cottage, a royal property, was well maintained and overseeing the online security of her three popular *bocadillo* shops—she sold the best sandwiches in the Monte, Salamanca, and Santiago de Compostela—he tended to avoid the woman.

Was his mama proud of him?

He'd done what she'd asked, taken that thing inside him and aimed it toward good, pointed it away from people he could hurt. He was glad there was little he could tell her during those scratchy calls home; she didn't have to bear witness to his talents at work. But being halfway across the world also meant that he hadn't been there for the woman who'd raised, loved, and treasured him when she'd needed him most.

He'd chosen to turn his back on his mama so he could do what he did best.

Maybe she'd been proud of him, proud when he'd stuck resolutely to the path he'd sacrificed her for. When he'd resisted allowing other people who could be sacrificed get in his way. But now, now that he planned on bringing Cenobia and her son into his shadow, two innocents who thought they could rely on Roman to put them first and above all else…

How could she be proud of him now?

Sofia touched his arm. She was eyeing his and Cenobia's captured hands, too.

"I'm getting more wine from the cellar," she said, gorgeously chic in an emerald-green silk jumpsuit with her hair in a loose, thick braid over her shoulder. *"¿Me ayudas?"*

"'Course, I'll help," he said, and excused himself.

As they chatted about nothing and strolled down the hallway toward the steps that lead to the wine cellar on the lower level, he knew she thought she was being sneaky. He'd already tracked his brother leaving the room a couple minutes ago.

Looked like he was heading into an ambush.

On the cool lower level, built into the mountain rock, he opened the door on the wine cellar, a gorgeous room of mountain-stone walls, black cedar racks, rich amber light, and comfortable chairs. He would have called it Mateo's man cave if his brother didn't spend so much time down here with his wife. Once, he'd walked in and had a chance to compliment his brother's fine, farmer ass—Roxanne had been mostly dressed—before Mateo had roared at him to get out.

This time, Roman yelled, "I know you're in here, Mateo," as he pulled the door closed behind him.

Sofia whirled on Roman as Mateo walked out from one of the aisles in a white oxford, olive cardigan, and black trousers.

"*Joder*, you told him!" he accused their baby sister.

"Did not!" she said.

Roman crossed his arms and leaned back against the door. "Well, y'all got me down here. What're you gonna do with me?"

Roman was two hours older than Mateo and five years older than Sofia, and he hadn't been raised with them. But even he'd noticed that they settled into a weird oldest, middle, baby dynamic when they got together. Before they'd forced a ring and an office on him, it'd been fun as hell to show up for a few months to give them a hard time.

Mateo would get the same wrinkle between his eyes that Roman got, and it showed the annoyance he was fighting now.

Sofia had a temper, too, but she'd been the conciliator between her negligent royal parents and the powerless villagers when Mateo had been in America. She put her skills to work as a moderator now as she said, "We want to talk about your plans for the holidays."

He'd known this was coming. "'Kay. Talk."

She put up a waylaying hand as Mateo gave an irritated huff. "Were you truly planning on spending them in Florida?" She left out *"instead of here with us,"* but it was in her voice. It was in the clouds in her pretty, deep-brown eyes.

"Maybe." Whatever decision Roman made, it was gonna be the best one for the people he cared about.

Mateo stepped in. "You'd rather risk getting your *polla* bitten off by a crocodile than opening your heart to that gorgeous woman out there?"

Roman straightened. "It's alligators." He'd walked into something he hadn't expected. "Gators do the dick-bitin' in Florida."

"Don't be an asshole," Mateo cursed.

"Then y'all don't stick your noses where they don't belong," he said coolly.

This wasn't an ambush. It was an intervention. And he was already feeling guilty enough about how much he was willing to give Cenobia. He didn't need them poking at the sore.

Sofia looked at him with naked, surprised hurt. She'd learn to protect herself around Roman.

But instead of lashing out, she said, with a practiced *princesa* level of calm, "You didn't hesitate to stick your nose in to help Mateo fix his relationship with Roxanne. You asked for a billionaire's financial intervention in our kingdom with barely a nod from us. You swooped in and provided security for my winery launch before I even realized I needed it. Why do you assume you must help us but can't accept it in return?"

"This ain't something I need help with," he said, gripping his ugly hands into fists.

"*Vale*," she said patiently. "Then...do you want to be king's advisor?"

He was gonna need a chiropractor after the whiplash she was giving him. "What's that gotta do with anything?"

"Answer the question," Mateo demanded.

Roman glared at him.

His brother looked fierce. But not pissed. He looked like a commander. He looked like a king.

For the first time, his king had given him an order.

Roman felt the weight of the gold ring in his clenched fist. "Y'all needed help and I—"

"That's not what we're asking you," Mateo said.

"Do you want to be the king's advisor, Roman?" Sofia asked again.

Roman felt prickles over his skin, under his Brunello Cucinelli virgin wool suit, bespoke starched shirt, and grey silk tie. He might as well have been in the holey jeans of his childhood, it was so cold down here.

"Do you want to be with that woman out there?" Mateo asked, his voice rough.

Roman licked his suddenly dry lips. "After the launch I've still have work to do to secure her home and company, but then I'll be back here to take care of what needs—"

"Stop, *hermano*," Sofia urged, gently and sadly. "Stop talking about your tasks and duties. What do you *want*?"

His nose was cold and his mouth was dry and he thought that something might have gone south on their buffet table. Something wasn't agreeing with his stomach.

He looked down at the alternating marble squares of the floor. "What I want's not important."

His sister's voice was coming from much too close. "It's important to me. It's important to Mateo. It's important to your family who loves you and every person in this kingdom." He felt his brother put a hand on his arm and didn't he know better? "It's important to that woman out there who is obviously in love with you. For each and every one of us, you've done so much. You protected me and my winery in a time of chaos. My husband is alive because of you. Our kingdom is thriving and Mateo is its king because you decided to get involved with your troublesome siblings and this tiny village in the middle of nowhere. But for all of that, we don't care about your happiness because of what you've done. We care because of who you are."

"You don't know who I am," Roman told the floor. He couldn't look them in the face. "You don't know what I've done. What I could do to all of you."

Mateo's hold on his arm was fierce and unflinching. "Whatever haunts you, I'm sorry it hurts," he said. "But, *hermano*, stop behaving like we're naïve about the choices you've had to make. We acknowledge them and we accept you. Don't push us away. You told me ten years ago I was a lucky bastard for the number of people who loved me, no matter how hard I'd tried to fuck it up, and you were right. I thought I wasn't worthy, and I almost made the biggest mistake of my life. You think—what—that you're dangerous? Now you're about to make the biggest mistake of yours. I'm begging you, don't do what you helped me avoid. It's criminal for such a worthy man to deny himself the people that love him."

Roman clenched his teeth together to keep from

shaking. He couldn't…have them and be loyal to her. He couldn't embrace a new path without dishonoring the sacrifice he made.

If they didn't get away from him, he was going to make them go away.

Thankfully, Mateo let go.

They stood in silence together for several moments.

"*Te amamos*, Roman," Sofia said softly. "A home, a family, and a purpose are waiting for you. All you have to do is choose them. What do you want?"

Roman knew a few words in a bunch of languages but didn't have a real great command of any of them. Right now, every word his sister said in English sounded like gibberish.

What did he want? To be loyal. To not hurt anyone else.

The knock at the cellar door was as welcome as a black hole opening up in the floor.

"Go away," Mateo commanded, kingly as all get out.

But Roman stepped back and wrenched open the door.

"Sorry," Henry said, looking harassed in the doorway. "You guys got no wifi connection down here."

"No shit," Mateo said.

Henry ignored him. "Roman, Glori's trying to get ahold of you. I've got her set up on the office computer upstairs. Cenobia's already waiting."

"What's happened?" Sofia asked.

Henry shrugged as Roman passed him.

This. The mission. This is what Roman was good for. What did he want? To use his talents for good. To catch the bad guys. To keep Cenobia and her family safe.

To kill the man who'd abused her.

He took the stairs two at a time.

Chapter Twenty-Seven

Monte del Vino Real, Spain

When Roman came through the doorway of Mateo's office in his slim dark-grey suit, his muscular, weaponized body taking purposeful steps toward her at the desk, his jaw hard, and his bright-green eyes furrowed into a warrior's focus, Cenobia's brain fired shocks of anticipation.

She would never get tired of seeing all the faces of this man: the soldier, the brother, the caretaker. The commanding and consuming yet gentle lover. The man who let amusement slip through his gruff facade.

She prayed Glori had good news. She wanted to stop running and start living the rest of her life with this incredible man.

She knew he loved her, regardless whether he could say the words or not. He showed it in every tenderness, every sweat-soaked act, and—most tellingly—every time he stood at her back supporting her next move. She wanted hours, days, years to tell him repeatedly that she loved him until he learned the words from the press of her lips.

She clicked the key to connect with Glori before he'd fully rounded the desk.

She let out a huff of shock when Lance Vasquez appeared on the screen.

Roman whipped around to face the monitor. Glori, Cenobia's head of security, and an unknown man also sat at the conference table with Vasquez. Roman sat in the desk chair next to her and rolled close. "Glori, we're here," he said.

She looked up at the camera from her computer, her dark skin free of makeup. She looked exhausted.

"Hi, sorry," Glori said. "Sir, things have been crazy. Intel has been coming in so fast this has been our first chance to give you an update."

Vasquez was slumped in his seat in a stained shirt. The man's usually perfect highlighted hair was rumpled like he'd been running his fingers through it. "No problem," Roman said. "Looks like you're getting another bonus."

"A double bonus," Cenobia chimed in.

Glori gave a tired smile. "Thank you, sir. Señorita. Okay, Señor Vasquez has quite the story to tell so I'm going to let him talk. FYI, we're halfway through the zip drive he provided, but right now, the documentation is backing up everything he's saying. We've already got Hernán Rodriguez, the liaison to Las Luces Oscuras, in custody, and eyes on Blake Anderson, head of Alphawind Autos. The FBI are on their way to arrest him."

Cenobia pushed her lips together to prevent them from falling open. What did the American automobile manufacturer have to do with the drug cartel? When she'd seen Anderson at her father's party, he'd apologized for attempting to co-opt her launch in Frankfurt. And she'd accepted.

"One other thing, sir. Señor Vasquez and his attorney…" Glori nodded her head at the unknown man. "…They came to us. We've agreed to a few conditions to get his story. But we haven't taken prosecution off the table."

Vasquez dropped his eyes to his fingers that were curled together.

"Okay, go ahead, señor," Glori said.

Vasquez eyed a bottle of water in front of him, and then wrapped both hands around it like it was a handhold on a flailing raft. He raised the bottle, but before he drank, he said, "No one was supposed to get hurt."

He drank deeply before he sat the bottle down.

"Cen, I…" He breathed then finally looked at the camera. "Señorita Trujillo, *lo siento mucho*. They told me no one was going to get hurt."

She could feel irritation enlarging Roman beside her. She put her hand on his strong thigh beneath the view of the camera.

"Tell us what happened, Laurencio," she said.

"Anderson approached me a year ago with concerns about La Primera," Vasquez began, his eyes back on the bottle. "Alphawind Autos invested millions developing a hybrid car for the Mexican market, but it still wasn't ready. La Primera would have destroyed them; it certainly would end Anderson's reign. I told him that as long as Daniel was in charge, the car would stay a little pet project that kept you out of trouble until you caught a husband."

Roman's thigh felt like marble beneath her hand and she flicked it with her nail. Her taciturn, tactical soldier was about to reach through the computer and wring Vasquez's neck. He was going to have to get used to this. Even when the reins of her company were firmly in her hands, it wouldn't end sexism in her industry, Mexico, or the world.

"I was…angry when Señor Trujillo named you CEO," Vasquez muttered. "I said things to Anderson I am not proud of. Those words might have inspired Blake to believe that I was open to…conversations about stopping the car launch. He proposed methods to harass your efforts."

Vasquez's obstinacy and his ridiculous attempt to force Cenobia into sharing a stage with Alphawind Autos.

"The sabotage of the cobots," Roman said.

Vasquez nodded.

"Then, with the launch of the car gathering steam, he said he'd used a method before to distract the Trujillos that might work again."

Cenobia's breath left her. For a moment, there was no oxygen to draw on. When Roman put his massive, hot hand over hers on his thigh, she found air again. She quieted her heartbeat with measured breaths.

"Thirteen years ago, your father had spearheaded an effort to increase foreign companies' investment in Mexican workers. He wanted them to pay a small tariff on certain made-in-Mexico car parts. The tariff would go to improving worker benefits. Alphawind Autos would have been more affected than others, to a tune of about 150,000 American dollars annually. It needed to be approved by the Mexican Automotive Industry Association before it would go before Congress.

But with your father's support, many felt it had a good chance of passing."

She didn't know who was squeezing harder, her or Roman. "When did the vote take place?" she asked.

Vasquez muttered the date. It was a week after she was kidnapped. The kidnappers had asked for $150,000 ransom.

"Your father was absent from the vote," Vasquez said, unnecessarily. "Without his advocacy, it failed."

The room was quiet.

After several moments, Vasquez said, "Anderson told me that the havoc Roman wreaked to rescue you had been unnecessary; you were going to be returned unharmed."

Rage like a bullet shattered Cenobia's shock. "He's a liar," she snarled.

"We're taking a break," Roman demanded. But Cenobia grabbed his arm.

"No, we finish this," she said. "Who is PazYGuerra? Who is Tyler McKinney?"

Glori and Cenobia's security chief looked like they would have gladly taken off Vasquez's head for her. Vasquez and his attorney looked ill. "He's American CIA gone rogue; Anderson hired him for both jobs. He was the one who contacted Las Luces Oscuras to be the muscle and throw investigators off track. When Anderson called him back for this one, the man you know as Tyler said he knew a way in."

Through her son. His son. If PazYGuerra hadn't known when he'd first connected with Adán, he'd certainly figured it out after he saw the boy's slate-grey eyes, the same color as his own.

"They were just supposed to scare you enough to get

you out of the way," Vasquez said, his finger adamantly poking the table. "But PazYGuerra began acting erratic. That attack on the compound—Señor Trujillo was only supposed to suffer a flesh wound."

To this man, his mentor suffering a flesh wound was acceptable collateral.

"One of the men reported that PazYGuerra grabbed Adán, actually looked like he was trying to take him. That wasn't part of the plan. No one was supposed to get hurt."

If he said that one more time, Cenobia was going to scream.

"And then, after my press conference...we lost contact with him."

Roman leaned forward.

"Anderson did not approve that job in Kansas," Vasquez mumbled, shaking his head. "We didn't provide any resources. PazYGuerra was on his own."

"Have you been in communication with him since?" Roman demanded.

Vasquez shook his head. "He's a madman. *No sé* what he'll do next. I don't know...who he'll come after."

Cenobia now understood Vasquez's confession. He was more afraid of PazYGuerra than he was of a Mexican prison.

Roman took out his phone and started messaging.

"Is that everything?" Cenobia asked coolly, surprising herself. She didn't feel numb or distant. She didn't feel like she was telescoping away. This felt like the hard structure of reality.

An unfair, unjust, sick, twisted, and cruel reality. But her nightmares had just come out of the shadows and stood in the harsh light.

She'd been raped and her life transformed because a company didn't want to pay a miniscule amount — 0.00015 of its annual revenue — so the people who made its goods could live a better life.

"Cen, *lo siento mucho que*—" Vasquez began.

Cenobia cut him off. "No. Never say my name again. You have connected the dots and provided proof, so we will not press charges. But you will leave the country. You will leave the industry. Your greed threatened everyone I love. If I ever see your face again outside of a courtroom, I will direct every drop of anger and all my vast resources into destroying you. Do you doubt me?"

The pale skin he prized so much looked a little green as Vasquez shook his head. His attorney didn't attempt to argue.

They agreed on next steps with the security team and wrapped up the call just as Henry came striding in.

"Roman, I've got to talk to you," he said urgently.

The big blond man carried that soldier's readiness she'd become accustomed to. His blue eyes skittered over her before they spoke volumes to Roman.

"Not without me, you don't," she said.

Roman looked at her for a beat—she met his eyes and let him see that she was coping with the revelations—before standing. "What is it?" he asked.

"One of the movement sensors outside of your home was tripped."

"Goats?" Roman asked.

Henry shook his head once. "We caught an image. It's a man."

Icy fear showered over Cenobia as Roman went marble still. Cenobia blinked. And in that shutter click of time, she saw Roman transform.

He started removing his jacket.

"I want all the teams mobilized ASAP," he commanded, neatly snapping his coat into a folded half and precisely hanging it over a chair back. "Lock down the village, and harden our defenses."

"It's already done," Henry said.

"Tell the men at my house to hold. Fall back to the perimeter and do not engage." He was rolling up his sleeves, crisp bends with the cuffs, and stopped. The gaze he aimed at Henry demanded absolute obedience. "You make that clear; do not engage. Lock down this house, gather everyone into the living room, and don't take your eyes off of them until you hear from me."

The uncomfortable kernel in Cenobia's stomach bloomed when Roman took off his dented black bracelet. "What are you going to do?" she asked.

He tossed the bracelet to the desk along with his heavy watch. "I'll take care of this." He reached inside his shirt to remove a small chain and pendant. "Henry, you just keep them safe."

The head of castle security seemed to be getting the same uncomfortable feeling. "Brother," he said, startling Cenobia. Then she remembered that Henry, too, was former military. These men would always be brothers in arms. "Let me arrange backup. You need the right guys to—"

"You need to follow orders," Roman said, his voice lethal.

He was sliding the king's advisor ring, the thick gold that gave him the right to command Henry, off his finger.

"Roman, I—"

"Henry," Cenobia cut him off. "Give us a moment."

The serenity in her voice belied the growing panic inside her as she watched Roman remove his ornamentation.

Henry looked her over then nodded. Once Roxanne Medina's bodyguard, he was used to taking direction from women. If she couldn't talk some sense into Roman, she could rely on Henry to use his linebacker-shoulders to block the exit.

He left the room and closed the door behind him.

When she turned back to Roman—him with his lover-boy eyes and bee-stung mouth, his perfectly styled hair and precisely tailored pants, a runway model preparing for war—he was stroking his thumb over the ring's face.

"Why aren't you taking backup, Roman?" she asked, quiet and measured as she stood, although she wanted to throw herself at him and hold him down with her body.

He straightened and tossed the ring on the desk. It landed with a surprising *thunk* for such a small thing. "My only use here is to protect these people. I'm not gonna risk one of them getting hurt on a job I already should have handled."

There was so much wrong about what he'd just said. "But you don't have to do this alone," she said, clinging to her calm. "What if he hurts you?"

He raised his chin as he looked down at her, his body as rigid as if he wore armor. "That'll never happen," he said. "He's never gonna get the chance to hurt anyone again."

What was he saying? "What are you planning to do?"

For just a moment, that icy general's stare broke as his eyes furrowed. "I'm gonna make sure he doesn't hurt you," he said, voice deep and methodical. "He's not gonna talk about you or Adán at a trial. He's not gonna make a deal and threaten you again."

Her brave, compassionate, family-loving warrior prince was saying exactly what she was afraid he was saying.

"Roman," she said, carefully and succinctly. "I don't want that."

He looked at her like she was going AWOL right in front of his eyes. "This is who I am. I thought you understood that. You said you loved the soldier."

"I do," she said, moving slowly toward him, as delicately as if she were disarming a bomb. "I also said I see you. That's why I know that the soldier is only one small part of who you are. I don't want you to kill for me." There. She'd said it. "You have so many more gifts than that."

In another shutter click of time, her man that had navigated her out of a dark and bloody bunker looked hopelessly lost. Then he dropped his eyes to the floor. Bent his head.

"I really don't, Cenobia," he finally replied. He reached for his neck and those capable hands began tugging at the perfect Windsor knot of his tie. "But I'm glad you're finally gettin' it." With the tie loosened, he unbuttoned the collar of his shirt, exposing his strong neck. "You're finally startin' to understand why I never contacted you." He pulled the tie carefully apart. "You finally realize why I'm never gonna say... what you want me to say."

When he raised his chin to look at her again, he was all male aggression. He slowly pulled the tie from around his neck, the silk hissing.

He looked terrible and haunted and beautiful.

"Getting the bad guy is all I want to do." Running the tie through a scarred and mighty hand, he moved toward her like a panther trapping its prey. "And not family or kingdom or…falling in love is going to get in my way."

Only his tiny pause kept his words from tearing out her heart.

"That's not true," she said, desperately searching his eyes as his huge hands surrounded her waist, feeling the heat and life of him although his eyes were empty. She saw him. How could she make him see himself?

He leaned close and his plush, soft mouth brushed over her cheek. She felt muddled at his hot breath at her ear. "True or not, it's my mission." The carelessness was maddening in his voice as he began to gently maneuver her backwards. "I gave up the only person who ever loved me to choose it. I won't turn my back on her to choose something else." He kissed her jaw. "And I won't hurt someone I care about again."

He lightly bit her neck and she arched into it.

Every word was wrong. But he was gripping her and kissing her and moving her with a destination in mind—the couch? a wall?—and that left him too preoccupied to do the destructive thing he thought he was cursed to do.

"You're more than someone who gives pain," she implored, tugging him against her as he nuzzled against her pulse. "You're more than a soldier, you're more than a warrior, and you're more than a prince." She wanted to inject her words into his heart. "You're Roman. You're our Roman. And we love you."

Even while he pleasured her, she would mentally summon all the people who loved him into this room to help her with her battle.

His good, strong hands, still holding the tie, surrounded hers. He pulled them off his shirt, bent his
head to kiss her knuckles, then yanked her against him
to kiss her mouth. Hard.

She felt one arm slide behind her.

"My mama used to be the only person who loved
me," he said against her mouth, low and awful. "And
I let her die. I knew who I was and what I was good
at. I made a choice. And that was to let my mama die
all alone."

He pushed her a step back and his sultry, heavy-
lidded eyes looked so tired. She wanted to hold him
until he rested his head in her lap. She wanted to tell
him they'd figure it out in the morning.

"I'm so sorry, Cen."

He pushed her with a light shove. She stumbled back,
through a doorway.

Standing with the lamplight behind him, he looked
like a primitive stone statue infinitely guarding a castle gate.

"I'm sorry I can't choose you."

He swung the door closed.

Stunned and standing in the dark, Cenobia grabbed
the knob. "Roman!" She felt the pressure of his weight
against the door.

He'd just pushed her into a closet.

The door creaked as he moved away. She jiggled the
knob wildly. It would turn, but the door wouldn't open.

What had he done with that necktie?

"Roman," she yelled again. The only response was
her pounding heart. She pressed her ear to the door.

And heard the slide of a window opening.

He was going out a window. He was going alone.

The dark in this closet was immense. When she'd been in the dark, in the bunker, Roman had been her light. He'd saved her.

Now Roman was in the dark, engulfed by a sacrifice he believed defined him. That devoured his light so intensely that he believed a lifetime alone, rejecting love and encased in duty, was his only option. His only value. All he was worth.

Nobody could gauge worth better than a billionaire CEO heiress.

She kicked off her heels. Then she wiggled up her restricting skirt until it was up around her hips, giving her legs freedom. She squared her body into a fighting stance. Faced the door.

She kicked, driving her heel into the weakest point, near the knob, with everything she had.

Thankfully, this closet door in the home of a royal family was made of the same cheap foam core of closet doors everywhere. A good-sized crack appeared near the knob.

When she kicked again, she could see lamp light.

She inhaled deeply. Then screamed, "Henry!" with all of her might.

She was a warrior queen and she had a Roman to go save.

Chapter Twenty-Eight

Monte del Vino Real, Spain

Speeding through the dark on winding roads, Roman demanded reports from the teams at the airport, train station, village, and Castillo. There'd been no alerts triggered or suspicious activity spotted. He was confident that PazYGuerra had come alone.

No one in the Monte would be hurt by this monster.

A window had been breached at his home, triggering another alarm. He'd again ordered the guards to remain on the road then silenced his phone, ignoring repeated calls from Henry and Mateo.

He climbed the rocky hillside to his house now with everything he needed: a Glock 19 in his hands, a Ka-Bar Tanto knife in the sheath on his hip, and one of Mateo's baseball caps in his back pocket.

An image of Cenobia, her dark eyes huge and disbelieving as she'd stared back at him from inside the closet, popped into his brain. He wondered if it was his mama's same look when she realized her son wasn't coming to her bedside.

If he'd been lucky, he would have broken his ankle on the ten-foot drop from Mateo's office window to the ground below. But nothing was left to luck or chance, now. Each movement and decision was based on lethal skill.

This is what he was born to do.

Even in the dark, he knew his security layout well enough to miss various sensors and alarms on his approach. There was a secret hatch in the floor of the laundry room. He'd installed it to allow an escape; he'd never anticipated using it to sneak inside.

Leaning against the side of his home, impervious in his rolled-up shirt to the cold, mountain wind whistling over rocks and boulders, he checked his home's hidden cameras on his phone. Most of the views had been obscured.

He shouldn't be surprised that a CIA-trained traitor was also good at this job.

Roman looked up and, for just a second, took in the view of the village of the Monte del Vino Real. It looked peaceful down there. Even after Roman said goodbye, he'd make sure it stayed that way.

He slid aside a rock-shaped panel then crawled under the foundation of his home. After some belly wiggling through the dark, he popped the hatch without a sound, then pulled himself up onto his laundry-room floor.

He'd always like his laundry room, which he'd specifically designed for a man of his clothing tastes. It smelled of the The Laundress fabric shampoos he preferred. Tucked away in cabinets over his front-loading Bosch washer and dryer were fabric-care tools that an award–winning costume designer had taken notes on when Roman had assisted her with some stalking threats.

On the upper-tier drying bar hung one of Cenobia's pretty dresses, mint green with melon polka dots. On the rack beneath it dried a pair of Adán's narrow jeans. The kid was going to start outgrowing his clothes like the Hulk.

When Roman hit puberty, he had crazy leg aches that his mama had Bengay-ed up, wrapped in warm towels, and medicated with hot tea laced with whiskey. He wondered if Cenobia knew to do that. And Bartolo and Daniel were fine dressers, but they didn't seem to know a lot about men's fashions. Adán, with his impending growth spurt, was going to need a look that made him feel comfortable while...

What the hell.

He was sitting on the floor of his laundry room mooning over a pair of kid's jeans. *Ranger up*, he commanded himself. Stay on mission. Do your fucking job.

What did he want? To guarantee that Cenobia and Adán got long, safe lives.

Shaking and cursing himself, he rose to his feet. Focused. Readied his weapon. Felt the weight of it in his hands. It fit so much better than a gold ring.

He crept to the laundry room door. Hearing nothing, he pushed it open.

He could hear nothing out in his hall. Every light was on.

Roman moved silently and slowly, checking the open doorways.

As he crept toward the living room, he came to a realization with each footstep that this breach of his own home felt different. Something was missing. He was calm. Ready.

And empty.

He was missing that growing eagerness he was used to. The building exhilaration. The rush of adrenaline.

At this critical point in the mission, when it was kill or be killed, his spidey-senses were usually tingling.

His training had kicked in, he was alert and prepared. But for the very first time, there was no thrill. He felt… outside of himself. Like he was simply letting his training control him. He wasn't engaged in the danger and excitement of an oncoming battle.

He wasn't thinking about all that he'd turned his back on when he jumped out that window.

He crouched down where the hallway met the entry into the living room. He pulled Mateo's worn baseball cap out of his back pocket.

His Spanish-royalty born, Ivy-league educated, PhD-wielding brother had a huge collection of disgusting, grimy, sweat-soaked, threadbare ballcaps he wore in the vineyards. Mateo never knew that sometimes Roman threw them into the wash for him.

Who was gonna do that when Roman was gone?

Holding the baseball cap stretched over his head, he allowed the bill to appear around the hallway wall.

A shot from a Sig Sauer P228 ripped the cap out of his hand. And gave away the man's position. He was low, about eight feet away, in the center of the room. That sonofabitch was hiding behind the overstuffed armchair where Roman had held Cenobia and she'd told him Adán was hers.

The man who'd raped Cenobia and terrorized Adán had invaded his home as a predator.

He was about to discover he was prey.

The woman who'd been raped and whose son had been terrorized didn't want this.

I don't want you to kill for me, his warrior queen had said.

With that flash of memory, Roman did something he'd never done before—not on the playground or in training or at Ranger School, not in a hundred death-hazarding missions, or dozens of combat jumps, or in thirteen years of saving people's lives.

He hesitated.

Go. You're losing the advantage. Go. Kill. Do what you're good at. Do what you want.

Cenobia had said clearly and plainly what she wanted. She wanted Roman. She wanted a future with him. She didn't want him to throw that away on this kill-or-be-killed mission.

What did Roman want?

A home, a family, and a purpose are waiting for you, his sister had said. All *you have to do is choose them.*

He'd chosen a path when he'd abandoned his mother and broke her heart. And he'd loyally followed that path until, by some miracle, he'd hit this fork. Would he stay on the long and lonely road and abandon his fierce warrior queen? Abandon his family who'd offered him love and devotion and a community on a silver platter? Abandon the smart, loving boy who, even with all his resources, had real challenges ahead of him?

Would he stay on mission instead of going home?

It's criminal for such a worthy man to deny himself the people that love him, his brother said.

The soldier is only one small part of who you are, said his love. *You have so many more gifts than that.*

All his mama had ever asked of him was to use his gifts for good.

What would she have wanted of him in this moment?

What did he want?

He wanted his mother to know he loved her.

He wanted Cenobia.

He wanted to choose a new path.

He wanted to stay alive.

Which, he realized with a feeling that grew volcanic, would be unlikely if he stood here much longer.

There was an advantage to being a master tactician playing another master: You could anticipate each other's every move.

Except when the move was a rookie one.

With hot, panicked terror flooding his system, Roman turned tail and ran back down the hall, pulling out his phone and pressing a button as he went.

"Henry!" he screamed like a baby shoved out into a bright, new world. Roman slammed the laundry room door behind him just as a shot winged off it. "Get everyone not protecting Mateo's up here and surround the house. We're gonna wait this asshole out. If he won't come out on his own, we'll bomb the place."

He locked the laundry room door behind him, his heart beating like a drum roll. Heading into the unknown meant accepting fear. It was awful. It was exhilarating. He waited a couple of seconds, then slammed the secret hatch he'd left open as hard as he could, the metal giving a good, loud bang. PazYGuerra yelled and shot into the door, insulting his masculinity and promising horrors on Cenobia and Adán. Roman squeezed himself behind the washing machine and tried not to scratch its beautiful enamel surface.

Decorated Army Ranger Roman Sheppard—Medal of Honor winner, reluctant warrior prince, savior of young heiresses, and stud of a hot CEO—was cowering next to his high-end laundry detergent.

"We're pulling up to the house now," Henry said.

What? How could he already be...

Cenobia.

His warrior queen had been defying men for too long to listen to Roman now.

PazYGuerra kicked in his poor shredded laundry room door.

In a slice of a second, training and instinct took over and Roman shot the man in his right elbow then left knee in rapid succession. PazYGuerra's weapon went down, then the man went down, too.

Roman shoved himself out from behind the washer, kicked the gun away from the groaning man, then lifted his phone to his ear.

"Roman, Roman!" Cenobia was shrieking into it.

"Shh, shhh, baby girl, I'm here." Bending his head to his phone, he picked up the gun, disarmed it, and stuck it up on a drying rack, all while keeping his own weapon aimed on the man. "It's all right. I'm okay."

"And is he?"

Roman looked down at the tall man, now cleanly shaved, with a prosthetic nose and black hair, who cursed him from the ground.

"Yeah, Cen. He's fine too."

"Gracias a Dios."

"I thought you didn't pray," he said.

"I said I don't pray for me."

The man was issuing threats to Roman, Cenobia, and Adán if Roman didn't let him go.

"You're not going to let him monologue, are you?" she asked as Roman heard guards entering from both sides of the house.

Roman looked around, picked up a dirty sock that had missed the hamper, kicked the man's shattered knee, then stuffed it in when the man screamed. "My woman said no monologuing," he told him. "There's nothing we need to hear from you."

Henry and the other guards came running down the hall and squeezed into the doorway.

Roman held up the phone and pointed at it. "You had one job," he told Henry.

"The house is protected, and guards are with her down at the entrance. But the only way she wasn't coming is if I knocked her out or roped her down with that tie you left. I didn't think you'd greenlight those options."

He put the phone back to his ear as the guards secured PazYGuerra then began staunching the blood flow. The man was going to be alive to stand trial.

He stepped over him, still yelling behind a dirty sock, and hustled down the hall to his living room before he said, "I'm still not sure leaving him alive is the best thing." Guards streamed into his house. "A lot can go wrong between now and prison. Even if he goes to jail, he's gonna talk. He's gonna tell people who he is to you and Adán."

"I don't care," Cenobia said fiercely. "He doesn't define me. He doesn't define Adán. We're more than a violent act. So are you."

God, he loved her. He gripped the phone close to his mouth. "I'm sorry I tried to leave you."

"Don't do it again," she commanded.

"I won't," he said, like a private saluting. "I can't. I figured out the one thing I'm good at."

"What's that?"

He looked at all the people buzzing through his house, saw Henry making a beeline down the hall toward him.

"Let's get this taken care of," he said. "Then I'm gonna spend the rest of my life telling you."

Chapter Twenty-Nine

Monte del Vino Real, Spain

It was late by the time Cenobia, Roman, and Adán returned home. Guards had taken away the shattered door and cleaned up the blood.

Blake Anderson was in FBI custody. PazYGuerra had been life-flighted to a hospital in Santander with Henry and five of the castle's best-trained guards who would watch him until he was released into Interpol's care. Rodriguez had given up high-level members of Las Luces Oscuras who'd helped to arrange Cenobia's kidnapping and the compound attack.

In two days, she, Roman, and Adán would fly to Frankfurt to prepare for the launch of their unassuming but revolutionary car. When she spoke to her father, he told her that her fiery condemnation of the efforts to stop the car from going to market had increased interest in La Primera to the point where their overwhelmed and leaderless marketing and PR departments had asked him get involved from his recovery bed.

He sounded twenty years younger, Bartolo had told him, on the three-way call from his own recovery bed in Kansas.

Glori had already shared with Cenobia's fathers everything known about the current and original attacks, including Anderson's motives. The three, who'd all been changed by what Anderson had wrought, took a moment to rage and mourn together.

It would take time. It would take help. But Cenobia was confident that the happiness of what was to come would ease the anger and sorrow about what had happened.

After the car launch, Cenobia told them, she and Adán planned to take a brief rest in Spain. When Bartolo returned to Mexico in just a couple of days, the two men would have the house to themselves, she'd said innocently.

"Los quiero, papas," she'd murmured at the end of the call. *I love you, dads.* Bartolo sniffed as they hung up, but she'd never point it out.

Then Cenobia faced the scariest thing she had to face that evening: she sat on the side of Adán's bed, looked down at her exhausted and beloved boy, and told him that if he needed anything in the middle of the night, he should knock on Roman's door.

A smile interrupted his jaw-cracking yawn.

"Do you have any questions?" she asked gently.

"Will he be coming back to Mexico with us?"

"Do you want him to?" she asked. "You can tell me the truth."

Her son sat up and began a ritual she hoped to repeat most nights until he left for college: he wrapped his arms around her, hugged her, and kissed her cheek.

"Buenas noches, mamá," he said. "Yes, I would like him to come with us."

Cenobia hugged her precious boy back, wished him the very best of dreams, then headed to Roman's room.

By the time my mama got a diagnosis, the cancer had already spread to her liver and lungs. The doctors said she could get another year or two with chemo, six months without it.

Our unit's area of operations was the whole northeast region of Iraq and we were getting the prime cuts, with a lot of high-value target captures and kills. With my squad's success rate, command was willing to let me take a week to go see her.

But mama decided to get the chemo. And we had this operation to go rescue a POW.

"Never shall I fail my comrades" is the Ranger creed.

I hated down time. That's when the adrenaline wore off. That's when I started to reflect.

We spoke on the phone a couple of times. Even through the static I could hear how weak she sounded. The calls were monitored, which was nice 'cause then I had an excuse not to tell her what I was doin'. Not to confess.

She only asked it once, each we time we talked. When was I coming home?

But the doctors had scheduled a bile duct bypass surgery, which was supposed to give her more time, and they'd even talked about putting her on a clinical trial. And we'd gotten the location of a death squad that killed innocent men, women, and children after using them as human shields.

Every one of those motherfuckers I shot filled me with satisfaction. I was using my gifts for good.

One night, about a month after her diagnosis, we were all in our room playing Halo, hanging out in the 130-degree heat in our T-shirts and Ranger panties (you woulda liked it), when our beepers went off. We sprinted to the ready room, donned our kits, and linked up at our MH-60.

As the squad leader, I got the details: It was a capture/ kill mission of a high value target. I was sitting in the door-way of our helo with my feet dangling out when they gave us the 30-second warning and I looked back at my nine guys. I knew they'd do anything I'd tell 'em without question. Their lives were in my hands. And I was the perfect tool for the job.

On mission, you stop noticing the sweat pouring down your body and the smell of the shit ditches you pass. You look around at the men you're with, and they're grinning like crazy, standing a little taller. If you're hurtin', you suffer that shit in silence. Ranger up. Remain tactical.

I never felt scared when the bullets started flying.

Our target building was at the top of a hill. Each team separated to cover different sides, traveling through open field. When we got to the top, there was another building that hadn't been in imagery. Me and two of my guys went to clear it.

I'd barely turned a corner when a storm of small arms and machine gun fire started raining down on the entire squad, who had to go prone in the open field; we'd just walked into a hornets' nest of fighters.

The two guys who'd come with me were trapped against the building, the rest of the squad were count-ing on the dark and dirt to save 'em. There was nowhere to go but up some outside stairs.

As I went up, insurgents were comin' at me, and I was just takin' single shots. Never missing. Never hitting someone who didn't deserve it. I finally got to the rooftop—it felt like it had been hours, with my guys laying out there like targets, but it turned out only to be about 45 seconds. Then, I took the bad guys out. They were as surprised to see me as I was to make it up there.

I was righteous.

I believed I'd finally found my purpose. I thought I was exactly where I was supposed to be, doing exactly what I'd been put on this Earth to do.

At that moment, it was the best feeling of my life.

"We captured our target and they were already talking about the Medal of Honor by the time we got back to base," Roman said, his elbows on his knees as he sat on a chair he'd pulled close to the bed. His thumb caressed the large ring on his finger that Cenobia had returned to him. "I was in the middle of a beer baptism when I got word that my mother had died. I made them tell me time of death three times, and then I had two other guys check my math.

"The only thing I was grateful for was that she hadn't been dead when I'd killed so many, so well, with so much joy in my heart. She hadn't been able to look down and see what I'd abandoned her to become."

"She loved you," Cenobia said from the edge of his bed, where she sat in her nightgown listening to this heartbreaking story. "She doesn't blame you."

He dropped his hands to grip the edge of his seat, his head still bent. "No one was with her when she died. That was the choice I'd made. If I'd gone to see her, maybe she would have kept fighting. Or maybe I just coulda been there to hold her hand."

"And your squad might be dead," she answered.

He knew. She knew he knew; he'd sought counseling for his PTSD and continued to do the work. But he was giving her this story, and she would reply with how much she still admired him.

"I decided then I had to be the best damn soldier I could be. To make her sacrifice worth it. I had to give in to my gift for pain and use it for good." He shook his head. "Problem was, in the six months after I was discharged, I spent as much time contemplating my gun as I did setting up Sheppard Security. There were days the only reason I didn't do anything was because I liked my landlord; I didn't want him finding a mess."

Cenobia had to curl her fingers together to keep from combing them through his dark hair, to keep from tugging him against her so she could staunch his pain. But a bandage wasn't what mended a wound. A wound healed when the infection was leached and the skin was allowed to mend with time and care.

Roman was doing the work to clean that wound now.

He raised his heavy-lidded eyes and looked at her, bright green in the low-lit room.

"Then Daniel called," he said, low and gruff. "And I found you. I was able to save you.

"I knew then I could still do my job and help people even after I betrayed her. That's what got me into a counselor's office for the very first time. You saved me, Cen."

He straightened in the chair.

"You did it again tonight. You're the reason I hesitated and almost got my damn fool head shot off." The way he drawled it made him sound pleased. "You're the reason I didn't do what I'm so good at and kill that asshole. I had another choice to make. And this time…"

His eyes on her were open and unflinching and filled with his heart. "I came home."

Joy ached in her throat.

He raised his hand, a hand he'd always called ugly but one she thought was beautiful for all of the truth it told, and tapped the gold on his finger. "This time, I think I'm gonna hang up my sword and wear this ring."

Tears glistened in her eyes. Her reluctant *príncipe* was no longer going to be so reluctant.

Because she'd never gained anything by hiding, she said, "I'd like to put another ring on your finger."

For a moment, he looked at her like she'd shot him.

But then he pursed his lips and lifted his chin and looked down at her from under those thick lashes. Her warrior might stand down. But he was never going to go away.

He rose slowly, giving her his smile-not-smile while his green eyes roamed over her like in every best fantasy. "You're wealthier than me, scarier than me, and you can kick my ass. This ain't ever gonna be a traditional relationship, is it, baby girl?"

He became huge as he loomed closer, massive shoulders in a prince's shirt, and she had to lean back on her hands to continue giving him a challenging stare. "Unlikely," she said. "You've already seen how good I am behind the wheel."

"But there's one road you haven't taken yet." He rumbled like the engine of a precision-built vehicle as he carefully put his hands beside her hips and leaned over her to fill her vision. "I'm the driver who's gonna get you where you want to go."

He searched her face, whatever he was going to say next on the tip of his beautiful tongue, and she loved watching her commanding prince check in with her, the collision of her dreams and an even better reality.

"I'm the only driver you're gonna have for the rest of your life," he promised, staring into her eyes.

Happiness exploded through her and she wiggled her hips between his hands and breathed, "That's right," over his lush lips.

"That's right?" he asked.

"Yes."

"That's a yes?"

She nodded wildly, looking into his eyes, the sea-glass, the soft lines, the worry. All hers.

"Should we be doing this in car metaphors, Cenobia?" His deep, luxurious voice sounded like it was breaking against her mouth.

She couldn't imagine a more perfect marriage proposal. "You see me. You know me. I see you. You'll be mine and I'll be yours, in front of my fathers and your family and our son."

"But..." As he searched her eyes, this is how she knew he loved her. Because he was willing to show her the bare, naked terror in them. "Are you sure? Are you sure you want to share your life, him, them, with me? Even knowing...how I let her down?"

Roman had been flogging himself with this for too many years for him to change that compulsion in minutes. But she had even more years to help him believe and trust what a magnificent man he was.

She laid flat on the bed, made herself vulnerable to

him, and framed his face with her hands so he would see all her truth and devotion. "You never let her down, *mi amor.* She asked you to use your gifts for good. And look what you've done with them. You saved your men. You saved so many others. You've wholly given your heart and mind and time and care to those who needed them. You found a family and built a home. The only way you could have let her down is by giving up. And you never did that. What a tribute to the woman you loved. Now Adán and I can love her as well. We'll love her together."

With tears slowly gathering in his eyes, making them swim an unimaginable ocean green, he nodded and lowered his head to press it against her skin, to kiss between her breasts. Her heart. She felt the fall of his quiet tears against her, and felt blessed by them, blessed by a man who trusted her to bear his burdens just like she trusted him to bear hers.

When his tears subsided, she ran her fingers into his hair and tilted his ear to her mouth.

"Make love to me, *mi amor.* My only. My one. Let's begin the journey of the rest of our lives."

He reached down to gather the bottom of her nightgown and, with gentle hands, pulled it up and over her head.

"Jesus, Mother Mary, and Joseph, I fucking love you," he breathed as he wiped his eyes on his shirt then looked down at her again like she was a mirage.

She smiled wildly up at him, dizzy with the impact of his passion and the glory of his declaration. Her perfectly molded and taciturn warrior prince was a spectacular mess. "You've seen this all before."

"Not like this I haven't," he moaned. "Not when it's mine."

His. She was so happy she felt like she glowed. "Kiss me, Roman."

What a miracle it was to say those three words, a miracle she'd get to indulge in for the rest of her life.

Roman kissed her. He kissed her mouth, soft, tender sips before pushing in, wet and deep. He kissed her ear then her neck then her shoulder before tasting the weight of her breasts, then lapping at her nipples. Then he trailed kisses down her stomach, slid to the floor, spread her knees, and kissed between her legs, delicately licking at her clitoris, trapping her thighs apart when she was too close and tried to shove him away.

"No, Roman, not… Come inside me," she begged, one hand clenched in her own hair while the other was clenched in his. "Please…inside me."

His lush lips shined up at her as he leaned his face against her trembling thigh. "I will, baby girl. My Cen. My sweetness." His voice sounded like the honey he prompted from her. "But I want you wet and relaxed. I want you to come first. It's gonna feel weird and invasive and it's gotta be good for you. Open up and let me eat your cunt, love."

Only Roman could make romance out of filth. Her first orgasm was against his mouth while she bit the thin skin of her hand to stifle her cries.

Her next orgasm was while he kneeled gloriously naked on his haunches between her bent-up knees on the bed. He looked powerful and massive as he used both hands to pleasure her *michi*, the muscles in his thick arms and hair-covered torso flexing as he worked her and watched, all that skin beginning to glisten with sweat. When he sucked on his thumb and fingers to get them wet, she stared like an addict. She rode the sight of him to orgasm as much as his thick, greedy fingers.

By the time she felt the tip of his hard penis at her entrance, she was molten with wet and ease.

"Cen, sweetheart, my sweet Cen, you ready, love?" She could feel heat and smoothness tapping at her as he leaned over to kiss her, hovered over her on his big, muscled arms. He held her head in his hands, kissed her lips then her nipple.

"Yes Roman," she sighed, floating on his leather smell and his words. He made her feel like a drip of syrup he was desperate to lap up.

"Okay…" He slid his arm under her, arching her lower back. "Okay."

She felt his penis, Roman's big wide-headed penis, push just inside her channel. It was hot. It was weird. She put her hands on his huge shoulders.

"Okay, okay, c'mere," he said and he scooped her up, settled back on his haunches and pulled her upright, and onto him, kept an arm around her waist to keep her from taking what could become too much too quickly but moving—ooh, she could feel that—making little circles with his hips as he watched her face.

She slid her hands over those glorious shoulders and rocked her hips and…oooooh. He slid in another inch. It was invasive. It was weird. It was also…it was also like having thick, hard, hot flesh moving into a wet place eager to take it. This was *nothing* like a toy.

He stretched out his legs beneath her as both of his hands wandered down to hold her butt.

"Gentle, sweetheart, take it slow…yeah, slide down it easy, baby. Nice and…" She ran her fingers into the hair at his nape and pulled him close to kiss him and circled her hips to get him deeper and he groaned into her mouth like he forgot what he was saying.

She leaned back, hanging on to his strong neck and panting, and rolled her body until he was all the way in. He grabbed her breast and squeezed it, rubbed his hand up her neck and over her face, watching her like she was a miracle.

He was hot and deep and filling. Her Roman was inside.

He slowly laid back, bringing her forward so she was hovering over him. "Take me for a spin, baby girl," he breathed against her mouth. "Play. Find out what feels good." Even as he offered himself up, a road of delights spread out beneath her, he palmed one butt cheek, thrust and slid inside her wetness, and she was thrilled that it felt too good for him to be entirely unselfish in his pleasure.

She ran her hands over his mounded chest, gripped into his hair, then slowly lifted up before rolling down, feeling what it felt like, what felt natural, what she could improvise to make it feel good. Heat, smell, sweat, sensation created a fog around her. She was in her body yet floating, aware of the cotton sheets against her knees, the hot slab of his torso between her thighs, his hands squeezing her breasts, and yet filled with the awareness that she was something grander than her parts.

She squeezed her pelvic muscles and felt a gasping shower of sparks, felt him jolt and thrust in response. If she sank down too straight and fast, it hurt, and he grabbed her hips to stop her. If she leaned forward and rolled her hips, pressing her clit against him as she rode the pleasure, he stroked his hands up and down her torso

and stared down at where he disappeared inside her like
he, too, couldn't believe how good it felt.

When she wrenched her body one way and he popped
out, she got embarrassed.

"Sorry… I…"

"Hey…no…" he cooed, pushing her sweaty hair back
from her face, looking into her eyes with sweat on his
brow. "You're fine. Never be embarrassed with me." His
voice was so gravelly and intimate she wanted to rub
against it. "The fun of sex is tryin' stuff—sometimes
it won't work and sometimes it's ridiculous but, fuck,
you always feel so good. Look…now I have a chance
to do this…"

His muscular arms circled behind her and then he
was using the head of his penis to thrum at her. She
was so wet and open. She could hear the squelch of him
playing with her. She never knew something so big and
hard could tease and tickle like that.

He grinned when he saw the surprise and pleasure
on her face. Joy lived in his laugh lines.

She rotated her hips until his long penis bumped
against her soft butt. She reached up and pressed it
against the crevice, between her two soft globes. Held
him there as she rubbed herself up and down it. His
smile melted away to something…wonderful. His hand
slid up to caress her neck and face, to hold her as he
looked at her with that amazed expression as she rode.
She pressed him flat against the bed and he moaned.

She looked behind to see it—to see that hard, red-
flushed rod poking between her ass cheeks, so dirty
and decadent looking—and realized that her hand on
his chest had accidentally slid up to press against his
throat. She turned back quickly to remove it…and saw

his closed eyes, his raised chin, and the look of ecstasy on his gorgeous face. She pressed into the soft part of his throat while she pressed the rod of his penis between her silky, muscled cheeks, and his mouth dropped open in a groan she had to let go of him to stifle.

It appeared they were going to share driving duties.

The rest of their lives was going to be so much fun.

He flipped her over and suddenly was on top of her.

"I need in," he demanded, eyes flashing down at her as he lifted her ass. "Let me back in."

She squeezed his torso with her knees. "Yes, *mi amor.* Now."

He kissed her deep, pushed up on his hands but stayed close, and entered her in one smooth, long slide, watching her face the whole time for her pleasure and discomfort. All the way in, he tasted her deeply as she buried her fingers in his hair.

Hovering over her, he pulled back and the creamy slide of him was just…filthy. He tickled her nipple with his tongue. Slid back in and sucked her ear. Out and bit her neck. He was watching and testing and tasting and she felt overwhelmed and gasping and helpless in the most glorious way.

Then he tucked his thick, strong thighs under her, grabbed one of her feet in his huge paw, kissed her neck, and began to thrust in earnest. She gave some guttural, out-of-control sound. He thrust and thrust, put that warrior strength behind his hips, jarred her whole body as he bit her neck, and when she grabbed his rock-hard ass to ground herself in the pleasure, he dragged her arms up and over her head and then pressed them down, bound them there with his massive body stretched out over her and then began to really give it to her, his hips getting that thick, massaging penis so good and deep, fucking her pussy because she could take it, watching her and teasing her with his mouth, and then he stopped pounding and just worked his hips, held her down as flashed that dick in an out of her, so fast, so good, and she was making some high, reedy sound to try to keep quiet and he was grunting against her face.

Suddenly, he pushed up on his elbow and wrapped those pouty lips around his thumb. He reached down and her clit, he was rubbing her clit while he thrust fast inside and he was looking down at her and he looked…

Well… This was a look meant just for her.

She fell apart.

Eyes wide, she came with both hands pressed against her mouth, lower back arched with her pelvis pressed against him and doing its own shouting, singing an angel's choir of wet pulses, as Roman held her up and against him with just one strong hand as she writhed because the other white-knuckled hand was stretched over his mouth, eyes equally wide and shocked as he thrust and ground and shuddered.

He didn't look like a prince or a fantasy or a dream. He looked like her man.

Her man was coming inside her because his woman had made his fantasies come true.

Five months later...

Monte del Vino Real, Spain

With the toast about to be given and all of the teams as alert and on point as they always were, Roman begrudgingly plucked the earpiece out of his ear and placed it into the outstretched palm of his COO and partner, Glori Knight.

"Lord be praised," she said, grinning as she stuck the piece in the pocket of her short, chic black dress. "Miracles do happen, si—Roman."

As the new lead at Sheppard Security, she was getting used to calling her partner by his name.

"Yeah, yeah," he said grumpily, although in reality, he liked seeing her dressed up for the celebration, curls high, big earrings, makeup on point. Giving her an equal stake in the company allowed her to have her own second-in-commands who were doing the legwork for securing this anniversary party on El Castillo's grand front lawn. "You tell my sister I kept my promise."

She gave a mock salute before turning and grabbing a glass of wine off a passing tray.

Watching her walk away, he fingered the spare earpiece in his pocket. It was more of a security blanket than a necessary tool. Taking a step back from Sheppard Security wasn't easy, but his company and all the people it would continue to save were in the best of hands.

He turned and began making his way across the lawn crowded with villagers laughing, banners fluttering, children running and playing, and banquet tables groaning under wine bottles and tapas platters and fountains flowing with cava. It was a stunning mid-May day, warm but not hot, snow at the top of Pico Viajadora like whipped topping against the drenched blue sky. The vineyards were lush and leafy, with flowering just beginning to happen. For growers, this time was the deep breath and a prayer before the rush of the growing season.

If their father had ever given them a gift, it was dying so that they could have this one-year anniversary party of the new king's reign on this gorgeous, calm-before-the-storm day.

Mateo, ever the penny pincher, had resisted having it at all.

In the past, he'd argued, celebrating a new king's peaceful transition made sense when coups and plagues and gold goblets laced with arsenic made the transition less of a sure thing. But now, the only threat to his throne was a two-hour-older brother who repeatedly and vehemently declared he had no interest in the role.

It had taken arguments from Mateo's older brother, little sister, powerful wife, and then the double-barrel blasts of his twin children's puppy-dog eyes to change the king's mind. They weren't celebrating *him*, they said. (Even though they were, they were celebrating both the new *rey* and *reina*, because why wouldn't they celebrate this hard-working, fair, empathetic genius of a couple who brought prosperity and excitement and the light of a bright future to this ancient kingdom?)

They were celebrating all of them.

With the children in bed, while the three siblings and their loves sat around Mateo's massive dining room table and got slowly drunk on Sofia's excellent wine, they convinced him that the party would be a chance to celebrate how far they'd come. How much they'd accomplished. How lucky there were. They gently tapped their glasses together and looked at each other and marveled.

Ducking behind a manicured shrub to avoid a group of village *viejas* who would trap him in conversation for an hour, Roman surreptitiously marveled now as he caught the sight of Daniel Trujillo and Bartolo sitting close together, their shoulders touching, at one of the many linen-covered tables as they quietly spoke with Father Juan, the Catholic priest who all but raised Roxanne. Since meeting Father Juan at a small family event a month ago, the two men had been considering asking him to officiate their vows.

For the last month, Cenobia had been serenely supportive in their company and going crazy with impatience when they weren't around. For her sake—and for his—Roman hoped they made a decision today.

They hadn't shared what they meant to each other with anyone but close family and friends, wanting to wait until the vows were spoken to tell the greater world. But Cenobia had nearly lifted off with happiness when, during an after-dinner stroll in the village, Daniel had slipped his hand into Bartolo's and they'd walked the lantern-lit granite streets hand-in-hand.

The Monte had a way of making what once seemed impossible come true.

For example, the impossible image of his sister, Princesa Sofia, leaning against her husband's hip, as she chatted animatedly with her mother, Dowager Queen Valentina in all her platinum blond hair and slinky dress glory. There'd been a time when the Queen would have no more talked pleasantly with her daughter while standing among a crowd of villagers than she would have flown to the moon. But since repairing her relationship with Sofia five years ago, she'd taken an active role in getting to know her people and advocating internationally for Monte wines.

Now, she greeted him with a kind nod and a "Señor Román" as he approached their little group.

"My wife says I have to stick my finger in your ear," Aish Salinger said, looming over Roman by a couple of inches with his shit-eating grin.

"Try it and say goodbye to your guitar-playin' days," Roman said with his smile-not-smile.

Aish used a lanky hip slide to hide behind his tiny spitfire of a wife.

Roman gave her a real smile and a put-upon sigh. "Yes, I gave Glori my earpiece."

Sofia pushed all of her glorious tawny-colored hair—it almost reached her waist now—back behind her shoulder and grinned. "I don't know why you resist me," she said haughtily. "I always know what's best."

Yeah, she kinda did. She used her best knowing for her kingdom, its winemakers, her winery, the villagers, and her family. Especially her brothers. When she wasn't here taking care of all of them, she was opening a new factory that produced her wine chemical or in California helping to support Aish's new status as a partner in his uncle's vineyard or simply on the road with Aish, enjoying the rock-n-roll lifestyle. He was glad she sometimes got to come up for air from being so universally needed.

"Is it time?" she asked.

Roman nodded and they took their leave of the Dowager Queen, Sofia on Aish's arm as they strolled across the lawn.

An eight-year-old tornado suddenly grabbed him around the waist.

"Tío," his nephew Gabriel said, already sweaty and dirty, his tie knocked askew, as he hung off Roman. "I thought you were going to be late."

Adán, equally sweaty, gave a look that his recently acquired teenager status allowed him. "I *told him* that you couldn't be late when you're one of the reasons they're giving the toast."

Liliana finally arrived, making her slow progress on pink flats without a scuff on them. *"Sí,"* she said. "Adán tried to tell him."

Roman held on to his nephew and brushed grass off Adán's sport coat and ached for his poor, sweetheart of a niece.

Silent, sustained crushes were the worst.

"Look, gang, just hold it together for five more minutes. Then y'all can change and enjoy yourself. Adán, I put a bag with your NASA T-shirt and your Abercrombie shorts in the car."

"Yeah?" he said, the teenage falling off him like the tailored sport coat would in a few minutes. Okay, maybe the kid wasn't going to be the clothes aficionado that he and Cenobia were. Roman didn't care.

Adán was safe. He was happy. And he didn't seem to mind Roman joining the already impressive ranks of his dads. Roman would keep picking out the kid's clothes and hanging them in the closet down the hall from his own bedroom and, he thought with a touch of selfish gladness, he'd be the dad most often saying goodnight.

"Let's go find your parents," he said. As Sofia inserted Liliana between her and Aish and whispered consoling words in her ear, Roman slung his arm around Adán's shoulders and tugged him against his side.

At last, next to a small stage set up on the lawn, he saw who he'd crossed a lawn and an ocean and a lifetime of mis-thinking to find.

As his nephew slipped out of his arm to run to his parents, Roman sighed, "How does your mom keep getting prettier?"

"You've got it so bad," Adán said, turning and grinning up at him. It was Cenobia's wide, teasing grin, complete with dimples. "Do you want to set up a Pinterest board? I can show you how to do it."

That earned Adán a precise, militaristic tickle under his expensive sport coat. The boy laughed and giggled then wiggled away.

Roman let him go so he could take the boy's beautiful mother into his arms.

"Adán knows how to break that hold," Cenobia said as she slid her arms around his neck.

"I know," Roman said, nuzzling her and recharging himself on her summer-flower sweetness. "But because y'all raised him to feel safe, he knows he doesn't always have to."

Working together, as a family, they were training Adán to protect himself, each move practiced in their home gym led by the philosophy that it was only to be used as defense and as a last resort. But neither Roman or Cenobia were willing to let Adán—young, wealthy, powerful, and soon to be heartbreakingly gorgeous—go into the world without realistic tools.

Those tools would never need to be used against PazYGuerra. He'd disappeared into the bowels of Interpol where he would stay, monitored by Roman's many trusted sources.

With the help of a counselor, Cenobia had told Adán the reality of the man's identity. It had been…an awful two weeks. Roman hoped to never watch his boy suffer through weeks like that again. But with constant interaction, open answers to every question, and a repeated refrain from Cenobia, Daniel, Bartolo, and Roman— *We love you. We would change nothing. He doesn't define you.*—Adán's pain eased. They met with their own therapists as well as a family counselor every week.

In a quiet one-on-one interview with a journalist Cenobia respected, Daniel and Roman just outside the camera's eye while Bartolo stayed back at the house with Adán, she told the world who Adán was to her. She let people assume their own suppositions about his conception. But telling the story had freed her voice to become a fiery advocate of sexual assault victims and a bill with her name on it that would change the way Mexican police investigated crimes against women was already working its way to Congress.

With the eye-popping success of La Primera, and Mexicans hailing her as a new Adelita leading the revolution for improved industries, better wages, and a cleaner environment, the bill was certain to pass. Her name was already being bandied about for soon-to-bevacated political seats. But when she'd celebrated her one-year anniversary as CEO, she'd declared publicly that she had no plans to take on politics.

Right now.

"*Mi amor*, it's time," she whispered in his ear.

He gave one last, fortifying nuzzle before he turned, keeping an arm around her.

At the top of the stage stairs, his brother—his arm around his own hard-won billionaire—gave his Golden-Prince smile and beckoned. So did his sister, in the cozy arms of her husband. The three kids, Adán included, squirmed excitedly.

The *rey*, *reina* and *princesa* of the Monte del Vino Real waved *Príncipe* Roman and his new bride to join them. That small family event a month ago? That had been their wedding.

His baby girl was now Roman's warrior queen.

Can you believe it, Mama? he said in his nightly prayers.

Ten years ago, pure angry curiosity dragged him to a kingdom he'd never heard of to take stock of siblings he didn't know he had. Duty and responsibility kept him here longer than he'd planned. He'd done what he was good at and surmised that this little kingdom and his well-intentioned but emotionally mixed-up siblings needed a soldier around to kick a few asses.

Or maybe, just like when Cenobia had stepped off the plane, it had been love at first sight.

Because as he walked to the stage with his wife on his arm, it wasn't duty or responsibility driving him there. Duty or responsibility wasn't why that ring fit on his finger now, wasn't why he was stepping back from his company to focus on advising the king.

It was choice. It was love. He wanted this woman and this family and the Monte del Vino Real.

At the top of the steps, he took his brother's and his sister's hands and the group of them exchanged smiles and kisses and hugs like they hadn't seen each other in a year. They'd all come so far. They all had so much to look forward to. They were all so lucky. The crowd was starting to notice and gather, starting to fill up their wineglasses with the glorious past, present and future of this vine-rich kingdom.

Up on the stage, they all wiped their eyes and grabbed wineglasses.

Then they turned to face their people.

Here, his siblings and in-laws and wife and the squirming future of the Monte would raise a glass and toast not only the last successful year, but the miracle of the last ten. They'd toast the exciting potential for the future.

Roman would toast the fact that he was home.

At long last, as Mateo's voice boomed over the crowd and their people looked up at them and the vines shushed in the breeze and the mountains encircled and protected them, they were home.

* * * * *

Acknowledgments

I can't ever thank editor Kerri Buckley and agent Sara Megibow enough for seeing my vision through with this series. I wanted to tell a series of stories about what power looked like when women wielded it, and never once did these powerful ladies ask me to compromise my vision. Their belief in me made me believe in me, a strong elixir for a debut author. Thank you, friends. I can't wait to see what we get up to next.

I tackled cultures that weren't my own in this book, which is widely intimidating. Thank you Angélica Lozano-Alonso for your help with Mexican culture and language, and thank you Jessica Snyder for helping me properly and respectfully write about the military. I wanted to showcase both cultures with infinite respect. If I was successful, it's to their credit, and if you think I failed, it's my fault.

Thank you to Dreamscape Media and narrator Scarlette Hayes for the phenomenal audiobooks. Scarlette, you made my books come alive. You made me laugh and blush and cry as if I didn't know what was going to happen next! When I re-read these books now, I hear your gorgeous voice in my head.

And, as always, thank you to Peter, Gabriel and Simon. Look what you helped me do! During a pandemic!!!! Thank you for being my biggest cheerleaders.

About the Author

Angelina M. Lopez wrote "arthur" when her kindergarten teacher asked her what she wanted to be when she grew up. In the years since she learned to spell the word correctly, she's been a journalist for an acclaimed city newspaper, a freelance magazine writer, and a content marketer for small businesses. Finally she found her way back to "author."

Angelina writes sexy, contemporary stories about strong women and the confident men lucky to fall in love with them. The fact that her parents own a vineyard in California's Russian River Valley might imply a certain hedonism about her; it's not true. She's a wife and a mom who lives in Houston, Texas. She makes to-do lists with perfectly drawn check boxes. She checks them with glee.

Her debut book, *Lush Money*, was named a Top 10 Romance Debut of 2020 by ALA's Booklist. *Lush Money* and *Hate Crush*, received rave reviews from Entertainment Weekly, NPR, and Booklist. You can find more about her at her website, *AngelinaMLopez.com* and at @AngelinaMLo on Instagram and Twitter.

A marriage of convenience and three nights a month.

That's all the sultry, self-made billionaire wants from the impoverished prince.

And at the end of the year, she'll grant him his divorce...with a settlement large enough to save his beloved kingdom.

January: Night One

Mateo Ferdinand Juan Carlos de Esperanza y Santos—the "Golden Prince," the only son of King Felipe, and heir to the tiny principality of Monte del Vino Real in northwestern Spain—had dirt under his fingernails, a twig of *Tempranillo FOS 02* in his back pocket, and a burning desire to wipe the mud of his muck boots on the white carpet where he waited. But he didn't. Under the watchful gaze of the executive assistant, who stared with disapproving eyes from his standing desk, Mateo kept his boots tipped back on the well-worn heels and his white-knuckled fists jammed into the pits of his UC Davis t-shirt. Staying completely still and deep breathing while he sat on the white couch was the only way he kept himself from storming away from this lunacy.

What the fuck had his father gotten him into?

A breathy *ding* sighed from the assistant's laptop. He granted Mateo the tiniest of smiles. "You may go in now," he said, hustling to the chrome-and-glass doors and pulling one open with a flourish. The assistant didn't seem to mind the dirt so much now as his eyes traveled—lingeringly—over Mateo's dusty jeans and t-shirt.

Mateo felt his *niñera* give him a mental smack upside the head when he kept his baseball cap on as he entered the office. But he was no more willing to take his cap off now than he'd been willing to change his clothes when the town car showed up at his lab, his ears ringing with his father's screams about why Mateo couldn't refuse.

The frosted-glass door closed behind him, enclosing him in a sky-high corner office as regal as any throne room. The floor-to-ceiling windows showed off Coit Tower to the west, the Bay Bridge to the east, and the darkening hills of San Francisco in between. The twinkling lights of the city flicked on like discovered jewels in the gathering night, adornment for this white office with its pale woods, faux fur pillows, and acrylic side tables. This office at the top of the fifty-five-floor Medina Building was opulent, self-assured. Feminine.

And empty.

He'd walked in the Rose Garden with the U.S. President, shaken the hand of Britain's queen, and kneeled in the dirt with the finest winemakers in Burgundy, but he stood in the middle of this empty palatial office like a jackass, not knowing where to sit or how to stand or who to yell at to make this *situación idiota* go away.

A door hidden in the pale wood wall opened. A woman walked out, drying her hands.

Dear God, no.

She nodded at him, her jowls wriggling as she tossed her paper towel back into the bathroom. "Take a seat, *Príncipe* Mateo. I'll prepare Roxanne to speak with you."

Of course. Of course Roxanne Medina, founder and CEO of Medina Now Enterprises, wasn't a sixty-year-old woman with a thick waist in medical scrubs. But "prepare" Roxanne to...

Ah.

The nurse leaned across the delicate, Japanese-style desk and opened a laptop perched on the edge. She pushed a button and a woman came into view on the screen. Or at least, the top of a woman's head came into view. The woman was staring down through black-framed glasses, writing something on a pad of paper. A sunny, tropical day loomed outside the balcony door behind her.

Inwardly laughing at the farce of this situation, Mateo took a seat in a leather chair facing the screen. Apparently, Roxanne Medina couldn't be bothered to meet the man she wanted to marry in person.

Two minutes later, he was no longer laughing. She hadn't looked at him. She just kept scribbling, giving him nothing to look at but the palm tree swaying behind her and the part in her dark, shiny hair.

He glanced at the nurse. She stared back, blank-eyed. He'd already cleared his throat twice.

Fuck this. "Excuse me," he began.

"Helen, it sounds like the prince may have a bit of a dry throat." Roxanne Medina spoke, finally, without raising her eyes from her document. "Could you get him a glass of water?"

"Of course, ma'am."

As the nurse headed to a decanter, Mateo said, "I don't need water. I'm trying to find out..."

Roxanne Medina raised one delicate finger to the screen. Without looking up. Continuing to write. Without a word or a sound, Roxanne Medina shushed him, and Mateo—top of his field, head of his lab, a goddamned *príncipe*—he let her, out of shock and awe that another human being would treat him this way.

He *never* treated people this way.

He moved to stand, to storm out, when a water glass appeared in front of his face and a hair was tugged from his head.

"Ow!" he yelled as he turned to glare at the granite-faced nurse holding a strand of his light brown hair.

"Fantastic, I see the tests have begun."

Mateo turned back to the screen and pushed the water glass out of his way so he could see the woman who finally deigned to speak to him.

"Tests?"

She was beautiful. Of course she was beautiful. When you have billions of dollars at your disposal, you can look any way you want. Roxanne Medina was sky-blue eyed, high-breasted and lush-lipped, with long and lustrous black hair. On the pixelated screen, he couldn't tell how much of her was real or fake. He doubted even her stylist could remember what was Botoxed, extended, and implanted.

Still, she was striking. Mateo closed his mouth with a snap.

Her slow, sensual smile let him know she'd seen him do it.

Mateo glowered as Roxanne Medina slipped her delicate black reading glasses up on her head and aimed those searing blue eyes at him. "These tests are just a formality. We've tested your father and sister and there were no genetic surprises."

"Great," he deadpanned. "Why are you testing me?"

Her sleek eyebrows quirked. "Didn't your father explain this already?" A tiny gold cross hung in the V of her ivory silk top. "We're testing for anything that might make the Golden Prince a less-than-ideal specimen to impregnate me."

Madre de Dios. His father hadn't been delusional. This woman really wanted to buy herself a prince and a royal baby. The king had introduced him to some morally deficient people in his life, but this woman... His shock was punctuated by a needle sliding into his bicep.

"*¡Joder!*" Mateo yelled, turning to see a needle sticking out of him, just under his t-shirt sleeve. "Stop doing that!"

"Hold still," the devil's handmaiden said emotionlessly, as if stealing someone's blood for unwanted tests was an everyday task for her.

Rather than risk a needle breaking off in his arm, he did stay still. But he glared at the screen. "I haven't agreed to any of this. The only reason I'm here is to tell you 'no.'"

"The king promised..."

"My father makes a lot of promises. Only one of us is fool enough to believe them."

She took the glasses off entirely, sending that hair swirling around her neck, and slowly settled back into her chair. The gold cross hid once again between blouse and pale skin. She stared at him the way he stared at the underside of grape leaves to determine their needs.

Finally, she said, "Forgive me. We've started on different pages. I thought you were on board." Her voice, Mateo noticed, was throaty with a touch of scratch to it. He wondered if that was jet lag from her tropical location. Or did she sound like that all the time? "I run a multinational corporation; sometimes I rush to the finish line and forget my 'pleases' and 'thank yous.' Helen, say you're sorry."

"I'm sorry," Helen said immediately. As she pulled the plunger and dragged Mateo's blood into the vial.

Gritting his teeth, he glared at the screen. "What self-respecting person would have a kid with a stranger for money?"

"A practical one with a kingdom on the line," Roxanne Medina said methodically. "My money can buy you time. That's what you need to right your sinking ship, correct? You need more time to develop the *Tempranillo Vino Real*?"

Mateo's blood turned cold; he wondered if Nurse Ratched could see it freezing as she pulled it out of him. He stayed quiet and raised his chin as the nurse put a Band-Aid on his arm.

"This deal can give you the time you need," the billionaire said, her voice beckoning. "My money can keep your people solvent until you get those vines planted."

She sat there, a stranger in a tropical villa, declaring herself the savior of the kingdom it was Mateo's responsibility to save.

For centuries, the people of Monte del Vino Real, a plateau hidden among the Picos de Europa in northernmost Spain, made their fortunes from the lush wines produced from their cool-climate Tempranillo vines. But in recent years, mismanagement, climate change, the world's focus on French and California wines, and his parents' devotion to their royal lifestyle instead of ruling had devalued their grapes. The world thought the Monte was "sleepy." What they didn't know was that his kingdom was nearly destitute.

Mateo was growing a new variety of Tempranillo

vine in his UC Davis greenhouse lab whose hardiness and impeccable flavor of the grapes it produced would save the fortunes of the Monte del Vino Real. His new-and-improved vine or "clone"—he'd called it the *Tempranillo Vino Real* for his people—just needed a couple more years of development. To buy that time, he'd cobbled together enough loans to keep credit flowing to his growers and business owners and his community teetering on the edge of financial ruin instead of free-falling over. He'd also instituted security measures in his lab so that the vine wouldn't be stolen by competitors.

But Roxanne Medina was telling him that all of his efforts—the favors he'd called in to keep the Monte's poverty a secret, the expensive security cameras, the pat downs of grad students he knew and trusted—were useless. This woman he'd never met had sniffed out his secrets and staked a claim.

"What does or doesn't happen to my kingdom has nothing to do with you," he said, angry at a computer screen.

She put down her glasses and clasped slender, delicate hands in front of her. "This doesn't have to be difficult," she insisted. "All I want is three nights a month from you."

He scoffed. "And my hand in marriage."

"Yes," she agreed. "The king has produced more than enough royal bastards for the Monte, don't you think?"

The king. His father. The man whose limitless desire to be seen as a wealthy international playboy emptied the kingdom's coffers. The ruler who weekly dreamt up get-rich-quick schemes that—without Mateo's constant monitoring and intervention—would have sacrificed the Monte's land, people, and thousand-year legacy to his greed.

It was Mateo's fault for being surprised that his father would sell his son and grandchild to the highest bidder.

"I'm just asking for three nights a month for a year," Roxanne Medina continued. "At the end of that year, I'll 'divorce' you—" her air quotes cast in stark relief what a mockery this "marriage" would be "—and provide you with the settlement I outlined with your father. Regardless of the success of your vine, your people will be taken care of and you will never have to consider turning your kingdom into an American amusement park."

That was another highly secretive deal that Roxanne Medina wasn't supposed to know about: An American resort company wanted to purchase half the Monte and develop it as a playland for rich Americans to live out their royal fantasies. But her source for that info was easy; his father daily threatened repercussions if Mateo didn't sign the papers for the deal.

In the three months since Mateo had stormed out of that meeting, leaving his father and the American resort group furious, his IT guy had noticed a sharp rise in hacking attempts against his lab's computers. And there'd been two attempted break-ins on his apartment, according to his security company.

Billionaire Roxanne Medina might be the preferable devil. At least she was upfront about her snooping and spying.

But have a kid with her? His heir? A child that, until an hour ago, had only been a distant, flat someday, like marriage and death? "So I'm supposed to make a kid with you and then—what—just hand him over?"

"Didn't the king tell you...? Of course, you'll get to

see her. A child needs two parents." The adamancy of her raspy voice had Mateo focusing on the screen. The billionaire clutched her fingers in front of the laptop, her blue eyes focused on him. "We'll have joint custody. We won't need to see each other again, but your daughter, you can have as much or as little access to her as you'd like."

She pushed her long black hair behind her shoulders as she leaned closer to the screen, and Mateo once again saw that tiny, gold cross against her skin.

"Your IQ is 152, mine is 138, and neither of us have chronic illnesses in our families. We can create an exceptional child and give her safety, security, and a fairy-tale life free of hardship. I wouldn't share this responsibility with just anyone; I've done my homework on you. I know you'll make a good father."

Mateo had been trained in manipulation his whole life. His mother cried and raged, and then hugged and petted him. His father bought him a Labrador puppy and then forced Mateo to lie about the man's whereabouts for a weekend. Looking a person in the eye and speaking a compliment from the heart were simple tricks in a master manipulator's bag.

And yet, there was something that beckoned about the child she described. He'd always wanted to be a better everything than his own father.

The nurse sat a contract and pen in front of Mateo. He stared at the rose gold Mont Blanc.

"I know this is unorthodox," she continued. "But it benefits us both. You get breathing room for your work and financial security for your people. I get a legitimate child who knows her father without…well, without the hassles of everything else." She paused. "You under-

stand the emotional toll of an unhappy marriage better than most."

Mateo wanted to bristle but he simply didn't have the
energy. His parents' affairs and blowups had been filling the pages of the tabloids since before he was born.
The billionaire hadn't needed to use her elite gang of
spies to gather that intel. But she did remind him of
his own few-and-far-between thoughts on matrimony.
Namely, that it was a state he didn't want to enter.

If he never married, then when would he have an
heir?

Mateo pulled back from his navel gazing to focus on
her. She was watching him. Mateo saw her eyes travel
slowly over the screen, taking him in, and he felt like a
voyeur and exhibitionist at the same time.

She bit her full bottom lip and then gave him a smile
of promise. "To put it frankly, *Príncipe*, your position
and poverty aren't the only reasons I selected you.
You're…a fascinating man. And we're both busy, dedicated to our work, and not getting as much sex as we'd
like. I'm looking forward to those three nights a month."

"Sex" coming out of her lush mouth in that velvety
voice had Mateo's libido sitting up and taking notice.
That's right. He'd be having sex with this tempting creature on the screen.

She tilted her head, sending all that thick black hair
to one side and exposing her pale neck. "I've had some
thoughts about those nights in bed."

The instant, searing image of her arched neck while
he buried his hand in her hair had Mateo tearing his
eyes away. He looked out on the city. *Jesus.* She was
right, it had been too long. And he didn't need his little
brain casting a vote right now.

She made it sound so simple.

Her money gave him more than the three years of financial ledge-clinging that he'd scraped together on his own, a timeline that had already caused sleepless nights. The only way Mateo could have the *Tempranillo Vino Real* planted and profitable in three years is if everything went perfectly—no problems with development, no bad growing seasons. Mother Nature could not give him that guarantee. Her deal also prevented his father from taking more drastic measures. The chance for a quiet phone and an inbox free of plans like the one to capture the Monte's principal irrigation source and bottle it into "Royal Water" with the king's face on the label was almost reason enough to sign the contract.

Mateo refused to list "regular sex with a gorgeous woman who looked at him like a lollipop" in the plus column. He wasn't led around by his cock like his father.

And that child; his far-off, mythical heir? The *príncipes y princesas* of the Monte del Vino Real had been marrying for profit long before Roxanne Medina invented it. He didn't know what kind of mother she would be, but he would learn in the course of the year together. And if they discovered in that year they weren't compatible…surely she would cancel the arrangement. After the initial shock, she'd seemed reasonable.

Gripping on to his higher ideals and shaky rationalizations, he picked up the pen and signed.

The nurse plunked an empty plastic cup with a lid down on the desk.

"What the…?" Mateo said with horror.

"Just the final test," Roxanne Medina said cheerily from the screen. "Don't worry. Helen left a couple of magazines in the bathroom. Just leave the cup in there when you're finished and she'll retrieve it."

Any hopes for a reasonable future swirled down the drain. Roxanne Medina expected him to get himself off in a cup while this gargoyle of a woman waited outside the door.

He stood and white-knuckled the cup, turned away from the desk. Fuck it. At least his people were safe. An hour earlier, his hands in the dirt, he'd thought he could save his kingdom with hard work and noble intentions. But he'd fall on his sword for them if he had to.

Or stroke it.

He had one last question for the woman who held his life in her slim-fingered hand. "Why?" he asked, his back to the screen, the question coming from the depths of his chest. "Really, why?"

"Why what?"

"Why me."

"Because you're perfect." He could hear the glee in her rich voice. "And I always demand perfection."

Don't miss Lush Money *by Angelina M. Lopez,*
available now wherever ebooks are sold.
www.CarinaPress.com